kissing
in
technicolor

kissing
in
technicolor

jane mendle

AVON
TRADE

An Imprint of HarperCollins*Publishers*

HarperCollins books may be purchased for education, business, or sales promo-
tional use. For information please write: Special Markets Department, Harper-
Collins Publishers Inc., 10 East 53rd Street, New York, NY 10022.

FIRST EDITION

Designed by Elizabeth M. Glover

Library of Congress Cataloging-in-Publication Data

Mendle, Jane.
    Kissing in technicolor / Jane Mendle.—1st ed.
        p. cm.
ISBN 0-06-059568-X
1. Women motion picture producers and directors—Fiction. 2. Motion picture
industry—Fiction. 3. Actors—Fiction. I. Title.

PS3613.E483K57 2004
813'.6—dc22
                                                        2004047710

04 05 06 07 08 WBRT/RRD 10 9 8 7 6 5 4 3 2 1

prologue

The truth? I always knew I was destined for great love. Heart pounding, tongue seeking, stomach fluttering, hair tossing, bodice ripping, madly passionate great love. If my life were *Casablanca*, I'd never have to make the choice between Humphrey Bogart and Paul Henreid. If it were *An Affair to Remember*, I'd somehow avoid getting hit by a taxi and spending months bedridden, so Cary Grant and I could get right down to business. If, God forbid, I were Scarlett O'Hara, tomorrow would never need to be another day because I'd manage not to lose Rhett in the first place. Harry Connick and Pavarotti would alternate singing the soundtrack of my life. My life would be one long lovely montage of having my romantic cake and eating it too.

Or so I'd always assumed. At dismal present, my romances more accurately resemble *Nightmare on Elm Street*. Or maybe *Godzilla*. Rather than emulating Vivien Leigh or Ingrid Bergman, I've evolved into the Bride of Frankenstein type.

This is not a pleasant thing to face if you are a budding screenwriter.

To be fair, I've only wanted to *live* the Hollywood fairy tale—not write it. I have every intention of making my much-needed fortune by writing heartrending screenplays about real people and real situations. I love characters who are neurotic and flawed and not always sympathetic. In fact, most of my screenplays contain elements of my own hum-drum life. Every conversation, every interaction, every minute of my own day is narrated as a screenplay within my own head. It's all fodder for a future scene.

For example:

Scene: Crowded Duane Reade drugstore

CHARLOTTE, "CHARLIE," FROST stands impatiently in line. She is a petite brunette wearing a faded Columbia University sweatshirt and yoga pants. She has a red pen stuck through her sloppy bun and is staring happily at the VERY SEXY GUY in line behind her. The PIMPLY TEENAGE CHECKOUT BOY is staring at CHARLIE.

          VERY SEXY GUY:
Excuse me?

CHARLIE'S eyes widen in pleased anticipation.

          CHARLIE *(coos)*:
Yes?

          VERY SEXY GUY:
There's a pen in your hair.

          CHARLIE:
What?

    PIMPLY TEENAGE CHECKOUT BOY *(loudly)*:
He said you have a pen in your hair.

Blushing, CHARLIE gropes wildly at her hair.

    PIMPLY TEENAGE CHECKOUT BOY *(hopefully)*:
It's really cute.

*Camera zooms for close-up of CHARLIE looking
disgusted, then cuts to VERY SEXY GUY
looking bored.*

I once read something in *Entertainment Weekly* about how film school is the glitzy playpen for trendsetters and It kids. Whoever wrote that obviously didn't get in. I spend the majority of my time in pajamas writing very intellectual papers about how the emotional distance between Character A and Character B mirrors the split-screen technique used in the classic film of the professor's choice. Blah blah.

My neurotic, flawed, not entirely sympathetic parents have been fairly grumpy about my persistent dream chasing of both men and movie fame. This is another sore spot. Let's picture another scene. Three years ago, twenty-four-year-old Charlie gleefully announces her acceptance to a top film studies graduate program. Her father calmly glances up from the Sunday *Times* crossword (which he is, naturally, working entirely in ink) and replies, "So you've decided to be a tramp in mud time."

Bizarre, right? My father is spacy enough that he is often inadvertently rude, but he's hardly the sort to call his daughter a tramp. I was gearing up for an offended tirade when he started laughing. "It's both an allusion *and* a compliment, Puffin. 'Two Tramps in Mud Time' is a Frost poem about combining love and work."

This is a good time to mention that one of the more aggravating consequences of having an English professor father means that I get poetry spouted at me when I want (or need) parental advice. Robert Frost tends to get quoted a lot because—don't laugh—my father's name is *Herbert* Frost. By virtue of sharing nine letters in their names, Dad feels that he has a special connection with Robert Frost. Like maybe they could form the Bert Frost Club and have rollicking sleigh rides in the miles they go before they sleep. Assuming someone managed to resurrect Robert Frost.

On the other hand, when I told my mother the same wonderful news, she sighed dramatically. "Puffin, darling, you *hate* your job."

At the time, I was working as a script reader for a production company owned by an aging diva too vain to surrender her hand in the film industry, but too lazy and too forgotten to be a real player. It was a despicable, despicable job, but it had the enormous advantage of no dress code. That meant I could wear black plastic clothing to work and still be considered professional.

"That's exactly *why* I need to go back to school, Mom. I can write better screenplays than the trash I see at work, and I want to write them."

"You used to want to be a doctor."

"That was in elementary school."

"So?'

"So then I threw up in ninth grade biology because the rat I was dissecting turned out to be pregnant. There was this little rat fetus all pickled in formaldehyde."

My mother snoaned at me. That means she made this particularly revolting sound that only she can make. It's a cross between a very nasally snort and a very throaty groan. I live in great fear that I will someday spontaneously inherit this trait and start snoaning at people. In my mother's case, snoaning generally accompanies disgust. I wasn't sure if she was disgusted with me or with the image of the rat.

"Charlotte, aren't there enough little blond girls from Kansas hotfooting it out to Hollywood, only to spend five years waitressing before resigning themselves to a career in porn? This is a pipe dream. I know you like movies—but don't sacrifice yourself. People just don't make it big in the film industry. Not in real life."

She was definitely disgusted with me. But I was used to that.

To: Third-year seminar <thirdyears@columbfilm.edu>
From: Rhonda Bain, Ph.D. <rbain@columbfilm.edu>

Dear class:

If you are receiving this e-mail, it is because you are currently registered to take Film Studies 771 as your required third year graduate seminar. This class will focus on exploring the development of Russian and Soviet film throughout the twentieth century. This is a highly advanced, work-intensive course. For that reason, I prefer not to waste the first class reviewing the syllabus. A copy of the syllabus is attached to this e-mail; please read it and reply with any questions you may have. Come to class prepared to discuss the first eleven chapters (pp. 1–379) of Vladimir Rokov's *The Advent of Silent Cinema in Post-Revolutionary Moscow* and the film *Masha*. *Masha* will be on reserve in the graduate film library for the next two weeks.

I am excited to work with you this semester. See you on September 3!

Rhonda

one

For perhaps the first time in my life, I was glad it was Labor Day.

Normally, I cherish summer. I love swimming pools and fireworks and long lazy days and free opera in Central Park and the way it feels to be squeaky clean and drinking a gin and tonic with lots of lime at the end of a long and sweaty day. But there is a very good reason why no one ever made a movie glorifying summer in New York. It's revolting. The entire city reeks like medieval London. Rationally, I know that people do not cease bathing and begin throwing their garbage directly out the window and onto the street whenever Memorial Day rolls around, but it absolutely smells that way. The Hamptons are not merely an elitist droolfest; they are a public health sanctuary.

I had spent most of the summer camped in my apartment as my cheap little window AC huffed and puffed to the best of its 5000-BTU capacity. (That's another gross thing about summer in the city. Practically no one has central AC, so window units spit these foul little drips of water on anyone unlucky enough to be traipsing the streets in mid-August.) Karen, my roommate, hightailed it to her parents' beach house every weekend. Had it not been for my monumental thesis fear, I might have taken better advantage of her open invitation to tag along. But my screenplay, *Honey and Helen*, was hardly writing itself. In fact, it was a more arduous process than even I, the over-achieving worrywart, had anticipated.

Three days before classes started, in a daze fueled by exhaustion and calcium-infused tea, I finally sent a draft over to my advisor with a note:

Horton—

Sorry to have vanished over the past couple months. Enclosed is the reason. I know it isn't exactly what we discussed for my topic, but I got inspired. Are cameras ready to roll?

—Charlie

Horton e-mailed back:

Charlotte—

A lesbian love triangle between a paraplegic, her sister, and a nurse? You are ambitious, but we should talk.

I wouldn't say that I *literally* started gnashing my teeth at this reply, but it certainly incited some mental grinding. Admittedly, I had always feared that *Honey and Helen* might be a tough sell. But honestly. Reducing such an intricate plot to "a lesbian love triangle" was unnecessarily salacious. I liked to think of it more as *Ethan Frome* meets *The English Patient* meets any Tennessee Williams story of mangled, dysfunctional families. Having spent the past three months welded to my laptop, wasn't I entitled to wish for a reply more along the lines of *Charlie, in my forty years of teaching film, I have never read a screenplay with such promise?*

Suffice it to say, I descended on Horton's office the Tuesday after Labor Day, ready to win him over. When I got to school, I could hear *La Boheme* floating from under his door into the hallway. (Horton and I are both opera buffs. Anachronistic, I know). I knocked. There was no response. Knock. Knock. The music was approaching atomic blast–decibel level. I opened the door, warbling "Rodolfo!" in full operatic splendor (and, if I do say so myself, completely in synch with whichever molasses-voiced soprano played Mimi).

Horton jumped about twelve feet. Maybe that was a bad call. After all, I was here to convince him I had the maturity and wisdom to make a sensitive, heartfelt movie about a paraplegic. I stood there sheepishly.

"Hey, kid." He grinned and adjusted the volume. Horton Lear is pushing seventy. He has rimless glasses and a beautiful white shock of Boris Yeltsin hair and has this whole Harley-Davidson-meets-nineteenth-century-German-philosopher aura. It's an odd look, but it works. Horton could have been a contender. He made three classic romantic comedies—sort of Billy Wilder-ish—back in the sixties. But he considers film an interpretable art form. He prefers pondering and analyzing movies to making them, so he's ended up teaching and doing the occasional review for the *Times*. I adore him. I fully agree that movies serve a deeper purpose than entertainment. I even relish the dissection of a good film into its requisite symbolic components. But when I make it big, you can be damn sure that I'm not going to skulk back to academia with my tail between my legs five years later.

I moved a pile of videotapes and loose papers from a slouchy armchair and sat down.

"So I take it you have a draft for me that's bleeding with red ink?"

Horton rubbed his hand across his chin. "Well, yeah, Charlie, I have to tell you that I'm less than enthusiastic about this latest brainstorm of yours."

"I gathered as much from your e-mail. It was, um, curt." I began to muster my arguments.

"I can tell you've worked really hard on this," Horton began. *Well, yes, that's one way to put it. Slaved or agonized over might be more appropriate, though.* "It just feels a bit contrived to me. There're a lot of good moments. I'd like to say I believe in the idea. But, in all honesty, I'm not sure you've got either the depth or the experience to pull it off. It doesn't work, Charlie."

I've never been told that a screenplay doesn't work before. I felt myself recoil slightly from the shock. I wasn't ready to relinquish *Honey and Helen*. Wondering what to say, I bit my lip for a second, before deciding to damn the torpedoes. Full steam ahead!

"Horton, listen, I know that *Honey and Helen* has a lot of flaws," I said. "It's a limited story about unglamorous people. It would require some unusually talented actors and be difficult to direct. I run the risk of being stereotyped as someone who can only make a small movie. But . . ." I paused for emphasis. The torpedoes were rocking and rolling now. "But it's absolutely unique. Because funds are going to be limited, a small, character-driven story is actually preferable. I anticipated extensive revisions because the story is so difficult. But I'm excited about this, and I'm willing to put in the time to fix it."

"Charlie, it's not a question of fixing." He stared piteously at me. "You know that I think you have tremendous talent. In ten years you can come back to this screenplay and rework it and it'll be a phenomenal, beautiful piece of work that'll probably win an Oscar. At that time, I will back you one hundred percent and help you in any way I can." He leaned forward. "At this time, there is no way I can commit departmental funds to the production of this screenplay. It's not going to happen, kid."

I wanted to vanish. Or die. Where was a merciful lightning

bolt to strike me down and put me out of my misery? The catastrophe of not being funded had simply never occurred to me. After the Summer of Sweat and Tears, there was no way this could be happening.

"Horton . . ." I began. He smiled at me, a slow, grand-fatherly grin. I didn't know how to respond to the sudden warmth. "Horton, what about my thesis? If I don't do this, I don't have a project."

"Charlie, you've written so much. I'm not worried about you finding a project. You can use one of your old screen-plays."

"They're not good enough."

"I suggest you reread them. There's a lot of material there. You are nothing if not a prolific writer."

"I don't *want* to do an old screenplay. I want to make *Honey and Helen*." Great, Charlie. Way to start whining. "Horton, everything I've done before has just been an imita-tion of something I've seen. This is different. This is some-thing I created. I know it's not marketable—but that shouldn't matter in grad school."

"I understand." Horton nodded his head so the Boris Yeltsin shock wobbled. "For the record, it's possible to write something marketable that doesn't compromise your artistic vision."

OK, could we have the debate about artistic vision *after* settling the fate of my graduate school career?

"What about the Jablonski?" I asked. The Jablonski Fellow-ship is a prestigious grant that will fund the production costs of an entire student film—eliminating the need for Horton to give me departmental money.

"I had a hunch you'd ask about that. Look, Charlie, you are free to apply for the Jablonski, and I think you have a shot at winning it. I'd love you to prove me wrong about this screen-play. I'll even write you a recommendation. But I think you should go home and mull everything over. This just isn't a screenplay that seems worth your time right now. You can do better."

My throat felt hot and scratchy. I was probably getting sick. I probably picked up diphtheria or consumption on the subway and was going to die a hideous death like Mimi in *Boheme*, only there would be no Rodolfo to weep over my faint, blue body. Horton waved the thick sheaf of *Honey and Helen* at me.

"Go home, Charlotte Frost. We'll talk later in the week. Get some sleep. You look pale."

"I was aiming for heroin chic." How dare he call me pale after I earned my jailbird pallor working on a screenplay that he so cavalierly rejected? Normally, I think Horton is God's gift to graduate students, but at that exact moment I would have gladly shipped him to China in a wooden crate. The one redeeming aspect of this entire monstrous meeting was that at least I hadn't started to cry. And I was damn well going to apply for the Jablonski. Abandon *Honey and Helen*? After we'd shared so much this summer? Honestly, Horton might as well be on crack.

I repeat: Damn the torpedoes! Full steam ahead!

When Karen came home later that afternoon, I was halfway through my third margarita and about three steps away from being the "before" poster girl for an antidrinking campaign. Yes, I turn to alcohol in times of trouble. Also—embarrassingly enough—Nancy Drew. I was almost done with *The Clue of the Velvet Mask*, having already laid waste to *The Haunted Showboat* and *Password to Larkspur Lane*. I watched Karen survey the scene tentatively: me, splayed out on the couch, surrounded by the detritus of kids' books, the 119 crumpled pages of *Honey and Helen*, a bottle of embarrassingly cheap tequila, and an empty box of Lindt truffles that were a gift and had somehow survived miraculously uneaten until now. I could almost see the cogs spinning in her head. Should she play the role of long-suffering, sympathetic roommate or put her psychology training to good use and act as therapist to the wretched pulp of a human who was so clearly in need of her expertise?

"If this is a substance abuse problem," she said, "I can't really help you. We don't learn that until next semester."

"Will you bring me five more martinis, Leo? And line them right up here," I deadpanned in my best Myrna Loy. Ten points to Charlotte Frost for an appropriate film noir quote. Of course it was wasted on Karen, who has the movie preferences of a thirteen-year-old boy. She actually watches action films and weird, trashy movies about the devil taking over present-day Manhattan.

She sat down next to me. "Oh, I don't care about the margaritas," she said. "But you've got to stop these Nancy Drew benders."

OK, that was funny. I love Karen. I forced myself to sit up, despite a sudden and crushing head rush. I think I need to grow another four inches and gain twenty pounds before deciding to drink three margaritas on an empty stomach again. Talk about no tolerance. What a cheap date I'd be. If I ever went on dates . . .

"So, what's up?" Karen reached for my margarita and took a sip.

"Horton's not going to fund my thesis!" My voice cracked a bit at the end.

"What?" Karen sounded genuinely shocked, which made me feel better. I rehashed the whole grisly conversation. At the end, my throat was all scratchy again. I was definitely coming down with consumption.

Karen's head was tilted a precise forty-five degrees to the left. I might have been more impressed had she not already told me about twenty times that this is a trick they teach you in psychology graduate school to convey active listening. "You're really going to apply for the Jablonski?" she asked.

"I have to!" I wailed.

"Horton knows his stuff, Charlie. You always tell me that."

"But, Karen, I want to make *Honey and Helen.* It's the only remotely camera-worthy screenplay I have."

"Oh, come on." She gestured to the bookcase bulging with various drafts of my screenplays. "Surely you could find something there you could use instead."

"I can't use anything there."

"Why not?"

"I don't want to!"

"Maybe you should think about it, Charlie."

"Look, I need you to be Supershrink right now," I snapped. "Do you think you could maybe dive into the nearest phone booth and come out wearing your empathy cape? I don't want to resurrect an old, crappy screenplay. I want to make the movie I spent all summer writing."

"Charlie," Karen began. The phone started ringing. I got up. I didn't want to talk anymore.

"I'm going to my room. If it's for me, tell whoever it is that I'm in the process of expiring from galloping consumption."

The phone was ringing so loudly that I didn't exactly hear what Karen said. But it sounded like "Charlotte, grow up."

two

Four A.M. is a hateful hour.

I had been staring at the blinking digits on my clock for forty-five minutes before deciding to abandon the whole idea of getting back to sleep. Every part of me ached with exhaustion, but I was feeling so scared and wormy and fretful that it was no use. I went into the living room and retrieved the untidy pile of my latest *Honey and Helen* draft. I read the whole thing through, strenuously avoiding the urge to pick up a pen and make changes.

My weeks of continual nitpicking meant that I didn't exactly have as fresh a perspective as would come with time. But I still liked it. Maybe taking out the lesbian angle would neutralize Horton's objections. Perhaps Honey and her sister, Helen, could both fall in love with a male nurse? Naaah. I rejected the idea as immediately as it came. What I liked most was the way the love was such a surprising and unprecedented event for all three women, how it came even after they each surrendered their traditional dreams for it, in a form they had never anticipated. I would have to improve the dialogue, somehow infuse the odd story with reality.

My alarm beeped in the midst of my reverie. It was five-thirty and I had to be at work in an hour. In a fit of insanity, I had agreed to sub for the Ashtanga Sunrise class at Harmony Yoga. The only practical thing I have done in the past year is to get certified as a yoga instructor. Rather than spending $100 a month on yoga classes, I actually get *paid*. (Don't even get me started on the level of abject poverty grad school entails). With a sigh, I set aside my unwieldy screenplay and went to find yoga clothes.

The lobby at Harmony was empty when I got there, but I was surprised to see that the class was full. (Did the word *sunrise* not frighten these people?) I slid my disc into the CD player. I burn my own yoga discs. I'm not overly fond of the "sounds of nature" pseudo-music that dominates most classes. If I wanted to hear birds chirping and leaves rustling, I wouldn't have moved to New York in the first place. Today's disc blended female vocalists like Sarah McLachlan and Shawn Colvin with some seventeenth-century German sonatas.

"Hi everyone, I'm Charlie Frost. I'm subbing for Nishtha today. If you have any questions, please stop me at any point. We'll start standing up with a half sun salutation." The class obligingly stood at the edge of their mats, hands in prayer position. This is something that totally surprised me when I first started teaching. A whole roomful of people doing what I tell them! Imagine!

The best thing about teaching yoga is that there is no mental activity involved. It's all what you feel—and if you can disconnect enough from the physical exertion of the class, it's possible to enter a very different zone. There are always two or three students in every class who get it. Then there are about ten women who want arms that look like Madonna's, five who have been told by their therapists to learn to relax, two who enjoy being trendy, four leonine and buff men more flexible than I am, and one or two really stiff guys who can barely straighten their legs. For some reason, they always show up with cushiony mats, then blush like thirteen-year-olds when I explain that those are used for pre-natal yoga.

By the time we bent forward, murmuring *namaste* in clos-ing, I was in a phenomenal mood. Forget Horton or the Jablonski: I could take on the world. Gathering my hair into a sweaty knot, I bounced up to the lobby, waving at Sahra, Harmony's owner, as I passed. I was so busy barreling along that I just barely stopped myself from crashing into a guy who was coming in the door.

"Oh, sorry! Sorry!" I gasped. Then I SAW. He was beauti-ful. Better than Tom Cruise, better than Pierce Brosnan, bet-ter than Kenneth Branagh ten years ago, possibly better than Adonis himself. I felt my mouth turning up into a weak, in-advertent smile.

"Not a problem." He skirted around me and entered the studio. Did he go here? We might meet again. We'd gotten off to a very good start, really. *Sorry. Not a problem.* That was promising dialogue . . .

I had enough time to go home and shower before heading to my first class of the semester. Despite the momentary dis-traction of the hot guy at Harmony, my one-track mind was busy composing my Jablonski personal statement as I pushed through the turnstile exit at West Ninety-sixth Street.

I didn't see the mugger until he was on me.

He lunged as I started to go up the stairs, pushing me down with his knee until I was pinned to the floor. I could feel his hands tugging at my purse. Automatically, I yanked back.

"Give it," he commanded. I turned my head away from the fetid, rotten smell of his breath.

"No!"

I said it without thinking, a reflex born not out of fear but

entitlement. It was *my* purse, after all. Common sense kicked
in. "No. You can take my wallet, but not the purse," I bab-
bled. "I need stuff in here, like notes for my thesis. They're
worthless to you. Please. You can have the wallet. But not the
bag." I found the wallet and handed it to him. It took him a
while to get off me. Nothing felt real. Despite my total pho-
bia of subway liquid, I was crouched on the gray cement, my
face mere inches away from a murky puddle.

"Don't scream." He started up the steps. I hadn't seen his
face, didn't even know what race he was.

I screamed anyway. Loudly. A real 1980s horror movie,
bring-on-the-ketchup-and-fake-blood scream. Then I charged
up the stairs behind him. He stuck out one filthy leg and I
tripped over it. There wasn't time to react to the pain. I got
up and raced after him.

"Somebody stop him! He stole my wallet! Help! Help!"

God bless New York.

I saw a doorman drop the taxi door he was holding open
for a woman and take off after the mugger. The woman said
something to the driver and came over to me. A small crowd
had gathered. Two other men joined the doorman in the
chase. Someone put a coat around my shoulders. I hadn't
been frightened until then. Now I started to shake. I could
hear fragments of the conversation swelling around me.

"Just now it happened? Here?"

"I've been living at this subway stop for fifteen years.
Never saw anything like this."

"Was there anyone else there?"

"You poor girl. I bet he was just waiting for a little thing
like you to come along."

"It's eight A.M., for crying out loud."

The woman from the taxi leaned forward and touched my
arm. "Are you OK?"

I could feel my lip quivering overtime. I nodded. My head

felt flimsy and uncontrollable. I kept nodding and nodding and nodding. The woman guided me inside the lobby of her building.

"You just wait here. Robert will come back in a second, and he'll call the police for you. Do you want to tell me what happened?"

I shook my head. And shook. And shook. We sat there in the lobby for what seemed an eternity until Robert came back. My ears were buzzing. I vaguely heard Robert and the woman conversing; the woman left and Robert said something to me that I didn't hear. I sat on the bench in the lobby, buzzing, for a long time.

"Thank you," I said at last. "I guess I should go."

Robert shook his head at me. "The police are coming. You should talk to them. I'd offer you tea or something, but I don't want to leave the lobby empty." He paused. "Sorry I couldn't get your wallet."

"It's OK." Robert had closely cropped black curls and looked to be about my age. "I'm Charlie. I live up the street." We shook hands.

"You have a big bruise here." Robert pointed to my shoulder.

"Do I? I fell when I was running after him." I leaned against the wall and closed my eyes. Getting mugged at eight A.M. seemed like a perfectly plausible excuse never to venture out for sunrise yoga again. After a while Robert tapped me on the nonbruised shoulder. I looked up and saw the police were here. There were two of them, one burly and redheaded, the other older with thinning hair and gray, papery skin. They asked a lot of questions, most of which I couldn't answer.

"Honestly, I didn't even notice him waiting there. You see so many sketchy people in the subway that you just start to tune them out," I repeated for what seemed like the twelfth time. I suppose if you have a police car and the freedom to park illegally, you can remain in blissful ignorance of all the freaks that inhabit the subway.

"OK," the redheaded one said. "Let me phone this in. Where do you live? We'll take you home."

"Three blocks up. Ninety-ninth. I can walk."

"We'll take you there. You still look kind of shaken."

He and the older cop walked over to the car. Robert looked at me.

"This is going to sound very strange, but I was wondering if you'd want to go out sometime, maybe for dinner. You know, under better circumstances."

Did he just ask me out? Did he have a victim complex? Or a fetish for sweaty women with bruises? On the other hand, he had just chased a mugger down the street for me. Plus I was much too addled to come up with a polite excuse. I wrote down my name and address.

It would be a romantic way to describe how we met. *He chased my mugger down the street.*

three

"What I don't get," Karen said, "is how you can be so totally melodramatic about burning a bagel but brush off a mugging." She was upside down at the time she said this, attempting a shoulder stand on my new yoga mat. Her legs were separated. I pushed them together.

"Well, it's not that I take it lightly," I defended myself. "But it's almost like this is something too big to dwell on. It's been a week already and I still don't want to go out that same subway exit. I can't afford to get too emotional about this or I'd never venture outside again." Karen wobbled a bit. "Hey, Kar, you're shaky because you're not straight. I'm going to lift you by your feet up into the air so that you can readjust your arms. Try and bring them as high up your back as you can." She nodded, very red in the face. I tugged her into the air. When I let her back down onto the mat, she was much more stable.

"Besides, I can think of this as just one more classic New York experience that I've now had."

"All I can say is that I have lived in New York my entire life and never been mugged," Karen said. She rolled slowly out of her shoulder stand the way I'd shown her, bringing her legs over her face first. "Well, you look nice. The doorman will be very impressed."

Robert was due any second now. He'd called promptly

the day after we met, but I'd put off going out with him. Now that I thought about it, I wasn't sure I wanted to date anyone who reminded me of that whole grisly episode. Besides, I'd barely had time to shower lately, let alone go out to dinner. Why is it that disaster never strikes when you have time to deal with it? The Jablonski application was due next week. I'd missed the whole first day of classes. Requesting new credit cards and ID had involved at least ten hours wading through automated systems. There was a pimple roughly the size of Montana looming on my chin. If he hadn't mentioned Gennaro's when he called, I might have turned him down all together. But I'd have to be one picky fish not to fall for that bait.

The buzzer rang. I dabbed a bit more concealer on my chin and blew Karen a kiss goodbye. Aside from my chin, I did look good. With the four-inch heels on my boots, I was almost five-six. Robert apparently liked the result.

"Wow. You look a lot better than the last time I saw you," he greeted me.

OK. So sometimes people say things that are probably harmless, but I get touchy anyway. This was one of those times. Could he have come up with a more backhanded greeting? Translated, he meant, "I didn't expect you to be so hot because you looked like a blobby lump when I asked you out."

(I really am trying to increase the level at which my automatic bitch reflex kicks in.)

I smiled brightly. "Do you often ask out women who are mugged on your corner?"

"You're the first."

"To be mugged or to be asked out?"

"Both."

We were walking downtown. It was colder than I'd expected. I buttoned the front of my mesh cardigan.

"Do you like being a doorman?"

Robert looked at me as though I had asked him if he enjoyed snorting pulverized beetle. What was so odd about that? People ask me if I like film school all the time. Besides, when you've lived for four years in a walk-up, doormen become fascinating.

"It's OK," he answered. "It's a job, you know. I like the neighborhood a lot." We entered the restaurant. Gennaro's is the size of a fingernail and doesn't take reservations. There was already a hefty line. Robert gave his name and we settled ourselves to wait on the bench outside. He really was very nice looking. Not hot, precisely, but I knew that if I got close enough he would smell like soap and flannel shirts and other comforting things. He probably coached Little League in his spare time.

"Do you live around here?"

"No, in Brooklyn."

"That must be quite a commute."

"It's not that bad unless it's really late at night. The subway's under construction, you know."

"I know."

I longed to be at home in my sweatpants. This date was scoring a million on the Dead Conversation Scale.

"And then he leaned over and said, 'I think you've got tomato sauce on your chin' and tried to wipe off my zit!!!!"

Karen and Marisa shrieked with appreciative laughter. It was the following night and we were in the middle of a marathon Whine and Wine session. Marisa had managed to score a palatial house-sitting gig on Riverside and Eightieth for six months while a woman at her job worked out of the company's London office. It lent an air of respectability to our gatherings.

"What on earth did you do?" Karen was flopped on the floor, wearing a pair of absolutely archaic sweatpants and a T-shirt that said "Homecoming '92."

"There wasn't much I could do. I just blurted out, 'I think that's a pimple.' He jumped back and started apologizing profusely, and we had another ten minute conversation damper." I grimaced at the memory. "I am never dating again. I think I'm going to be celibate. I wasted an entire night that I could have been working on the Jablonski application." I reached for another scallion pancake. Chinese food can heal all wounds.

Karen rolled her eyes. "I hate that feeling—the I'm-wasting-time-just-by-being-here feeling."

"I get that every day at work," Marisa offered. Karen and I looked at her and she shrugged. "It's true."

"I don't know why I agreed to go out with him," I said, diverting the conversation back.

"Well, you were in *shock*," Marisa said. "Give yourself a break, Charlie. You'd just been mugged."

"Sure. But I think I went out with him simply because he asked. I'm not like you, Maris. I don't get asked out all the time." I shrugged. "I was flattered."

"Which is fine," Karen said. "There's no reason to be ashamed of that."

"Thank you, Doctor." I said. "But do you want to know something horrible? Something that I probably should be ashamed of?"

"What?"

I studied the oil congealing unattractively on my pancake before I answered. "I didn't like that he was a doorman." Karen and Marisa were quiet. "I think the conversation was so terrible because we had absolutely nothing in common."

"Do you mean to say that there are people in this world who *haven't* checked out the Walker Evans exhibit at the Met?" Marisa gasped dramatically to emphasize her point. "And he hadn't made it to Lincoln Center for that Lebanese film noir thing you dragged me to?"

I made a face at her. "OK, yes, that was part of the problem. But it was more that he's happy being a doorman. He has absolutely no other ambitions in life. I don't like to be around people who feel that there's nothing worth working for in life or that they've accomplished their entire life before the age of thirty."

"Charlie, you're so intensely ambitious that maybe that's exactly the kind of guy you need," Karen said seriously. "I'm not saying that you should reconsider Robert, but maybe you should think about whether a relationship could sustain another ambition as driving and all-encompassing as your own."

Could she have picked anything more depressing to throw in my face? Where were those empathy skills she was supposed to be learning in school?

"Could you separate the doorman and the lack of ambition bits?" Marisa asked. "Would it have been OK if he were a completely unambitious Ivy-educated lawyer?"

"I don't know." It was a good point. "Probably not. I don't think I could ever be happy with someone who didn't at least understand why it's important for me to be ambitious." I sighed. "I really, really don't like talking about this. It makes me feel like I'm some horrible uppity geek destined to be lonely forever."

Marisa ran a hand through her curly hair. "Charlie, you're not destined to be lonely forever."

"That's good."

"But you are definitely an uppity geek."

There are times when you just don't want your friends to tell the truth.

To: instructors@harmonyyoga.com
From: sahralove@harmonyyoga.com
Re: Class attire

Dear instructors:

In light of Harmony's growing celebrity clientele (how exciting!), I am writing to request that you devote some thought to your teaching attire before coming to class. It is up to us to project the confidence, balance, and poise associated with Harmony Yoga. In particular, I feel that old, stained, or holy clothing is not appropriate for teaching. (By holy, I mean clothing with holes in it, not spiritual). To aid you in selecting the best possible garments, I am offering all instructors an additional twenty percent discount on clothing sold in the Harmony store. We have just gotten in new colors for the SpiritMove support tanks and pants—including beet, sage, and mushroom!

Sahra

To: Charlie <cfrost@columbfilm.edu>
From: Katherine Frost <katherine_frost@spacecom.net>
Re: Your Safety

Charlie dear—

I tried to send you a care package but the post office wouldn't let me because I had included several bottles of mace and pepper spray. In light of recent events (which I won't go into because you have said that you don't want to talk about them and I respect this), I feel that it is imperative that you carry some personal protection with you. Mace and pepper spray are available at any hardware store. I know you're busy, but please try to pick some up.

I have just gotten the new Margaret Atwood book. You can have it when I'm finished.

Love,
Mom

To: Horton <hlear@columbfilm.edu>
From: Charlie <cfrost@columbfilm.edu>
Re: Return of the prodigal grad student

Horton—

I hate to ask—but do you have a copy of *The Battleship Potemkin* anywhere? We are supposed to watch it for Russian and Soviet film, but it's been checked out of both the library and Kim's Video for a week now. If you don't, that's OK (the ship goes down, right?), but it would be helpful.

Also, thanks for proofing the final *Honey and Helen* draft. I guess I'll hear about the Jablonski in a few weeks. It's really good to know that even though you don't support the screenplay, you support me.

Let me know about the movie,

Charlie

four

Having stomped through September like Attila the Hun, I decided to make some October resolutions:

1. I will not be such an asshole to other people when I am in a foul mood—no matter how justified.
2. I will work diligently and with good humor on whatever thesis project I end up doing.
3. I will spend more time with my parents and grandmother.
4. I will be more vigilant about tweezing my eyebrows. There's no need to look like a Neanderthal.

This is how the morning of October 1 began:

Scene: Ninety-ninth Street, New York City

Camera pans CHARLIE as she leaves her building, waving cheerfully at her sleazy neighbor MR. MARCELLO. CHARLIE is dressed more chicly than we have seen her before. MARCELLO'S eyes follow CHARLIE as she walks to the corner. As she turns uptown,

*we see a close-up of her face: blemish-free,
a hint of Chanel Nude lipstick, marvelously
arched brows. She enters Starbucks.*

*Scene: Crowded Starbucks, buzz of
conversation fills room*

CHARLIE approaches counter.

> BARISTA *(chirps)*:
> Hi! I'm betting you want a grande skim
> caramel macchiato with extra caramel. *Camera
> off CHARLIE'S startled face.*

What can I say? Obviously, giving up caffeine was not on my list of improvements. There are some things that shouldn't even be attempted. Still—you know it's been a bad month when Starbucks has your order memorized.

I hadn't had the guts to make it an official resolution (even to myself), but I also wanted to improve the whole relationship part of my life. Robert was more than par for the course in my dismal romantic career. Despite my persistent, outrageous fantasies, I flit from date to date, feeling trapped or bored or generally aggravated. It's been years since I've had a second date with anyone. I can't even remember what it's like to have a real boyfriend.

The truth? Sometimes I wonder if I am even capable of love.

"So why does Kuleshov choose to emphasize the shadows in this scene?" Professor Rhonda Bain hit pause on the VCR and looked expectantly at the class. "What does he accomplish here?"

"It's character establishment." My least favorite classmate, Miguel Reynard-Arora, was the first to answer. "He places the husband and wife in darkness to show that they are evil. The guest is bathed in white light to show innocence."

"But the guest isn't innocent," I countered. "He's killed someone."

"And the husband and wife aren't evil," Chris Martin added. "They're stupid and vengeful, but also pious. They believe that they are enacting the will of God."

"Why the shadows then?" Rhonda repeated.

Theories are batted about the room. White is meant to represent the blankness of the guest's past. When the guest sits at the shadowed table with the couple, he enters their world. It could be a way of reinforcing the cultural differences between the characters since black is the traditional color associated with death in the West whereas white signifies mourning in Asian countries. What a yawnfest.

"Maybe," I said slowly, "we're trying too hard to attribute meaning to something that has none. If you take the shadows to be just that—shadows, rather than something symbolic— the scene looks exactly like a painting. The contrast between the light is so purposeful that it's like religious art during the sixteenth and seventeenth centuries. It reminds me most of something Caravaggio would paint, but it could be referencing anything from that era."

The room was quiet for a second. "Tell me more," said Rhonda. "Why would Kuleshov want to make an allusion to that period or that type of art?

Good question. I hadn't thought my theory out that far before voicing it. "Well, the film is filled with religious themes, so this could be another way of emphasizing that imagery. But also, artists from that time were commissioned to paint certain topics, whether or not they believed in them. Kuleshov lived in a time when the themes of art were similarly dictated by the government. He was essentially ordered to make Soviet propaganda movies. Maybe it's a silent reference to that lack of choice—a nod to the artists who are told what to paint or film or write."

I could tell Rhonda liked the theory. Charlie Frost dazzles again.

"It seems totally farfetched," said Miguel sulkily.

Please. Just because we didn't buy your Mickey Mouse white-is-good-and-black-is-evil bit . . .

Anyway, I was not going to blow Resolution #1 on such an unworthy specimen. I smiled sweetly at Miguel and raised my magnificent new eyebrows.

"Why do you say that, Miguel?" Rhonda inquired with greater diplomacy than I could have managed.

"You can't expect Kuleshov to assume his viewers would know about sixteenth century art. This was a propaganda film for the proletariat. I mean, *hello??!!*"

What can I say? He had me at *hello*. Once I heard the derision in his voice, I was up and running, all resolutions temporarily suspended.

"Hello??!!" I echoed sarcastically. "That's precisely my point, Miguel. Kuleshov could *only* get away with making a subtle, veiled protest against government control over art. He had to find a reference that wouldn't be understood by the viewers and the censorship committees. Nevertheless, Kuleshov was aware that his films constituted his legacy to filmmaking. He envisioned people debating the imagery of his mise-en-scène. I know he wrote something about this after he defected."

"It still seems like kind of a crackpot academic theory," Miguel broke in.

I ignored his jibe and began scanning Kuleshov's autobiography for support. "Here," I announced triumphantly. "On page 176, he writes: 'I played games with the censors, hiding bitter and arcane messages within my films. Look carefully, and you will find them.'" I paused to let the quote sink in. "Later in the same passage, he writes, 'I don't approve of obvious symbolism. A film should be like an onion, with layers and skins waiting to be peeled apart.'" I had the little stinker tied up in knots now. "Don't you think that interpreting black as evil is a little simplistic for a symbolist of Kuleshov's magnitude? Listen, Sherlock, that's hardly an onion of a theory. As far as I'm concerned, the only similarity is that it brings tears to my eyes."

I didn't think the last bit was that funny, but a roar of laughter greeted my diatribe. Game, set, and match to Charlotte Frost.

After class, I realized that I was going to have to pass Horton's office on my way out of the building. I hadn't exactly been avoiding him. But I didn't want to talk to him until I knew about the Jablonski funding. Horton's door was open, but I was pretty sure he wouldn't notice me. Frankly, if Horton is working, the entire Big Apple Circus could prance by without comment. I sauntered past.

"Charlie?" he called. "Do you have a second?"

Shit.

"I heard that!" Oh no, had I said that *aloud?* Could I possibly dig this pit of mortification any deeper? At least he sounded amused. Grumpily, I retraced my steps.

"Hi, Horton."

"Are you avoiding me because you don't know if you've gotten the Jablonski?"

"No." *Yes.*

"Really?"

"Well, OK, yes. I was trying not to talk to you. But now I feel like a total fool. Am I that predictable?" *Or transparent. Or neurotic.*

Horton shook his head. "I know you pretty well, Charlotte. Look, I don't care about the Jablonski. Whatever happens is going to happen. I had a favor to ask of you." Horton began to rummage through the waist-high towers of screenplays on his floor. Two towers toppled before he found what he was looking for.

"Can you read this? I want your opinion."

"Sure." There was a big coffee stain on the front of the script. "What is it? Is it someone applying for next year?"

"Naw, just something a friend wanted me to take a look at. I had mixed feelings and wanted a second opinion."

"I love that you just used the term *second opinion* to refer to a script rather than a possible medical disease."

Horton shook his head again, this time in feigned exasperation. "By the way, Mallory and I have tickets to *Rigoletto* that we're not going to be able to use. Do you want them?"

"Are you kidding me?" I squealed. "Absolutely!"

"I'll put them in your mailbox. They're for next month. Mallory also wants you to come for dinner. She's planning to send you an e-mail to set it up."

"Did you tell her I was avoiding you?"

Horton looked sheepish. "I may have mentioned it."

How embarrassing. I studied the floor intently for a few seconds. "Horton, I hate that I'm applying for the Jablonski and you don't think I deserve to get it."

"Oh, Charlie," Horton said sadly.

It was a little hard to tell with all the papers on the floor, but as far as I could see there were seven tiles running the width of the office and twelve down the length.

"Whatever I think about *Honey and Helen*, I still want you to get the fellowship. You absolutely deserve it. I just feel that some of your other work is more promising. But I know that, for whatever reason, you feel very strongly about this screenplay. And I respect that. I'd be disappointed if you had let me talk you out of using it even though *you* thought it could work." He squeezed my shoulder. "You're acting the way real filmmakers act."

"Thanks." I looked up. I wanted to say something more, but didn't know what or how.

"It's the truth. You can repay me by e-mailing Mallory. Also, maybe you could stop slinking past my office and cursing."

Resolution #5: I will make it through an entire conversation with Horton without humiliating myself.

five

Despite Sahra's e-mail, I had not invested in a new sage-colored yoga outfit. If I am so poor that I have to take the subway home at four A.M., I am not going to drop $40 on a tank top that makes me look seasick. My concession to projecting confidence and poise was to brush my hair before class.

Had I known the Yummy Stranger I'd seen a few weeks earlier would be in the class, I might have gotten the tank, a haircut, Bliss facial, full body wax . . .

As it was, I just looked like myself. He was the same chiseled jaw, wavy hair, sculpted perfection. And he absolutely stunk at yoga. His downward dog was so precariously upward that I was afraid he might injure himself. Halfway through the third round of sun salutation, I moved to help him. Sometimes the only way to teach a student having that much trouble is to place him into the correct pose. The hottie's shoulders were pulled up to his ears. I tapped them.

"You want to bring these down. Good—that's much better. Now curl the toes under." I moved his feet for him. "Now, quick, push back into downward dog. Keep the hips high in the air. Keep your legs as straight as possible." I ran my finger behind his knees, feeling the muscles buckle and strain under the faint pressure. Sweat gleamed faintly across his neck. "There you go. Take a moment to feel where you are now." He let out a deep, shuddering exhale that I hoped was due more to Zen awareness than plain exhaustion or pain. I moved on to the next student, proud of myself for resisting copping a feel. He was really, really beautiful.

Sahra corralled me as I was leaving the studio. "Charlie, wait, can you do another class today? Miriam just canceled."

"Oh." I thought for a second about my resolution to spend more time with my family. "I'm having dinner with my parents. Is the class now?"

"Half an hour." Sahra looked expectantly at me. "I'll pay you extra."

It was four-thirty. If I taught the five-to-six-thirty class, I would make it to Long Island—unshowered, in my yoga clothes—around seven-forty-five.

"Sahra, I don't know. Can't you get anyone else?"

"I've tried. I could teach myself, but would rather not. Charlie, you can make it there in time for dinner. It's only the suburbs."

"I won't make it there for the obsessively early hour when my family likes to eat. Six was already a bit wild for them." On the other hand, I was very broke. "How much extra?"

"Class plus half."

"What about double?" I was pushing it. But if I was going to break my resolution, it was going to be worth it.

A sour look flitted across Sahra's usually beatific features. "Fine."

I walked over to a bench along the wall and pulled out my cell phone. There was no one home. They were probably all waiting at the train station for me already.

"Hi, it's me. I'm really sorry, but I have to teach this extra yoga class tonight and I'm going to be later than I said. I'll call when I know which train I'll be on. Go ahead and eat if you're starving and I'll be there in time for coffee and dessert."

I was a rotten, rotten daughter. They should have left me on a mountaintop to be devoured by wolves when I was a baby. But no doubt some kind goatherd would have found me and I would have grown up to fulfill my destiny of being self-absorbed and poverty-stricken anyway.

"Hey. I'm sorry to interrupt. Can I ask you something?"

I looked up. The Yummy Greek God Stranger smiled at me. *Of course you can ask me something. Would you like to do it before or after we ride off into the sunset together?*

"Sure," I said aloud.

"I didn't quite get what we were doing in class. So you're here . . ." He put himself into a very awkward Warrior II pose. "Then you lean forward and what next?" He was about to keel over.

"It's like this." I demonstrated. "Place your hand six inches on the right side of your foot. Lift the other leg. When you can keep your balance here—and that can take months to achieve—look up at the ceiling."

"Months?"

"It's yoga. You can't rush it. You're supposed to be spiritual enough to appreciate the quest." Ooops. That might have been too sarcastic. The Yummy Stranger didn't look too offended.

"Even when you teach two classes in a row?"

"Did you hear that?" I shook my head. "Sorry."

"It was my fault. I wanted to ask you about the pose. I shouldn't have been eavesdropping. Is your family going to be upset?"

I rolled my eyes. "Yes. My grandmother will start squealing about how hard I have to work and offer me money about ten times. My father will be essentially silent except to quote some obscure poem that is barely relevant to the situation and that I won't recognize as a poem. My mother will claim that it's not a problem and that she understands but she will snoan periodically in disgust."

"Snoan?"

"Uhhrrhhhrssg," I demonstrated. "That is a snoan. It is obvious to me that I am slowly turning into my mother. But if I ever start snoaning, I may have to have my vocal cords surgically removed."

He smiled. There were dimples. "Well, you're very good at yoga and I'm sure the next class will be glad to have you."

I shrugged modestly. "Especially when I start to introduce headstands again. Seriously, thanks. I love teaching."

"Well, I'll probably see you again." He slung a perfectly battered leather jacket around his shoulders, flashed me a ladykiller smile, and loped off.

Be still my throbbing heart.

six

When I finally got to my parents' house, my mother and grandmother were camped out in the kitchen drinking champagne. This is a pretty typical scene in my family. My grandmother drinks nothing but champagne, coffee, and (occasionally, in dire circumstances, when forced), a very dry white wine. Every day at four o'clock, she has a glass of champagne while she watches *Judge Judy*.

"Sugarbaby," she squeaked when she saw me.

"Hi, Gran." I kissed her. "Hi, Mom." At five-two, I towered over them both. "Any champagne left?"

"Don't you want dinner?"

"Sure, what is there?"

They both went into a flurry of Tasmanian Devil activity. Much as I play up the drama of going home, I always feel better when I get here.

"I can't believe you had to work so late," Gran said. "My poor baby."

I shrugged and began to devour some pasta.

"Mom, please," said my mother. "Charlie couldn't help it."

"But she's so overworked. I haven't seen her in absolute ages."

"I was out here last week, Gran. Remember?"

"Really? Well, anything seems like ages when it's my only granddaughter."

No wonder I feel guilty all the time.

"How's your social life?" Gran asked. This, translated, meant "Are you dating anyone yet?"

"It's social," I replied. My policy is that if you ask a vague question, you get a vague answer.

"Well, are there any new boys we should know about?"

"Nope," I said.

"What about the doorman? He sounded safe."

I made a face. "I see him all the time. Every time I go in the subway. Every time I go out of the subway."

"But are you dating him?" Mom asked.

"I don't think we have enough in common. He likes the Yankees."

My mother emitted a petite mini-snoan. This was definitely not a topic of conversation I wanted to pursue.

"What about you, Gran? Any new men in your life?" Since my grandfather died three years ago, I have become the central excitement in Gran's life. It wouldn't be the worst thing in the world if she were to find a nice Gentleman Caller somewhere.

"Ooooh, aren't you the fresh one?" She laughed, flattered.

I really, really needed some champagne.

In the interest of familial bonding (and because I was dog-tired), I ended up spending the night on Long Island. When I woke up, there was an envelope on the night table. I opened it.

Charlie—

Just in case you ever want to buy an ice cream soda.

Love,
Granny

There was a check for $100 inside. Hmmm. She must have left it there last night. I had crashed before Dad drove Gran back to her house.

Downstairs, the kitchen was quiet, with the *New York Times* already disheveled on the table. Someone had left out a pot of hot coffee. I poured a cup and picked up the phone.

"Gran, that was completely unnecessary," I said when she answered.

"What?"

"Playing Tooth Fairy and leaving me money by my pillow."

"Oh, well, I thought you could use it."

That was an understatement. "I can. But I don't want you to feel you have to give me money. I can always use more, but honestly I'm doing OK."

"Didn't you just have to buy books?"

"Well, yeah, but—"

Gran cut me off. "Charlie, take it and enjoy it. I won't make a habit out of it."

"OK."

"Treat yourself to something fun. I just saw these nice yoga tanks with the bra built right in. It's amazing what they come up with these days. And they had the most exquisite colors."

What was it with yoga clothing? I didn't think I looked that disreputable. "Maybe. Thanks, Granny."

"Bye, sweetheart."

I read the screenplay Horton had given to me on the train back to the city. It was excellent—witty and charming with lots of adorable, fanciful scenes. But I had a sneaking fear that he had given it to me as a possible directing project in case I didn't get the Jablonski. Not only did I want to direct one of my own screenplays, I definitely didn't want to do something adorable and fanciful.

If I didn't get this fellowship, my life was going to devolve into utter hell.

To: Charlie <cfrost@columbfilm.edu>
From: Sahra <sahralove@harmonyyoga.com>
Re: Keep up the good work!

Charlie—

I saw you giving Hank Destin a little extra help the other day. Just so you know, that's more than fine with me. I'm hoping he'll be a big link for our studio.

Sahra

To: Sahra <sahralove@harmonyyoga.com>
From: Charlie <cfrost@columbfilm.edu>
Re: Keep up the good work! [2]

Who's Hank Destin?

Charlie

To: Charlie <cfrost@columbfilm.edu>
From: Sahra <sahralove@harmonyyoga.com>
Re: Keep up the good work! [3]

Darling, maybe you should think about leaving your ivory tower one of these days. Just a bit of advice.

—S

seven

There are few things less Zen in this world than standing over a toner-less Xerox machine with a half-copied chapter on Eisenstein and less than twenty minutes to go before a yoga class almost forty blocks away. It was with some effort that I refrained from tapping my foot impatiently as the undergraduate library assistant tinkered with various knobs and cartridges. I was going to have to take a cab to get there on time, which would mean that I would spend almost a third of my paycheck for the class just *getting* there.

"Um," said the library assistant, standing up. "I can't get it to work. You might have to come back." She was covered in ink, with a large black smear across one cheek, and looked as close to a forlorn Dickensian orphan as you could be expected to find on the Upper (Upper) West Side.

"There's no way I can get back today. Are you sure I can't just check the book out?"

"It's noncirculating."

"I know—but I need it for a paper that's due tomorrow," I lied, "and I'm a graduate student." For some reason, grad students always get better library privileges than undergrads. It's assumed that we have such rich and vital academic lives that a due date under six months is an imposition. "Is there any way you could make an exception?" I begged.

The assistant shifted from foot to foot, looking uneasy. "I'm not supposed to."

I looked at her. She faltered a bit. Apparently, I had taken to menacing young girls as a new hobby. I increased the pressure on my look.

"But maybe I could leave a note explaining everything for my supervisor and if I got your phone number, you could bring it back if there was a problem, right?" she offered.

"Absolutely," I agreed, following her to the front desk and handing over my student ID with relief.

While I was scrawling my name and phone number on a slip of paper, Miguel Reynard-Arora slithered up to the front desk.

"I can't seem to find this book," he said huffily, shoving a printout at the assistant. "That section is so disorganized," he fumed. "Hi, Charlie," he added, as an afterthought.

"Hi, Miguel," I said obligingly. I was pretty sure we were targeting the same section of books and that I might be responsible for some of the alleged disorganization. I checked my watch. Fifteen minutes till class. Crud.

"I'll be with you in a second," the assistant said. She still had the black smudge of ink on her cheek. As she flipped my book over to stamp the inside, Miguel caught a glimpse of the title.

"I didn't realize that was a circulating book," he announced.

"Oh, um," the student said.

"It is now," I said brusquely, cutting off any explanation she might feel the need to make. I swept the book into my bag and turned to leave. Fourteen minutes.

"I might need that book for my paper," Miguel said.

"It'll be back soon."

"Like today?"

I flipped to the due date. "Looks like I've got it till Saturday."

"How come you can check it out?" Miguel demanded. What an aggravating bastard.

"If someone else needs it, you'll have to bring it back today," the assistant broke in, looking worried. She was probably already regretting her minor lapse in protocol.

"The copier is broken, Miguel," I said. "Tell me what chapters you need and I'll be glad to copy them for you."

"How can I tell if I can't look at the book?"

The assistant began to look excessively frightened and waifish.

"Maybe I shouldn't let you take this out," she said timidly.

It was impossible that there could be a more irritating human on this planet than Miguel. Impossible.

"OK, I am very late for yoga," I said with effort. "I will have this book back in the library by seven tonight. Just give me time to teach my class and get to a functioning copy machine, OK?"

"Oh, of course," Miguel agreed magnanimously. "How's your thesis coming, by the way?"

"It's coming," I replied. "Miguel, I am really, really late. I have to go."

"Are you applying for the Jablonski?"

What a nosy asshole.

"Like I said, gotta run!" I eased my way out of his slimy claws and headed for the door. The sensor began beeping wildly as I passed by with my illicit checkout. I let it go and headed for Broadway as fast as I could. Twelve minutes till class.

Halfway through Surinamascara B I noticed that the superstud from last week was back, all dimples, biceps, and an abominable downward dog pose. I adjusted his arms and feet and hips. Repeatedly. I wondered if this was Sahra's mysterious Hank Destin. And if so, why was he so important?

He lingered after class again, catching me as I twisted my sweaty hair up into an awkward bun.

"Hi. I have another question for you."

"Sure." I ejected my CD and put it into the case.

"I forget the name of it, but this"—he paused and arched into crescent pose—"is just killing my back." He straightened.

"Actually, do it again. OK, first of all, you need to angle your back foot inward. That's better. Now let's try bringing your hand a little higher up on your leg." I helped him balance as he readjusted. "Does that help?"

"Some. It still hurts."

"Crescent requires a lot of flexibility in your back. You may want to modify it until you're a little stronger. Do you remember the bridge pose?" He nodded. "If you practice the bridge at home, it'll help strengthen your back." I flicked the lights off and picked up my purse. We walked out of the studio.

"How long have you been doing yoga?" I asked.

"Just a month or so. My agent thought that I was getting a little too beefy from weight training. I guess the no-neck look isn't in."

"I just cannot stand those no neck monsters," I vamped reflexively. He looked puzzled. "*Cat on a Hot Tin Roof*?" I questioned.

"That's right! I forgot about that."

Phew. He had some knowledge of Tennessee Williams.

"I was Brick once, actually, for a scene in acting class years ago," he continued.

We had hit the lobby by now. Sahra, thank goodness, was nowhere to be seen. She was probably off weaving herself a tunic from organic flax.

"So you're an actor? That's why you have an agent."

"Yup. Just another New York cliché, I'm afraid."

"I'm one as well: grad student slash yoga instructor."

"In English?"

"Film, actually."

"Really!"

We walked outside, and the real world intruded unpleasantly, with taxi horns blaring at full volume.

"Are you heading downtown?" he asked.

"Up."

"I was just thinking we could have split a cab."

Can I take that back? The thought of rumbling across town in the back of a cab with him was absolutely enchanting. We both paused for a second. I didn't want to say goodbye and fervently hoped he was experiencing some of the same bittersweet leavetaking.

"Look, I know it's kind of tacky to do this on such short notice," he began. "But I don't have any plans for Saturday night and was wondering if you'd want to go to dinner." The beautiful dimples appeared. "I'd like to hear about film school."

My heart was skipping multiple beats. The most beautiful human alive had just asked me out.

"That sounds great. I was planning to spend the weekend writing my midterm on Soviet film, so I'm sure that I'll be in dire need of distraction by Saturday night." Ew. Why had I let him know what a geek I was? Sometimes I think my tongue has a life of its own. "I'm Charlie, by the way."

"I know. I caught your name at the beginning of class." He looked highly amused for a moment. "I'm Hank."

OK, evidently he was somebody. I had no idea who. Considering the amount of time I spend planning my fantasy film cast, it was kind of odd. I tend to keep tabs on actors with good reviews.

I scribbled down my phone number and ripped the page

out of my notebook. "Here's my number, so we can get in touch."

I'm not inventing this: as I walked to the subway, the sun emerged from behind a cloud.

eight

I was tempted to e-mail Sahra as soon as I got back to campus but couldn't deal with any more cryptic drama. Instead, I Googled Hank Destin on the Internet.

Never before had I entered such a lucrative search term. For a second, I thought the computer might erupt and spew microchips across the library. As best I could distill, here's what popped up: thirty-two articles from *Soap Opera Digest*, eleven from *Soap Stars*, one from *Entertainment Weekly*, five from the *New York Post*, nine from *The Hollywood Reporter*, three from *Variety*, six from *TV Guide*, one official Web site for *Troubled Passion*, and ninety-three fan sites, including www.hankisbuff.com.

Soap opera: that's why he had never popped up on my radar of talented actors. Not that there aren't talented actors with soap backgrounds (hello—Susan Sarandon?), but I tend not to follow soaps. Frankly, I wade through so much of my own melodrama that a daily dose of someone else's fictional problems has never seemed enticing. I checked the time of *Troubled Passion*. There was no way I was ever going to watch it unless I either figured out how to set my VCR or entered the TiVo generation. I glanced around me. I didn't see anyone in the library that I knew. Furtively, I double clicked on www.hankisbuff.com.

Let me just say that I thought I knew that Hank was

buff. Apparently, I had only scratched the surface of his superior buffness. Hank was more than buff. He made Michelangelo's *David* look like Chris Farley. His agent was crazy. There were many, many pictures proving that Hank was not turning into a chunky, Tennessee Williams no-neck monster.

For a brief second, I had a major eighth-grade anxiety attack. What could Hank Destin, burnished daytime love god, want with me?

Despite the looming Soviet film paper, I called an emergency Whine and Wine session on Friday night.

"They weren't kidding," said Marisa as she gazed at the computer screen. "Hank *is* buff!"

"I know! So did you bring me something to wear?"

"Just a second." Marisa enlarged one of the photos on the Web site. She made a slurping sound.

"Maris, please. Hands off and no drooling."

"I don't see how you can complain about no love life. First you had that doorman and now a soap star. That's two dates in two months, Charlie."

I hoped she was being sarcastic.

"I read somewhere that Pinot Noir is the new Shiraz," Karen announced out of the blue.

"Huh?"

"Well, you know Shiraz used to be the It wine, but now I think Pinot Noir is replacing it." Karen had downed her first glass awfully fast and was now twirling a second glass between her fingers.

"Well, I'm glad I brought something trendy," Marisa said.

"Did you bring anything trendy and wearable?" I asked.

"Yes, yes. Calm down. I brought you lots of clothing to try on."

"Had either of you guys ever heard of Hank Destin before now?"

"Honestly?" Karen asked.

"Honestly."

"No. But we share a television, Charlie. It's never on and we don't have cable."

"*Troubled Passion* is network, not cable."

"Whatever." Karen rolled her eyes. "I am practically *failing* statistics. I can't afford to stare at anything other than my computer screen right now."

"Marisa?"

"Unfortunately, not having the disposable graduate student schedule, I'm actually unavailable from two to three every day. My boss insists that I find the great American novel before Christmas, remember?" One of the consequences of climbing the publishing ladder as quickly as Marisa has means that she never engages in anything that remotely resembles a relaxing activity.

"So you guys think that people who watch soaps are people with nothing better to do with their time?" I asked.

"Maybe." Karen wrinkled her nose. "That's so snobby, though. If we had cable, I'd probably watch a lot more TV. But not soaps. They just don't appeal."

"To me either," I admitted. "I don't think I've ever watched a whole episode of any soap. I've never even heard of *Troubled Passion*. But I don't really like television in general. I'd rather read or watch a movie. Or talk to you guys." I drank some wine. "I can't believe this guy asked me out."

"Why?"

"I guess mainly because of how he looks, but also I can't imagine why me. He could have some spectacular leggy model. Besides, we don't have anything in common. What are we going to talk about? I guarantee that this is going to end up a repeat of Robert."

"It's not going to be a Robert repeat," Karen said definitely.

"Why not?"

"Because you're going to be so caught up in how he looks, you probably won't be able to carry on a conversation anyway."

nine

In preparation for my glamorous date with the man who launched a thousand Internet hits, I spent the day in sweatpants writing about religious imagery in Soviet film. Overnight I had somehow developed a horrible sore throat. By three, my head was whirling. I darted out for cough drops and Starbucks. With my luck, I'd have laryngitis by the time dinner rolled around.

Marisa had talked me into borrowing a soft black wrap dress that seemed tremendously low cut. (Being an A cup, I tend to shy away from baring my nonexistent cleavage.) But there was no denying that the dress was flattering, and this would be a perfect occasion to wear the Shoes of Sin. I had gotten them last year reduced from $200 to $50. Admittedly, I had no business buying ankle strap stilettos when I had to pay off $500 worth of textbooks. But they were so spectacular and so temptingly on sale that I caved on my resolution not to spend money unnecessarily, wore them once, accumulated seven blisters and relegated them to the depths of my closet.

I would endure more blisters for Hank Destin.

We had planned to meet at a restaurant in the West Village at eight. At seven-twenty, I tripped down to the subway, sneezing wildly. I had once heard that three sneezes meant luck was on its way. Was it possible that nine sneezes meant triple good luck? As I went into the subway, I heard a wolf whistle behind me.

"Got a hot date, Charlie?" It was Robert. Then again, maybe nine sneezes meant karmically disastrous luck.

"Hey, Robert. How are you?"

"Things have been slow lately. No muggings, nobody screaming from the subway . . ."

"I'll try and stir up a little petty crime to entertain you."

"You can entertain me without crime, Charlie."

I sighed. "I'm not going on a date, Robert. I just have dinner with a friend." I was overtaken by a massive coughing fit that was no doubt punishment for my lie.

"Like I'm buying that. He better be Brad Pitt if you're going out with that cough dressed like that."

Brad Pitt? Considering the circumstances, it wasn't a bad guess. I sucked in as much air as was possible through my strained chest.

"You know, Charlie, if you ever want to reconsider"—he grinned—"my *door* is always open." Not unless his sense of humor improved. Subtle and sardonic is always preferable to the weak pun.

When I finally got downtown, Hank was already talking to the bartender. He won major points for the restaurant. It was tiny, with orange and yellow walls, glowing wood tables, and thousands of little candles. *La Traviata* was playing softly in the background. The bar was some sort of coppery metal. I slid on the stool next to Hank, resisting the urge to leer "Well, hey there, sailor."

"Charlie, hi." He leaned over and kissed my cheek. The pit of my stomach plummeted. It was probably just the music. Opera has been known to have a similar effect on me as PMS: I get all weepy and emotional and overcome. "This is Vincenzo," Hank said, gesturing to the bartender. "I was just telling him about you."

He was telling someone about me? My stomach began another flip-flop. I shook hands with Vincenzo, who looked about fourteen.

"Do you come here a lot?"

"Oh, Vincenzo and I go way back," Hank said. Then he and Vincenzo began snorting and giggling like third graders. I raised my eyebrows. Hank let me suffer in confusion for a few minutes before adding, "I've been coming here for years; I used to live around the corner. His parents own this place. I used to take Vincenzo and his little brother to Knicks games."

"It's adorable," I said, looking around. "I love it."

"Do you want to sit down?"

"Sure."

Hank led the way to the back of the small room. We sat down at a table next to a cheerfully crackling fire. Any second now, I might overdose on charm.

"Actually, this is perfect," I said. "I've had the most dismal day. Both my roommate and I have midterms and we've just been camped out in front of our laptops all day."

"Is your roommate in film school also?"

"No. Karen is in psychology and she's been attempting to do statistics all afternoon. About once an hour, she's been screaming things like 'why can't you be a nice computer and do as I ask?' Then thirty seconds later, she stomps into my room and announces that there is a reason statistic rhymes with sadistic."

Hank laughed. I continued, "It's kind of off-putting. I mean, she *is* the reigning expert in my life on how to manage emotion."

The waiter came over and handed us menus. "Would you like wine?" Hank asked.

"Definitely."

"Let's get a bottle."

We bent over the wine list together. "Which looks better to you," he wondered, "the Montepulciano or the Chianti?"

Each bottle was over $40. I am the queen of the $8 Australian red. "Let's go for Montepulciano," I said. "I can rarely tell the difference between the two, but Montepulciano sounds so much better."

"I know what you mean. Sometimes I feel like a hick ordering Chianti in Italian restaurants." He signaled to the waiter and ordered. "Have you been to Italy?"

"Never. It's my number one place that I want to go. Mainly . . ." I paused. "Well, this is a little geeky, but it's mainly because of the art. I love sixteenth- and seventeenth-century Italian art, and to see the best of it, you have to go there. It's not the kind of thing that ever tours." I was babbling. "Have you been?"

"Several times. It's unbelievable. You have to go."

When I make my millions. The wine arrived and was uncorked with great fanfare. It was excellent. Hank and I decided to split braised artichokes as a starter. Clearly this was fate: we both loved artichokes. It takes a sensitive man to eat a baby artichoke.

"So you're an actor," I said.

"Mmm-hmm."

"Why did you decide to do that rather than something else?"

"You mean rather than get a real job?"

"No," I said, even though that was exactly what I had meant.

"It's OK. I get asked that all the time. Seriously, college just wasn't my thing. I mean, the partying was OK, but I wasn't into the academics and it all just seemed sort of silly."

College had definitely been my thing, *especially* the academics. I would go back in a heartbeat. In many ways, I don't think I have ever felt so challenged or nurtured or capable of growth. The rest of my life has been spent trying to eke out the same potential that I managed so effortlessly to evince at the tender age of twenty.

"Where were you in school?" I asked.

"Southern New Jersey State."

That was slightly unfortunate. I come from the kind of background where people don't go to the sort of state schools that also have geographical directions in the name. Michigan is one thing. Southern New Jersey State, on the other hand, would be snoan inducing. Still, there was no need to be so offensively elitist. It didn't mean he wasn't bright.

"So I dropped out and moved to New York and did the whole bartender routine," Hank continued. "I modeled for a while, but got really bored, so I took some acting classes, did some really awful theater so far off Broadway that I might as well have been back in Jersey. Then I got cast in a couple of soaps and it was all history."

"Is that what you do now?"

"Don't you know, Charlie?" he teased. "I'm Dr. Kendall Reston on *Troubled Passion.*"

I looked down into my wineglass for a second. Should I confess to my foray onto www.hankisbuff.com? What was I thinking? Definitely not. "How long have you been doing that?"

"Soaps in general, about seven years. I've been Kendall for almost four now. Eventually, I want to do something more serious, but for now, it's fine. The one thing that soaps have over theater or film is that every time I'm on a set, I'm doing something completely different. All the plot changes keep the work interesting."

I hadn't thought of television in that way. That's kind of how I feel about screenwriting. It's the one thing that's difficult enough for me to find consistently interesting. Every new scene presents a different challenge, a different puzzle to sort through.

"Plus, soaps pay more than bartending," Hank added.

The artichokes arrived and were phenomenal. We inhaled half the plate within five minutes.

"You know, Charlie," Hank said, "I don't think one plate of these is going to be enough for both of us."

"Possibly not." I stabbed one of the larger, juicier artichokes.

"Hey, I was going to eat that."

"Well, that's the risk you take when you invite a starving yoga instructor to dinner."

Hank motioned to the waiter and ordered a second plate of artichokes. I hoped he didn't think I was a monumental glutton. I'm sure the willowy models he usually dated didn't go through braised artichokes like they were beer nuts.

"How long have you been teaching yoga?" he asked.

"Not that long, actually. Maybe ten months? When I was working, I took yoga all the time, but when I went back to school I just couldn't afford to go that often. I was going to a place downtown then, and one of the instructors there suggested I take a certification course. It's my only West Coast affectation."

I drank some wine. We were almost down to the bottom of the bottle. What a decadent meal. Karen was at home drowning her statistics sorrow in Chinese food while I was plied with artichokes and Montepulciano.

I liked Hank. To be fair, I especially liked the way he looked and the fact that he had taken me to a charming, pricey West Village restaurant rather than a grotty grad student den. But it was also surprisingly easy to talk to him. A lot of times I feel bored on dates. Being with Robert, for example, had felt like work, whereas this whole meal was effortless. It was as though the entire affair had been elaborately choreographed especially for me. By the time we were drinking our after-dinner cappuccinos, I was lulled with so much wine and arti-choke and crackling fire that I felt comfortable sharing the *Honey and Helen* debacle with Hank.

"I'm just so confused," I said. "On one hand, I feel so strongly about this screenplay. The problem is that I trust Horton's judgment so much. If he feels that it doesn't work . . ." I paused. I had never said this aloud before. Even with all the wine, I felt frightened voicing it. "If he feels that it doesn't work," I repeated, "then there's probably some truth to that, no matter what I think."

"How typical is this of your screenplays?" Hank asked.

"In some ways, it's very typical. I tend to write small, character-driven pieces. This is certainly more ambitious than anything I've done before and it has the most entangled plot."

"Do you think you managed to keep that same intensity of characterization even with all the new plot elements? It sounds like what your advisor likes about your work *is* the focus on the characters—and it's really hard to maintain that kind of personal dynamic when you're juggling a compli-cated plotline as well." He smiled. "Take it from someone who has had two near-death experiences and three affairs on camera in the past month."

What a cutie. "You've got a point," I agreed and sat quietly for a moment. "It's just that applying for the Jablonski Fel-lowship seemed like such a good idea at first. In many ways, it seemed like the only option I had. Now I'm starting to worry that I've put myself in a lose-lose situation. If I get the fellowship, it'll be weird and awkward between Horton and me. He's going to be advising me on a project that he thinks is awful. If I don't get it, I'm going to be so embarrassed and upset and I don't have another project for my thesis." I ran a hand through my hair. "Let's not talk about this anymore. Please. It's depressing."

"Should I get the check?" Hank asked.

"OK." I would have preferred to stay in the restaurant forever. If it turned out that we had fallen into some weird Rip Van Winkle time warp and it was really twenty years later, I would consider it twenty years well spent.

Hank placed his hand on the small of my back as we walked out of the restaurant. It was slightly cold outside. I shivered, absurdly conscious of the pressure of his fingers against my spine.

"Well," I said, for lack of anything better to say.

"Well," he replied.

His fingers were precariously close to my ass.

I wanted Hank to kiss me. But I wanted him to kiss me like Ryan O'Neal kissed Ali MacGraw or Tracy kissed Hepburn—like I was the only woman in the world with lips. I didn't want the patented Destin soap opera tongue, nor did I want the same kiss that he gave to every dyed-blond model with gazelle legs.

He kissed me.

I forgot about notches and belts.

It had been a *long* time since I'd kissed anyone. My whole body turned to a gooey, gelatinous mass. I clung to Hank's neck and shoulders for support. I wanted to go home with him. I wanted to tear his clothes off and spend all night romping through bedclothes with him. I envisioned him leaving a slow trail of tiny, snail-shaped kiss imprints down my spinal cord.

After a few minutes, he whispered, "Charlie," into my hair.

"Mmm," I moaned softly in reply.

"Charlie, I have a confession," he said.

Was he going to tell me how much he adored me? The timing was perfect for a romantic declaration. I opened my eyes and gazed (sexily, I hoped) up at him.

"Your yoga class is way too hard for me. I can't go back. It just hurts too much."

That's not what I had wanted to hear.

"Shhh," I whispered, nestling up to his chest.

"I'm serious. I've been sore since Thursday."

I stroked the back of his head. His fingers still lingered palpably on my back.

"It's meant to be an advanced class. There are others you can take that are easier. I think there's even an all male beginner class." I didn't want to talk about this. Chatter was fine if there were artichokes and a fire. But if you were on a darkened, scenic street in the West Village, the stage was set for something slightly steamier. I, for one, was perfectly happy to continue necking on the streetcorner like a thirteen-year-old.

"I don't know that I'll be keeping up yoga," he said. "But I want to keep seeing you."

My already gelatinous body melted completely into one oozing puddle.

"Well, I want to keep seeing you," I purred in agreement.

"I have to be up really early tomorrow. But let me get you a cab home and I'll call you later this week."

This was it? After all the food and wine and wooing and fire, I was going to be unceremoniously dumped in the back of a taxi? Didn't he want to take me home and spend the rest of the night having wild, passionate sex?

"OK," I said glumly.

He leaned in and kissed my hair. "Let me know if anything develops with your screenplay."

"OK," I repeated.

And so the curtains came down on the most spectacular, though aborted, date of my life.

Dear Ms. Frost:

Thank you for your application to the Jablonski Student Film Fellowship. While your screenplay holds much merit, we received an unusually large number of qualified submissions this year. Unfortunately, we are unable to offer you financial support for your project at this time. We wish you the best of luck in your future endeavors.

Sincerely,

R. Thatcher Lemmons
Executor, Leo Jablonski Trust

ten

If I were Cher and I could turn back time, I would want it to be Saturday night again. By Wednesday, I was completely wretched. The burgeoning cold I'd managed to ignore during dinner with Hank had erupted. This time, I was sure that it was consumption. I had coughed so much that my abs ached. I even canceled my yoga class on Tuesday.

Hank hadn't called. It was probably because I was a really lousy fish-mouthed kisser with artichoke breath.

Even more painfully, I didn't get the Jablonski. I had looked at the rejection letter with horror and stamped into the kitchen to gulp some more cough syrup.

A while ago I had told Horton and Mallory Lear that I would come for dinner Wednesday night. I had thought that it would be better to wait and talk to Horton in person about salvaging my graduate school career, once I was feeling better. As I dressed for dinner, though, I began to regret not e-mailing him about the fellowship. It was going to be difficult to pretend that I didn't know the outcome. I am not good at covering my feelings at the best of times; who knew what I would admit to in such a fevered state?

The Lears live only a fifteen-minute walk away, but I felt that my weakened condition necessitated a taxi.

When I got there, there was a small crowd assembled in their living room: Horton; Mallory; their son, Richard; his wife, Serena; and Chris Martin from my program. Horton's also his advisor.

"Charlie!" Mallory leaned forward to air kiss my cheek. "I'm so glad you came. I've been telling Horton we needed to have you and Chris over for such a long time."

"It's been really busy this fall." I said feebly. Mallory's warmth is overwhelming. I am fairly certain that (unlike me) she has never felt the need to resolve to be less bitchy. For some reason—beyond her natural amiability—she has always been open about how much she likes me. It's flattering. I wish there were more people so actively involved in the Charlotte Frost Fan Club.

"Well, I'm glad you're here. Serena wants to talk yoga with you, and I want to talk opera with you." She pressed a glass of wine into my hands. I probably shouldn't drink with all the medicine I was taking. On the other hand, I might not survive if I didn't. I took a tentative sip and sat down on the couch next to Chris.

"I missed Rhonda's class today," I said. "Did anything important happen?"

"I was barely awake for it myself. We talked a lot about *Alexander Nevsky* and Miguel mouthed off for twenty minutes. I wish you'd been there to cut him down to size. Rhonda just let him blab. I think she's given up on pointing out the flaws in all of his arguments."

I glanced around before replying. Mallory had vanished into the kitchen, and Horton, Serena, and Richard appeared deeply ensconced in conversation. "Excuse me, but Miguel is a total dickwad. I think I could deal with him if it weren't for the fact that he's both so arrogant and yet so stupid. It's a foul combination."

"I know. It's just going to get worse now that he's gotten the Jablonski." Chris sighed.

Miguel got the Jablonski? He wrote like a six-year-old. I set my wine down with a clunk. This was monstrously unfair.

"How do you know?"

"He mentioned it about every thirty seconds in class today."

"But he writes like an idiot!" I protested. I wondered if anyone would notice if I left and went home to bawl my eyes out. This was too much to take.

"Does Horton know?" I asked.

"I don't think so," Chris said. "They just announced it this afternoon. I hope not," he added wryly, "because I applied for the Jablonski too and I hadn't gotten around to telling Horton that I got rejected."

I felt a little better. "I applied too," I admitted.

"Really?"

I nodded.

"How the hell did Miguel beat you out, Charlie?" Chris sounded surprised. "I didn't even know that you applied, but you're—" He stopped. "You're so much better than he is."

That was sweet. "I think we're both better than Miguel, but unfortunately that doesn't seem to be helping us." I stood up. "Come on, I think it's time to eat. Our mission is to keep Horton off the topic of the Jablonski."

Had I been able to taste the food, I'm sure dinner would have been delicious. Despite managing to feign nonchalance with Chris rather successfully, I was collapsing inside. I couldn't face the thought of having to start over on my thesis, of plastering a smile on my face whenever I saw Miguel, of pretending I didn't care that a prestigious committee felt that someone as immature and vile as Miguel Reynard-Arora was more talented than I was. Had I been stubborn and egotistical to submit *Honey and Helen*? To be fair, I had applied partly to avoid starting a new thesis topic. But there was a tiny bit of me that craved the glory as well, that longed to show Horton he was wrong, that wanted people to whisper, "That's Charlotte Frost; she's got the Jablonski, you know."

Somehow I made it through the meal, mechanically chewing my food, laughing at jokes, and nodding thoughtfully at conversation I didn't hear. Everything about me hurt, even my fingernails.

After dinner, everyone went into the living room for coffee. This was clearly the evening that was never going to end. Apparently, I was the only one fantasizing about my sweatpants. At some point, Mallory wandered back into the kitchen. I followed her, figuring my chances of being alert enough for a conversation were better with Mallory than the rest of the bunch, who were arguing about a *New Yorker* article as though they were on *Crossfire*.

"Mallory, do you need any help?" The kitchen was a total wreck. Mallory (and Horton as well, I hoped) would be spending all night cleaning.

"Not a thing, unless you want to keep me company. I'm just obsessive enough not to be able to relax while the kitchen looks like this."

"That's easy enough. But are you sure there's nothing I can do?"

"Charlie, you're so sick that you're about to keel over. Why don't you sit down, give me back that cup of coffee you have, and let me make you some herbal tea instead?"

"That sounds great," I admitted. I felt about six. It was both comforting and disconcerting. Mallory should consider forming a Rent-a-Grandmother service. She'd be perfect— aside from her hair, which is dyed flaming red, cut quite short, and slightly spiky.

"I knew there was something wrong when you didn't defend the Mets," Mallory continued. She was bustling about the kitchen with so much energy that it was tiring just to watch. "I was afraid for Richard's life when he called them 'New York's other team,' but you didn't even blink an eye."

"He called them *what*? Mallory, I must have been spacing out. I apologize. I'm not sure if it's ruder for me to admit that

I wasn't really listening or to have bitten your son's head off had I noticed. It's been a really long week."

Mallory set down a steaming mug of tea in front of me and added a generous slug of brandy. I raised my eyebrows.

"It's medicinal," she said tartly, capping the bottle.

I rolled my eyes and drank a little of my spiked tea. It hurt to swallow, but I felt better once the first gulp went down.

"If you want to talk about anything, I'll be happy to listen," Mallory offered.

"No. Not really. Thanks though." As nice as Mallory is, I couldn't envision myself venting to her about the Jablonski or charming soap stars who don't call.

"I'm sure all of this stress about your thesis is beginning to take a toll," Mallory said sympathetically. "Horton was saying just the other day that he wished it could be resolved."

"Yeah," I muttered. Talking to anybody—let alone my advisor's wife—about the travesty of my thesis was not high on my list of enjoyable activities. Especially when I was the only one who knew exactly how things had been resolved. To my horror, I felt my eyes getting hot and watery. I blinked several times, hoping Mallory had been too absorbed in cling-wrapping leftovers to notice.

"The screenplay that you submitted for that fellowship—what's it about?"

There was no way this conversation could get any more horrific. I drank some more tea before answering. "Two sisters, one of whom is a paraplegic, and their relationship with a nurse who comes to take care of the paraplegic."

"Kind of like *The English Patient*?"

"Not really." I could not deal with this conversation. "There's the nurse similarity, but that's it. It's really more about what happens when somebody novel and different charges up a cloistered, emotionally devoid atmosphere." I needed to think of a way to change the topic immediately.

"Are there any new exhibits I should see at the museum?" Mallory is the curator for a small folk art museum.

"Yes, I'll give you a brochure before you go. Back to your screenplay, though," she continued.

Shit. Shit. Shit.

"Did you find it easier to work with only three characters? I've never been able to decide whether it would be harder to create something with lots of plot and characters to juggle or something so tiny that everything has to be perfect for it to work at all."

"Oh, I don't know. I want to hear about the museum. Really." To my absolute horror, there were tears puddling up in my eyes. I hadn't cried when Horton said he wouldn't fund *Honey and Helen;* I hadn't cried when I was mugged; I hadn't cried when I got the Jablonski rejection letter; I hadn't cried this morning at four A.M. when I spent a solid half hour coughing up phlegm, but now—*now!*—in the most awkward place I could have ever picked, I felt the tears sliding down my face as uncontrollably as a thunderstorm. Mallory turned away from the pot she was scraping and saw my face.

"Charlie?" She pushed a box of Kleenex over and sat down across the table from me. "Oh, Charlie, what's the matter?"

I shook my head, afraid that if I opened my mouth, I would start to blubber. I didn't want Horton or Chris to hear me. In the Annals of Charlotte's Most Embarrassing Moments, this was going to rank right up there with the time in the eighth grade that a bunch of really popular boys caught me singing "Leader of the Pack" (all three parts, at the top of my lungs) as I walked home from school.

I took the Kleenex and began to mop myself up.

"I'm sorry," I whispered.

"Why?"

"This!" I gestured to my face. "I'm so mortified."

"I wouldn't worry about it," she said. "Believe it or not,

I've done worse. Once, I was makeup shopping at Saks and the saleswoman suggested I use this antiwrinkle eye cream and I just overflowed then and there. I think I was massively hormonal."

I smiled, more to show that I appreciated her effort than because I felt any better. The tears were beginning to slow, thankfully.

"I'm mortified," I repeated. Mallory smiled sympathetically at me. I took a deep breath. "If I tell you something, will you promise not to tell Horton? I just need to tell him myself." Mallory nodded. I smashed my lips together for a second to collect myself and to control the tears that were once again threatening to escape. "I didn't get the fellowship. I got the letter yesterday."

Mallory patted my hand. "So?" she asked.

"So I didn't get it!" I repeated.

"And you probably deserved it," she said. "But you know what, Charlie? It doesn't matter."

"Yes, it does." I didn't understand what she was talking about. I should never, ever have opened my mouth. I shouldn't have come to dinner. I should have stayed at home buried under five blankets, getting high off Robitussin.

"Mmm, not really. It's a big blow to you. But it doesn't diminish your talent in any way. You're the same screenwriter you were yesterday, or last month, or three years ago when you applied to grad school."

"You don't get it." I shook my head. "I am in such a pit, Mallory. I don't have a thesis. I dread telling Horton. Everyone kept telling me to listen to him and find another project, but I was so stubborn and arrogant that I just charged ahead and did what I wanted and now—" I stopped. My voice was beginning to crack. "Now, I am so incredibly embarrassed, and I should have started casting my project by now, and I don't even have a screenplay, and I'm so behind that I probably won't stand a chance at any of the end-of-the-year awards, and I am so, so embarrassed." I stopped and buried my face in my hands.

"Charlie?" I took my head out of my hands. Mallory continued, "Charlie, I repeat: so what? You'll figure something out. I know that Horton thinks that you are destined for a wildly successful career. You'll have that regardless of what happens with your thesis. So you lapsed in being omnipotent, brilliant Charlie Frost for a few months—now you've learned from the experience and it's time for you to get on with the rest of your life."

I sat there, reluctantly absorbing her words. Behind me, I could hear Horton's booming voice.

"Mallory? Charlie? Where have you vanished to?"

I began wiping my eyes frantically. He was *not*, damn it, going to know that I had dissolved into tears in his kitchen.

"There you are! Don't you want to come join us? I'll help you with the dishes later, Mal." He paused, taking in the scene. "Is everything OK?"

I concentrated on staring down at the table in case my bleary face gave me away. "Mmm-hmm," I murmured perkily.

"Charlie, have you been crying?" he asked incredulously.

"Oh no, I'm just sick."

It didn't sound plausible, even to my own ears. Mallory, bless her, chimed in, "Horton, no. Charlie's just been keeping me company. We'll come to the living room in a second."

Horton stood there in the doorway, shifting his weight uneasily from foot to foot. "OK," he accepted. As he turned to leave, something in me clicked. I couldn't stand to have him walk out, halfheartedly buying my ineffective lie.

"Horton," I called. "Wait." He swiveled back around. I felt vaguely nauseated. "I didn't get the fellowship. I was going to tell you at school, but then I sort of dissolved here. I'm sorry. I've been a total moron about the whole business and I should have listened to you in the first place." It wasn't as horrible to say as I had anticipated. In fact, I felt slightly better.

The crinkled skin by Horton's eyes furrowed even more deeply. "Oh, Charlotte." He sighed. "At the risk of hurting your feelings, I'm not surprised. In fact, I'm a little relieved. Come talk to me tomorrow and we'll brainstorm thesis plans." He gave me a wise old man look. "Trust me, kid, this is not worth crying about."

"I think it is," I shot back defensively. Mustering half-serious prissiness, I added, "You shouldn't belittle my choice of when to express emotion."

Horton's bushy eyebrows shot up. "Charlie, I'm glad to see this whole experience hasn't leveled your sense of entitlement," he said wryly.

I went to wash my face before rejoining everyone in the living room. Despite the embarrassment factor, I felt as though all possible proverbial weights had been lifted from my shoulders.

"Whenever the good Lord closes a door, he opens a window," I solemnly announced to the mirror in my best Mother Superior voice.

eleven

I had almost forgotten about my enchanted evening with Hank Destin when he called the next day.

"Charlie, doll, I am so sorry not to have called you sooner," he said breezily, sounding like the major TV sleazeball he probably was. "I had to go to L.A. for a couple of days."

"It's OK," I snuffled.

"Are you sick?"

"I have the plague, or maybe consumption. Something dreadful and anachronistic." I held the phone away from my face and blew my nose as delicately as possible. I've been to L.A. They definitely have telephones there. He could have called.

"That doesn't sound like fun."

"It's not. I even skipped teaching yoga."

"Yuck." Somehow, he made the word *yuck* sound like the most heartrending and honest expression of sympathy. I found myself warming up to him. He probably had something vastly important to do in L.A.—like meet with the president of Sleazeball Soaps, Inc.

"Anything else happening?" he asked. "Did you hear about your screenplay?"

Whatever little bit of me had thawed began to ice over again. I was done talking about the Jablonski.

"I didn't get the fellowship. I don't want to talk about it," I said curtly.

"OK."

"I mean, I don't want to be rude. It's just that I need to figure out how to salvage my graduate school career and I managed to dissolve into tears at my advisor's house last night, which was one of the more appalling moments of my existence. It hurts my brain to think about it."

"OK," he repeated.

"The thing that totally pisses me off," I continued, "is that this guy I hate ended up with the fellowship." For some reason, I was incapable of shutting up. "You have no idea what a moron he is. There's no way he deserved it."

"Not the sharpest knife in the drawer?"

"Hank, he's a *spoon*!" I started giggling and sniffling at the same time. Control, Charlotte, control. No more tearfests in front of people you want to impress.

"You don't have to talk about it if you don't want. I just called to check in with you. I have an invite to a screening of this new movie and I thought I'd see if you want to come."

"What movie?"

"*Three Days*."

"The one Carmen Reynolds wrote? Absolutely."

"I don't know who wrote it. It's got Nick Vasey in it, and we've got the same agent." Nick Vasey was a beautiful young thing. I wondered if his agent specialized in gorgeous men and, if so, how I could learn to do the same.

"Well, let's go." I was attacked by violent coughing. "Sorry," I croaked. "When is it?"

"Monday night, at the Ziegfeld."

"OK, well, I can meet you there."

"Seven?"

"Sure. Thanks for asking."

"Take care of your cough, Charlie."

"What, this little thing?"

Hank laughed. "Goodbye, Charlotte."

"Bye." I crawled back to bed. I should probably go to the doctor. I didn't want to be dead before Monday night.

Three hours later, the doorbell rang.

"Delivery."

I pushed the buzzer to unlock the door. I hadn't ordered anything, though comfort food from the diner wasn't a bad idea. I wrapped a bathrobe around my vaguely indecent pajamas and opened the door.

"For you, miss."

The deliveryman handed me a massive bouquet of flowers.

"Oh, you must have the wrong apartment," I said regretfully.

"Charlie Frost?"

"No, that's me." I took the card.

Charlie—

I thought you might need something to help you recover from the plague before Monday night.

Hank

He sent me flowers. *He sent me flowers.* What an adorable, nonsleazeball thing to do. I hoped I hadn't wandered onto the set of some reality TV show and all this careful wooing was eventually going to be revealed as a cruel joke. Dazed with mushy contentment, I signed the delivery slip.

"This is for you too." He handed me a plastic I ♥ NY bag.

Inside, there was a container of matzo ball soup and a menu from the Second Avenue Deli. The magnificent flowers paled in comparison. The Second Avenue Deli is in the Village and makes legendary matzo balls. I couldn't imagine what kind of bribery was involved in getting them to deliver this far uptown. It was two-thirty-three. I carried my soup into the living room. For the next twenty-seven minutes, I drooled at Hank Destin on the television while I ate lunch. I wondered vaguely how he had managed to find out where I lived, but decided that if you were the most perfect human who ever lived, it couldn't be that hard. I was in the phone book, after all.

It really was that simple: Hank Destin was the most perfect human who had ever lived.

Needless to say, the soup had put me in a humdinger of a good mood for my meeting with Horton. I practically floated into his office.

"You're in a better state than when I last saw you."

"I am," I sighed. "Horton, I am a totally new Charlotte Frost. No more moping and weeping and drama and rebellion. I promise. I am out to conquer the world, and I am going to write the best damn thesis you ever read."

"Glad to hear we're back in business."

"Definitely." I remembered the screenplay he'd given me to read. "Only, Horton, I want to direct a thesis that I've written."

"Of course." He seemed surprised.

"What about that screenplay you gave me?"

"What about it?" I could see my question suddenly dawn on him. "Charlie, that was just for you to read. It has nothing to do with you other than I wanted your opinion."

"Really?" He nodded. "In that case, I loved it."

"You did?"

"It's charming, Horton. Obviously, there are a couple of things I thought could be improved, but overall, it's great."

"I was pretty taken with it as well." He paused. "I hate to ask you to do any more work."

"But you're going to anyway, aren't you?"

"Yes. You used to have to write story memos for your old job, didn't you?"

"Thousands of them. I can do one for this." A story memo is basically an analysis of a script plus possible improvements.

"It would be really helpful for me. But what about you?"

I shrugged. "I guess I'm behind schedule. There's no way I can write something new. I thought about using that script I wrote last spring, but I'm not wild about it."

"*Poker Face?*"

"Yeah, that's the one."

Horton tugged the forelock of his white hair absently. "I'm not wild about it either. Plus, there are so many settings that it might be difficult to film on a small budget." He pulled a screenplay off his desk and handed it to me. "Do you remember this?"

"Of course." It was the first screenplay I had ever written. I'd written it for a class in college and ended up using it as my submission sample to grad school. " 'Do you think I should film *The Doctor's Wife?*"

"I think you should revise *The Doctor's Wife*."

"Really?"

"I read it again a couple of weeks ago. It's a very smart screenplay, Charlie."

The Doctor's Wife is a retelling of *Madame Bovary* set in 1950s America. I've never been crazy about *Madame Bovary* as a book. But it's sort of fascinating that everything about the story is so Betty Friedan—except that it was written by a nineteenth-century syphilitic French male. I looked at the screenplay nostalgically.

"I'll reread it. I'd almost forgotten it existed."

"You've come a long way as a writer since you did this, so it's hardly camera-ready. But just think of it as something to revise."

"OK. I'll take a look at it over the weekend." I stood up to leave.

"Charlie, just so you know . . . you are a much better writer than Miguel Reynard-Arora."

"I know. That's the problem, Horton." I sighed. "Chris is a lot better too."

"See you next week?"

"OK."

"I'm glad to see you're back to normal, Charlie."

I smiled indulgently at Horton. I wasn't back to normal. I was soaring thirty feet above normal. As I walked home, I found myself inadvertently clenching my jaw in exactly the same melodramatic way as Hank did on *Troubled Passion*. Maybe somewhere in a studio he was clenching right now. We were clenching in unison.

This was great love.

twelve

Monday was hot. The Channel 4 weatherman had referred to it as an "unseasonably" hot day, which didn't exactly do justice to eighty-eight degrees in the middle of October. This should have been hiking boots/football game/hot cider weather. Instead, after twenty desperate minutes sweating on the subway, my favorite little black dress was notably wet and crumpled.

I hoped I dried off before Hank got there.

I'd been standing in front of the Ziegfeld, rereading *Madame Bovary* and making notes, for about ten minutes when I heard my name.

"Charlie! Charlotte Frost! Get your head out of the book."

In retrospect, I really think that I just turned around. Marisa swears that I was so completely engrossed in a Flaubert reverie that I hadn't heard her call my name the first three times and finally whirled around, violently, as though risen from the dead.

Either way, I turned around. As I did so, the straps on my favorite little, now-sweaty, black dress snapped. The front of the dress fell to somewhere around my bellybutton. They were very skinny straps. I was not wearing a bra.

There I was, Charlie Frost, Boobs to the World, for all of Fifty-fourth Street to see.

"Oh shit!" I screamed, calling more attention to my half-naked self.

Marisa clapped her hands over her mouth. "Charlie, I'm so sorry," she squeaked.

I was due to meet Hank in all of thirty seconds.

I clutched my dress together. I couldn't believe that I had just been worried that it was wet and crumpled. At least I'd been *decent*.

"Maris, what do I do?"

She rummaged through her bag and handed me a sheer black sweater. I put it on gratefully, even though there was no way I'd fool anyone. It was very sheer.

"Marisa, I'm half naked!" I hunched over to make my chest less visible. "And why are you here?"

"I work two blocks away," she reminded me. "I was on my way home. The subway's on the corner. Do you want to find a bathroom and swap clothes?"

"What'll you do?"

"I'll get safety pins or something."

"OK." Marisa was wearing a sort of businessy gray button-down and black pants. Not exactly my idea of date gear, but desperate times call for desperate measures. As we were scurrying off to the deli across the street, I heard my name again. This time, I turned very gingerly around.

It was Hank. I was definitely cursed. Five minutes earlier, I would have been wearing my dress; five minutes later, I would have been safely ensconced in Marisa's work clothes. But he had arrived, fatefully, just in time to observe my humiliation.

I had no idea of the protocol for getting caught half naked in midtown Manhattan.

"Hi," I said sheepishly. Hank stared at my chest very obviously. I hunched over even further and did my best to hold my dress together. "Um, Hank, this is my friend Marisa. Marisa, Hank. Marisa just called my name and I turned around and well . . ." I gestured toward my chest. "The dress kind of broke."

Hank started laughing.

"It's not funny."

Hank kept laughing.

"So we're going to go swap clothes and I'll be back soon."

"We can skip the screening, Charlie. Take a cab back to your place and you can change," he offered.

I thought for a second. That sounded awfully nice.

"Don't you want to see the movie?"

"Well, yeah, but I can see it another time. We can go for dinner instead."

"There's a dry cleaner on the corner," said a guy walking past us.

"What?" I turned around.

"Dry cleaner." He pointed. "You can get a safety pin." The guy walked on, as if advising bare-breasted strangers were a completely normal occurrence.

I looked at Hank and Marisa. "Maybe I should do that."

"Sure," Hank said agreeably. He looked at Marisa. "Do you want to come to the screening? I can get another seat."

"Yeah, thanks!" Marisa said, immediately. She didn't even look at me to see if I would mind her impinging. I was a bit miffed. Didn't Hank want to spend all night talking to me . . . and only me? On the other hand, my nerves were vibrating at warp speed. Having Marisa around would help— sort of like having a human security blanket.

"Charlie, see that door over there?" Hank pointed to the side of the building. "We'll wait for you inside it. Just knock when you get done."

The woman at the dry cleaner's thought that somebody walking in half naked and asking for two safety pins was the most amusing thing in the world. Ha ha. What a knee-slapper. Maybe she and Hank could form a laughing-at-the-nudity-of-others club.

"I'll pay for the safety pins," I offered, attempting to re-mind her that the sooner I was clothed, the better. My back was beginning to cramp from being hunched over.

The woman stopped her cackling for a second. She pointed to a curtain. "Go behind there, honey, and hand me the dress. I'll sew it back together. It'll just take a second." She giggled some more as she reached for a sewing kit.

I was embarrassed that I'd been impatient. "Thanks."

In less than ten minutes, I was wearing my little black dress and strolling back toward the Ziegfeld. The woman at the cleaner's hadn't even let me pay for the repairs. Talk about the kindness of strangers. I knocked on the theater's side door.

A publicity assistant, wearing one of those *Star Trek* head-sets, opened the door. She was young and perky and wearing the tightest possible black pants.

"Hi, I'm with Hank Destin," I said tentatively.

"Great," the assistant said. "Destin #3 has arrived," she said into her headset. I felt very important. Maybe if I went to enough of these with Hank, I could get a Secret Service type code name: Filmgirl or Seebreast or something.

The assistant led me past a massive line of people and into the theater. Hank and Marisa were sharing popcorn. There was tape on the seat next to Hank. The assistant ripped it off. I sat down, and Hank offered me popcorn.

"Glad to see you're clothed," he said.

I rolled my eyes. "Please, neither of you ever remind me of this again."

"She doesn't mean that," Marisa explained to Hank. "She'll be retelling the story before tomorrow."

"Marisa and I decided we should all go out after this," Hank said.

I ate some popcorn. "Well, after my traumatic experience, I certainly deserve more nourishment than popcorn."

"Dinner at Vynl?" Marisa suggested. Vynl is practically my favorite restaurant in New York and only a ten-minute walk from the Ziegfeld. It's cheap and trendy and has hot wait staff and fantastic Bloody Marys. It is not a particularly Hank-ish type of restaurant, in that it is not quiet and expensive with solicitous waiters and a whole menu of fine Cognacs.

"Sure," I said. "We ought to call Karen while we're at it." If Hank wanted to hang out with Charlie and her friends, he might as well get the full experience.

Three hours later, Karen sailed into Vynl looking frazzled. Being a future psychologist, she's managed to build a fairly lucrative tutoring business for kids with test anxiety. She usually has about one or two kids that she works with at a time. They all seem to be named either after herbs (Sage, Dill, Cilantro) or after mid-sized American cities (Madison, Augusta, Salem).

"I need a drink," she wailed. "Let's play a game. Pretend I am tutoring you. I say, 'The formula for the area of a circle is Pi *r* squared.' Now you tell me: What is the formula for the area of a circle?"

"Pi *r* squared," Marisa said obligingly.

"Yes!" Karen shrieked. "Why is it so hard to remember that?"

Hank, Marisa, and I shrugged.

"No one at my office knows how to unclog a Xerox machine," Marisa said sympathetically.

"Sahra believes that I should only wear garments made from recycled yak hair," I offered.

"Let's not even get *started* on the craziness of my job," Hank added.

Karen looked at him. "Oh, you must be Hank," she said, coming back to earth. "Hi, I'm Karen. Obviously."

Hank nodded. "The roommate," he said. "And the psychologist."

Karen winced. "It's more like the psychology grad student currently moonlighting as completely unsympathetic and impatient SAT tutor." She reached for the drinks list and began scanning it desperately.

"At least tutoring's not your real job. Grad school has a goal that you work toward," Hank said. "Sometimes I get the hamster wheel syndrome. You know, I just keep running and running and getting nowhere and nothing ever changes." He took a sip of his beer and offered us a charming smile.

"Correct me if I'm wrong," I said, "but don't you actually get *paid* at your job?"

"Money is a fine consolation prize. But I wouldn't mind acting in something real. Like maybe the movie we just saw."

"You *liked* that? I thought it sucked." I exclaimed. "I liked it the first time they made it, when it was called *The African Queen* and had Humphrey Bogart and Katharine Hepburn in it."

"Oh, it was terrible," Hank agreed. "And I never thought about it before, but you're right. They really did rip off *The African Queen*. Still, Charlie, it was a movie, written—so you tell me—by somebody relatively well-known, opening in theaters, getting reviews, the whole nine yards." He opened his menu. "Hard not to be jealous when I'm sweating it out on set five days a week." I felt his hand squeeze my knee under the table. At least I hoped it was his hand and not Marisa's or Karen's.

I also opened my menu and stared at it, even though I always order the portobello mushroom sandwich at Vynl. Why mess with perfection?

"Tuna wrap looks good," Hank said.

I smiled at him. I couldn't help it. It was a way to occupy my lips so I didn't ask Hank if it was really possible that he liked hanging out with me and my friends, eating a $7 tuna wrap in a restaurant on Ninth Avenue.

If this kept up, I might have to invest in a red carpet to strew in front of my doorway.

thirteen

Going to Vynl was sort of the last hurrah of my social life. I spent the next few weeks absorbed in my thesis. It was very unglamorous. An actual incident:

SCENE: Charlie's apartment

CHARLIE is typing furiously on her laptop. Papers are scattered across the floor. There is a large blob of zit cream on her forehead. She pauses and stares at the wall for a moment, her eyes alighting on a large cockroach. CHARLIE sighs, reaches for a crumpled piece of paper, and deftly kills the roach.

CHARLIE: (aloud to the cockroach corpse): Someday, after I make my fame and fortune, I'll do all of my writing at a charming seaside cottage and the only arthropods allowed inside will be lobsters.

On Halloween, Karen sailed in at one A.M. to find that I was in the exact same position as she had left me six-

teen hours earlier: curled on my bed in yoga pants, surrounded by empty Diet Coke cans, typing on my laptop with
as much lackluster determination as I could muster. She
stared.

"Charlie, you've got to stop and take a break."

"Can't." I took a swig of tepid Diet Coke. Aspartame has
been shown to cause cancer in lab rats in extremely large
doses. I was undoubtedly up in the rat cancer range by now.
"It's now officially November and this needs to be completely rewritten by Thanksgiving."

"This is crazy."

"Is that your professional opinion?"

Karen crawled onto my bed. Her makeup was a little
smeared. She didn't look ready to run a marathon herself.
"Have you ever read *Save Me the Waltz*?" she asked.

"By Zelda Fitzgerald? Yeah, I thought it was a piece of
shit."

"So you know how she obsessively practices ballet for days
and days on end because she really wants to be a ballet
dancer? And at the end she gets some kind of toenail infection and has to quit?"

"Yeah." I wasn't sure where Karen was going with this
train of thought.

"Well, that really happened, except in life she didn't get a
toenail infection. She had a psychotic break and had to go into
a sanitarium. She wrote the book while she was locked up."

"And?"

"And I don't want you giving yourself a toenail infection,
Charlie!"

I started giggling. I hoped Karen was a little more direct
with her clients than she was with me. "I'm not going to give
myself a toenail infection. I promise. I've got it all planned
out, Karen. My thesis defense is scheduled for April 1. I'm
going to get the first draft to Horton by Thanksgiving. Between Thanksgiving and New Year's, I'll do revisions, then

start location scouting and casting in January. I can film in February, and take March for postproduction work." I rubbed my eyes. "But you're right. Maybe going to bed right now wouldn't be the worst thing in the world." I looked at Karen. "Hey, where were you tonight anyway?"

"I went to a Halloween party with Marisa and this guy from school. We were the only ones there not dressed up. I spent most of the night avoiding this creep who was dressed like Elvis."

"Young Elvis?"

"Old, fat Elvis. And to be perfectly honest, he looked a little too realistic for my taste." Karen stood up. "Night, Charlie."

"Night."

Karen was right. I was beginning to ossify in front of my computer. I couldn't afford the time for a real break, but getting out of the apartment was necessary. Lacking my perfect little seaside refuge, I took the train to Long Island on Saturday. Going home is exceptionally conducive to work. The food is good, the maid service excellent, and since my parents are dead to the world by eight-thirty every night, the distractions limited.

Hank called my cell phone while we were eating dinner. A little shiver went through me when I saw his number on the caller ID. We'd exchanged a couple of flirty e-mails over the past week, but there had been no vocal communication. I was itching to talk to him but couldn't face a familial Inquisition after getting off ("Was that a *boy*, Puffin?"). I let it go to voice mail. He left a very sweet message.

"Hey, workaholic, it's Hank. I know you're up to your ears this weekend, but I was wondering if I could pry you away from that screenplay next week. One of the producers for *Troubled Passion* is having a party. Come with me. It'll be an experience."

As if he had to ask. I would scrub floors with Hank Destin. I would groom dogs. Having never accomplished running a single continuous mile in my life, I would nonetheless agree to a marathon as long as he invited me.

I decided to save the message so I could listen to it repeatedly, cheering myself out of writer's block by the promise of real-life romance and adventure. I was having trouble with the bit in my screenplay where Emma decides to marry Charles. The part where she starts having affairs rang true (naturally, Emma has to search outside her lusterless marriage for validation). Getting her to agree to marry insipid Charles in the first place was more of a challenge. It just didn't feel plausible. Why would a fantasizing young girl agree to spend the rest of her life with a sleepy country doctor?

Not being the reigning expert on marriage, I went to find my mother for advice. She was reading in the den, an old plaid flannel bathrobe wrapped around her nightgown. Our cat, Brontë, was curled on the couch beside her. I reached down and rubbed Brontë on the back so that her tail stuck straight up in the air.

"Mom, what made you want to marry Dad?"

"Excuse me?"

"I was just wondering. What was it that spoke to you? You know, Dad's Dad. He's a dorky English professor in the suburbs. You must have known that he'd never be rich and he'd never be famous, but there had to be something that made you want this life."

Mom looked at me suspiciously. "Well, Charlie, it's not so much that I wanted to live in the suburbs stressing about how to pay for braces and college tuition. That part just happened. I wanted your father. I remember being about your age and riding the bus to his apartment and being so eager and impatient to see him that I got off and walked the last five blocks because the bus was moving too slowly." There was a look on her face that could only be described as sappy. "Why do you want to know?"

"Just for my screenplay, I guess. I'm trying to figure out why Emma would agree to marry Charles."

"And you thought you'd compare me to Emma Bovary? Thanks, Puffin."

I looked at my mother, swathed comfortably in her ratty bathrobe. Married or not, she probably wasn't the best pipeline into the mind of Madame Bovary. Emma would have never been caught dead in flannel, and my mom, to her credit, wasn't exactly the type to have affairs, get in debt, and die young and unfulfilled. Maybe Mom was more like Emma's dad. I could hear the undercurrent of hope in her voice. She didn't want me to ask questions about love because I was writing a screenplay. She wanted these questions to pertain to my own life, for me to be whisked off imminently to a life of minivans and picket fences by a sweet, albeit bland, doctor.

I couldn't live with those wishes. They weren't mine. Did that mean that Emma and I were alike? I wanted to believe that Emma could have been like me. I wanted her to be more than a frivolity. I thought for a second and then headed back to my computer.

fourteen

In an effort to prevent future embarrassment with Horton, Chris Martin and I agreed to read each other's screenplays before we turned them in. Chris doesn't exactly write my kind of screenplay. He's much more into the psychological faux-Hitchcock thriller, inevitably conjuring up some earth-shattering revelatory twist in the final scene. But he's a solid writer, brilliant with dialogue, and I trust his opinion. It was with some trepidation that I arrived at City Diner for our meeting.

Grabbing a handful of diner mints as an appetizer, I settled into a booth and began to read *Vogue* while I waited. It was the "shape" issue, purportedly celebrating women of all body types. Their example of a petite woman was five-six. I was mentally composing a letter to the editor (which I would never actually write and send) when Chris slid into the booth across from me. He plunked his copy of *The Doctor's Wife* on the table.

"Charlie, lunch is on me because I predict that you'll be giving me way more help than I'll be giving you."

"Did you like it?" I asked nervously. I had read bits and pieces of *The Doctor's Wife* out loud to Karen as I wrote them, but Chris was the first person to see the whole thing. I *thought* it was good. It felt right and had been an unusually fluid writing process. But I'd lost some faith in my internal screenplay barometer after the *Honey and Helen* debacle.

Chris cocked one eyebrow in a very wry and jaded film student way. "It's pretty fantastic, Charlie. I can't believe you pulled this together so quickly."

Fantastic. Chris is sort of a mini-Horton. He doesn't lie and he doesn't give unnecessary praise. I've sat through a million writing seminars during which he's aired his very honest, sometimes harsh opinions. I lapped up his words before replying.

"It kind of wrote itself," I admitted. "It was a lot of work, but it wasn't that same browbeating sweaty angst that writing my Jablonski project was." I shrugged. "Shows what I know about this stuff."

"Help me out, though, with the literary part. You said this is based on *Madame Bovary?*"

I nodded.

"OK, don't get upset, Charlie, but I've never read it. I am sure that this makes me a terribly uncultured person and that my life would be enriched were I to pick up a copy. Can you give me the thirty-second Cliff Notes? I just want to make sure I'm clear on the adaptation before I get into my comments."

"Sure." *Boys.* No self-respecting, now-grown teenage feminist would be caught dead having not read *Madame Bovary.* I synopsized the best I could. "Emma is this dreamy little naive farm girl who marries a much older doctor. She craves cities and excitement and wealth, but he's totally content with the simple, pleasant life he's carved out for them. He adores her; she feels really trapped and smothered by her marriage and keeps thinking that there must be more to life. She has a series of affairs, mostly with this one young sexy clerk named Leon, and gets into horrible debt because she keeps charging stuff she can't afford from an evil conniving merchant. Finally, she kills herself, having never gotten any of the things she wanted out of life."

"So you've kept the shell of the story intact, but transplanted Emma and Charles to some generic 1950s suburb." Chris pursed his lips for a second, thinking. "Do you want the film to have a message? I get the sense that you want this to make a point."

"I guess I just want to drive home that Emma's story is hardly unique and that, despite the suffrage movement, there was a substantial lack of progress in the societal roles for women between when Flaubert wrote his novel and the fifties."

"I get that somewhat. I think you could make the case even more strongly without coming across as preachy. Beef up this idea that Emma's unhappy and trapped even though she has the same life that most women get. Maybe play up the fact that there really isn't anything wrong with Charles. He's dull, but he wants to be a good husband, and he adores her."

"So maybe if I throw in another scene with Emma and her father . . ." I began thinking aloud.

"Then you could have her father not understand why she's complaining and that would show how the man and the woman are on two different wavelengths," Chris finished.

I nodded, mentally placing the scene in the first act. It wouldn't be hard to add.

"Another thing," Chris continued. "Emma's too likable. Don't be afraid to make her somewhat unsympathetic. You want to emphasize that the choices she makes are neither typical nor wise. Let her be foolish and human and impulsive. People will still be able to identify with her situation, but they don't have to agree with how she escapes it."

I pushed my menu to one side and leaned forward toward Chris.

"What else?"

* * *

Chris and I processed our screenplays until it was time for
me to teach yoga. I could have stayed there working with
him all night. Sahra was seated at the Harmony front desk
when I got there, overlooking her Zen domain like a slather-
ing Rottweiler.

"Hi," I said, breezing past her.

"Charlie, wait," she called.

I grudgingly paused. Sahra had been unusually irritating
lately. I was starting to wonder if it was on purpose. Maybe
she suspected that I was an uncentered basket case and was
trying to aggravate me until I cracked and outed myself.

"Yeah?" I asked tentatively.

"Here's your employee memo for November. I think
you've got enough time to read it before class. Basically, I've
decided that we need to give each class a theme."

"A theme?'

"Like a central focus. So, for example, a nice autumnal
theme might be to focus class around a celebration of the
harvest."

What a freak. How was I supposed to focus a yoga class in
New York City around a harvest celebration? I'd have to in-
vent cornucopia pose.

I opted for the path of least resistance. "What a lovely
idea," I oozed, skimming the memo. "Maybe I'll use a theme
of giving thanks. I think we could all use a little more gratitude in our lives." *Like maybe gratitude for instructors, particularly those who are consistently on time and never complain
about the meager pay.*

Grumbling under my breath, I went into the locker room.
Miriam, another instructor, was standing in front of the mirror, twisting her hair into a million little braids.

"OK, what's this theme garbage?" I greeted her.

"It's unusual," Miriam acquiesced, anchoring her braids in
place with a bobby pin. Since she had a substantial number

of green streaks running through her dark hair, she looked sort of like Medusa. "But I think it'll be helpful for us to center our classes more. Yoga shouldn't be just about exercise. It's time that we remembered that this is a spiritual, as well as a physical, journey." She twisted her Gorgon head so that she could better deal with her braids. "I'm glad that Sahra has reminded us of that."

Sometimes I think that if Miriam were accidentally to be locked in a coffin alive, she would emerge with a big smile, announcing that it had been so nice to have some time alone in the dark.

fifteen

I had masterminded my schedule perfectly, turning in an initial draft of *The Doctor's Wife* to Horton a mere three hours before I was due to meet Hank. I used the intervening time to battle the crowds at the Fifth Avenue H&M. Finishing *The Doctor's Wife* was an accomplishment worthy of some celebratory spending. And trust me: all H&Ms are not created equal. The Fifth Avenue one is definitely the best in the city. I have heard of different chain stores carrying different lines based on region of the country. But honestly—are the fashion tastes of customers shopping at H&M on Thirty-fourth and Sixth so radically different from those of customers shopping at Thirty-fourth and Eighth?

At any rate, I found a perfectly nice black halter top to wear to the party. Given how nervous I was about meeting the whole *Troubled Passion* entourage, my time would have been better spent at a yoga class than shopping at some Darwinian madhouse that operated on the survival-of-the-fittest principle. Even Mother Teresa would have been daunted by the dressing room line. (And let's face it—I am not one of those people who possess any form of innately benevolent calm.)

I had asked Karen for advice about the party. She suggested that I scrawl her name and phone number on the back of the bathroom door. Genius. But seriously—what if Hank's castmates convinced him that the captain of the football team shouldn't be dating the class grind? What if they told me that they liked me more than last week's girl? What if it turned out that they had all gone to my film program and ended up working on soaps instead of winning Oscars?

Frankly, I was officially flipping out.

The party was in a big gray Central Park West building with a mirrored elevator. Considering our last date, I was relieved to notice that my halter top was still adequately concealing my chest.

"Don't be nervous, Charlie," Hank said, as I reached for his hand.

"I'm not nervous," I lied. "I just felt like holding your hand."

Hank gave me a dubious look, then pulled me to him for a hug. I came up to approximately his armpit and stayed there, nestled under his bicep, for the remainder of the ride. The door of the elevator opened directly into the host's apartment, with the two of us still holding each other. As far as I could tell, the apartment took up the entire floor. There were an almost overwhelming number of people inside. I had a sudden flash of "Oh, Toto, I don't think we're in graduate school anymore."

"Haaaaannnnk," a woman drawled. "I thought you weren't going to make it. I thought you were going to leave us *all alone* and wishing you were here." She looked to be in her mid forties, with lots of platinum hair bouffanted on top of her head, and a shiny gold dress. Ivana wannabes were alive and well in the world of soaps.

I was suddenly acutely aware of my minimalist black pants.

"Hey, Pug." Hank replied. "Charlie, this is Pug Benedict, one of the *Passion* producers. Pug, I want you to meet Charlotte Frost."

"Darling," Pug said, extending her hand to me. "Help yourself to anything. I'm going to steal your boy away for a second. I need him to talk to someone."

I glanced around the roomful of people and back at Hank, willing my eyes not to be puppy doggish. I did not want to be left alone for Charlie's Adventures in Lamé Land.

"Sure, Pug. But give me and Charlie a chance to get our coats off, OK? I'll be with you in a second."

I hated that I was grateful that he said that. As Hank put his arm around my shoulders and maneuvered me through the crowds, I gave myself a mental pep talk. *You are smart. You are funny. You can handle these people. Please, Charlie, try to be normal.*

After we dropped off our coats, I took a glass of champagne from a circling waiter. When in doubt, drink like your grandmother.

"There's Maddie," said Hank, scanning the crowds. "Let me introduce you."

"Can you tell me who Maddie is?'

"She was my love interest on the show last season. But I cheated on her with Marina, who should be around here somewhere. Maddie just had a baby and I'm refusing to acknowledge it as mine, so she's now contemplating suicide."

Of course.

"Maddie," Hank called.

An absolutely dazzling six-foot-tall redhead turned around. "Baby!" she squealed.

"Maddie, I want you to meet Charlie Frost. Pug's corralled me and I am afraid I have to go deal with her right now. We just got here. Can you introduce Charlie to some people?"

"Of course." Maddie leaned forward and air kissed Hank. I watched him weave back through the crowds.

"Hi," I said to Maddie, taking a swig of champagne to fortify myself for my first ever conversation with a redheaded Amazon. I felt like a hobbit compared to her.

"So you're Hank's new little girl," Maddie said.

I didn't say anything. Agreeing that I was, in fact, Hank Destin's new little girl just felt too strange. Where were the Women's Liberation Police when I needed them?

"He told me you were a smartie."

"I guess."

"You teach yoga, right?'

Hank had been talking about me. I wondered what else he said. I felt vaguely violated. It was one thing for me to chaperone Marisa and Karen through a tour of www.hankisbuff.com. Discussing me with a redheaded Amazon wonder was a completely different situation. Obviously.

"Part-time. I'm in grad school."

Maddie and I chitchatted for a few seconds about my oh-so-fascinating life. She had never heard of *Madame Bovary* but thought it was real interesting that I was writing a movie.

"You should meet Bunny," she said.

"Bunny?"

"Our head writer."

Maddie led me over to two balding men talking. Her skinny hips swung like a pendulum as she walked. It was a mystifying gait. Hip sockets were not—as far as I knew—double jointed.

"Bunny, this is Charlie. She came with Hank."

The rounder of the two men held out his hand.

"Hey, sweetheart."

(For some reason I had assumed Bunny would be female.)

"Charlie's writing a screenplay. It's about a book. I forget the name."

"*Madame Bovary*," I supplied.

Bunny's eyebrows raised. "Ambitious."

"It's a retelling set during the fifties. It's my thesis project for grad school."

"Where are you in school?"

"Columbia."

"Good program."

I shrugged modestly. Maybe it was because he was a writer and maybe it was because he had heard of *Madame Bovary*, but I felt comfortable talking with Bunny. I wasn't sure how I felt about the names at this party, though. Pug. Bunny. If I wanted to fit in, I should probably start introducing myself as Puffin.

"Who's your advisor?" Bunny asked.

"Horton Lear."

"Right," Bunny nodded. "I forgot he was there. Now that's a name you don't hear too much anymore."

Whatever I think about Horton's reclusive tendencies, I was not going to let Bunny malign him.

"I'm very lucky to be working with him."

"It's your last year, right?'

"Yes."

"Listen, sweetheart, if you need anything after graduation, just look me up."

"Thanks," I said awkwardly. It was a generous offer to make to someone he'd just met—but I wasn't planning to go into television. I was planning to reinvent the character drama.

It was almost as if Bunny had heard what I was thinking. "I know you're probably in your artiste phase where you look down on soaps, but six months of unemployment will cure you of that. If you look at the plotline, *Madame Bovary*'s not so dissimilar from *Troubled Passion*. And the money more than compensates."

"I'm sure." I smiled weakly. Where was Hank? "Thank you, Bunny."

Bunny's companion nodded his head at me. The two of them returned to their conversation. For lack of anything better to do, I went in search of the bar, absently helping myself to a peapod shrimp as I walked.

"Glass of white, please."

The bartender handed me my wine, wrapping a napkin around the stem of the glass.

"Charlie?" he said.

It was Chris Martin. Talk about the bizarre power of coincidence. I had never been so glad to see a classmate.

"Hey! What are you doing here?"

Chris gestured to the table full of bottles and smiled.

"OK, dumb question," I admitted, taking a sip. It was terrible wine. Were it not for the visible corkscrew on the table, I might have suspected it had a screw cap. I checked the label. It was Wind Song White. Sigh. I suppose expecting someone who voluntarily went by "Pug" to have good taste in wine might be too much. But was it so outrageous to want wine that didn't sound like it would be more aptly located on the Duane Reade perfume aisle?

"I think I should be the one asking how you ended up here," Chris teased.

I looked down awkwardly. I wasn't sure that I wanted people from school to know about Hank. It still felt too unreal and possibly ephemeral for me to want to go public with it.

"I came with a guy," I admitted.

"Don't make it sound so lurid, Charlie. You're allowed a life."

"Of course." I felt silly. "This wine is practically fungal."

"Really?" Chris took my glass, sniffed it, and made a face. "How about I put my bartending course to work and whip up something exciting?"

I was about to protest that he didn't have to when I noticed a gaggle of blond starlets observing us. I didn't feel like reverting to my role as Hank's little girl. "Go ahead and impress me."

Chris began deftly pouring things into a cocktail shaker.

"Did you ever figure out the thunderstorm scene?" I asked, referring to a particularly tricky part of his screenplay.

Chris added something green and leafy to the shaker and looked up at me.

"We need to talk more about that. It's not working. The audience knows that Melanie has intercepted Arthur's letter; I just can't figure out how to write so that the audience gets more information but I don't give away anything that would give Arthur a clue that Melanie's read his letter."

I thought. "So Melanie needs to tell both the audience something and Arthur nothing."

"Exactly."

"Maybe—" I began but was cut off.

"I *said*, can I get a gin and tonic?" A rather florid man glared at us. "I've asked you twice."

"Sorry, sir," Chris said and set to work. I rolled my eyes sympathetically at him.

As the guest took his drink from Chris, I heard him mutter something about people not being paid to flirt. As if. I don't have much sympathy for people who misconstrue an intellectual discourse for flirting.

Chris looked at me. "You're mixing with the help, Charlie. We better talk about this later. Maybe lunch on Monday?" He shook my drink and poured it into a martini glass. It was pale green with specks of more green floating in it.

"What is this, an algae special?" I asked.

"It's a mojito—fresh mint and lime. It's Cuban."

That was nice of him. It was far better than the fungal wine. Even though I would have preferred to keep talking screenplays with Chris, I didn't want to get him in trouble. I went and found Hank, who was talking to Maddie by the fireplace.

"Hi," I said cheerfully, willing myself out of my neurotic, anxiety-driven insecure social slump. I was the only one who had to know how completely out of place I felt.

Hank reached down and messed up my hair. "Ready to go?" he asked.

I looked up at him, taking in the wavy dark hair and small, pebble-sized dimples. I put my arms around his neck, reveling in the surge of that increasingly familiar, safe and warm feeling that Hank gave me. I didn't care that Maddie was watching me hang on him like a small, but definitely clinging animal.

"Yes."

sixteen

Reader, I slept with him.

He lived in a spectacular waterfront apartment in Brooklyn, with floor-to-ceiling windows offering views of both the Brooklyn and Manhattan bridges. You could see boats going past.

We didn't spend too much time looking out the window.

The next morning, I crawled on top of his chest, letting my legs splay around his body.

"You are beautiful," I said, running a hand down his completely hairless, probably waxed chest. I've never had a particular fetish for the unhirsute, but Hank was testimony to the benefits of male salon treatments. He had a phenomenal chest.

Hank looked up at me. "You are beautiful," he replied.

I swooned briefly, but—for some reason—the thought of being beautiful unnerved me a little. It didn't feel right. I'm not hideous. Many people do find me attractive. But beautiful? I wasn't so convinced. I tend to reserve that category for redheaded Amazon queens. I nestled closer to Hank's perfect poreless pectorals and stared at the river.

This is your life, Charlotte Frost.

* * *

After coffee and bagels, I found the subway and rode home. Despite the scenic tugboat views, his apartment could be more conveniently located. It took me almost an hour to haul myself back. I had a hunch that Hank didn't spend too much time on the subway. If I were he, I wouldn't either. It could be considered an occupational hazard. You never know when you might pick up a case of flesh-eating bacteria on the train.

The rest of the weekend was devoted to nursing my hangover and recovering from—ahem—a sleepless night. (Chris's mojito had proved to be slightly more potent than expected.) Monday morning I woke to the ringing phone.

"Charlie, never in all my life, honestly, darling. I'm shocked!" It was my grandmother, sounding more addled than normal. "You tell me you have so much work and, of course, I believe you and have these visions of my poor, sweet granddaughter slaving on her screenplay day after day."

"I do slave," I muttered in drowsy defense of myself. I looked at the clock. It was seven-fifteen. My alarm wasn't due to go off for another forty-five minutes.

"Then *why*," Gran announced triumphantly, "are you on Page Six of the *Post* as the new love interest of TV star Hank Destin?"

I was suddenly very awake.

"What?" I whispered. There was no way we had hit the gossip columns. I hadn't even been ready to tell innocuous Chris Martin that I was dating Hank. Nothing like a little paparazzi to ruin a quality romantic buildup. Hank and I had barely started dating. There was just no way I was worthy of being a blip on the *Post*'s gossip radar.

" 'Rumor has it that the sexy *Troubled Passion* star has been spending more than a little bit of his free time with film student Charlotte Frost,' " Gran quoted.

"We've only gone out a few times!" I squeaked.

"Mmm-hmm." Gran sounded suspicious.

"Tell me that you haven't called Mom and Dad yet. Please." My parents sniff at the *Post*. Turning up on Page Six would be considered only marginally better than streaking down Broadway. I could already hear the snoans. Plus I didn't even want to deal with their frenetically optimistic hopes that I might (gasp!) have a boyfriend. I could already envision my father loading me up with volumes of love sonnets that I would obviously want to quote to Hank.

"Well, Charlie, you can't expect to keep this from them."

"I just wanted to feel a little more secure in the relationship before I broadcasted it. We've barely started."

"That's what you get for targeting the rich and famous. Honestly, Charlotte, I can't believe you didn't tell me. *One* date with a sexy TV star should have been noteworthy enough to mention to your grandmother. Now listen, I insist you come for dinner."

"I have too much work," I lied.

"That's what you said last week. But I find that you were actually living it up with this handsome young man. I'll pick you up at five-thirty. Goodbye, darling."

"Gran, wait." I was talking to a dead line.

I grabbed my coat and sneakers and threw them on over my pajamas. Three minutes later, I was at the magazine stand on the corner reading Page Six.

Destin's Destiny?

Notorious playboy Hank Destin seems to be cooling his wild ways. Rumor has it that the sexy *Troubled Passion* star has been spending more than a little bit of his free time with film student Charlotte Frost. According to sources, the pair met at a yoga class and have been inseparable ever since. Destin's reps refused to comment on

> the situation, but we suspect that brainy Char-
> lotte's got Hank twisted up in knots.

I reread it twice, unnerved by my newfounded blip-status. I needed clarity. I closed my eyes and willed all of my drowsy, shell-shocked brain to function. I began mentally ticking off questions in my head.

1. Why had his reps refused to comment? Surely they had to be aware of our amazing and fateful karmic draw to each other.
2. Notorious playboy??? Could the *Post* have made that up, along with the inseparable bit? (The real inseparable partner in my life was my laptop. We were joined at the fingertips.)
3. What would Hank think about this?
4. What would everyone else I knew on the planet think about this? I like to think that I'm destined for fame, but not for being the brainy paramour of an allegedly bed-hopping soap star.
5. I was his destiny? Not that the *Post was* the most reliable of sources, but at least they were insinuating we had a future. I wanted to squeak with joy and turn cartwheels, and march down Broadway wearing a sandwich board reading *Destin's Destiny*.

"It is your destiny, Hank," I growled to myself in a throaty Vader-esque voice.

"You gonna buy that, miss?" The clerk stared at me grumpily. I forgave him for attempting to evict me from his newsstand. I was, after all, standing there in my pajamas quoting a 1980s sci-fi blockbuster to myself.

I bought three copies of the *Post* for posterity and an iced tea to calm my nerves. As I walked home, I practiced pendu-

lum swinging my hips the way Maddie did. I didn't feel remotely sexy—more like a pregnant platypus.

Apparently brainy Charlotte, albeit Destin's Destiny, had
not yet mastered all the tricks necessary to achieve the status
of a millennial sex goddess.

To: Charlie <cfrost@columbfilm.edu>
From: Katherine Frost <katherine_frost@spacecom.net>
Re: Your Apparently Glamorous and Completely Unmentioned
Love Life

Puffin, forgive me, but I am VERY confused. Who is this Destin
person? Is he really on television? Your grandmother tells me
that you are being very ambiguous.

As you know, your father and I simply want the best for you and
we are very curious about these developments.

Love,
Mom

To: Charlie <cfrost@columbfilm.edu>
From: Herbert Frost <herbert_frost@spacecom.net>
Re: Something to consider

Love is anterior to life,
    Posterior to death,
Initial of creation, and
    The exponent of breath.
            —Emily Dickinson

Think about it!

Love,
Dad

To: Charlie <cfrost@columbfilm.edu>
From: Marisa <marisa.rosenbaum@citybooks.com>
Re: Page Six

Charlie, are you OK?

—M

seventeen

When you live in the ivory tower, there's no sense getting worked up about what goes on in the crass and lowbrow outside world. Apparently, no one at school had bothered to read the *Post*. Absolutely no one commented on my loss of paparazzi virginity. It was all cutthroat dialogue and critical analysis as usual.

After surviving yet another interminable Soviet film seminar, I found Horton in his office.

"I hate him," I announced grumpily, flinging myself into the slouchy armchair. "I absolutely hate him. If I have to listen to Miguel Reynard-Arora emit one more smarmy, self-satisfied remark about what a *trial* and a *burden* it is to have to consider the recommendations of the Jablonski committee when casting his screenplay, I will rip out his arrogant vocal cords with my bare hands."

Horton's glasses had slid down his nose. He gazed myopically at me over the tops of the lenses.

"Charlie, why don't you tell me how you really feel? Just for a change?"

"I'm serious!" I was wearing a black sweater with a big cowl neck. I pulled the cowl part up over my face so I didn't have to look at Horton.

"I read your screenplay," Horton said, interrupting my sheepish avoidance.

I pulled the cowl back to its normal position.

"You did?" My voice sounded very small. "Already?" I inhaled deeply—yogically—and tried not to look nervous.

Horton nodded. His Boris Yeltsin wedge of hair wobbled a bit. "It was tremendous. It's going to be a spectacular film."

I closed my eyes for a second. I almost wanted to pull the cowl back up just so that I could enjoy this moment of relief privately.

"Thanks." My voice was still small. I cleared my throat. "So what do I need to do to revise it?"

Horton pushed his glasses back up the bridge of his nose and grinned. "You don't waste time, kid." He handed me his copy of *The Doctor's Wife*. I began to study the comments.

"Charlie, I meant what I said."

"Yeah?" I said, flipping through his notes.

"Charlie, you've created something incredible. You seemed so down after *Honey and Helen*. Frankly, I was afraid that you would have trouble finding the enthusiasm to work on something new."

I looked up. "Well, you were right. This is going to make a much better movie. *Honey and Helen* wasn't working." I made a face. "I just wish I hadn't screwed my chances of winning any of the end of year prizes."

"I don't think you have."

"I'm behind, Horton. Lots of people are already casting. I probably won't have this ready to film before January."

"Don't rule anything out. I think you'll be able to pull this one off."

"If I can find the right cast." I crossed my legs into lotus. I was confused about Hank. Spewing about my love life to Horton was not my normal MO, but I decided to test him anyway. "Horton, I started dating an actor."

"Chris said you had someone new," Horton said knowingly.

"How exactly did that come up?" The thought of them discussing my romantic prospects was a little frightening. I

envisioned them hunched together, rubbing their palms together like conniving wizards. Not your business, gentlemen.

"He said you guys had been working together and that he
saw you out and even though you were at some glitzy party,
you were willing to talk screenplays. It came up in the context of 'Charlie's been a great help on this project.'"

"Oh. Well, yeah." The Page Six episode had made me a little paranoid, but reassuringly my love life was still more interesting to me than to other people.

"Do you like him?"

"Horton, I adore him. It's frightening. Just looking at him
makes me happy."

"That's nice, Charlie. That's the way it's supposed to be."

"Yeah." I looked at my watch. I didn't feel quite ready to
continue this discussion. I tend to treat Horton like a friend,
but he is my advisor, after all. A little professional distance
might not be the worst thing in the world. I personally
would be outraged were Miguel to be bitching about me to
his advisor. Maybe I should dredge up the Golden Rule and
start applying it to my own decadent and cynical life. "I have
to get to yoga. I'll let you know when I have revisions."

I wandered dreamily out of Horton's office.

*I'd like to thank the Academy. This is such an honor. Thanks
to Horton Lear, who has been a true mentor. This film would not
exist without him. Thanks to Karen and Marisa and to my parents and grandmother for always supporting me . . .*

My dad spent most of Thanksgiving weekend making various nauseating puns on the word *soap*. By the third time he
announced that "Charlotte's dating a soaper guy," I was contemplating the possibility that I had been switched at birth
and my real parents—the ones with brilliantly wry senses of
humor—were off living in Tahiti.

The Monday after Thanksgiving, Karen and I picked up
Marisa at her office (just two blocks away from the infamous

strap-snapping site) for a Whine and Wine session. She had pulled her hair back in a black binder clip and looked grouchy as hell.

"Ten minutes, I promise," she said, as she tossed a pile of papers into a messenger pouch. "Go find some books you want to purloin. Ned will help you." She cradled the phone receiver between her head and neck as she sealed the pouch. "Ned! Ned, these are my friends and I am going to make them wait here for me while I get this stuff out, so the least we can do is send them home with something wonderful."

Ned was Marisa's assistant. Karen and I had heard all about him when he was hired two months ago. ("He just graduated from Brown in May and he answers my phone! He says 'Marisa Rosenbaum's office!' I have an office!")

"Hi," I said to Ned. Did twenty-two year olds really look that young? Ned was practically a fetus, as far as I was concerned. "I'm Charlie. I call Marisa all the time."

"Me too," Karen confessed. "But I like to think that I camouflage my personal crises better than Charlie."

Ned led us into the main hallway. "What do you guys want? This'll be number seven on the *Times* list next week." He handed us a copy of the second novel by a chic Brooklyn author.

Karen wrinkled her nose. "I hated his first book. It was so incredibly smug and self-righteous."

"Really?" Ned asked, looking around. He lowered his voice. "It's the hot book right now, so I thought I'd offer it. But just between us, I thought it was trash."

"I thought *I* was the only one who thought that!" Karen exclaimed. "Everyone else acted like it was Styron's second coming or something. Please."

"There was that *Time* profile that called him the savior of modern fiction," Ned said.

"As if!" Karen squealed.

"So, what other writers do you like?"

Karen and Ned were off and running. I felt vaguely super-fluous as I listened to them rhapsodize over Henry James. (Like anyone will admit to not liking Henry James. It's sort of like admitting that you don't like the Beatles or failed re-medial English or something.) I studied the back of a mys-tery, trying to decide if I was too busy to invest in light reading or if because I was busy, I could *only* devote time to something undemanding.

Marisa reappeared in the promised ten minutes. "OK, I'm ready. Let's go. I need dinner."

I reached over and pulled the binder clip out of her hair. "Rough day?"

She glanced at Ned, then decided to say it anyway. "There are *only* rough days."

As we waited for the elevator, I saw Karen sneak a peek back toward Ned, who was standing over the fax machine.

"Ned seems nice," I said mischievously.

"Yeah, he's a good kid," Marisa replied.

"Don't you think so, Karen?"

"Hmm?" Karen looked up. "Sure, I guess."

Whatever. I know sparks when I see them.

eighteen

It was a real *Wuthering Heights* day—cold, blustery, as dark as ten at night even though it was ten in the morning. It would have been perfect moor-strolling weather, but—there being a lack of available moors on the Upper West Side—I had strolled to the Laundromat instead. There was this deceptively fine mist that looked too light for an umbrella, but I arrived soaked and frozen. Abandoning cleanliness for warmth, I found an old college sweatshirt in my dirty laundry and changed into it in the bathroom.

Twenty minutes later, I was slogging through my reading for class and evaluating just how desperately I needed a coffee refill. Not enough to venture back outside. It hadn't stopped raining for a week. If this kept up, I would no doubt develop rickets from lack of vitamin D.

For the record, I *hate* the Laundromat. Today the woman behind the counter happened to give me an extra dryer token by accident. Being the Good Samaritan that I am, I had tried to return it—at which point she started lecturing me on how dryer tokens were not, under any circumstances, to leave the Laundromat and how it is because of people like me that the Laundromat has to buy more tokens and then raise their prices to offset the cost of new tokens.

Frankly, I was waiting for her to blame the entire decrepit state of the economy on my alleged token hoarding. I could honestly see how embezzlers might get started. I should have just kept the stupid forty-five-cent token for my next visit. Needless to say, this had created something of a hostile environment. Every so often, she would glare at me suspiciously to make sure that I was engaging in no illicit activity.

(I will know that I have achieved some measure of personal and financial success when I finally have my own washer and dryer.)

I had just transferred my wash, making a great show of inserting each token into the dryer with exaggerated care, when Robert walked in. He was wearing a parka that looked suitable for exploring Antarctica. I bent my head studiously over my book. There are times when running into people in New York randomly makes me happy, like this is *my* city and I have taken one hell of a bite out of the so-called Apple. But the Laundromat is not one of those times and Robert not particularly one of those people. I watched as he approached the woman at the counter. She broke into a smile as he talked to her.

Nauseating.

She went into the little closet in the back and came out with a sack of laundry. It took me a second to realize that apparently Robert could afford to get his laundry done for him. Even more nauseating. I slunk further behind my book and hoped he would leave without noticing me.

"Charlie?"

I looked up and feigned shock. "Wow, Robert, hi! I didn't even see you. What a coincidence."

Robert shrugged. "Maybe not such a coincidence. I just moved around the corner."

"Closer to work?" I asked, pulling the sleeves of my dirty sweatshirt over my hands.

"Yeah and, well, you know," he said inarticulately.

"Well, good to see you again," I said brightly.

"Sure." Robert did a little shuffle toward the door and paused. "Hey, Charlie, would you do me a favor?'

"What?'

"Well, I've been thinking about going to school and I have to, you know, write this essay to apply. Do you think you could read it and just make sure that I don't have any errors or say anything really dumb? I'd pay you."

Maybe I should have been happy that Robert wanted to go to school, but I just felt sad that he was afraid of sounding stupid. It must be horrible not to trust your own writing.

"Oh, you don't have to pay me. That's silly. Just send it to me as an e-mail attachment and I'll look at it."

I scrawled my e-mail on a scrap of paper and handed it to him.

"Thanks." Robert did another awkward shuffle and hustled out the door into the *Wuthering Heights* mist. I stared out onto the street after him and decided it was time to call my real-life predestined Heathcliff.

That night I was curled up in bed (clean sheets—yay!) when Karen knocked on my door.

"Yeah?" I called, reluctantly setting aside my magazine.

She wandered in and proceeded to sit directly on the ninety-year-old velvet couch that belonged to my great-grandmother that nobody—be it God, Hank Destin, or the ghost of Flaubert himself—is allowed to sit on because it is too old and I am deathly afraid of damaging it permanently.

"Karen, the couch!" I yelped.

She jumped up. "What, what?"

"You know I don't like people to sit on that couch."

"God, Charlie, I thought something was wrong." She glared at me, then sat on the floor.

I moved my legs so there was an available corner of space on my bed. "Here." Karen crawled up next to me.

"What's up?" I asked.

Karen's forehead furrowed so there was a tiny dimple between her eyebrows.

"Ned asked me out."

"Ned, as in Marisa's assistant, Ned the fetus, Ned?" I asked.

"He's twenty-two."

"So that Ned."

"Yeah."

"You gonna go?"

"I don't know."

"I thought you were checking him out the other day."

"Yeah, but he's twenty-two."

I decided not to repeat the Ned-the-fetus comment.

"Do you think that's too young?" I asked instead.

"Well, yeah!"

"There's a six-year age difference between Hank and me."

"That's different."

"How?"

"It just is," Karen said morosely. "You know it is."

"Ahh," I said intelligently. She was right—there *was* a difference. I was sort of stumped on how to get around this. "Well, do you think he's cute?"

"Sure."

"Did you like talking to him about books?"

"Definitely."

"Then what's the harm in going out to dinner *once*? I'm dating Hank and, to be perfectly honest, dating college dropout TV beefcake is hardly my usual thing."

"Well, if we go out once, then I've opened the door."

"A *crack*," I emphasized. "You've opened it a crack and you can always slam it closed again. No harm done."

"Guess not." Karen stretched her legs out in front of her and wiggled her toes. She was wearing a pair of rainbow-striped knee socks that I had given her. The toe wiggling was especially effective because the socks had a separate space for each toe, like gloves.

"I think you should say yes."

Karen tilted her head. "I already did."

"You already did?" I repeated skeptically.

"Mmm-hmm. But I was thinking of canceling."

"Don't cancel."

"I won't."

Karen slid off the bed. "Sweet dreams."

"You too."

nineteen

When I'd called Hank from the Laundromat yesterday, we'd arranged to meet for dinner in Chinatown, then walk up to some chic bar in Soho or NoLita for martinis. Chinatown was my suggestion. He was going to have to handle the chic bar part all on his own.

I got to Chinatown early because I needed to pick up various stuff— Christmas/Chanukah gifts, new sequined slippers (my old ones had basically exploded) and multiple pairs of cheap gloves because I tend to lose them. I had accomplished most of this by seven and had a spare half hour to putter around before meeting Hank. I was especially proud of the red mandarin satin mules I'd gotten for my grandmother. They were perfect for shuffling around while sipping champagne.

I decided to kill time by trying on hats. Karen has this sort of 1930s black felt fedora-esque thing that she got in Chinatown. I call it her speakeasy hat. I covet it but, lucky for her, it's much too big for me to borrow. I look like a six-year-old playing dress-up.

Six hats later, I realized that either I had a pinhead or Chinatown hats were sized to accommodate Spock ears.

"Too big again!" cried the shopkeeper, as yet another hat slid down to the bridge of my nose, completely covering my eyes.

I laughed as I took it off. "I think they're all going to be too big. Thank you, though."

"No," the shopkeeper said vigorously. "We must find pretty hat for pretty girl."

I smiled at him. "Oh. Thanks." I watched as he darted into the store, emerging with a tower of new hats.

"Child-sized," he said.

I tried on a red Paddington hat. It wasn't as gigantic as the adult ones but still stubbornly fell over my eyes.

Oh my God, I really did have a pinhead.

"It's not as bad, but still too big." I checked my watch. Ten minutes left. I should probably start walking to the restaurant to allow myself adequate primping time in the bathroom before Hank got there.

"No, we find you one."

"No, I should go."

"You need hat."

"Well, I want a hat, but I don't need one." I held up my old knit cap. Admittedly, it looks like something Hans Brinker would wear to ward off frostbite during the big skating race, but it fits my pinhead perfectly. We could have continued this verbal tug of war but Hank appeared. Given that we were meeting each other five blocks away, it wasn't a total coincidence.

"You're early," I said.

"Few minutes." He reached out and put a black, broad-brimmed hat on my head. Too big.

"None of them fit," I explained. "Apparently, I'm a pinhead."

The shopkeeper watched as Hank substituted the black hat with a fuzzy gray *Newsies* cap.

"You are brother and sister," he said, holding out a mirror so I could check out the cap. I looked like a *Playboy* bunny.

"Noooo," Hank said, tilting the angle of the gray cap.

"I look like a *Playboy* bunny," I announced.

"You must be brother and sister," the shopkeeper said. He pointed at me. "Because I want the pretty girl to be available for me."

Hank and I both started laughing.

"Sorry," he told the shopkeeper, handing me a cranberry-colored cloche.

It fit.

I repeat: it fit. The shopkeeper clapped.

I stared at myself in the mirror. "Not bad. How much?"

"Fifteen dollars."

Did I like it fifteen dollars' worth? I adjusted the brim.

"OK, ten, just for you," the shopkeeper amended. That was the easiest bargaining I'd ever done in my life.

"Sold," I replied, reaching for my bag. The hat matched my gray coat perfectly.

"Hey, Charlie, I want to get this for you," Hank said.

"Don't be silly," I said automatically.

"I'm not. I'm being selfish. I want you to think of me when you wear it."

Swoon. Swoon swoon swoon swoon swoon. As if I didn't think of him enough already.

As we walked toward Mott Street, I slid my hand into Hank's. "Thank you."

"You're very welcome."

"You do realize that this is *exactly* like *La Boheme*. Rodolfo buys Mimi a bonnet from a street vendor at the beginning of act two."

"I know," Hank said earnestly. "That was my actual motivation. I wanted you to think of me as Rodolfo."

"Really?"

Hank looked at me as if I were on crack. "No, Charlie. I've never even seen *La Boheme*."

"Oh, you're losing points, buddy," I said. "You're going to have to get me some dumplings to make up for that one."

* * *

Two orders of shrimp and watercress dumplings, one order of ginger chicken, one order of string beans, and a thousand cups of tea later, I was in a very good mood.

"I should come here more often," Hank said. "I used to come to Chinatown a lot when I first moved to the city. But I don't think I've been down here in years."

"Up here," I reminded him. "You're a Brooklyn boy now."

Hank grinned. "Yeah, that's right." He drank some tea that had to be ice-cold. "Want to head out?"

"Sure." I yawned inadvertently. It had been a long day.

"If you want, we could skip the bar and go to my place," Hank said. "We could make drinks there."

Fantastic offer. *Fantastic offer.*

"That works. Maybe we could even work in some kind of a massage exchange."

"Where's the check?" Hank swiveled his head wildly and faked excessive eagerness to leave. Goofy boy. The waitress saw him and brought the bill to our table. She stood there timidly for a second.

"Thank you," Hank said. He flipped the bill over. This dinner had to have a cost an eighth of what our first date had. The waitress still hovered beside us.

"Dr. Reston?" she said softly.

Hank broke out a trademark smile. "Hank," he said. I sat there awkwardly, unsure how to deal with the unexpected intrusion of a fan.

"Wow," the waitress said. "Wow, wow, wow. Dr. Reston."

"Please," Hank said. "I'm Hank."

"Wow."

OK, I thought cynically, *we get it. Wow.*

"I love the show. I wish you and Serena would get back together." Serena was Maddie's character. "You treat her so poorly." The waitress frowned. "Terrible."

Hank shrugged. His dimples were very charming and very prominent. "Blame the writers, not me."

The waitress giggled. She looked at me. "He doesn't treat you like that."

"Certainly he does," I said mischievously. "He's a beast." I shook my head sadly. "Especially when no one's around." I shrugged. "Just brutal."

The waitress stared at me uncertainly. "Kidding," I said.

"Oh, oh." She got it. She curtsied slightly. "I get your change."

"Wow," I said after she left.

Hank gave me a wary look. "All part of the package," he said.

The waitress returned with a man who looked to be the owner of the restaurant, two other women, and a camera.

"Please," said the man, holding up the camera. "Is it OK?'

I had thought that Hank's trademark smile couldn't get any bigger, but he positively beamed. "Of course," he drawled. Getting up, he slung one arm around the shoulders of the owner of the restaurant and the other around the waitress. All three grinned. The flash popped.

"Next time you come," the owner said, "you'll be on the wall." He gestured to two other framed photos, one of the owner with Giuliani and one with someone I didn't exactly recognize but thought might be a Knick.

"Looking forward to it," Hank said. His professionally whitened teeth practically sparkled.

As we walked back to Canal in search of a taxi, I looked up at Hank. "Celebrity," I said.

"No," he scoffed. "Please, Charlie."

I wondered.

twenty

"Don't worry, Charlie. You'll be OK." Marisa's niece, Nina, took me by the hand and gently guided me down the stairs of the nosebleed seats at Lincoln Center. What a cutie. She had begun clucking over me the minute I said, "I hate heights." While being shepherded out of *The Nutcracker* by a seven-year-old was probably a new level of dorkiness, I was too touched by her ministrations to object.

"Did you like the show, sweetheart?" I asked.

She nodded vigorously.

"What was the best part?"

"When the big lady came out and all the little girls were under her skirts. And they did turns."

"Mother Ginger! Yeah, I like her too. My favorite part is when it snows."

Nina wrinkled her nose. "That was only OK. You told me it was going to happen before we got here, so I wasn't even surprised."

"Sooooorrrry," I replied.

"And you told me about the Christmas tree, too."

We had reached the exits. Thank goodness. I really do hate heights.

"What can I say, Nina? You're just going to have to find somebody else to take you to *The Nutcracker*."

She gazed uncertainly at me. "No, I like you. We're still going out for hot chocolate, right?"

"Of course, we're going out for hot chocolate," Marisa interjected. "Don't let Charlie fool you. She was begging to come with us."

"It's true," I admitted. "Got your gloves, Neeners? It's cold outside."

Twenty minutes later, Nina was completely absorbed in a cup of candy cane hot chocolate and I was giving Marisa an all-important Hank Destin update.

"I feel like a twelve-year-old," I raved. "I can't remember the last time I was so into a guy."

Marisa swirled her spoon in her cocoa. "Sophomore year," she said. "Elliott Fredrickson."

I did not want to be reminded of Elliott Fredrickson.

"I keep waiting for the catch, you know? He's just too good to be true. Any day now he's going to confess that he's gay or a Scientologist or has some weird sexual fetish for sheep," I admitted.

"Do you think that maybe you're being just a little bit paranoid?"

"Well, OK, maybe. But why would anyone so fabulously perfect land in my life? Guys like Hank just aren't single." I frowned. "Let me revise that: guys as great as Hank *seems* just aren't single."

"Maybe he's attracted to your low self-esteem."

"Very funny." I made a face at her. Nina looked up from her candy cane and made an even more gruesome face. For a few moments, we got caught up in a face-making spree.

"So are you guys going out tonight?" Marisa asked, when all three of us had exhausted our grimace repertoires.

"Nah, schoolwork."

"It's Saturday."

"And I still have exams." I drank the dregs of my cocoa. "Actually, Hank's in L.A. again, which rescues me from choos-

ing between love and career. I'll see him later in the week." I
stopped. "What do you suppose he does in L.A. anyway?
Troubled Passion films in New York. You don't suppose he has
a West Coast mistress, do you?"

"Doubtful."

"I worry," I said honestly.

"Relax."

There was a pause. "OK, I have a big question for you,"
Marisa continued.

I set down my mug and waited.

"What do you think about Karen and Ned?"

No way in hell was I going to get involved in this one.
"What do *you* think?"

"I don't know." Marisa stared at the table. "Well, OK, I
don't know what she's thinking," she amended. "He's so
young."

"A fetus," I agreed.

"And he's my assistant! She couldn't find someone who
wasn't my assistant?"

I shrugged. "He's cute and they had a conversation about
Henry James."

"Sure," Marisa agreed. "Cute and smart and has read not
just *Portrait of a Lady* and *Daisy Miller*, but also *The Bostoni-
ans*. It's impressive. But still."

"I wouldn't worry too much about it," I said. "Once they
go out, she'll realize how young he is and that'll be that."

"You think?"

"Absolutely."

Later that week, after turning in my final papers and teaching yoga, I embarked on what I sincerely hoped would be my
last shopping expedition for the season. I had debated the
present-for-Hank issue endlessly. I needed to find something
he would appreciate and enjoy, but not necessarily anything
that suggested that I considered him to be the love of my life

(which I did) or that I had spent hours pondering what to get him (which I had). Although I fully agreed with the *Post* that Hank was my destiny, I would hardly be so bold as to label him my *boyfriend*. Please.

I'd settled on a bartending kit—cocktail shaker, ice strainer, etc. It was tasteful and wouldn't embarrass either one of us. Plus he needed one. When he made martinis at his apartment, he'd used two glasses as a shaker—which, aside from being no way to treat Ketel 1, had involved some unnecessary sloshing.

What I'd told Marisa was true. I'd spent so much time fretting that Hank would be revealed as somehow disastrous and unacceptable that I was giving Chicken Little a run for his sky-falling feathers. The need to find *the* ideal cocktail shaker for him was only heightened by the fact that he pretty much showered me with presents. It was never anything big, just constant. For example:

SCENE: Union Square green market. HANK and
CHARLIE each have a Starbucks cup and are
wandering from merchant to merchant. CHARLIE
has a bag filled with something leafy
dangling over one arm. She stops before a
table filled with small African violets. She
picks up a pink violet in a pot and gazes at
it pensively.

          CHARLIE:
African violets are so pretty.

          HANK:
Yeah, they're nice.

          CHARLIE *(to the vendor)*:
These are beautiful. I wish I didn't have

such a tendency to kill all my plants,
otherwise I'd get one.

                    HANK:
Hey, let me get you a plant.

*CHARLIE's in-need-of-tweezing eyebrows raise
slightly.*

                    CHARLIE:
I *kill* plants.

                    HANK:
Better than killing people. Come on, let me
get you violets. Pick out the one that you
want. It's like the ASPCA—you have to
choose.

CHARLIE eyes the plants.

                    CHARLIE:
In that case, I want the one with the waggly
tail.

*CUT TO: Close-up of the VENDOR giving
CHARLIE a venomous look.*

Totally sweet, right? Plus it's been ten days and Franklin
and Eleanor, my two new plants, seem to be flourishing despite the harrowing subway ride uptown.

At any rate, I needed to find his present. In case you've
never tried, it is damn hard to find a good cocktail shaker.
One would assume that a city of eight million people might
be remotely amenable to such a quest. But after two hours,
I'd seen giant shakers, tiny shakers, phallic shakers, shakers

with strange spouts, shakers shaped like penguins, but not one single classic inoffensive silver cocktail shaker.

I was in a total funk by the time I wandered into ABC Carpet and Home. Were it not for the dire need to procure a suitable present immediately, I would have avoided ABC altogether. It's so ludicrously expensive that I'm paranoid that my bank balance might somehow diminish just by walking through the door.

But it's lovely . . .

The store was all decked out for Christmas, with huge golden garlands and holly strewn about and Renaissance-sounding carols playing softly in the background. A tankard of complimentary hot, spiced cider sat by the cash register. I helped myself to a cup, shifting my backpack and yoga mat bag to a more comfortable position. Forgetting my mission, I wandered happily through the store, toying with everything from teapots to wrapping paper. My feet stopped hurting. My headache vanished.

I was so thoroughly convinced that ABC was the promised land that I was neither shaken nor stirred when I finally found the perfect, gleaming, timeless shaker and swizzle stick set. It looked vaguely Art Deco. I turned it over. There was no price tag.

"Excuse me," I said to a passing salesman. "Can you tell me how much this is?"

"Oh," he replied in a strong French accent. Then he said something that sounded like "sevwef."

"I'm sorry?"

"Sevef decont."

I smiled apologetically. "Sorry—I didn't catch that."

"Les soldes. C'est un deecont."

I am a real dunce at languages. I learned next to nothing in four semesters of French.

"It's on sale?" I asked. The salesman nodded. "How much?" I asked for what seemed like the hundredth time.

"Senty."

"Seventy?" I asked.

"Senty deecont," he repeated.

I was beginning to loathe his smug Gallic imperturbability.

"It's seventy and there's a discount?"

He shrugged. "Senty deecont." Then he nodded.

Seventy dollars was a hell of a lot of money for a cocktail shaker and two swizzle sticks. On the other hand, if there were a discount on top of the $70, it wouldn't be so bad. It was the ideal present. I adored Hank and he had certainly given me way more than $70 worth of dinner, wine, cranberry cloche hat, and African violets since we'd started dating. Besides, I rationalized further, time was money and the sooner I got Hank's present out of the way, the sooner I could get on with final revisions to *The Doctor's Wife*.

"How much is the discount?"

"Sevwefcent."

I sighed. Whatever. Better to get it and figure it out later. I was simply not going to be able to understand this guy. I would never find a better shaker and I was sick of running through the city like a possessed madwoman.

"OK, I'll get it," I said, taking a last swallow of my cider.

The salesman led me to the cash register. He wrapped the shaker and swizzle sticks in tissue paper as he processed my credit card. He tucked a sheaf of marbled wrapping paper in the bag.

"Ees free," he said.

"The wrapping paper?"

He nodded.

"Wow, thanks," I said, scrawling my signature on the receipt.

It wasn't until I was on the train back uptown that I realized I had never looked at the receipt. I didn't know how much the discount was. I reached into the bag and found the receipt.

I gasped reflexively. The train went blurry for just a second. Blinking several times, I brought the receipt inches away from my eyes and stared at it hard, as if the numbers would somehow rearrange themselves into a more reasonable amount under such scrutiny. The discount (or "deecont") was seventy dollars. I had just purchased a $711.63 cocktail shaker.

I was indeed Chicken Little. The sky had indubitably fallen.

twenty-one

The sky had fallen. I had purchased a $711 cocktail shaker.

"Oh shit," I moaned. I was lying in corpse pose on my yoga mat in the center of the floor. I had gone straight from shopping to Whine and Wine at Marisa's. Marisa didn't even look up from packing clothes into a suitcase. She had to be out of her housesitting apartment in two days.

"I can't believe you were going to spend $70 on a cocktail shaker," Karen said dryly.

"No wonder they gave me free wrapping paper. It's probably complimentary after you spend $500."

"Actually," Karen continued, "I can't believe you even set foot in ABC. You can't afford anything in there."

"Karen, shush!"

"They'll take it back," she said. "Don't you think?"

I brought my knees over my head and curled, appropriately enough, into embryo pose.

"I have no idea what I'll do if they don't take it back," I mumbled. "I'll have to sell my eggs."

"Why didn't you look at the receipt before you signed it?" Karen asked.

"I don't know. I was tired and carrying all this stuff. I guess I just forgot."

"You forgot?" Karen asked.

"It just happened! I didn't realize I hadn't looked at the receipt until I was already on the subway." I took a deep breath and adjusted my position.

"What I don't get," Marisa said, "is why you just didn't go to Zabar's."

I sat up suddenly, wrenching my back in the process. Getting out of embryo pose correctly is sort of a three-minute procedure.

"That's right!" I exclaimed. "They have that whole kitchen-ware section upstairs."

Marisa nodded. She had a look of "Oh, Charlie, you are such an idiot" on her face.

"Uh-huh," she said.

"Marisa, you're brilliant," I said, twisting to relieve the cramp in my back.

"Is that *brilliant* in the British sense?" she asked.

I laughed. Marisa has this ongoing obsession with British people who use "brilliant" to mean OK. She claims that every time she calls her London office to tell them she's done something—sent a fax, talked to her boss, breathed—the person on the other end of the phone responds, with great enthusiasm, "Oh, that's brilliant! Just brilliant!"

"American," I confirmed. "Definitely American. Do you suppose Zabar's is still open?" We were only a block away.

Karen checked her watch. "At ten-thirty at night?"

"OK, maybe not," I admitted, flopping back into corpse pose. "They *have* to take it back. That guy spoke no English. I honestly thought he said $70." I paused. "Even if I were filthy rich and had $700, I don't think I'd spend it on a cocktail shaker. That's ridiculous. You could probably buy a small seventeenth-century Flemish drawing for that price."

Marisa picked up a stack of magazines and began sorting through them.

"OK, I have to ask," she said, tossing aside all but one copy of *Harper's*. "How was the date, Karen?"

"Did Ned say anything?" Karen said quickly.

"Do you think I would dare ask him for his opinion without asking you first?"

Karen smiled. "Point taken. Thank you." She paused. "It was OK but he's really young. Dinner was fine, but then we went to this party. They were playing actual beer pong. The apartment was the size of my shoe and they managed to squeeze an entire Ping-Pong table in there, which leads me to believe that they felt it was a necessary piece of furniture."

"Does Ned live there?" I asked.

"No, it was just some of his friends, but he was playing. In fact, he seemed to enjoy playing beer pong."

"I didn't know there were people in this world who appreciated both Henry James and beer pong," I said.

"Of course there are," Karen said. "I just prefer not to date those people." She shook her head. "He is way too young for me."

I rolled over onto my side and gave Marisa a smug, Cheshire cat smile.

I was batting a thousand on predicting human behavior.

Maybe *I* should become a psychologist.

I had gift-wrapped a copy of what I sincerely hoped would be the ultimate, final, set-in-stone version of *The Doctor's Wife* and dropped it in Horton's box at school before the holidays. Hank had asked me about a thousand times if he could read something I'd written. In a burst of courage, I printed out a copy for him as well and tied it up in a big, red bow. I'd managed to find an adequate bartending kit at Zabar's and, fortunately, ABC had taken back the ludicrous shaker without even a sniff.

Considering how nervous I get when people I know read my writing, I felt that a copy of *The Doctor's Wife* was a tremendous personal sacrifice worth far more than what I could have spent at ABC. Hank immediately understood this. He started laughing when he opened up the bar kit. But his face got serious and clenched up in a *Troubled Passion* way when he saw the screenplay.

"Charlie-doll, thanks. But are you sure? I don't want you to give me this if you're not ready."

I let my hair out of its ponytail. "I'm ready," I said. We were at his apartment, having gone to dinner first at the same adorable restaurant as on our first date.

He leaned over and kissed my neck. It tickled. I squinched my shoulder and head together inadvertently.

"Tickles," I said.

Hank kissed me in the same spot again.

"Stop going for my neck, you vampire," I said.

He did.

"I have something for you too," he said. He handed me a small flat package. "It's sort of appropriate now that I have your screenplay."

I have never been the sort to open presents painstakingly, so that the paper can be reused and the pregift excitement is drawn out for as long as possible. Instead, I shredded the wrapping ecstatically.

Inside was a small leather-bound brown book. I looked at the spine. It was a really old copy of *Madame Bovary*. I opened it and began flipping through the pages. There were beautiful color illustrations. I was about as speechless as I ever get.

"Where'd you find this?'

"Secret."

"It's beautiful."

"I thought so too."

"I love illustrated books."

Hank smiled a real smile, not the Kendall Reston lady-killer look.

"I love old books," I continued.

Hank's smile widened.

"I'm glad," he said.

I stared at the book some more. "This is a perfect present. This is way better than the bar kit." I sat there quietly for a second. I wanted to tell Hank that I loved him. I could feel the words hovering on my tongue, waiting to erupt, poised to transform our relationship into something more elevated and passionate and historic. I could see the pride of a successful present lurking in his eyes, the dimples growing more uncertain with each passing second of my silence.

I wanted to say it.

But for some reason (probably fear) I stroked the cracked leather binding of my book and pretended I'd had no such urge.

AUDITIONS:
Three men, one woman, and assorted extras needed for full-length student-written and directed feature film.

Auditions January 7–10.

For more information, e-mail:
cfrost@columbfilm.edu

To: Karen <kstein@columbpsych.edu>,
Marisa <marisa.rosenbaum@citybooks.com.>
From: Charlie <cfrost@columbfilm.edu>
Re: Too much?

Is it excessive to make eleven New Year's resolutions?

—C

twenty-two

Lacking an office, I'd taken over Starbucks as my substitute headquarters. The Monday after New Year's, I camped out there for five hours. During that time, I met with the students who were going to be cinematographer, film editor, sound person, and costume, lighting, and set designers for *The Doctor's Wife*. I'd spent Christmas vacation reviewing their résumés and portfolios and listed my top choices for each position. The crew had also had the chance to read screenplays by all of the thesis students and list their preferences. We'd supposedly been paired together by this computerized algorithm that's like the match system for medical residencies. However, professors have been known to interfere with the process. Given that I'd managed to get my first choice for everything except sound editor, I suspected that Horton had exerted some muscle on my behalf.

(I did ask him. He stared at me blankly and said, "Ever heard of gift horses, Charlotte?")

Sarah Wong, the costume designer, was my last meeting of the day. I was pretty sure that—despite Horton's intervention—I'd been the only person to request Sarah. She was a junior fine arts major and the only undergraduate who'd applied for any of the positions. While she was obviously inexperienced, her costumes for a campus production of *Macbeth* were (in my opinion) nothing short of sensational. I didn't care how much better she would be with some graduate design classes under her belt; I had a hunch that, even in her inchoate collegiate form, she had more than enough talent and vision.

I was even more convinced after our meeting at Starbucks. Sarah showed up with a sketchpad of ideas.

"These look great," I said, flipping through the pages. "But don't forget the budget."

Sarah pushed her glasses up her nose. "I don't think it'll be an issue," she said. "I priced some of this stuff at vintage stores and on eBay yesterday." She handed me a sheet of figures. "These are rough estimates, but it looks like I could outfit the entire cast for about $500."

I'd initially allotted her $1,000 and fully expected that she would request more money. I stared at Sarah's estimates. She'd listed things like "1950s silver taffeta ball skirt with zipper and hem damage; $30 at Timeline on Eighth Street. Can be altered to fit size 0–6."

"Do you know a good place to get the repairs done?" I asked.

Sarah looked surprised. "Oh, I have my own sewing machine. I planned to do repairs and alterations myself. And obviously I'd sew any frocks that we didn't purchase already made. Certainly, I'll want to come up with something for the dinner party scene myself."

I nodded. What a little star she was going to be. Despite her vibrant sketches, she was wearing plain black pants and T-shirt that looked straight from the Gap.

"Why are you at Columbia?" I wondered. "Why not art school?"

Sarah shrugged. "Parents," she said honestly. Then, changing the topic, "Do you like the idea of the color theme?"

"Color theme?"

"Yeah, see, look. Emma starts wearing pastels and then

moves into richer, more jewel-toned colors for her affairs. As the movie progresses, the color slowly leaches out of her wardrobe so that by the time she dies, she's just wearing grays and blacks. Here. I made a chart matching colors to scenes."

It was a great idea, but I didn't want the imagery to be too obvious. Sarah was leaning forward in a nervous way that reminded me of the way I sometimes sat in meetings with Horton. I watched her for a second, then handed the chart back without even looking at it.

"Sarah, I suspect you're a genius. Do what you think is best."

If only finding the perfect cast were as simple. After four nights of auditions, I was fairly certain that I would go with Sabrina Waters (*not*, I was convinced, her real name) as Emma. She'd given a solid, albeit not stupendous, audition and had a vulnerable, doe-eyed look that would work for the character. I'd updated Flaubert's villainous merchant Lheureux into the cold fish character of Joshua LaRue and struck gold with a chronically unemployed actor named Walsh Ryan. Walsh had a pasty, prim look that was spoiling his chances of a career in TV or film but that suited LaRue perfectly. I was blown away by his audition. He had managed to be both seductive and repellent at the same time.

I was having more trouble with the two male leads, Charles and Leon. I left the second round of callbacks slightly worried. I could tell that Sabrina was the sort of actress who responded to her castmates. If I could find the right Leon and Charles, she would take off. I was toying with giving Leon's role to a sexy undergrad with wooden acting skills. In the best-case scenario, his pouty playboy looks would inspire genuine chemistry in Sabrina and camouflage any other deficiencies. I wasn't satisfied with the casting, though. And when it came to Charles, I was stumped.

It was Karen's birthday that weekend. I baked twenty chocolate cupcakes and spelled *Happy Birthday, Karen!* on them, one letter (or punctuation mark) per cupcake. Karen invited a slew of friends from school and I asked Hank, Chris Martin, the still-forming cast and crew of *The Doctor's Wife*, and a few friends from college. It would be the first time Hank had seen my apartment. I only hoped that he wouldn't be so put off by the grad student squalor of my apartment that he dropped me for somebody who could afford a cleaning service and an elevator building.

I was sitting on the windowsill talking to an incredibly boring chemistry student when Hank got there. Our living room is the size of a fingernail, so he had to squeeze through the crowd to get to me. (Had these people no class? Didn't they understand that they were to part in Red Sea fashion before his buff, notorious playboy self?)

"Charlie-doll," he greeted me.

"Hey, baby," I replied. I was learning to speak Sleaze. Maybe I could list that on my résumé: reading knowledge of French and Latin, fluent in Sleaze. "This is John. He's in chemistry. He was just telling me that he makes movies, too. Only his are about chemistry."

John nodded vigorously. "I do computer simulated films of catalysis at a molecular level."

"So you could call your movie *A Molecule to Remember,*" Hank said.

I loved it. Who knew that such a stud could engage in stupid academic humor? John did not look amused.

"*To Kill a Molecule?*" I offered.

"*Atom's Rib,*" Hank challenged.

"Oooh, very good." I thought for a second. "*Lord of the Molecules,*" I said, as John moved off with a disgusted look on his face. I took his absence as a cue to wrap my arms around Hank. I despise PDA. I think it's revolting. I have been known to snarl "Save it for the bedroom" under my breath to publicly necking couples. But at that particular moment in time, I just wanted to revel in his Hankness. It was a reflex. I had to do it. Maybe I was still reeling, three weeks later, from the old copy of *Madame Bovary*.

"Would it be really, really awful to say, 'Welcome to my humble abode'?" I asked.

"Yes."

"I made cupcakes. And there's beer and wine and stuff."

"You made cupcakes?"

"Of course," I said. I took his hand and maneuvered us over to the food. Hank looked down at the table.

"What's that?" he asked, pointing to the comma cupcake.

"It's a comma. Happy birthday comma Karen exclamation point."

"Of course," he said sarcastically. "Cupcakes should be no excuse to sacrifice grammar."

I giggled.

"Charlie, Charlie." Marisa appeared beside us. "Hi, Hank," she said, distracted. "Do you see what I see?"

"What?"

"Karen!" she wailed. "And Ned! Did you invite him? Why is he here?"

I scanned the room. Ned was indeed here. His arm was around Karen's waist and he was feeding her a bit of cupcake.

Talk about PDA.

"I didn't invite him," I said slowly. "And since you didn't either, I'm assuming Karen did."

"Would it be completely unethical to fire him for hitting on my friend?" Marisa asked.

"She's not exactly beating him off with a stick," Hank said.

"He's my assistant. He's twenty-two." Marisa did not look pleased. "He's not supposed to be her birthday present."

I shrugged. "You can control when he takes his lunch break, Maris. You can't control whether or not he feeds cupcake to your friend."

"Well, she should know better! I'm the one who has to look him in the eye at work tomorrow. How am I supposed to ask him to Xerox something when he's been playing nookie with Karen?"

I hugged Marisa. "Maybe they'll both be too drunk to remember anything."

I looked at Karen and Ned. Her head was tilted back, and she was laughing.

I predicted ensuing melodrama.

twenty-three

Hank and I took a cab back to Brooklyn after Karen's birthday party. I wasn't sure what was going on with the Karen and Ned situation and, anyway, his apartment was more private than mine. It also didn't have empty beer bottles and wrapping paper shreds strewn everywhere.

One of the things that I like about Hank is that he always listens to me talk about school and is either interested or pretends to be. I told him about Sarah Wong (who hadn't come to the party, which was just as well since I wasn't sure she was twenty-one. The last thing I needed was to be caught with a liquored-up, underage costume designer). I told him about Sabrina and my casting concerns. It was about two in the morning and we were curled in bed. Hank reached out and smoothed my hair.

"I read your screenplay," he said.

"Oh." I wasn't sure if he had. I had also wondered if, given the atrocious writing to which he's accustomed, he'd be able to appreciate a different genre. I stared down at the blanket. Maybe I didn't want to know his opinion.

"I thought it was brilliant."

Is that brilliant in the British sense? I thought inanely.

"Oh," I repeated aloud. I'm not very good at accepting compliments.

"I wasn't surprised, though," he continued. "You're so obviously smart and I could tell from the way you talked about Horton and school that everybody thought you were going to be a success."

I felt myself smile. I wriggled a little so I wasn't quite so close to Hank. "Oh," I said for the third time. Considering my chronically inept conversations, it's amazing that I can write brilliant dialogue for fictional people.

Hank had seen me wiggle. He stretched out his hand and played with my hair again. I felt myself melting automatically and closed my eyes.

"I know you're upset about the Charles-Leon casting problem," he said. "I'm actually sort of glad to hear about it."

I opened my eyes. Hank wasn't smiling, but his dimples were prominent nonetheless.

"Maybe I could solve part of that problem," he continued. He took his hand out of my hair.

"How?" I asked.

"I think you know some actors besides the ones who turned up at your audition," he said simply.

It took me a second to get it. "You?'

He nodded. "I'd do it in a heartbeat."

"You'd really be in my thesis?"

"Of course."

All of a sudden, my life made sense. It was so beautifully clear. I couldn't believe I hadn't thought of it before now. I didn't need the wooden, sexy undergrad to play Leon. I had a much more famous wooden, sexy actor at my disposal. Even though no one I knew had heard of Hank, his performance in a Columbia student film would undoubtedly spike interest. I'd get so many more reviews and my chances of admission at indie festivals would skyrocket. I seriously couldn't believe I hadn't thought of this.

"I think you're the brilliant one," I said. "Let's do it. It'll be so much fun." I leaned over and nibbled his ear. "Won't it be a blast? The two of us working on a film?"

Hank reached out to me. I threw myself on top of him and kissed him happily. We stayed that way, just quietly kissing, for a long time.

"I can't believe I didn't think of this," I said at last, sitting up. "You'll be the perfect Leon."

"Leon?" he repeated.

"Yeah, sexy soap actor stars as sexy paramour. Come on," I teased. "Aren't you used to having on-screen affairs?"

Hank's jaw clenched in a very Dr. Kendall Reston way.

"Charlie," he said.

"OK, I'm *not* making fun of *Troubled Passion*," I said hastily. "But seriously, this is great. Sabrina can't fail to have chemistry with you. And the audience will understand exactly why she wants to have an affair." I giggled. "Who'd turn down such a stud?"

"Charlie," Hank said again.

"What?" I smiled at him.

"I don't want to play Leon."

"What? But you just said . . ." I trailed off.

"There are two male leads in your screenplay."

"You want to play *Charles*?"

"I assumed I'd play Charles," he said. "It's a much better role, Charlie."

"Well, sure, but, it's not really your type of role, Hank."

"What do you mean, my type of role?" Hank sounded frosty. I rolled off him. If we were going to have a serious conversation about this, I didn't want my judgment clouded by the fact that I was straddling his chest.

"You know," I said.

"No, actually, Charlie, I don't. I think you better tell me."

"Hank," I said pleadingly.

His eyebrows raised. The jaw clenched more tightly. I had

to tread carefully here. I didn't want to hurt his feelings more than I already had.

"It's not that I'm typecasting," I began. "But you are a very sexy guy and Leon is meant to be a very sexy guy. Charles is the bland and boring husband."

"It's a better role."

"It *is* a better role," I agreed. "He's a much more complicated character. But I happen to think that, given your talents and what my screenplay needs, you'd be better suited for Leon."

"So you think that how I look is a *talent*? That's not a talent, Charlie. It's an accident. Had a different sperm connected with a different egg, I could have ended up like Lyle Lovett."

I smiled despite myself.

"Why do you want to play Charles?" I asked. "Is it just that it's a better role?"

"Look, Charlie, I know I don't complain much. But believe it or not, I find *Troubled Passion* as silly as you do. They pay me a lot, and it's acting, which is what I want to do with my life. But I've wanted a chance at a better character than Kendall for a long time now. That's why I keep going to L.A. for auditions. Except like you, apparently everyone out there assumes that someone who does soaps can't do more than that. So I'm stuck." His face was very tight. He didn't look like Kendall Reston anymore. "When I read your screenplay, I thought it would be my chance to do something real. I was so happy that *you* were the one who'd written this rich, beautiful screenplay." He paused. "I thought, *Surely Charlie will understand; surely she'll give me a chance.* I guess I was wrong. I'd love to play Charles. But if you think that having me as the lead would spoil your screenplay, that's fine. It's your choice as director." He frowned. "And because I've decided that I want to be in *The Doctor's Wife* no matter what, I'll even consent to play Leon if that's what you want. But think about it, Charlie, because you could do worse than me. I'm a professional actor and I take my work seriously. I know I can do better than Kendall Reston. I just need the chance."

"I never knew you felt that way," I said. "I thought you liked soaps."

"I do. I'm just getting to the point where I want something more."

I wasn't sure what to say. I wanted to thank him for confiding in me but "Thanks for sharing" was a bit much. We sat there for a while, not saying anything.

"You don't have to let me know about Charles now," Hank said at last. "Take some time to think about it."

"I will."

"I'm going to get some sleep," he said, rolling away from me.

But despite what he said, I think it took us both a long time of staring at the ceiling before we drifted off.

twenty-four

Because Horton flat-out refused to come to my make-shift office at Starbucks, I went into school to meet him. Since my thesis counted as all of my course requirements for the semester, I hadn't been to campus since before Christmas. It hadn't changed much. Horton was in his office, playing some kind of strange bluegrass music and wearing overalls. He looked ridiculous. We were in the middle of Manhattan, after all.

"Farmer Lear, I presume," I said as I moved a stack of papers so that I could sit down.

"Listen," he said, holding up one finger. I heard a faint pinging beat among the guitars and fiddles. "It's the hammered dulcimer. It's very rare."

"Great," I said. "You know, if we were meeting at *my* office, I'd be able to offer you coffee."

Horton adjusted the volume of the music. "Charlie, if you save your receipts, I'll see what I can do about getting your caffeine habit reimbursed. But forgive me for having a senior moment. I can live without meeting in the middle of seven hundred pompous graduate students."

I debated whether I should comment on the "pompous graduate student" part and decided against it. Instead, I pulled out my notes and gave him an update on all of my meetings. He didn't say much, just nodded thoughtfully.

"Tell Kent to e-mail me," he said at one point. Kent was the set designer. "I think I've got some friends whose house we can use for the outdoor scenes. It's in Connecticut. I'll check but don't anticipate it being a problem."

"What's the house like?"

"The neighborhood is *American Beauty*–type suburbia. Big houses, lots of trees . . ." He waved his hand rather than completing the thought. "The house was built in the forties and has a yard big enough to accommodate cameras. If my friends agree, you can take a field trip there to make sure you like it. But I think it's perfect."

"I trust you," I said, flipping through my notebook. "Casting is more of an issue at the moment." Horton had come for part of the audition process and had seen both Sabrina and Walsh do their monologues. I told him what I thought about them.

"Walsh is a no-brainer, you're right," he agreed. "I think Sabrina will be good, as well. The audition was fine."

"That's what I thought. It wasn't jaw-dropping, but it was solid enough and I suspect she's malleable."

"What about Charles and Leon?"

I guess my face must have given something away because Horton sat up a little straighter in his chair. "Charlie, don't go perfectionist on me. You don't need to hold a second round of auditions." The thought *had* crossed my mind. I wondered how Horton knew. "I was at those auditions," he continued. "You've got enough actors who will work in the roles. I know that maybe they don't match whatever idealistic plans you've got floating in your head. But they'll be OK."

"Do you remember Noah Essen?" I asked, referring to the sexy undergrad.

"For Leon?"

I nodded.

Horton shrugged. "He fits the role, but can't act to save his life. What about the Moses kid?"

We talked for a few minutes about various casting options. Horton lobbied strongly for a less decorative, more talented actor than Noah. "Look, Charlie, skill is ultimately the most important thing," he announced. "Don't trash what you've got with Sabrina by pairing her with someone if you have any doubts about his acting whatsoever."

I licked my lips nervously, then rummaged in my bag for Chap Stick so I could have a moment to think about how I would explain the Hank situation.

"OK," I muttered, devoting an unnecessary amount of attention to rolling exactly the right amount of Chap Stick out of the tube before applying it.

"Think about it. You have a day or two before you need to decide. Have you let Walsh and Sabrina know?"

"I was waiting to talk to you first."

Horton's lips moved in a way that made me think he was repressing a smile. I didn't get what was so funny about wanting his advice. If I learned one thing from the *Honey and Helen* debacle, it was that maybe my instincts aren't unerring.

"So that just leaves Charles."

"Yeah." I took some time making sure my Chap Stick was stored in the pocket on the side of my bag. That way I'd be able to find it more quickly next time I wanted it.

"You got any thoughts, kid?"

"Sort of."

There was a long pause.

"Well?" Horton said at last.

"Remember I told you about that actor I was seeing?"

"Yes." Horton's voice was sharp. I plunged ahead anyway. "He wants to play Charles. I let him read the screenplay."

"Do you want him to play Charles?"

I hate that Horton always asks the most important question right off the bat. Is it really necessary to be so blunt? I began counting the cinder blocks on his wall.

"Charlie?"

"Sorry," I smiled nervously. "I was just counting the cinder blocks on the wall so I didn't have to think about this."

"Cinder blocks?"

I shrugged.

"I think you need to think about it," Horton said.

Like I didn't know that . . .

"He's a soap actor. He's sort of famous, if you follow that stuff," I offered.

"Yeah, Mallory saw you on Page Six," Horton said blandly.

"*What?*"

"Couple months ago, right?"

"You never said anything!"

"Was I supposed to? I figured that if it were my business, you would let me know."

"I didn't know Mallory read Page Six," I said, even though that was hardly the point.

"Religiously," Horton said. "You're lucky you haven't seen her since then. Unlike me, she'd have no such compunctions about asking nosy questions. She thinks the whole thing is fascinating."

Grand.

"Well, he may be in soaps, but he's still a pretty big name for a student thesis."

"Undoubtedly," Horton agreed. "You'd get some press."

"Which would be great. I need publicity if I want to be able to get writing gigs after graduation."

"Well, I'll help you out if you're worried about that," Horton said. "It won't be hard to set you up with an agent."

"Thanks."

"Can this boy of yours act?"

"He's thirty-three," I said. "He's not a boy."

"Charlie," Horton said warningly. I sighed. I did *not* want to delve into this.

"I've only seen the soap," I admitted. "He tends to clench his jaw a lot." I began clenching my jaw furiously in imitation. "Serena," I said in a deep voice. "I don't love you. I've never loved you."

Horton grimaced.

"He wants to do something real," I said, feeling like I wasn't giving Hank enough of a shot. "He thinks it's time to transition out of soaps."

"Why *The Doctor's Wife*?"

"He thinks it's a good screenplay."

Horton tilted his head. "At least he recognizes that."

"Horton, don't stereotype him because he's in soaps. I *really* like him. And he's not an airhead. I'm serious."

"OK." Horton began stroking his jaw. "Charlie, I have to tell you that my gut is against casting a friend—any friend—in your thesis. You're the director. You need to be professional and in control. I really believe your ability to do that will be hampered by the presence of someone who knows you in a different context."

I was quiet. I'd thought of that too.

"To say nothing of the fact that it's grossly unfair to the people who auditioned to cast your boyfriend as the male lead. It's one step off nepotism."

"And film is certainly an industry that frowns on nepotism," I said sardonically. Half of my class, plus all my former coworkers, were kids of actors or industry moguls.

"Since you can't guarantee that this guy—what's his name?" Horton continued.

"Hank," I said glumly.

"Since you can't guarantee that Hank will be any better in the role of Charles than your other options, I think it's a bad idea."

"There's one more thing," I said.

"What?"

"Hank's really good-looking. I mean, spectacular-looking."

Horton looked at me suspiciously. "Given that he's working in soaps, I would assume that."

"So," I continued, "I was thinking that this would add a new psychological dimension to the film that I couldn't get with another actor."

Horton made a small rolling motion with his forefinger that I took to mean "Go on."

"With a husband who looks like Charles, why would Emma need to look outside her marriage for fulfillment? I think it could be a very powerful statement about what we consider vital in a relationship. *Especially*," I added triumphantly, "if I cast someone ordinary-looking for Leon."

"Possibly," Horton said.

"Think about it," I added. "It could be helpful for character development. It clearly demonstrates why Emma would be attracted to Charles in the first place, but also shows why she might grow disillusioned with him. If there's nothing captivating under the face, then naturally she'll want to search for something else."

"It's an interesting idea," Horton agreed. "But I still think you should find another actor for Charles and brainstorm something around him instead of Hank." I looked at the wall.

"Are you counting cinder blocks again?"

"No."

"Ultimately, Charlie, it's up to you. But I would advise against mixing business and pleasure."

"Maybe I'd be mixing pleasure and pleasure."

Horton shook his head. "Do you have anything else you want to talk to me about, kid?"

"That's it."

"Then let me get some work done. I have a whole pile of screenplays I want to read."

"For what?" Horton wasn't teaching screenwriting this semester.

"Because I want to read them. Go home. Count the tiles in your kitchen or something. Let me know what you decide."

I paused in the doorway for a second before I left.

"He's *really* good-looking, Farmer Lear," I said. "And you can tell Mallory that I said that."

twenty-five

Horton's office is almost twenty blocks north of my apartment. I'd barely left the Columbia gates when I realized that the question wasn't to cast or not to cast. Somewhere along the way I'd decided to risk Hank in the role. The real issue was how to make it work. I needed someone talented and not super-attractive to play Leon. If he weren't too old, I would have switched Walsh from LaRue's small role to Leon's more pivotal one. I was contemplating rewriting portions of the screenplay to account for the differing levels of talent in the cast when I walked straight into a fire hydrant.

Suffice it to say that my subsequent curses would have put any ninetieth-century, scurvy-ridden sailor to shame.

Vowing alertness from now on, I held on to the treacherous hydrant and rubbed my leg. It was already stiffening into a bruise. This better not interfere with yoga. I envisioned myself announcing to the class, "Now lunge into Warrior II. I'm actually not going to do this because I walked into a fire hydrant, but make sure to keep a ninety degree angle at your knee."

Four blocks later, I was contemplating the possibility that my life might be slightly more traumatic (or eventful) than that of most people I knew when I spied the chairs. *I did not walk into them.* There were maybe ten or

eleven, with the legs toppled every angle and extending spi-
derlike from the trash heap. I might not have given the un-
gainly pile a second glance were it not for the two women
busily stuffing chairs into the less-than-capacious trunk of a
VW bug.

"Don't worry," one reassured her friend in a thick Queens
accent. "We're gonna fit *all four* in the car."

I watched her readjust the chair within the trunk, three of
the four legs protruding stubbornly. I studied the chair heap
more closely. The chairs were filthy, scabbed and textured
with years of use. But they were obviously oak, solidly built,
with wide, slick seats and spindles extending down the back.

"Are these yours?" I asked.

"They're anybody's," she replied. "But I'm taking four of
them," she added, with a jealous glance toward her bounty.

Given that I kept throwing people off my great-
grandmother's velvet couch, it wouldn't hurt to have some
substitute seating. I envisioned one of the chairs, painted a
gleaming white, sitting in my room. Gingerly claiming the
least grimy of the bunch, I proceeded down the street, glowing contentedly with my own spontaneity.

A few blocks later my arms felt as leaden as if I'd spent
the afternoon hurling shotputs. I set the chair down and sat
in it for a moment. Even though I was practically home, it
was time for a cab. I lugged the chair into the street and
spent a solid ten minutes attempting to hail a cab before I realized that no one was going to stop for me and my chair and
that I could have been home already. Sighing, I flipped my
unruly throne upside-down, balancing the lip of the seat on
my head, and grasped each armrest firmly. Though perhaps
not the ideal way to walk, I thought I could make it. Humming "She's Got the Groove" as a little theme music, I re-
sumed marching home. I really regretted not having a VW
bug and loyal friend with a Queens accent to help me out.

A block later I reattempted hailing a cab.

Again, drivers wouldn't stop, even though I could tell they were unoccupied by the lights on top of the car. I growled to myself. Flipping the chair upside-down again in despair, I started walking again. My bruised leg hurt. I had gone all of another block when I nearly crashed into a policeman leaving a Korean grocery.

"Sorry," I muttered.

"Not a problem," he said. "You got a chair on your head, you know."

Ha ha. What a comedian.

"Something wrong with that?" I asked curtly.

"It's funny."

"Glad to make your day," I said, wobbling away from him. My arms hurt. My leg hurt. My head hurt. I envisioned my obituary in the *Post*:

> Charlotte Frost, 27, died suddenly today after overexerting herself carrying a chair found on the street back to her apartment. Frost is mourned by her family, friends, and soap star Hank Destin. Destin expressed sorrow over Frost's death, but our reporter saw him cast a roving eye at a glam blond walking past. In an especially tragic twist, the chair Frost was carrying was later revealed as infested with termites.

"Why don't you take a cab?" the cop asked. He was burly, with red hair and either a lot of freckles or three freckles, each the size of my fist.

"I tried. Twice. No one would stop for me."

"Scared by the chair, I expect." The cop nodded. "They're not supposed to do that." He laughed again. "You sure look silly with it on your head."

A small idea popped into my head. I debated, but then decided that I was at an all-time low and had nothing to lose. "If you're going to laugh at me," I said slowly, "the least you could do is give me a ride home."

"Where do you live?"

"Ninety-ninth."

"It's only a few blocks away."

"It's kind of slow going with a chair on your head," I said.

"I bet."

I waited. "OK," he said at last.

"Really?"

"Sure." We made our way down the block to his car. There was another cop in the front seat, an older man with grayish skin. The redhead leaned over and said something to his partner, who gave him an obvious look of disgust. My cop then loaded my chair into the trunk and let me into the backseat of the cruiser. The first thing that I noticed was that there were no door handles in the back. I should have expected that, but it was a shock nonetheless.

I looked at the cops again. They seemed familiar. "Wait a second," I exclaimed. "I know you guys! You helped me when I was mugged in the subway. Last fall, Ninety-sixth Street." I love it when New York feels like a small town.

"Oh yeah," the older one said. "I remember that. You look a lot better today."

"Surprise," I said.

"I think we need sirens," the redhead said. He flipped on the flashing lights, honked his horn, and moved into traffic. For the next five minutes, I was fully aware that I was in the process of living one of the best-ever New York stories. I thanked them profusely when we pulled in front of my apartment.

"You need help getting that upstairs, girlie?" the older cop asked.

Girlie shook her head. "I'll be OK. Thanks, though." I

waved goodbye to my saviors and headed toward the front door.

My annoying neighbor, Mr. Marcello, was sitting on the front stoop even though it was about ten degrees outside. He had on a pair of fluffy red earmuffs. As my chair and I lumbered past him, he screeched.

"Coming home in a cruiser," he leered. "Miss Charlie must have been doing something baaad."

"Yeah, I murdered a stoop-sitting busybody," I retorted, heading upstairs.

That afternoon I taught yoga in my bike shorts. Sahra noticed the bruise right away.

"Charlotte! What is that?" she demanded, pointing from across the locker room at my leg.

"Bruise."

"Why it's ghastly," she said, coming over for a closer look. "How'd you do it?"

Rough sex, I thought. Aloud, I said, "I walked into something." I had to come up with a better excuse.

"What?" Sahra reached out and fingered the bruise lightly.

"Um, you know." I hedged for time. "A fire hydrant."

Sahra's mouth twitched, but she didn't laugh.

"I have some witch hazel in my office," she said. "That should help some. Does it hurt?"

"Yes."

"Let me get the witch hazel."

She was back in about five minutes with a fluff of something soft and cream-colored and the bottle of witch hazel. She detached a wad of fluff and soaked it in witch hazel. She handed it to me and I dabbed at my bruise, which immediately began tingling.

"Thanks," I said. "This kinda stings."

"It's cleansing," Sahra said. "This'll help it heal quicker and reduce scarring." I hadn't even thought about scars. What if I were marked for life from walking into a hydrant? The mild tingling progressed to a stabbing prickling sensation. I sat down suddenly. Sahra sat down beside me.

"I haven't seen you in a while, Charlie," she said.

"Busy," I gasped through the pain.

"So I gathered. I read about you and Hank."

"You and the rest of the world," I said. My leg was burning. What the hell was this stuff? It was *burning*. "This stings a lot."

"Cleansing," Sahra repeated. I refrained from saying that I preferred my bacteria-ridden bruise. She continued, "Hank's a really nice guy. Very down-to-earth. His agent has sent over quite a few people. That Nick Vasey kid and some others."

My leg my leg my leg my leg my leg my leg my leg my leg my leg my leg.

"Mmm-hmm."

"Certainly helpful to the studio. How's your bruise feel now?"

"Not so good," I whimpered.

Sahra looked down at my leg. "Charlie, are you *allergic* to witch hazel?" she asked sharply.

"I don't know," I whispered. I felt dizzy. Moving my head as little as possible, I looked down. My entire leg was bright pink and covered in erupting violet welts. I couldn't even see the offending bruise anymore.

"That's not normal. You have to go the emergency room."

"I said it stung," I told Sahra.

"I didn't know you were allergic. Come on, get your stuff. Hurry. You could go into shock any second."

As Sahra bustled me and my stinging, cramping, flaming leg upstairs, I realized that I was going to ride in both an ambulance and a police cruiser in the same day.

My life was *definitely* more eventful than most people's.

twenty-six

SCENE: *Charlie's parents' living room.
CHARLIE, her PARENTS, and GRANDMOTHER are
sitting in front of a fire, each with a
glass of champagne. CHARLIE is wearing
boxer shorts and a sweatshirt. Her right
leg is fuschia-colored. She dabs at the
welts with a tube of ointment.*

        CHARLIE'S GRANDMOTHER:
I still don't understand what happened to
your leg.

        CHARLIE:
Gangrene.

CHARLIE'S MOTHER snoans loudly.

        CHARLIE:
Sorry.

        CHARLIE'S GRANDMOTHER:
I didn't hear what you said.

                    CHARLIE *(mutters very softly)*:
Rough sex.

                    CHARLIE'S MOTHER:
I didn't hear what you said.

        CHARLIE'S GRANDMOTHER *(who clearly has
                managed to hear Charlie)*:
Well, dear, nothing I ever did made my leg
look like *that*.

I was never going to let Sahra live down the witch hazel
episode. I didn't precisely care once the doctors had assured
me that there would be no lasting scars. Still, it's so rare that
Sahra displays anything resembling guilt that I figured I was
entitled to milk her conscience a bit. Her herbal remedy had
sent me to the *hospital*, after all. Unasked, she had offered
me a week of paid recovery time, either out of remorse or
from a genuine fear that Harmony clients might glimpse my
hot pink leg. I should have used this time to develop a shooting schedule for *The Doctor's Wife*, but spent most of it
doped up on prescription-strength, turbocharged Benadryl.
The welts weren't receding as quickly as I had hoped. Truth
be told, I was revolted by my own leg.

Two weeks to the day after my run-in with witch hazel,
the cast and crew of *The Doctor's Wife* assembled at Vynl. We
would start rehearsals later that week. Horton very generously offered to arrange for our dinner tab to be billed to the
department. That was nice of him and made *The Doctor's
Wife* seem more like a real production than a student film. I
wasn't too surprised, though. It was becoming clear that the
film would come in under budget—especially with the
money Sarah Wong was saving me on costumes.

I hadn't been quite sure how necessary it was to convey to
the cast and crew that Hank and I were dating, but figured

openness was the best policy. I wasn't going to announce it, but neither would I camouflage it. Sabrina and Walsh had been delirious when they heard that there would be a name actor in the film. Nick Barone, who would play Leon, had never heard of Hank. Nick had a spacy, serene quality that I hoped was natural and not due to some tranquilizing hallucinogen. He and Sarah Wong spent most of dinner conversing intently. Sabrina batted her eyes at Hank a lot. Walsh was quiet. Hank kept putting his hand on my lower back and referring to me in very familiar terms, thereby removing any doubt anyone might have had about what he was doing among the nameless and uncelebrated.

After dinner, I stood up. The restaurant wasn't very crowded and we had a long table along the wall. I *hate* making speeches, but some sort of formal kickoff to filming was necessary.

"Hi everyone," I began. "Can everyone hear me OK?" A few people at the far end of the table shook their heads, so I raised my voice. "I don't have much to say. I just wanted to thank you for your participation in *The Doctor's Wife*. There is a lot of talent sitting at this table right now. I am thrilled to have all of you as part of the cast and crew." I blabbed mundanely for a few more seconds about everyone's ability. "I'll be scheduling individual meetings with each of you in the coming weeks. In the meantime, here's the shooting and rehearsal calendar. Anyone with conflicts should let me know immediately." I gave Hank the calendars. He took one and passed the stack on. "You will notice that I have placed all my contact information at the top of the page." I paused. I hate this kind of senseless speech. "I'm looking forward to working with you all. For those of you who *haven't* read *Madame Bovary*—and I suggest you keep yourselves anonymous—you might want to pick up a copy."

Kent, the set designer, made a show of covering his face in shame. Everyone giggled. I rolled my eyes and sat down.

Hank reached out and patted my knee. I smiled at him, then at Sabrina, who was watching us intently.

Hank and I walked down Ninth Avenue slowly after dinner, holding hands and gossiping about our impressions of the cast. When we hit Forty-second Street, I turned us east.

"I better get home," I said.

"You're going home?"

"Yeah, I can pick up the express at Times Square."

We walked on for a few seconds.

"I have to be up early tomorrow," I explained. "There's this guest yogi at Harmony and he's running a special two-hour training session at six-thirty." I shuddered. "Not that anything would make me more peaceful and centered at six-thirty in the morning than being asleep." I hoped Hank wasn't annoyed that I wanted to go home.

I could see the garish lights of Times Square ahead. If there is one place on the planet that I think could be excised at no cost to civilization, it would be Times Square.

"We could hop in a cab and I could drop you off," Hank offered.

"I'm fifty blocks out of your way," I replied.

"So?"

I kissed the top of his nose. "So I'm fine on the train."

Hank looked a bit puppy doggish. "OK," he said. "When will I see you next?"

"I don't know." I frowned. "This week is probably going to be hellish. Let's try to get together sometime before rehearsals start, but no promises." I kissed his nose again and descended into the subway.

To: Chris <cmartin@columbfilm.com>
From: Charlie <cfrost@columbfilm.edu>
Re: blather

C—

Have you given the kickoff speech to your cast and crew
yet? I blathered senselessly through mine and am now too
embarrassed to face everyone. Hopefully, they were all too
liquored up on Columbia-sponsored booze to notice or
care.

If you have not yet engaged in this lovely inaugural ritual,
might I suggest that you prepare something in advance,
memorize it, and insert charming little jokes that will appear
spontaneous but are, in fact, so well-practiced that they only
appear effortless?

Morosely,
Charlie

To: Charlie <cfrost@columbfilm.edu>
From: Chris <cmartin@columbfilm.edu>
Re: blather

Dear Morose in Manhattan:

I am afraid your warning came too late. I blathered as well.
I am beginning to suspect that our education has been
devoid of practical lessons. Wouldn't we have benefited
far more from a class entitled "Faking Directorial Authority"

than Rhonda's useless, but intellectually stimulating,
seminar?

Up for lunch one day this week?

Yours,
Film Student Faker

twenty-seven

When you are a graduate student, and do not have disposable taxi funds, getting from Ninety-ninth Street and Broadway to the Lower East Side is a bit of an undertaking. I brought several copies of *The New Yorker* that I'd taken from my grandmother's to entertain myself on the trip. For a while, I'd had my own subscription. But the problem with having a subscription to *The New Yorker* was that no matter how diligent and industrious I was about reading it, I eventually got behind. Then I inevitably ended up in a situation where someone brought up an article in the latest issue and I either had to be silent and unopinionated (i.e., stupid) or 'fess up that I hadn't read it yet.

It is *so* much simpler just to read batches of my grandmother's old issues. Since I'm not technically a subscriber, I avoid self-imposed guilt. Plus I can easily eliminate the awkward cocktail party situation by murmuring that I've let my subscription lapse. My father happens to think that I exaggerate the eventuality of *New Yorker* guilt, but Karen says she gets it too.

Of course, as Hank and I were having dinner with Maddie and her new boyfriend, there was a good chance that I would make it through the night without any *New Yorker* references. That's why I was going to be on the train for an hour. It would never occur to any of my friends to set foot in such a distant and trendy outpost as Rivington Street. I was actually looking forward to the evening. I'd subjected Hank to my friends so many times that I felt I sort of owed it to him to spend some time with his. I also found Maddie fascinating. I didn't precisely like her—though she'd been friendly enough to me—but something about her intrigued me. Maybe I'd put a redheaded actress in my next screenplay.

I was the last one to get to the restaurant. Hank, Maddie, and an extremely good-looking guy, who looked as young as Ned, were already sitting there drinking martinis. I settled in next to Hank and squeezed his knee in greeting. I *love* that we have progressed enough that I can fondle him at will.

"Charlie, this is Declan," Maddie announced. She was wearing a black strapless corsetlike top and a hot pink silk skirt. The skirt looked as though it might flare when she stood up. The combination of the pink and her red hair was fairly dramatic. To say nothing of the fact that wearing a tube top in January basically screams out taxi. (I was wearing black pants and a sweater and high-heeled boots with thick socks underneath and my gray coat with the cranberry cloche hat and a thick wool scarf that Marisa had knit for me two winters ago. That, as far as I am concerned, screams poverty-stricken, graduate student subway rider.)

I smiled politely at Declan. He was very, very attractive. I may not get *New Yorker* insecurity with soap opera people, but I'm certainly intimidated by their looks. It's like one of those old *Highlights* magazine games: which of these is not like the others?

"Good to meet you," Declan said. He had an Irish accent. His attractiveness score instantly doubled.

"Want a martini, Charlie?" Hank asked.

"Maybe just some wine," I decided. I am not a martini person. I think they taste like Listerine.

"Are you going to want my olive?" Hank asked.

I love olives. "If it's up for grabs."

Hank fished it out of his drink and handed it to me.

"So are you an actor, Declan?" I asked.

"Not me. I'm a bartender for now."

I nodded.

"The visa problem, you know."

"You don't have a work visa?" I asked.

"They're hard to get." He went off into a fairly technical monologue about immigration restrictions. Given the brogue, I didn't quite catch all of it.

"So you basically came to New York knowing you wouldn't be able to work legally but knowing you would eventually have to support yourself?"

He nodded. This was baffling.

"Why?" I asked.

"Ah, man, it's *New York*," he said. "Been dreaming of it all my life."

Still. There are many foreign locales that I think would be a blast to inhabit. Sydney, for one. London also. But I would never do it illegally. It just seems like the risk would take the fun out of it. I am basically a practical person. Perhaps this was yet another way that I was separate from my freewheeling, life-by-the-horns tablemates.

Declan looked as though he sensed my apprehension. "What's the worst that'll happen?" he twinkled at me. "If I get booted out, I can always go bartend at home."

Maddie reached out and stroked his arm.

"We'd think of a way for that not to happen," she teased.

Was she thinking of *marrying* this guy? That was an awfully suggestive statement. I stepped on Hank's toe for confirmation. He stepped back on mine. I learned nothing from the podiatric interchange. She was probably just flirting.

The waiter brought our menus and I pretended to give mine full attention while I tried to figure out what it was about Maddie that inevitably made me feel so colorless beside her. I didn't think it was just the attractiveness factor. I also didn't think it was insecurity about Hank's fidelity. If he'd wanted to date her, he would. Hankisbuff.com was filled with rumors about him and various gorgeous women, but Maddie wasn't even on the list. Maybe it was just that—despite not being the greatest brain of the century—Maddie had an ease with herself that I envied. Right now, she and Declan were huddled over their menus, pointing out various delectables to each other and giggling. I closed my menu and stared out at the restaurant. There were eleven other tables, occupied by thirty-two people.

(Karen once said that counting while nervous is an obsessive tendency. I replied that they obviously weren't teaching her much in school, because even I recognized that. I suspect that it is also the most accessible way to distance myself from a situation that is freaking me out. Like right now . . .)

I closed my eyes and pretended I was wearing something less drab than my sensible sweater and pants. All that glitters is not Maddie.

Dinner was better after that. While we were having coffee (but not dessert, because everyone but me was on a strict dietary regimen), Maddie gave me a dazzling smile.

"Charlie, I think it's so exciting that Hank is going to be in your little film."

I bristled a bit at the "little" description, but gamely smiled back. "Certainly exciting for me as well. The rest of the cast seems very taken with the idea of working alongside him."

"Sabrina's a trip," Hank said. "She's a great actress."

"You think?" As far as I was concerned, neither Sabrina nor Hank had distinguished themselves at the first rehearsal. "I think Walsh is going to be the real find." I realized Maddie and Declan were probably lost. "He's got a fairly small role as the villain, but he's sort of staggeringly good at being icy.

Hank hasn't seen him yet, because they don't share many scenes."

"You're the husband?" Maddie asked.

Hank nodded.

"The husband is a lot like the villain, actually," I said. "They're both cold fish and make the main character—that's Sabrina—unhappy. Walsh's character, LaRue, can turn on the charm when necessary, and that's why he's so dangerous. But the husband can't."

"I don't see Charles as a villain."

"Well, he's sort of inadvertently villainous simply because he's so pitiful," I amended. "He's not cruel on purpose."

"I disagree that he's pitiful," Hank said. "I just think he and Emma are on completely different wavelengths."

"He's weak."

"I'm not so sure."

"Look, I *wrote* the thing. He's a weak character."

Maddie and Declan exchanged glances at that.

"I think he's open for interpretation," Hank said easily. "The words on the page don't mean much without the directorial influence."

"Well, since I'll be directing as well . . ." I trailed off meaningfully.

"She's got you there, baby," Maddie said.

"I think it is to be discussed," Hank replied. He wiggled his eyebrows suggestively at me.

"We can discuss, but I created the character. I know what he's supposed to be."

"Are you fighting your director?" Maddie teased.

Hank looked sheepish.

"Does he do that on the show?" I asked her.

"No, he's real good about following orders there."

"Charles is a complex character," I said. "Well, not that Kendall isn't complicated, it's just that Charles is especially, you know." My attempt at diplomacy was failing miserably. There was no way my foot could be any more immersed in my mouth. "I guess he could be interpreted in different ways," I added tactfully. "But I have a pretty good vision for how he should be."

Hank's brows were drawn together. I nudged him. "OK?" I finished.

"Sure, whatever," he said.

I stared at his eyebrows intently, waiting for the minute furrows to smooth out. Honestly. The last thing I needed was for Hank to turn into a major artistic diva over this. I certainly hoped that casting him as Charles hadn't triggered my own disastrous remake of *A Pretentious Star Is Born*.

twenty-eight

Sigh.

I was either naive or delusional. Somehow, despite nearly six years working in or studying film, it had never occurred to me how much effort making a movie would be until now. I arrived at Gennaro's almost an hour late to meet Marisa and Karen. Luckily, the line was unusually long and they were still huddled by the door waiting. I had taught yoga that afternoon, and my mat was still strapped to my back like a papoose. I shrugged it off.

"Sorry I'm late," I apologized breathlessly. "I didn't even go home and change. Things just kept getting out of hand. Did you get my messages?"

"Yes," Karen said shortly.

"Everything OK?" I asked.

"Mmm-hmm," Marisa replied.

She sounded sort of weird also. I wondered if they'd been talking about me. Were they irritated that I was late? I looked at Karen more closely. She looked tense enough that I figured it had nothing to do with my getting caught at rehearsal.

I stood there obliviously for a few seconds before realizing that it was Ned—not my extended rehearsal—that they had to be discussing. Marisa continued to be less than pleased about the burgeoning assistant–best friend romance while Karen was essentially head over heels. She had airily explained Ned's reemergence by the fact that he had flooded her inbox with witty, charming e-mails. He was also heir to some kind of Vermont bottling plant fortune and tooled around Manhattan on a bright red Vespa. Even I found it sexy—and I tend to rank motorcycles (or mopeds or whatever a Vespa is) up there with go-carts and unicycles in the category of "transportation I will never use, no matter how desperate."

"Are you sure everything's OK?" I repeated.

"*Yes*," Karen said testily.

Got it . . .

"How was rehearsal?" she added, in a gentler tone.

"Fine, mostly. It was Emma and Leon's meeting. Nick— that's the guy who plays Leon—is sort of soft-spoken. I need him to be a bit more forceful. But I think it'll be OK."

One of the waiters motioned to us. I was careful not to bop anyone with my yoga mat as I made my way to the table.

"I guess not having to wait in line is one perk of the never-ending rehearsal," I joked as we sat down.

"How's Hank?" Marisa asked.

"Do you mean how is Hank in the role of Charles or how is Hank in general?"

"In the role of Charles."

"Jaw-clenching," I admitted.

"Charlie, he can't do it *that* much."

"No, not really. I don't know." I reached for my menu. "Are we getting wine?"

"Yes," Karen said. "But get back to Hank."

"I don't know," I repeated. "I still pretty much adore him. But he's been a bit of a pain at rehearsal lately."

"How?"

"I think he and I have very different ideas about the character of Charles. And I think I'm right. Aside from the fact that I essentially did him a favor by casting him as Charles, I did *create* the character."

"Do you really think you did him a favor by letting him in the film?" Karen asked quietly.

"No," I said wryly. "I think he probably did me a favor by agreeing to be in it. I let him do it not just because of the publicity, but because it's more interesting to have a sexy Charles. I told you guys that. But maybe I didn't realize what an ego he has."

"Are you sure his ideas are all worthless?" Marisa asked.

"It's not that they're worthless," I said slowly, thinking aloud as I spoke. "It's that I have a particular concept of the character and I feel that, as writer and director, my concept should be respected. If he must challenge it, I would prefer he come to me and do so in private."

"He's challenging you in front of everyone?"

I shook my head. "Not directly. What happened yesterday is that I gave him directions on how to play Charles and he basically did something completely different. When I called him on it, he pretended to understand and agree with me, but then kept doing something different."

"Do you think he thought he was doing what you wanted?" Marisa wondered. "Maybe you're overestimating his acting abilities."

"No, I think he's being passive-aggressive," I said. "And he better stop before we start filming because it's pissing me off."

"You should talk to him about it," Karen said.

"Not yet. Maybe at some point." I closed my menu. "I can't believe it's after nine. God, I'm tired."

"All of us are, I think," Karen said.

"Yeah," I said softly, my mind still on Hank. "The other thing is that I know that Hank considers this his big entrée into 'smart films.'" I made a quotation mark gesture with my hands. "So I suspect he may be going overboard with the serious acting. I mean, he's hardly the odds-on favorite for Stanislavsky's heir."

"What do you want from him?" Karen asked.

"That's kind of a loaded question," I said, laughing. "Sex, a trip to Tahiti, for him never to know that I'm killing the African violets he gave me . . ."

"You're killing the violets?" Marisa asked.

"Haven't you seen Franklin lately? The bloom is definitely off."

"Figures Franklin would be weaker than Eleanor," Karen said. "But that's not what I meant and you know it. What do you want out of Hank in terms of a performance?"

"I want him to be as innocuous as possible. He wants to convey great passion and I want him to convey well-meaning befuddlement. If he would be even an iota more malleable, I could get exactly what I want." I bit my lip. "Enough of my bitching. What's up with Ned, Karen? We may as well process all romantic drama at once."

Karen looked down. Then she giggled. *Who are you and what have you done with my sensible roommate?*

"Ned is surprisingly fantastic."

"But indiscreet," Marisa added.

"Maris, he knows we're friends and assumes that you're his friend too. I think that's all. Just relax."

"What's up?" I said.

"Ned and I had, um, a rather prolonged night last night and he used this as his excuse for being an hour late to work this morning."

"What exactly did he say?"

" 'God, Marisa, I'm so sorry. Karen and I didn't get *any* sleep last night.' Wink wink," Marisa mimicked.

Yeesh. Aloud, I asked, "Is that OK with you, Karen?"

"I think it's a little more public than I'd be normally comfortable with, but he did say it to Marisa. He knows how open I am with you guys."

"Yeah, but that's the point," I interrupted. "*You're* open with us. It's different when it's your new boyfriend who's open."

"Oh, I don't know if we're at the boyfriend label yet," Karen mused. "I think we're still 'just dating' for another month or so."

"Karen, you are dodging this just as much as I dodged the Hank-acting issue," I squealed.

"I know," she said ruefully.

"We don't really need to rehash this," Marisa broke in. "I am so happy that you're enjoying being with Ned. Really. I would just prefer that he didn't use a wild night with you as an excuse for being late. It's not even the fact that you're my friend. If I were to sit down and announce that any other assistant had claimed hot sex kept him from being on time, you guys would die laughing and assume that it was someone really gauche and unprofessional."

"Probably. But that's my point," Karen said. "I don't think he would use it as an excuse with another boss. It's because you're my friend that he feels he can say that."

Marisa looked down.

"Enough," I said suddenly. "How great was the night, Karen?"

Karen broke into a smile. "Pretty damn wonderful," she said. "Hey, are we getting wine?"

twenty-nine

The next morning, I attempted to write directorial notes for our next rehearsal. It was one of those sleepy, pointless attempts at work that involves frequent games of solitaire and e-mail checks.

After about half an hour, I began to contemplate Starbucks. It was fairly arctic outside. I had pulled my space heater next to the couch, which was probably bad for the laptop, but certainly good for attempts to wean myself off caffeine. I bent over my script and reread Leon's conversation with Emma.

> LEON:
> You want it to be simple, Emma, but
> things can't always be that way. Life is
> neither as pleasant nor as cruel as we
> wish to believe.

I envisioned Nick Barone's features and decided that he should look down and light a cigarette rather than confronting Emma directly at this point. I scanned the rest of the scene. I had put on *The Marriage of Figaro* and it was playing a little too loudly. My kingdom for a cup of coffee. Maybe I could coax my favorite, multipierced barista into delivery.

```
                    LEON:
I've always been terribly in love with you
and I'm not convinced that's been a
blessing.
```

My writing seemed suddenly shlocky and horrid. Was it possible that I had spent the past four months carefully crafting a piece of trash? I moaned aloud to the empty living room and clicked back on the Internet Explorer icon. There was a new message from Horton, telling me that he had heard about an article that was on *Slate* or maybe *Salon* (but one of those Web magazines that only organized people read) about film adaptations of great novels and I should be sure to check it out. I closed my eyes and listened to the opera for a second. Normally *Figaro* makes me want to dredge up all my forgotten ballet and dance around the apartment, but today I felt thirty seconds away from sleep.

Rather than dealing with *Slate* (or *Salon*), I Googled Hank. Ever since the Page Six incident, I've sort of thought that I would prefer to notify myself of all Hank Destin publicity. It had been a few weeks since I'd last checked and there were some updates on fan sites about Kendall Reston's suicide attempt. *Has the heartless Dr. R. grown a heart?* one of them blared.

Shifting my laptop to a different position, I clicked on the link to *Love Lives of the Stars*, then clicked again on the article about Hank.

Oh, shit. There I was again, continuing in my starring role of Destin's Destiny. My modem chugged along at an infuriating speed as it downloaded a photo of Hank, Declan, Maddie, and me from the time we'd all gone out. I was laughing and appeared to be all nostrils. I hadn't noticed any paparazzi that night, but I wasn't particularly adept at identifying them. (Hank, on the other hand, could sniff out the photographer on an Outward Bound retreat. I wondered if he'd spotted the photographers while we were at dinner.)

Doing my best to ignore the picture, I read the article, which was about how Hank and Maddie were dating normal, nonindustry people.

> While some friends expressed surprise that Hank has fallen for curvy Columbia student Charlotte Frost, Maddie thinks it's simple.
>
> "Charlie makes Hank laugh," she said, tossing her red mane.
>
> As for Maddie? She's not spending too many nights at home, either. Since meeting Declan Fitzgerald . . .

I leaped for the phone and called Marisa.

"Ned, it's Charlie. It's an emergency."

When Marisa picked up, I didn't even bother saying hello but immediately gave her the Web address.

"Love lives of soap stars?"

"Click on the Hank link."

A second later I heard her laughing. "It's not a *bad* picture, Charlie."

I'd forgotten about the nostril shot.

"Yeah, except for the fact that I'm all nostril, but I'm not talking about the picture. Check out the next to last paragraph."

After a few seconds, Marisa asked, "So?"

"THEY SAID I WAS CURVY," I screeched. "That means I have a big butt!"

Marisa started laughing. "No."

"Yes! Curvy means fat, Marisa. It's a total media euphemism."

"Charlie." I could hear Marisa trying not to laugh.

"Don't laugh. You're not the one who was just labeled fat by a substandard gossip Web site."

"Curvy does not mean fat. It means . . . curvy."

"Please."

"Maybe they just mean . . . I don't know," she trailed off. "You're not fat," she added definitively. "What are you, a size two?"

"That's irrelevant. It doesn't matter whether I *am* fat; it matters that they called me fat."

"They called you curvy."

"OK, we're going in circles, Maris." There was a long pause. "I hate this scrutiny," I admitted. "It makes me feel like the entire multimillion viewership of *Troubled Passion* thinks I'm not good enough for Hank."

"Which, of course, is reinforced by the fact that *you* don't feel like you're good enough for Hank."

"Yeah, sometimes," I admitted. "It's that whole cool kid versus geek thing."

"Well, just remember that Danny really fell for Sandy at the end of *Grease*."

"Except she gave up her identity!! Am I supposed to do that?"

"OK, no, it's a bad analogy, you're right." Another pause. "Johnny Castle fell for Baby in *Dirty Dancing*," Marisa added timidly.

"So he did." I sighed. "I'll let you get back to work."

"Hank likes you, Charlie," Marisa said. "And you like him. That matters a lot more than whether or not *Love Lives of the Stars* likes you."

"Yeah," I agreed. I did like Hank. Even though he was driving me up the wall about Charles, I liked Hank.

"Thank you," I said to Marisa, even though I still felt unreassured.

"Not a problem."

After I hung up with Marisa, I stared into space for a very long time. I needed a break from life. I went to the Metropolitan Opera Web site. In precisely three hours, there would be a matinee of *The Marriage of Figaro*.

Now *this* was fate.

Bella, bella.

thirty

The opera did the trick. I left the Met lulled into serenity. No spa could possibly be as effective an indulgence.

The next day I was glad I'd pampered myself. At Hank's suggestion, Maddie and I met to find a dress for me to wear to the Soap Opera Awards. Maddie had generously offered to lend me something but—given that she's almost a foot taller than I am—it never seemed like a real possibility. Instead, we met at a boutique on Crosby Street that had offered to supply dresses for the cast of *Troubled Passion*. Hank was pretty sure that we could get my dress comped as well.

(The perks of dating Hank Destin just kept getting yummier.)

Maddie rushed in nearly twenty minutes late and actually greeted me by air kissing me on both cheeks. I was flattered by her effusive gesture—even though I've never seen anyone outside of a Christopher Guest film do that.

"We're supposed to have a consultant to help us," Maddie said as I held out the handful of basic black Audrey Hepburn–ish dresses I'd selected. She went and spoke to the sales clerk, who promptly disappeared into the back of the store and returned with another woman.

"Maddie, darling, I'm so glad you're here. We just outfitted Marina in the most fabulous silver McQueen. Is this Charlotte? I'm Gretchen."

Gretchen was plump and bustling. She had on a black button-down shirt that was so tight that the buttons gaped—purposely, I assumed—across her chest. You could see that she had on a red bra underneath. Gretchen seized me by the shoulders and held me at arm's length. Then she circled around me, stroking her chin and mmm-hmming. At one point, she reached out and rubbed my hair between her fingers, as though it were a bolt of cloth that she was testing for quality.

"We've gotten in a new Japanese designer, Hatsura, that I think would be perfect for you. How are your shoulders?"

What kind of a question was that?

"Muscled," I replied tentatively. "I teach yoga."

Gretchen smiled. "Honest child," she said. "Why don't you go into the dressing room and start changing and I'll bring you things."

"OK," I said. "I usually prefer simple and black. I picked some stuff out."

Gretchen patted my shoulder. "Go change," she said, tilting her head toward the dressing room. "Let *me* do my job."

A few minutes later, she knocked on the door of the dressing room. I opened it and she handed me an armful of dresses. Not one was black.

"Now I want you to start with the orange Hatsura," she instructed me.

"Orange isn't really my color," I began.

Gretchen pressed her lips together. "Charlotte, can I bring you something to drink? Maybe a Perrier?"

Or a gin and tonic.

"I'm OK," I said aloud. I shut the dressing room door and wriggled into the Hatsura. It was very, very orange. There was a beaded vine running across the chest. I opened the door.

Maddie was perched on a poofy white cube outside the door and sipping a glass of sparkling water with lime.

"Charlotte, you look darling," she exclaimed.

Gretchen made a small clucking sound. "I'm not sure the orange is doing you justice," she said.

Duh.

"Try the emerald one," she continued.

I obediently went back inside the dressing room. There were two green dresses. I pulled down the darker one and examined it. It was sort of like a dress made from a bunch of sarongs. There were lots of crisscrossing fabric strips wrapped on top of one another. Each strip was a different texture and slightly different color. Very mermaidy. I unbuttoned the strips and the entire dress came apart. I attempted to reconstruct it around myself, which required some contortionist skills. After a few futile minutes, I poked my head out of the dressing room door.

"Um, I think maybe I need a little help," I called.

"That's the parrot dress," Gretchen said. "The emerald is the Zac Posen."

"Gretchen, I am so sorry you're saddled with me and my unfashionable self," I said sincerely.

Gretchen began unfastening the strips I'd fastened incorrectly. "I'm not," she replied. "You're going to be such the swan. Isn't she, Maddie?"

"Oh, sure." Maddie joined Gretchen in unfastening the strips. "Charlotte doesn't know how pretty she is," she said to Gretchen.

That was really, really nice.

"Don't be silly," I protested.

Maddie and Gretchen both looked at me. "Hush," Gretchen said.

The two of them began circling around me as they wound the fabric strips into an intricate pattern.

"I feel like a Maypole," I said.

Gretchen laughed.

"Or maybe a mummy."

"*Hush*," Maddie said emphatically.

I hushed.

At last they finished and stood back to gauge the effect.

"No," Maddie immediately said.

Gretchen clucked agreement. "Definitely not." They began unwinding me.

"It's probably just as well. I don't have a staff available to dress me," I said.

Gretchen gave me a little push toward the dressing room. "Now try the Posen."

The Posen didn't work, nor the copper satin, nor the midnight blue rubber, nor the silver flapper dress.

"You're too short for these," Gretchen clucked. I wondered if clucking was her personal version of snoaning. "They dwarf you."

"Maybe something black and simple?" I asked.

"Charlie, once you get to the awards, you'll be glad you have something colorful. It's the thing to wear," Maddie said.

Gretchen walked away abruptly and went into the back of the store. She returned with a brown bag.

"This young woman brought us by some samples of her stuff the other day. She's just getting started and sews out of her apartment in Alphabet City. If it works, you'll be very trendy, my dear." She pulled a dress out of the bag and handed it to me. It was rose-colored silk, very shiny, very simply cut.

I opened my mouth to announce that I was not the pink type but thought better of it when I saw the steely look in Gretchen's eye. I closed it without saying a word and went to try the dress on.

"Yes," said Gretchen when I came out.

"Yes," said Maddie.

I looked at myself in the mirror. It was a pretty dress.

"It needs to be shortened," I said.

"That's easy," Gretchen said. "How do you feel in it?"

I looked at myself again.

"I love it," I said honestly. "Thank you."

After a seamstress named Anoushka pinned the dress up, I changed back into my clothes. I thanked Gretchen again profusely, said goodbye to Maddie, and headed for the subway to get to rehearsal. I felt a bit flat for some reason.

Maybe I was just upset that my carriage had turned back into a pumpkin and my coachmen were back to their normal mousy selves.

thirty-one

The inevitable had happened: Franklin the violet had shriveled away. Instead of a green thumb, I had the Thumb of Death. I sincerely hoped that his demise held no symbolic, portentous value for my relationship with Hank. I deposited his brown remains in the kitchen trash and headed to Harmony. Filming for *The Doctor's Wife* started tomorrow and I had one last brainstorming session scheduled with Horton that afternoon. While I probably could have used the time to review the shooting script and plans for lighting and sound, I was so nervous about filming that I was practically having palpitations. An indulgently long yoga session was far more necessary than any addled preparation I might attempt.

When I got to Harmony, Sahra greeted me with relief.

"Charlie, thank goodness! Miriam can't make it in today. Can you take over her two-hour advanced class?"

I don't know why she seemed surprised. Counting on Miriam to show up for class is rather like expecting a genie to emerge conveniently from a lamp just when you need three wishes. I sub for her at least once a month.

"If necessary," I said, wrinkling my nose to indicate how unenthused I was by the idea. "I sort of wanted to *go* to her class. My thesis starts filming tomorrow and I need to work off the nervous energy."

Sahra nodded. "Very impressive. You've made it, my dear."

"Not yet. I'll be amazed if I pull this off. I sort of feel like I'm wandering around with one foot on a banana peel."

Sahra actually smiled, which is one of the few times she has indicated having any sense of humor since I'd started working at Harmony. Of course, the witch hazel incident had connected us more deeply. Some people can only relax after nearly killing an employee.

"You win, Charlotte. I'll teach the class and you can just be a normal student."

"Really?"

She nodded. "I don't think you'd be doing anyone much good as an instructor at the moment, anyway." She pursed her lips. "You're giving off some very bad energy."

"I thought I was emitting calmness and serenity," I called as I headed into the locker room.

By the end of class, I was drenched in sweat, so exhausted and soothed by the physical exertion that I was basically a piece of pulp. I so often associate Sahra with all of her unfortunate nitpicky managerial qualities that I forget that I was initially drawn to Harmony because she was such a good yoga teacher. I took a purposely long time rolling up my mat to prolong the residual relaxation.

"Thanks," I said as I headed out.

Sahra ejected her disc from the CD player and looked up at me. "Ready for filming?"

"I think it's sort of like paying my bills. I'll never be ready to do it, but I have to anyway. But thanks for class. It's exactly what I needed."

"Well, you certainly pushed yourself hard enough."

I wasn't sure how to respond to that.

"That's quite a forearm stand you've developed," Sahra added. "Have you started working into lotus from there?"

"What do you mean?"

"Here, go up again. I'll show you."

"Sahra, I might faint if I do any more yoga," I said, but knelt on her mat anyway. I put my arms on the ground at a right angle, pushed back into downward dog for a moment, then kicked into the air so that I was upside down, using the front part of my arms to hold myself up. I was more wobbly than usual; I could definitely feel the effects of two hours of hard-core yoga.

"Tilt your head more," Sahra said as she reached down and adjusted it for me. "I'm going to move your legs into lotus now. It's going to take a little more balance so you'll want to contract your bandas."

I obligingly tightened my abdominal muscles, feeling increasingly off-kilter as my legs twisted over each other.

"Good," Sahra said. She let me balance by myself for a few moments and then showed me how to lower my lotus-bound legs down over my face to the floor and back up again. After I came back down, I lay on her mat for a few extra seconds, too exhausted to move. Maybe if I clicked my heels together three times, I'd suddenly be home.

"You've got a good body for yoga," Sahra said, looking down on my curled form.

Sahra was never this complimentary. Maybe I should let her douse me with toxic witch hazel more often. I muttered an embarrassed thank-you and added, "According to *Love Lives of the Soap Stars*, I'm curvy."

"What's that supposed to mean?" Sahra sat on the floor next to me.

"Probably that I have a big butt."

"Surely not."

I was quiet. I could already feel my muscles stiffening. I was going to feel like hell tomorrow.

"I better get to school," I said. "Thanks for class."

"Charlie, maybe it's not my place to say this," Sahra began tentatively.

"When you begin like that, I can hardly wait to hear the

rest," I said sourly as I pulled my damp hair back into a tighter ponytail.

"There's no need to be so hard on yourself. Just give yourself a break. Do something to relax once in a while."

She was right: it wasn't her place. I stood up and gestured to the empty studio.

"And what do you think this class was?"

"Even when you relax, you push yourself. It's not healthy."

"How about we stop analyzing me?" I said, walking to the door.

"Just think about it," Sahra called after me.

I was so annoyed I didn't even say goodbye. What right did a noxious, celebrity-drooling hippie have to comment on the way I conducted my life?

To top it all off, I was so sore the next morning that I spent the first twenty minutes of wakefulness howling for Karen (who wasn't even home) to bring me Aleve. Despite the intense muscle pain, I really thought Sahra was wrong about me pushing myself too hard. Screenplays didn't get turned into movies (or yoga classes taught, for that matter) if you wafted through life in oblivious, Miriam-ish bliss. Tranquility could be debilitating.

Couldn't it?

To: Dad <herbert_frost@spacecom.net>, Mom
<katherine_frost@spacecom.net>
From: Charlie <cfrost@columbfilm.edu>
Re: A rolling camera gathers no moss

Just checking to let you know I am still alive and that filming is
going well. I will try to make it out for dinner on Sunday, but no
counting chickens.

Love,
Charlie

P.S. I'm exhausted, btw. Or else developing a case of late-onset
narcolepsy . . .

To: Charlie <cfrost@columbfilm.edu>
From: Katherine Frost <katherine_frost@spacecom.net>
Re: Narcolepsy

Puffin, dear, I think that prolonged family contact has been
shown to decrease symptoms of narcolepsy, chronic fatigue
syndrome, fibromyalgia, and other wearying disorders.

Love,
Mom

thirty-two

The interiors for *The Doctor's Wife* were filming at a large warehouse Columbia had rented in the Bronx. Since it was shared among eight thesis students, the filming schedule was fairly restrictive. I'd scheduled three weeks of filming interiors, then a week doing exteriors at Horton's friends' home in Connecticut, with the option to film a final week at the warehouse if there were any problems.

Because I felt my life was hard enough without having to take the subway to the Bronx every day, I'd borrowed my grandmother's car for the duration of filming. Frankly, I was schlepping so many costumes, scripts, lights, etc. back and forth that the subway probably wasn't even an option. What I really needed was a pack mule (and probably an intravenous drip of Valium to take with me on set).

On the fifth day of filming, I drove downtown fifteen blocks and picked up Horton. He was going to watch the filming today. I was dying for his input. Because I'd started by filming all of Emma's scenes in LaRue's shop, I'd just been working with Walsh and Sabrina so far. Today would be Hank's first day on set. We would be filming some of the more intimate scenes between Emma and Charles. Hank had been unusually good in rehearsals lately. I hoped to submit Horton to eight full hours of "I told you so."

Horton came out of his apartment building carrying two travel mugs. He had on a gray wool overcoat buttoned to his neck and looked suddenly very old for some reason. Maybe because I usually see him seated behind a desk, I'm just not used to how slowly he moves. Horton handed me both coffees as he opened the door and settled into the car.

"Bless you," I said gratefully. "Or is this just another ploy to get out of visiting Starbucks?"

Horton took a long time to remove his gloves, buckle his seat belt, adjust the visor to block out the sun, adjust the placement of the seat, breathe into his hands, and put his gloves back on.

"Repay me by giving me a detailed update on the filming."

Considering that all I had wanted to do for the past five days was get his opinion on everything from when we should break for lunch to how to get Sabrina to stop overacting, that was hardly much of a request. I pulled away from the curb and began talking.

Half an hour later we pulled up to the warehouse. Some of the crew were already there, tinkering with cameras and lights. Hank was sitting in a metal folding chair reviewing a script. I wandered over to him. Although I wanted to lean over and nibble his earlobe, I pulled up another folding chair beside his and sat down backward in it.

"Hey there, sailor," I said.

Hank looked up and wiggled his eyebrows. "Go away, wench. I'm already committed to a four-ten grad student in another port."

"Four-ten?" I asked.

"I may have been a bit generous," he acknowledged. "She could be only four-eight."

I made a face. "We are not amused," I said loftily.

"Good morning, Charlie-doll."

"Morning. Come meet Horton."

Horton was talking seriously with one of the cameramen, but turned when he saw me leading Hank over.

"Mr. Destin, I presume," he said grandly.

Hank smiled. "Hey," he drawled. "It's great to meet you finally. Charlie's obviously told me all about you."

"It's all lies," Horton replied easily.

"Don't offer such a quick disclaimer," Hank said. "Some of it was flattering."

As Hank and Horton continued their cocktail party banter, I spaced out for a second. Here's the thing: I know how much work goes into making Hank look like Hank. I know about the macrobiotic diet and the recently bleached teeth and the regular workouts that no longer include yoga. But watching him kid around with Horton, I was just conscious of how absurdly wonderful he was.

I was the luckiest person on the planet.

Except four hours later, I wished I'd never laid eyes on Hank's magnificent self. What kind of feeble idiot had I been to let my artistic ideals be compromised by my libido?

We had rehearsed the scene until every line, every breath, every inflection was the way it should be. It was soon after Emma and Charles get married, when she first begins to feel dissatisfied. I wanted Charles to be obliviously eager to please his beautiful young wife. Hank had managed to capture Charles's ominous ignorance painfully well during rehearsals.

Now, with cameras rolling and Horton watching, he had puffed Charles up with premature sorrow and anger. It had to be on purpose. He was too experienced an actor not to know what he was doing.

"Cut," I called. "Hank, I want you to play the scene *exactly* as we practiced in rehearsal. Charles doesn't know what's going on. He adores Emma and, because he is so happy with her, he can't imagine that she doesn't reciprocate." I gave a few more directions with Hank looking blandly at me. When I finished he nodded.

"OK, doll."

I wished he hadn't said *doll*. It's not that I want to be referred to as Madame Director, but I'd prefer something that wouldn't remind everyone that we regularly rolled out of bed together before coming to rehearsals. Frankly, *Charlie* would have sufficed.

"Let's start again," I called, giving the go-ahead signal to the camera and sound guys. I pulled on my headset and watched Hank and Sabrina settle into the faux-1950s living room again.

After about three lines, I realized Hank was playing the scene exactly as he had before. I stared unhappily at the cameras. Each take whittled enough money from the already slim budget that I couldn't afford to have whole scenes be useless.

Damn the bastard.

Damn the bastard.

I took a deep breath and waited out the take. This time, I began my instructions with Sabrina so as not to offend the Master Egoist.

"Really nice, Sabrina. You've got a good sense of Emma's desperation. I want you to lower your voice a bit more when you tell Charles you love him. 'Of course I love you,'" I modeled for her. She bit her lip, looking even more waifish than normal.

"Of course I love you," she repeated in a hollow voice, getting the tone I wanted immediately.

I beamed. "That's perfect." I turned to Hank and chose my words carefully. "Hank, that was also really nice. I had the sense that you were overacting a bit, though. Let's try to

keep Charles as quiet and subdued as we did in rehearsal.
The image of Charles that you're projecting now is very different from the one we worked on. I want you to try to get
back to that old Charles, which you played so well. OK?"

"Sure." Hank winked at me. I stared at him with exasperation. It was going to take a lot more than a wink to make up
for this debacle.

"OK, guys, let's go." I noticed Horton looking at me, but I
turned away from him. I could envision the unappealing
conversation we were going to have on the way home. Annoyed, I reached for my headset again and tried to concentrate solely on the set.

"Cut!" I screamed halfway through the scene, ruining the
take completely. I knew the editors could have rescued and
spliced together some of Sabrina's lines from this scene into
the final print, but I didn't care. "Everyone, take ten. Hank, I
want to talk to you about the scene."

I could feel eyes following me as I made my way to Hank.
"Sit down," I said, indicating the mustard yellow couch on
the set.

"Are you going to send me to the principal's office?" Hank
asked, eyes twinkling.

"I *am* the principal," I snapped. We both sat down. "What
the hell are you doing?"

"I don't know what you mean."

I pressed my lips together in frustration and stared at him.
He looked back. I envisioned the blurb in *Love Lives of the
Stars*: "Sexy Hank Destin and loser girlfriend Charlotte Frost
often play games of Stare Wars during breaks on the set of
The Doctor's Wife, Charlotte's silly film that Hank has agreed
to grace with his presence. *Troubled Passion* fans can't wait
till Hank stops starring in Amateur Hour and is back on set
as Kendall Reston . . ."

Hank broke the staring first.

"Charlie, relax," he said.

"I am relaxed. I just want to know why you're not acting Charles as we rehearsed."

"I am acting the way we discussed; I just think the scene needs a little more than that."

"This isn't *Troubled Passion*, buddy. If anything, it's quiet, understated, discreet passion."

"None of these characters is particularly discreet."

"Hank, please. I *loved* the way you did this scene in rehearsal. I don't know what power struggle you're trying to pull here, but I would appreciate it if you would have the courtesy to act the scene as directed." I looked at him in a way that I hoped could be described as *unflinching* rather than *pleading*.

Hank patted my knee. "You're not the only one who knows about acting, Charlie," he said as he got up.

Talk about metaphorical daggers in hearts.

"I know I'm not," I said quietly. "I just know how I want this to be acted."

"Give me a kiss," Hank said suddenly.

"We're on set," I said shortly. "Let's just get the scenes out of the way." I looked at the lock of hair falling shaggily over his eyes and brushed it off his forehead. He was so beautiful. "We can roll in the hay later, sailor."

Hank smiled at me. "Yo ho ho," he said.

thirty-three

Horton and I didn't say much on the ride home. I concentrated unnecessarily hard on driving. I hate driving in the city. We were almost back to Manhattan when we got completely entrenched in traffic on the West Side Highway.

I sighed as I pulled the car up to a dead halt.

"Maybe I need a Pegasus-type flying horse instead of a pack mule to get to the set. Think that'd be the best way?"

Horton shrugged. "Or a hot air balloon."

We were both quiet again.

"Do you want to talk about what happened today?" he asked.

"I didn't realize there was anything to talk about."

Horton adjusted his glasses. "I thought you did a good job of handling a belligerent actor."

"Oh, please. Hank wasn't being a belligerent actor. But I don't know what was going on."

"Has he done anything like this before?"

"Like what?"

Horton made a sound. He wasn't my mother, so it wasn't precisely a snoan, but it was definitely the sixty-eight-year-old male film professor equivalent. "Charlie, you are many things, but you are not stupid. I'm not going to force you to talk about anything, but at least do me the courtesy of acknowledging that what happened in the living room scene was not what you had planned."

I stared at the road.

"He's not normally like that," I said quietly. "I think we just have different ideas about the character of Charles."

"Mmm-hmm."

"I'm sorry you didn't get a good impression of him. Hank is really great." My words sounded a bit phony but they were true. I'd wanted Horton to like Hank and to think he was a good casting choice. I closed my eyes for a second. I had a headache. It was probably a brain tumor. I was probably going to black out and crash the car, killing both Horton and myself. When people reviewed *The Doctor's Wife* posthumously, they'd look at each with bewilderment. *This could have been a great movie*, they'd say, shaking their heads sadly. *Although Charles is overacting. Strange that such an obviously accomplished director could have made such an amateurish error in her stage directions.*

"Are you OK?" Horton asked.

"I have a headache."

"Long day," Horton said.

"It's probably a brain tumor."

Horton ran a hand through his hair, slightly disheveling the Boris Yeltsin wedge. "Charlie, what does Hank think about the script of *The Doctor's Wife*? Has he told you?"

"He thinks it's brilliant," I replied.

"Good. If he gets that much, I think everything will be OK."

"I never doubted that it would," I said tersely.

Horton didn't say anything for a while. The traffic inched painfully forward. At last, he turned his face away from me and stared out the window.

"Your thesis has been a rough process. I would like for you to experience a smooth filming." He paused. "I don't want you to be sour and cynical at the end of this film, Charlotte. Nor do I want your thesis to destroy a relationship that obviously has given you a great deal of happiness."

"Horton, honestly—" I began, but he shushed me.

"That's all I think we should say about it for now."

"But—"

"Enough."

When I got to my building, I could hear music blaring. Somebody was evidently having a party. The music got louder as I climbed the stairs. It didn't stop at the third floor, and as I made my way up the last flight of stairs, I began mentally composing how I would ask my next-door neighbor to temper the volume. I reached the fourth floor landing with my mouth set in a firm line. Then I paused.

The music was definitely coming from my apartment. Apparently, *I* was having a party. I unlocked the door and slowly walked inside. The smell of garlic nearly knocked me over. Karen and Ned were in the kitchen cooking. I looked around for a makeshift mosh pit, but as far as I could tell, they were alone.

Karen reached out and lowered the volume when she saw me.

"We're making fresh pasta with goat cheese and olives and tomatoes," she announced. "And there's salad and bread." She was sitting on the kitchen countertop.

"And a very nice bottle of Pinot Grigio," Ned added as he stirred a pot on the stove.

"Hank called, but you'll have dinner with us, won't you?" Karen added. "It'll be ready soon."

Either the elves had come while I was on set or Karen had cleaned the apartment this afternoon. The various drafts of *The Doctor's Wife* that had been scattered all over the living room were now neatly piled in one corner. I didn't particularly feel like facing Hank. Pasta and sweatpants sounded exactly like what I needed tonight. I took off my hat and set my bag on the floor.

"Come on," Karen urged.

"Come on," Ned repeated. "Don't rush off to Brooklyn. Why would you want to see Hank when you have such glamour in your own apartment?" He struck a ridiculous movie star pose, one hand tucked behind his head. Karen imitated him, affecting an equally exaggerated stance.

I laughed. "Of course." I reached into the salad and pulled out a strip of red pepper and began nibbling. "You guys are awesome. Here I've put in a long, hard day toiling in the mines and look what I get to come home to."

"The mines?" Ned said.

I nodded, reaching for another piece of pepper. "Salt mines. Or maybe coal. But nothing as pleasant or exotic as diamonds."

Ned turned around and kissed Karen on the forehead. "Dinner is almost ready, my darling." She lifted her face up and they began a series of revolting little baby kisses. Kiss kiss kiss kiss kiss kiss kiss . . .

Charlotte, the intruder, decided she had best absent herself from such an intimate situation.

"I'm going to call Hank back before we eat," I announced.

Neither Karen nor Ned paid me any attention. Ned was now stroking Karen's hair. I was glad they were happy together, but honestly. Restraint is not the least desirable quality that one could cultivate. I picked up the phone and wandered into my bedroom.

Hank answered the phone with a breezy, "Charlie-doll, is that you?"

"I'm sorry, this is Her Majesty's social secretary. The queen is not receiving calls tonight," I said in a fussy British accent.

"Hey, baby," Hank said. "I miss you already."

"I just saw you an hour and a half ago."

"That was a long time ago."

I didn't miss Hank at all, unless you count missing the opportunity to string him up by his beautiful, arrogant thumbs and dangle him from the ceiling.

"Definitely a long time when you're stuck in traffic with your advisor who insists on quizzing you about why your boyfriend slash leading man can't follow your directions," I agreed.

"Aw, doll, I did what you wanted."

"On take number four!" I squeaked. "Hank, this is a student movie, not a soap. There's no money for you to screw up takes, and besides, I'm the director. You've got to do what I ask." I stopped. "At least on set," I amended.

"Don't be pissy, Charlie," Hank said. "Come on down and visit me."

Pissy? *Pissy?*

"I just got home. I don't want to go to Brooklyn," I said in the least pissy voice that I could manage.

"Drive, sweetheart. Put that borrowed car to use. It'll take you twenty minutes."

"It will *not* take twenty minutes," I said petulantly. "It will take a hundred million years, the same way it always does."

"I want to see you. I miss you."

"Why don't you come up here? Karen and Ned are making a fabulous dinner and we'll be that much closer to the warehouse in the morning."

"Privacy."

"There's a door that closes."

"Come on, sweet Charlotte. What if I were to have a car come pick you up in an hour and bring you down here? No subway. No driving. Door-to-door chauffeur service and I promise to give you a long massage when you arrive."

Sweatpants still sounded like a good idea.

"Please."

"Can there be a bubble bath?" I asked. Hank has a large, baroque bathtub with jets.

"I think we could arrange that. And I promise we can go to Starbucks in the morning."

I gave in. It was very hard to stay annoyed with such a solicitous studmuffin.

"Don't worry about the car service. I'll drive. But I want to have dinner with Karen and Ned."

"Sure. That'll give me time to alert the servants that the queen would like her ermine robe tonight."

I smiled. "See you soon, bratty, mule-headed, egotistical actor."

"See you soon, demanding, equally mule-headed, pretentious director."

We hung up. When I left for Brooklyn after dinner, I was in a much better mood than I would have thought possible earlier in the day.

thirty-four

On Sunday afternoon, I was lying on Marisa's floor painting my toenails with her new Chanel polish and fending off a wave of fatigue. We had rented the Ingmar Bergman movie of *The Magic Flute*. Marisa was curled on her couch with a cumbersome manuscript from which she would occasionally read aloud truly awful, overwritten lines.

"Why are you still reading that?" I asked, after a particularly bad passage.

"Steven asked me if I would." Steven was Marisa's boss.

"But surely you knew by page twenty that it wasn't anything you'd want to publish."

Marisa shifted on the couch. "No. I knew by page twenty that it wasn't anything I would want to read for pleasure. But, believe it or not, this type of thriller sells very well and the author has a good track record."

"What's it about again?"

"A psychopath who blows up bridges."

"Anything else?"

"The studly FBI agent who catches him has a lot of sex with a blond engineer who designs bridges."

"Of course." I had smudged my pinky toenail beyond recognition. I reached for the polish remover and a Q-tip.

"You know who I saw yesterday?" I asked, as I excavated my cuticle from underneath a glob of polish.

"Who?"

"Robert the doorman."

"Really? Where?"

"Outside the subway. He's always so weird around me. Very nervous."

"Maybe he still likes you."

"God, I hope not. I can't deal with that kind of obsessive torch-carrying. I mean, we went out once."

"Does he know about Hank?"

"You'd have to be on Mars not to know that Hank has taken time off from *Troubled Passion* to act in his nobody girlfriend's student film." I dipped the Q-tip in the remover again and went back to my toenails. "His *curvy* nobody girl-friend's student film."

Marisa set the half of the manuscript that she'd already read on the floor. "If you follow soaps. My hunch is that Robert doesn't. But he could still have heard about you and Hank and finds it awkward."

"Maybe. He asked me once to read an essay that he'd written and I said I would and then he never sent it to me. And when I asked him about it yesterday, he started blush-ing furiously."

"So he gets nervous."

I capped the polish remover. "Socially inept people drive me up the wall."

"Socially overadept people drive *me* up the wall."

"Like Hank?" I asked. "He's as glib as they come. If he had lived a hundred years ago, he'd be one of those con-artist traveling salesmen who made millions off some phony tonic that he'd invented. Dr. Destin's Pick-Me-Up Pills," I mocked.

"Hank's pretty smooth, all right," Marisa agreed. "But it doesn't bother me."

"Kind of bothers me, though." I rolled on my back and

stretched one leg in the air so that I could admire my toes. "He's being a complete brat on set, and when I screw up my courage to talk to him about it, he's so adorable that I capitulate almost immediately."

"Brat how?"

I wasn't sure exactly how to explain it. "Bratty like he knows more than I do about everything. He thinks he knows the best order to film scenes, the best way to angle a camera, the best way to move so the mike doesn't frizzle dialogue, and—most irritating of all—the best way to play Charles."

"Is he right about that stuff or does he just think he is?"

"Well, sure, he's right about some of it. He's got a lot more experience working in front of a camera than I do. I'm glad he's so interested in playing Charles, but I wish he would remember that a student film is meant to be a learning experience. He doesn't give me any chance to figure things out for myself. Plus, I'm the director, and it really, really undermines my authority to have my boyfriend correct me all the time."

I paused, reached for the nail polish, and began applying a second coat to my right foot. "To say nothing of the fact that, regardless of his experience, there is a huge difference between TV and film. The only film Hank has ever been in was *Sorority Spring Break* and he had a really tiny role."

"So?"

"So *The Doctor's Wife* is a different type of movie. It's a remake of *Madame Bovary*, remember? It's a different type of acting and a different type of character than he's used to."

Marisa lowered the volume on the movie. "Charlie, there's no need to be snotty about Hank and soaps. Practically every famous actor has had a stint in soaps at some point."

"I know. I'm not being snotty about soaps. I'm being snotty because he's making me nervous and it's the only defense I can muster."

"My, what good insight you have, Grandmother dear," Marisa said in a Little Red Riding Hood voice.

"Yes, well, I do live with Karen." I finished the right foot and began a second coat on the left toes. "This is a pretty color."

"Yeah, I like it."

"I don't want to talk about Hank anymore," I said. "It's upsetting me."

"Sure?"

"Yup."

"Karen would say that maybe you should talk about it because it's upsetting you."

"Which is why she is the psychologist and I am the melodramatic, neurotic screenwriter."

We watched the opera for a few minutes in silence.

"Karen and Ned are totally in love, aren't they?" Marisa asked suddenly, right in the middle of the Queen of the Night's best aria.

I reached for the VCR and paused the movie. I couldn't concentrate on both the conversation and the aria at the same time.

"I think so. They're pretty cute together. Nauseating, at times, but cute."

"Yeah. Neither one of them is telling me much at the moment. It's strange. Like I don't want to know about the details of what's going on, but I don't want this to affect my relationship with either of them."

"Well, it's got to affect your relationships with them *somehow*," I said honestly. "That's inevitable. Do you think that their dating is a problem?"

Marisa sighed. "I don't know." She played with a couch cushion for a minute. "With Ned, not so much. He's sort of annoying. I know he doesn't mean to play the Karen card all the time, but every time he wants or needs anything, somehow her name gets worked into the conversation. With Karen—" She stopped. "I guess I worry that this is going to set us apart somehow."

"Oh, surely not," I said.

"I can feel it happening."

"Maybe, at the moment, you guys find it a bit awkward to be around each other. But eventually all the things that seem unsettling and bizarre about Karen and Ned are going to become normal and a fact of life."

"I guess."

"Plus, we don't know how Karen and Ned are going to fare. They haven't even been together for two months." I capped the nail polish and bit my lip thoughtfully. "They have gotten awfully serious about each other awfully quickly, though."

"Hello, pot, have you met my other friend, the kettle?" Marisa asked.

"What's that supposed to mean?"

"You and Hank were walking into the sunset together after one date."

"Not exactly. After two dates. He didn't call me for almost a week after we first went out, remember? I probably scared him off by talking about Caravaggio."

"Whatever. You know what I mean."

"Yeah. Don't you think it's a little strange the way things have worked out?"

"What do you mean?"

"Well, up until this year, you've always been the one with the boyfriend and I've always been the third wheel."

"Yeah. I don't feel like dating much now."

"Because?"

"Because I'd rather be at home with a good book and my sweatpants."

"That's exactly what I used to say in the pre-Hank days."

"I remember."

"So?"

"So maybe there are just other things I want to focus on right now. Like getting my job on track."

The pause time on the VCR expired and the Queen of

the Night came on, cursing her daughter at full blast. I reached for the remote and hit stop.

"Ned's not the only problem at work, is he?" I asked.

"I just need to get out of there. I hate it. I love editing. But I hate it there." She stopped. "Karen and I were talking about this a lot. But, honestly, Ned has dropped a lot of hints lately that make me think that Karen's told him stuff."

"Really?"

"Yeah. More than dropping hints. I told Karen that I thought *Hard Times* was sexier than Georgia Barlow's supposedly erotic book and people have been coming up and teasing me about it. I never say what I think about authors to people at work. Ever. I make such a point of that. I also told her that I thought Joe, our accountant, had a comb-over as long as my arm."

I laughed.

"And Ned now refers to Joe as the Comb-over King."

"That's awkward, but none of that is precisely classified information. Especially if the comb-over's that exaggerated."

"Sure, but I've said stuff about Steven and about the way the company is run that isn't exactly the kind of thing that should get out."

I wasn't sure what to say. "Could you talk to Karen about it?"

"Maybe."

"It could help."

"Maybe."

I looked at my watch. It was three-thirty.

"Hey, want to come to dinner with my family tonight?"

"Are you driving or taking the Long Island Rail Road?"

"Driving." I wiggled my eyebrows enticingly.

"OK. Will they care?"

"No, they love you and, besides, you can help divert conversation away from what's happening on my film. I really don't want to talk about it to them at the moment."

"When are you going to bring Hank to dinner?"

"You sound like my mother. Now stop. I already let you interrupt my favorite aria."

Marisa reached for the remote and rewound the tape so that we would get to hear all of the Queen of the Night's curse uninterrupted.

"You know what we can watch next time?" she asked.

"The Zeffirelli *La Traviata*?" I replied.

"Bingo."

"Hank doesn't like opera, you know," I said.

"Throw him back," Marisa advised. "He's clearly too uncultured to keep."

To: Charlie <cfrost@columbfilm.edu>
From: Chris <cmartin@columbfilm.edu>
Re: Starbucks break

In lieu of my ability to take you out for coffee right now, this e-mail
serves as a virtual caramel macchiato.

Chris

To: Chris <cmartin@columbfilm.edu>
From: Charlie <cfrost@columbfilm.edu>
Re: Starbucks break

In lieu of my sanity, this e-mail serves as a virtual meltdown.

Charlie

thirty-five

The stress of filming was getting to me. Somehow, overnight, I had developed a flaming red zit directly between my eyebrows. It looked like a bindi. The Soap Opera Awards were tomorrow night and I was seriously contemplating wearing an actual bindi to avoid any catty comments about "rosy-faced Charlie Frost" on *Love Lives of the Stars*.

My cast, thankfully, had developed no such unfortunate marks. Sabrina looked positively dewy as she strolled through the set of LaRue's store. I watched as Walsh coaxed her into ordering new drapes and furniture that she couldn't afford and that would eventually fail to provoke the desired envy of her social-climbing neighbors. The scene was missing something, though. Midway through the third take, I sighed. Hank was sitting beside me on the side of the set and he reached out and scribbled on a nearby pad, *It's a hard scene.*

So? I wrote back. *Don't you think it's missing something?*

Hank shrugged and we went back to watching Walsh exude oily charm. After the scene ended, I approached Sabrina and repeated the identical stage directions for the third time.

"Charlie, that's what I've been trying to do," she protested.

"I know. But we need to see Emma's desperation. She doesn't care about the furniture, per se. She cares about feeling important and envied and making her life less mundane."

"I'm trying," she repeated.

"I know. Let's do it again, though."

Sabrina drew her brows together slightly. "I thought the scene was OK in rehearsal."

"It was. Let's just give it another shot."

I walked back to my seat and gave the signal to begin shooting. Hank passed me another note:

She's tired, C. Lay off her.

OK, who died and appointed him the Savior of Sensitivity? I ignored the note and focused on Sabrina's increasingly awful performance. After the take was over, I walked onto the set and said, as delicately as possible, "Sabrina, you're nervous. Relax. I know that you just want this scene to be over. But what comes out is apathy and a lack of caring, rather than Emma's genuine fear and desperation. We're going to try it again. I want you to work on lowering your voice and leaning more toward Walsh when you describe your house. You can do this."

Sabrina pursed her lips and gave me a look that suggested she would prefer to rot in hell than redo the scene.

"It's almost two," Hank said loudly.

"What?" I turned around.

"I think we need to break for lunch, Charlie."

I stared at him. "After the scene," I said curtly. I reached for my headset.

"She's tired, Charlie. She's not going to get it if you keep riding her. Let's break and pick up later."

"We'll finish the take."

"You ready for lunch, Sabrina?'

Sabrina glanced back and forth between Hank and me, like a kid caught between divorcing parents. She didn't say anything.

"Let's knock off for now. We'll come back in an hour and start over," Hank said loudly to the cast. "Everyone, take a break."

I was speechless. Should I ever be able to identify my eye-teeth, I would gladly swap them for the ability to come up with exactly the right response at moments such as these. Lacking a crushing reply, I narrowed my eyes and glared at Hank.

"Actually, no. Hank, if you'd like, you are free to go to lunch since we're not doing your scenes at the moment. I'm afraid I'll need Sabrina, Walsh, and the crew to complete another take," I said very quietly. I could feel eyes on me. Sabrina looked like she might start crying (which, frankly, made two of us). Hank looked at me coldly.

"You're pushing her too hard, Charlie," he said and walked out, slamming the door behind him. There was an ominous silence.

"Um, OK," I said softly. I couldn't believe the havoc that Hank had so shamelessly wreaked on my set. He was dead. He was fucking dead. Forget the Soap Opera Awards. I was going directly to *Love Lives of the Stars* with an invented potency problem ASAP. I stared at my cast, who stared curiously back at me. I remembered that I was in charge and decided to resurrect some of my authority.

"Sabrina and Walsh, Hank is right in one sense. I am being tough on you guys. I know that, but I'd like to explain why," I began. "This scene is pivotal in the establishment of Emma's downfall. I don't want to give you guys a lunch break just yet—though I'm sure you need one—because I want you to channel all of the frustration you feel with the scene, and probably with me as well, into your acting. I'm afraid that if we stop, we're going to lose some momentum and we'll temper some of the natural emotion that's running strong right now." I looked at them. "I hope you understand."

They both nodded. I walked onto the set of LaRue's store and hoisted myself onto the phony shop counter.

"We're going to take this slowly and really work on understanding what's going on in Emma and LaRue's minds. Let's start with you, Walsh. I want you to tell me everything LaRue might be thinking when he sees flighty Emma sail into his store."

I let everyone take the rest of the day off once we finished the store scene. After we spent the time talking about the characters, both Sabrina and Walsh had been essentially perfect. I was willing to call it quits after one take, but Walsh asked if we had enough film to do it again.

"I think we're on a roll and I want to nail this scene," he said. I was grateful for his implicit endorsement of me as director. Hank hadn't returned by the time I let everyone go. While it would royally screw my thesis were he never to return, I was much too angry to care at the moment. I cried all the way home, parked the car in a garage rather than searching for street parking, cried as I raced up to my apartment, and flung myself on my bed still howling.

After about twenty minutes, I lay there wetly and tried to figure out what had happened. Both Hank and I were probably right. Honestly, we could have taken a lunch break then. It wouldn't have destroyed the film. My preference had been to keep working and—as the final take indubitably showed—that had paid off. What I objected to was his challenging me publicly and then usurping my directorial authority. It wasn't an appropriate thing for an actor to do, let alone a boyfriend.

The phone started ringing. I let it go to voice mail. I didn't feel like talking to anyone at that moment, particularly if it was someone from *The Doctor's Wife.*

"Charlie, hi. It's Chris Martin. I guess you're on set. At any rate, I was just calling to see if you wanted to get together. I figure filming has got to be the most stressful thing ever. So I thought I'd offer to take you out to dinner sometime this week and you can reciprocate when I go into production. Let me know."

I hauled myself up to a seated position. I didn't really feel like facing anybody. But I would have to reenter humanity sometime and I'd rather talk to Chris, who would at least understand movie making, than deal with Karen (with her penetrating empathy), Horton (with his arsenal of I-told-you-sos), Hank (with his misplaced arrogance), Sahra (with her offensive tranquility), my parents (with their shocking cinematic ignorance), or anybody who had witnessed my heinous humiliation at the hands of the hunk I loved. I picked up the phone.

"Can we go to dinner right now?"

thirty-six

I stumbled up the stairs to my apartment at midnight, half looped from too much wine and emotion. Dinner had been exactly what I needed. Chris and I had brainstormed every single possible aftermath that might emerge from this afternoon's fiasco and how I should deal with it. Not once did he comment on what an obvious jackass Hank was. Not once did he say that it was a difficult situation or express anything that remotely suggested he agreed that I had pushed Sabrina too hard. Listening to his advice, I made another resolution to myself: I was not going to let my attachment to Hank get in the way of making *The Doctor's Wife*.

When I got upstairs, there was an enormous box, wrapped in orange and pink polka dot paper, in front of my apartment door. I sighed and opened the card.

Charlie-doll—

I was completely out of line today. I have no idea what came over me. I was tempted to charge up to Ninety-ninth Street and demand to see you, but thought that I might be the last person you wanted to deal with at the moment. So I've sent you this instead, because I thought that after your hard day, you might just want something to hug.

Sorry,
Hank

P.S. Check your e-mail.

I shredded the paper grumpily. Inside was a very large stuffed gorilla from FAO Schwarz. I couldn't deal with Hank being adorable right now. After coping with crazed Mr. Hyde all day long, I couldn't go back to thinking of him as tame Dr. Jekyll. It was too confusing and, frankly, too manipulative on his part. I left the gorilla on the doorstep and went inside. The lights were out, which meant that Karen was either asleep or at Ned's. I booted up my laptop and logged onto e-mail. Hank had sent a decorous and remorseful note to the entire cast and crew of *The Doctor's Wife* apologizing for his behavior. It ended with "See you on set tomorrow."

I turned off the lights, set my alarm, and fell asleep in my clothes without even brushing my teeth.

The next day was monumental for several reasons. First, it was the Soap Opera Awards. Second, it was Valentine's Day. (Don't ask me what marketing genius thought up that little ploy.) Third, it was the day after the power struggle that would live in infamy. I walked onto the set that morning with trepidation, but filming proved to be both productive and uneventful. Even though he was high on my list of people I didn't want to appreciate, Hank was rather sensational during the day's scenes. I had been wrong: He *was* a talented actor, with a breadth that extended well beyond the *Troubled Passion* clenched jaw.

Urg.

After we broke for the day, Hank and I arranged that we would each go home and primp for our upcoming date with the red carpet. The studio that aired *Troubled Passion* was going to send a car to pick him up first, then me, and then deliver us to the awards. It was a very businesslike conversation. It's funny how when there actually *is* troubled passion, it gets expressed in the most mundane ways. At least in my life.

In fact, we spent fewer than five of the thirty minutes that it took to drive from my apartment to the awards talking to each other. Here's what we said:

```
SCENE: Interior, Lincoln Town Car. We see
the door open and CHARLIE slither inside.
She sits down next to HANK. Neither moves to
kiss or embrace the other.


     HANK (commenting on Charlie's dress):
Pink.


          CHARLIE:
Yeah.


          HANK:
Not your typical style.


          CHARLIE:
No, but you should have seen the look the
fashion consultant gave me when I suggested
yoga pants and a Mets T-shirt.


          HANK:
Yeah, Maddie said it took a little coercion
to get you to find a dress.
```

*CHARLIE turns and stares out the window. Cut
to CLOSE-UP: There is a very small furrow in
her forehead, as if she is trying either not
to talk or not to cry.*

At any rate, having now paraded down a red carpet in a
free silk dress and Marisa's borrowed shoes, I can say with absolute certainty that it is overrated. Maybe at some time in
my life (say when I was eight), I would have enjoyed pranc-
ing in front of the wildly snapping paparazzi. But now I just
felt sort of sad that I was so unmoved by the glitter and by
the even more horrifying fact that it was Valentine's Day and
Hank and I hadn't even kissed.

I got sloshed at the after-party. It wasn't entirely accidental. Neither Hank nor Maddie won the awards for which
they'd been nominated. Both pretended not to care, but I
had a hunch that they were more miffed than they were letting on. *Troubled Passion* did win for best writing and directing. Bunny, the writer, hustled me into a corner and
proceeded to rhapsodize for fifteen solid minutes about his
golden statue.

"That's great, Bunny," I said, looking around for someone
(*anyone*) else that I recognized.

Bunny blew a whiff of cigar smoke into my face. "So three
seconds before they call my name, I lean over to Pug and I
say, 'Pug, I'm not going to get it.' And she says, 'Sure you are,
Bunny. Aren't you the best?' And I say, 'Nah, Pug, it's not going to happen.'" Bunny paused significantly. "And I'll be
damned, kid, but they called out my name."

"I know, Bunny. Congratulations."

"Sure, sweetheart, it's a good life." More cigar smoke assaulted me. I felt my lungs constrict and forcibly restrained a
coughing spasm. Bunny raised his glass to me. "So how are
things with you and our Dr. Reston?"

"Oh, they're great," I lied.

"I've got to tell you, I'm surprised you're still around. Hank's not one for monogamy."

I faked a sickly smile. "That's not exactly what I want to hear, Bunny," I said in what I hoped was a light-hearted tone.

"Oh, sweetheart, you know what I mean. You're certainly *my* type, but up until now, girls like you have never been Hank's thing." He raised his glass drunkenly. "But, hey, who am I to cast stones?" He nodded emphatically. "If you kids are happy . . ."

What did he mean by the "girls like you" comment? I smiled another fake smile. "We are," I said as I leaned over and pecked Bunny's cheek. "Congratulations again."

After I escaped from Bunny and his poison cigar, I realized I had nowhere to go. I couldn't see Hank anywhere. For lack of a better option, I went into the bathroom. Marina, one of the *Troubled Passion* cast, was in there. She'd opened the window and was sitting on the windowsill smoking. It was cold with the window open and I shivered inadvertently. Marina waved some smoke away with her hand and dangled her cigarette out the window.

"Sorry," she said in a voice that sounded as if she weren't particularly sorry at all.

"Not a problem," I said, examining myself in the mirror. My hair looked a bit scraggly. I hadn't thought to bring a brush with me. I pulled it back using the ponytail holder I always keep around my wrist. Marina watched me.

"You're the little thing that's keeping Hank so occupied, aren't you?"

Why did these people insist on diminishing me by using terms such as "little thing"? I dizzily turned away from my reflection. I really was drunk. I was going to have to be careful not to say something I'd regret later.

"We're dating," I said.

"It's a shitty place to be on Valentine's Day."

I rolled my eyes. "It happens, I guess." When I'd first heard the awards were to be on Valentine's Day, I was disappointed that Hank and I couldn't engage in something more passionate and solitary. But given our current woes, I was sort of relieved to have a scheduled Valentine's activity that absorbed all of our time and thoughts. "Besides," I added, "Hank spent all day acting in my student film, so it's only fair that I spend all night doing this."

"I'd heard he was doing that." Marina stubbed out her cigarette. She reached in her purse and pulled out a little mandarin satin change purse and a dollar bill. "Want a line?" She flicked open the purse. It was half filled with white powder.

"No thanks." The last thing I wanted to be was trapped in the bathroom with a coked-up Marina. I smiled apologetically at her and checked my watch. "I probably better get back to the party."

Marina was arranging her coke on a little mirror.

"Suit yourself."

I felt a little wobbly as I rejoined the party. Hank saw me and emerged from the crowds. He put an arm around me.

"I am drunk," I announced.

"Glad to hear that."

"I am very drunk, indeed," I repeated.

"You want to head home?"

"No." I shook my head emphatically. "I want to stay here and be drunk indeed," I said, slurring my words together. I leaned against Hank. "Marina's doing coke in the bathroom."

"Surprise," he said dryly.

"Do you do coke?" I asked.

"I have. Twice. Both times were around ten years ago."

"I've never done it. I don't think I've even been offered it before."

"Surprise," Hank said again.

"I am drunk," I repeated.

"Come on, Charlie. It's Valentine's Day. Let's go home."

Hank retrieved our coats and said the appropriate good-byes and led me downstairs to the waiting car. It was warm in the car, and I lurched against Hank.

"I knew you were the kind of unsavory creature who'd get a girl all liquored up," I mumbled. "Now you're going to ravish me."

"That sounds like an excellent idea," Hank said.

"All liquored up and about to be ravished," I groaned.

Hank reached out and stroked my hair. I rolled away from his touch and promptly fell asleep.

So much for Valentine's Day.

thirty-seven

It was eleven when I woke up the next morning. I lay there for a second staring out Hank's window at the boats going past and feeling generally parched. Resolution: No more getting drunk, accidentally or otherwise, and *especially* not on Valentine's Day. I felt like a jerk. What if I'd blown a chance to make up with Hank, who was certainly not lying in bed beside me at the moment?

"Agua," I rasped, doing my best imitation of the guy caught in the desert on *Sesame Street*. "Agua." There was no reply. I hauled myself upright and went into the living room. Hank was sitting with his feet propped up on the coffee table. There was an enormous stack of newspapers next to him.

"Here we go," he said, reading aloud from the *Daily News*. "*Troubled Passion's* sexy Hank Destin was accompanied by Charlie Frost, the Columbia film student who's been occupying his time of late. Ms. Frost was festively attired in a Valentine pink silk dress by an unknown designer."

I curled onto the couch beside Hank and rested my head in his lap. "Nothing about how the pink complemented Ms. Frost's shocking beauty?"

"Ms. Frost's shocking beauty was rivaled only by her

shocking intoxication," Hank said, his eyes still fixed on the newspaper.

I hit him lightly. "It does *not* say that."

"What makes you so sure?" he asked mischievously.

"Because if your publicist was good enough to get all these papers here before noon she's got to be good enough to suppress the less-than-startling story of a drunk date."

"How do you know that I didn't run out to the newsstand to get them?"

I rolled over so I could see his face. "Did you?"

"No, of course not. Sandi had them delivered."

"Mmm-hmm," I sniffed, reaching for the *News*. There was a nice picture of Marina. Her eyes were clear, so it must have been taken before she snorted most of her change purse in the bathroom. I snuggled closer to Hank.

"We never talked about the other day," I said quietly.

"Must we?" Hank said, flipping through the *Post* to find the style and gossip section.

"I appreciated your apology," I said. "But it was a little too late. Hank, I don't want to fight with you. But if we're going to fight, I would rather we fight about something personal than something to do with the film. I just can't afford to let you destroy my thesis."

"I have no problem with you other than what happens on set," Hank said, putting the *Post* back on the table.

I sat up. "What's that supposed to mean?"

"It means that I adore you."

"But . . ."

"But not when we're working on the film."

I felt my cheeks begin their inevitable flaming. "I don't get what you're saying."

"I don't like the way you think about filming, Charlie. I don't like the way you work with actors, and I don't like the way you schedule the takes. It's inexperience, mostly, but it's irritating. You got annoyed with me for wasting takes—but you overshoot everything because of your ridiculous perfectionism. You have no concept of when a scene is over."

"It's a student film, Hank. I'm supposed to be learning."

Hank shrugged. "Sure," he said lightly. "And I'm sure you'll be an adequate director eventually. But you ought to be more closely supervised than you are."

I could feel my throat getting hot and scratchy. I swallowed hard before answering. "I think Horton and the other faculty in my program are the ones who should make that decision."

"Horton's got such a hard-on for your writing he can't see past that to your directorial flaws."

What a classy reply. I couldn't believe I was dating someone who used the term *hard-on* in the same sentence as he discussed my writing. "I haven't heard any complaints from the rest of the crew. You're the only one who's being difficult. Maybe it's more your problem than mine." I winced as soon as the immature words were out of my mouth. I might as well have stuck out my tongue and chanted nanny-nanny-boo-boo.

"Perhaps," Hank replied calmly. "But I'm also the only one with enough experience to know the difference between what you do and how things ought to be."

"Well, maybe it was a mistake to allow you to be in such an amateurish project. Maybe I should have ignored your desperate begging," I said harshly.

"Oh, come off of it, Charlie. We both know I'm doing you a favor."

"I thought you *liked* my screenplay. I thought you *wanted* a more serious role," I cried. I felt dizzy. I ran my hand through my dirty hair and closed my eyes for a second. I was way too hung over to deal with this fight.

"You're a good writer. There's no doubt about that. And I admit that the way I acted on set the other day was unfair to you. I shouldn't have challenged you in front of everybody."

"Thank you," I said more loudly than I'd intended.

"But," Hank continued, "it's not all my fault, doll. The only way I could get you to pay attention to me was to be in your screenplay."

"That's not true!" I interrupted. Hank held up a hand to shush me. I felt sick. Very, very sick.

"You thought my acting was a joke," he said. "You assumed I was just some talentless pretty face. *You* were the artist. Let me tell you something, Charlie: there's no room in your little world for anyone else to have any talent. You always have to be the star."

"That's not true!" I cried again.

Hank looked at me. "Are you sure, Charlie?" he asked quietly. "Think about it and maybe you'll see that I'm more right than you want me to be."

I closed my eyes again. I was incredibly dizzy. This was worse than my one and only mountain-climbing-without-enough-water experience. I opened my eyes suddenly. I was going to be sick. I clambered off the couch and raced to the bathroom, retaining just enough presence of mind to slam the door behind me. I knelt by the toilet, retching and crying at the same time. I remembered the way Hank had looked sitting beside me on the couch, all calm and civilized and surrounded by newspapers. I shuddered as I threw up again. I stood up, enduring a tremendous head-rush in the process, and reached for the mouthwash. I rinsed my mouth out, splashed some cold water on my face, and sat back down on the floor, shivering. I started crying again.

After about ten minutes, Hank knocked gently on the door. "Charlie?" I didn't say anything. "Charlie, are you OK?"

I still didn't say anything. My lips felt essentially paralyzed. I wiped my eyes with the back of my hand. It was absolutely unfair that I could set new mortification records for myself at the age of twenty-seven. Never before had I been so hung over that I threw up. I didn't remember being *that* drunk.

"Go away," I said. My voice sounded a little more blubbery than I would have liked. I cleared my throat. "Go away," I repeated. "I'm too busy crying and curling into the fetal position to talk to you."

"I'm not going to go away."

"Thanks." For someone with a twice-weekly cleaning lady, Hank's bathroom floor was not as clean as it should have been.

"I'm going to open the door, OK?" Hank turned the knob and looked down at me. He was almost unendurably beautiful and self-possessed. I turned my head away.

"You lied," he said.

"What?" I felt myself getting heated again.

"You said you were in the fetal position," Hank replied blandly. I was sitting upright against the wall, with my knees hunched up in front of me. Hank sat down beside me. He reached out and patted my knee. I jerked my legs away from him. "It's OK," he said, patting the knee again. I let him. We sat there for a while, not saying much of anything.

"I'm just hung over," I said.

"I know. But that's not why you threw up."

"It could be."

"Yeah, it could be," Hank agreed. "But it was an upsetting conversation."

"I don't throw up because of upsetting conversations," I said stuffily. There was another long pause.

"Come on, Charlie," Hank said at last. "Why don't you get back in bed and lie down for a while?"

"I'm fine."

"I know you are. But could you let yourself be human for a little while?" He stood up and held his hand out to me. I let him pull me up and lead me into the bedroom. He tucked me in, as if I were a kid, and left the room. I closed my eyes. A few minutes later he was back, sponging off my forehead with a wet washcloth.

"Is that a cold compress?" I asked miserably, looking up at him.

"Yes," he said, still sponging.

"An actual Florence Nightingale cold compress?" For some reason, it amused me to think of Hank offering such a Victorian remedy.

"Yes. Now lie still."

I closed my eyes again and let myself be taken care of. "Thank you," I said.

"I still love you, Charlie," Hank said.

"Please don't be romantic right now. I can't take it." After a few more seconds of silence, I began to feel guilty. He was bathing my forehead, after all. "I love you too," I replied, even though I wasn't sure that was exactly true at this exact moment. Hank's erratic swings from cold and judgmental to tender and caring were entirely too addling and confusing.

"Oh shit!" I remembered suddenly.

"What?"

"I have to go to Great Neck this afternoon. I'm supposed to take my grandmother grocery shopping and then we're going out to dinner. My parents are out of town and I have her car."

"Want me to go with you?"

"Are you kidding me?"

"No, I don't have anything planned. I'll go with you if you want."

I lay there for a second, still feeling sick. Hank had never met my family. There had never been a time that seemed right and, truthfully, I had never wanted to suggest it in case he didn't want to. I was pretty wretched at the moment. It didn't exactly seem like the optimal family-meeting time.

Then I remembered what Hank had said earlier and repeated it silently to myself. *Let yourself be human, Charlotte.*

"I'm so embarrassed," I told him.

"Why?"

"Because I spent the last hour fighting, puking, and crying," I said honestly. Hank smoothed my hair.

"Stop," he said. "It's OK."

We endured the hundredth awkward silence of the morning. "Sure," I said at last. "Come with me to Great Neck."

"Really?"

"Yeah," I said. "I'd like it. Just let me lie here for a little while longer. I'd sort of like the world to stop spinning."

thirty-eight

After several years testing various, frightful routes from Ninety-ninth Street to Great Neck, I've decided that the simplest way is to go to the eighth circle of hell and head straight south. That will take you directly to the Long Island Expressway, aka the ninth circle. For the record, there has been construction on the LIE since I was approximately four years old. I don't understand how the past twenty-three years constitute enough time to create multiple third-world nations but not to rebuild Exit 22A. Please.

At any rate, Hank and I were only delayed for about twenty minutes or so, which is a record. I felt perfectly fine as we turned into my grandmother's neighborhood. Apparently, my early morning bout of insane vomiting had been temporary. No matter what Hank said, I didn't think it had been caused by the conversation. I have had far more revolting conversations in my life and none of them had driven me to bizarre, psychosomatic escape routes.

My grandmother was standing outside holding a champagne flute as we drove up.

"I promise I don't come from a family of lushes," I told Hank. "She always has a glass of champagne around this time."

Hank unbuckled his seat belt. I had told him about my grandmother and her daily champagne habit around fourteen times already. "And I thought you were short," was all he said. We got out of the car.

"Granny, I think there are laws about this," I said as I kissed her.

"About what?"

"Open drinks outside."

She stared at me, her eyes widening in surprise. "Oh, surely not, darling. How else would people have garden parties?"

I laughed. "Maybe it's only around college campuses that they have those laws. Gran, this is Hank. Hank, my grandmother."

"It's nice to meet you *finally*," Gran said, batting her eyelashes. I hoped the eyelash batting was intentional. We went inside. My grandmother's house is the architectural equivalent of Miss Havisham's wedding dress. She and my grandfather moved there in 1947 and furnished it lavishly. It has not been renovated since. There are holes the size of my head in the Persian carpets and a fully functioning hi-fi system in the living room. As we went onto the sun porch to watch *Judge Judy*, Gran turned around. Pointing at Hank, she mouthed, "So handsome."

Gran's infatuation with Hank continued from *Judge Judy* right through the trip to the grocery store. She subjected every single person in the store to an introduction.

"No need," she told a cute little old man as he reached to help her get down a bottle of seltzer. "My granddaughter or her boyfriend will help me," she added in a loud voice. "This is my granddaughter, Charlie. She's at *Columbia*. You've probably seen Hank before. He stars on a very important television show."

The man turned around and winked at me. "I've got it," he said, gallantly sweeping the seltzer off the top shelf and handing it to my grandmother.

I felt that it wouldn't have been overreacting to gasp, "My hero," but Gran merely sniffed and said, "Thank you" tartly. Moving down the aisle, Hank and me trailing her with the overstuffed shopping cart, she assailed a worker restocking cans of tomato juice.

"Hello, Albert," she greeted him. "My granddaughter and her boyfriend came with me today."

Albert smiled. "Hi there, Mrs. Frost," he said. To me, he added, "Congratulations on your movie."

Who knew my grandmother had such a booming social life at Waldbaum's? "Thanks," I told Albert, "but no congrats until it's done. There's still a long way to go."

"Hank's in Charlie's movie," my grandmother added. "But he's also on TV."

"Yeah, man, you look familiar," Albert said. "What show are you on again?"

"*Troubled Passion*," Hank said. Albert looked perplexed for a second.

"Yeah, sure!" he exclaimed at last. As we made our way to the all-important vitamin supplement area, Hank rolled his eyes at me.

"Sorry about this," I said quietly.

"I think it's great," he replied honestly. "Your grandmother's adorable. I wish my family got so excited about me being on TV. They just take it in stride." I have never met Hank's family, all of whom live within three hours of New York. He has five older sisters and a veritable slew of nieces and nephews. He seems more attached to Vincenzo and Franky from the Italian restaurant than his own blood. Perhaps taking things in stride was a family failing to which Henry Joseph Destin, Jr., was not immune.

My grandmother was talking to a woman about her own age. "Yes, well, I find it helpful when my granddaughter comes shopping with me," she announced at the top of her lungs.

"I don't have a granddaughter," the other woman said.

"Really?" Gran asked. "Well, they're marvelous creatures. You should absolutely get one."

"Did I ever mention that I come from a long line of eccentric women?" I muttered to Hank.

"It was unnecessary," he replied softly.

It was time to rescue the grocery store from my grandmother's gloating clutches. I pushed the cart up to her and allowed myself to be introduced.

"Ready for dinner?" I asked.

"Dinner, sure. What time is it?'

"Five-thirty."

"Five-thirty?? We're late!"

Behind me, I heard the unmistakable sound of Hank snickering.

Hank fawned about Gran half of the way back to the city.

"Yeah," I said at last. "I hope I'm that feisty when I'm her age."

Hank was driving. He changed lanes without signaling. "I have a hunch you will be." He reached out and attempted to mess up my hair but I ducked. "You're pretty feisty now," he added unnecessarily.

We were going over the Triboro Bridge. I turned my head so I could get a better view of the city. Much as I liked talking about my grandmother, Hank and I had some unfinished business if we were going to have our first-ever make-up sex.

"I'm sorry about this morning," I said.

"What are you sorry about?"

"That I was so, um, *untidy* in your bathroom," I said.

Hank snorted, presumably at my euphemism. "You're not sorry about what you said to me?"

"We both said some evil things. I was really hurt by what you said and assume you felt the same way about me."

I waited, but Hank didn't respond.

"I don't like fighting, Hank," I said at last.

"I don't like it either. Sometimes it can be necessary, though."

"I don't get what you mean."

"Well, Charlie, neither of us are the type to shirk conflict, particularly when it's related to something we feel strongly about."

I had no idea what he meant. I avoid conflict like the plague. I would rather surrender an aborted fight than engage in a full-fledged one. I said as much to Hank.

"Bullshit," he replied.

"Excuse me?"

"Charlie, you're about as nonconfrontational as Mike Tyson."

"I disagree," I said hotly.

"Point taken," Hank said.

I wanted to remain snooty but couldn't help laughing. "I *really* don't like fighting with you, Hank."

"Let's not do it, then. Let's make an effort to be more sensitive to each other."

"OK." Really, he was the one who needed to make an effort, but I would be good-humored about his one-sided delusion. Hank moved into the exit lane for the Ninety-seventh Street exit. "Where are we going?" I asked.

"I'm going to drop you home and get a cab from your place."

"You don't want me to come back with you?" I felt distinctly wounded.

"Not tonight. We have to start filming again day after tomorrow. I think it might be good if we had between now and then to focus on what's important—and that's making the best possible film we can."

I was so stunned I nearly started throwing up again. To be fair, I agreed that nothing was more important than the success of *The Doctor's Wife*. I just wished Hank didn't feel that way also. It would have been far more preferable had he believed that the most essential thing was our enduring couple-dom. I stared out the window. Hank and I were going to walk off into the sunset together. I was sure of that. But I didn't want time away from him, even for a night. Shouldn't we be rekindling our lust for each other? In my opinion, it was time to take the troubled out of our particular troubled passion. Did Scarlett and Rhett go back to separate apartments after their brouhaha? I think not.

"OK," I said in a small voice.

When I got to my apartment, Karen was working on her laptop in the living room.

"Excuse me," I said. "I have to know: are there sunsets in my future?"

Karen looked up. "Hang on just a second. I have to save this." She typed longer than a simple Ctrl-S would have indicated. I waited impatiently. At last she looked up. "OK. What's going on?"

"Are there sunsets in my future?"

"Happy endings, you mean?"

"Yeah." I took off my shoes and curled up on the other end of the couch. It had been a freebie from Karen's cousin, who had moved to L.A. and felt it wasn't worth taking with her. She had been a very spoiled cousin. I wasn't particularly crazy about the floral pattern, but it was a lovely, large down-filled creation.

"Why are you worried about this?" Karen asked, shifting her laptop onto the coffee table.

"Hank and I are squibbling with each other." I detailed the morning's fight.

"You *threw up*?" Karen asked.

"I guess I was hung over."

"Charlie, I've never seen you throw up."

That was comforting. Hank hadn't known me long enough to provide the much-needed confirmation that this was a fluke, once-in-a-lifetime (probably caused by astrological up-heavals) event. "Yeah, well, with my abhorrent luck, it had to happen for the first time at Hank's." I pulled my hair into a ponytail. "It was so embarrassing and he was so terribly nice about the whole thing and he even went out to Great Neck with me. My grandmother loves him, by the way."

"Not surprisingly. He makes a stellar first impression."

And second and third and fourth . . .

"I guess I'm worried that this film either will destroy our relationship or our relationship will destroy the film."

"Do you really believe that or is it a four A.M. sort of panic?"

"Karen, he is driving me up the wall!" I stared at a crack in the ceiling. "And I'd venture to say that the feeling is mutual. We're not getting along at all."

"You're spending a lot of time together. And you're tense about getting *The Doctor's Wife* finished and that's natural and you'd probably be tense right now regardless of who played Charles."

"That's true." I stared at the ceiling some more. "That's an awfully large crack."

Karen glanced up. "Yeah, it is."

"We're probably going to be crushed to death under two tons of asbestos and moldy sheetrock."

"Don't be such a fatalist, Charlotte."

I rolled my eyes. "How can I help it when I should be having make-up sex right now? It's not a just world, Karen."

Karen sat up and pulled her computer back onto her lap. "If you're going to talk about sex, then I have to work," she said.

Urg.

To: Charlie <cfrost@columbfilm.edu>
From: Katherine Frost <katherine_frost@spacecom.net>
Re: Dinner

Charlie—

Couldn't you have waited to bring Hank to dinner until your father and I were back in town? You know we're dying to meet him. Any night is fine. Just let us know.

Mom

RESOLUTIONS TO KEEP <u>THE DOCTOR'S WIFE</u> FROM DESTROYING
PASSIONATE ROMANCE WITH HANK AND VICE VERSA:

1. Engage in more non-filming outings.
2. Do not talk about filming during these outings.
3. Remember that filming is finite and that Hank is (hopefully)
   more permanent.
4. See if Hank can be discouraged from coming to set on days
   that he is not filming.
5. More yoga.
6. Listen to Hank's suggestions. Maybe it will help for him to feel
   his advice is wanted—even if it's not followed!
7. Do NOT let Hank know that both Franklin and Eleanor have
   kicked the bucket.
8. Do NOT let Hank meet parents on the off-chance he vanishes
   in horror.
9. Talk to Horton? Talk to Chris?
10. MORE YOGA!!!!

thirty-nine

Karen's question about four A.M. panic wasn't entirely off base. At four-sixteen, I was lying in bed staring at the ceiling and making up knock-knock jokes. Marisa had claimed that there could never be a truly funny knock-knock joke because there was something inherently flawed in the joke's predetermined structure. I maintained that although I had never heard a funny knock-knock joke, it wasn't impossible.

Knock knock. Who's there? *Ima.* Ima who? *I'm a fool to be in love with Hank.*

Knock knock. Who's there? *Starbuck.* Starbuck who? *Hank Destin is one star buck.*

Knock knock. Who's there? *Sexy.* Sexy who? *I'm too sexy for Hank Destin, too sexy for Hank Destin . . .*

Knock knock. Who's there? *Boo.* Boo who? *Boo hoo, why are you crying?*

After an hour, I had proven myself wrong—and entirely too obsessed with Hank. I rolled out of bed and wandered into the kitchen. Marisa, Karen, and I had planned on brunch together at the diner. Maybe I could occupy my turbocharged, fretful brain by cooking something and we could eat here instead. I pulled out *Joy of Cooking* and began scanning breakfast options. (When I was little, I thought that there was a series of *Joy* books and that this included both *Joy of Cooking* and *Joy of Sex*. Given a lifetime of being horribly, horribly wrong about virtually everything, it's amazing that I still trust my instincts at all.)

If I had cranberries, I could make cranberry orange scones. There was a twenty-four-hour Gristede's a block away. I grabbed my coat and put it on over my pajamas and headed out before I lost my rare burst of Betty Crocker momentum. The streets were hopping, despite the ridiculous hour. A group of surprisingly elderly men hovered on the island that ran down the center of Broadway. They grew silent as I passed by them. On my way back from the grocery store, one of them whistled at me. I turned around. It was my neighbor, Mr. Marcello.

"Shouldn't you be in bed, little girl?" he called.

"Likewise," I replied, pointing at him. His friends started hooting. I walked back to my apartment serenaded by catcalls and offers of various sleeping arrangements. Only in New York can you get propositioned by five different septagenarians during a four A.M. dash to the supermarket. Back at home, I turned the heat up in the apartment, made a cup of tea, and got to work. The baking did the trick. An hour and a half later, I left a note for Karen to call Marisa once it was a decent hour and invite her over, put on some nonfloury pajamas, crawled into bed, and slept dreamlessly for the next four hours. I was still in my pajamas when Marisa wandered in later that morning. She had brought two pints of raspberries with her.

"Do we have to have tea with scones and berries, or can we do coffee?" she asked.

"We can have coffee," I said. "Definitely." I pulled the coffee maker out from under the counter.

"I can do that if you want to get dressed," Karen offered.

"I'm OK. I'll consider it a sign of emotional progress if I can stay in my PJs past noon."

"Why is that progress?"

"I'm trying not to be so Type A."

"So staying in your pajamas makes you what—a slob or a Type A minus?" Marisa replied skeptically.

"Very funny," I said as I measured out scoops of coffee. I remembered my insomnia. "Knock knock," I said cheerfully.

"Who's there?" Karen asked obligingly.

"Orange."

"Orange who?"

"Orange you glad I made scones?" I said, turning the coffee maker on and brushing stray granules of coffee from my hands.

"I think it's supposed to be 'Orange you glad I didn't say banana,'" Karen said.

"Have you no sense of humor?" I said. "I'm *inventing* knock-knock jokes."

"No, I don't think I'm the one without a sense of humor," Karen said airily.

"We are not amused by your persistent cynicism," I said in my queen voice. I took the scones out of their Tupperware. "Should we heat these?"

Karen and Marisa both nodded. I frowned at the scones. "I think microwaving may affect the texture. I think I'll just warm them in the stove," I decided.

While we were waiting for the scones to heat up, I filled Marisa in on my recent Hank traumas.

"I think I'm glad that you're trying to relax. I think this will all blow over if you chill for a while," she said.

I sipped my coffee. "Easier said than done."

"Are you or are you not a yoga instructor?"

"I know, I know." I pulled butter and jam out of the refrigerator and set them on the table. "Aren't you proud that I baked scones rather than flipping out all night? That's a constructive use of nervous energy." Marisa and Karen didn't say anything.

The phone rang and I grabbed it.

"Hello?" I said.

At first I thought I had a heavy breather. Then I realized that the sound was my mother snoaning repeatedly into the receiver.

"Mom, is that you?" I asked resignedly.

"Puffin," she began. "Your father and I will be back on Tuesday. What about dinner on Wednesday? We'll come into the city."

"I'm filming, Mom."

"We could meet you on the set, if you want."

No.

"Mom, it's not really a good time. Maybe when I get done filming?"

"Puffin, I'm very curious about meeting Hank and we haven't seen you in ages. Now I don't want to pressure you, but—"

"Then don't."

"What?"

"You just said that you didn't want to pressure me. So don't."

"Oh, Puffin."

"Mom, I'm serious."

"Is everything OK?"

"Everything's fine. I just need to concentrate on working right now."

"Charlie," my mother said but I cut her off.

"I have to go," I said. I hung up the phone. My clock read twelve-oh-two.

At least I had managed to accomplish something today, even if it was only staying in my pajamas past noon.

forty

On Tuesday Hank and I had another on-set tiff. It dissipated fairly quickly. We both stared at each other after a few seconds. He spoke first.

"I don't want to keep doing this, Charlie."

"Me either."

I told the cast and crew to take a twenty-minute break, and Hank and I sat down and worked out a compromise shooting sequence. The day went smoothly enough after that, but I felt like Hank might be developing into the cinematic equivalent of a tapeworm. No matter how much I yielded to him, he always needed more. In the absence of a miracle, I decided I needed guidance. We quit filming at four. I drove straight to campus and raced up to Horton's office. I caught him just as he was locking his office door, his hat and coat already on.

"Hey, kid," he greeted me. "We didn't have a meeting, did we?"

"No, I just need to talk to you, but I guess you're on your way home. It can probably wait."

It couldn't. I wasn't exactly on the verge of exploding. Implosion was more probable. If something didn't change soon, I was going to shrivel into a fragile shell of my previous self. I would be the Chrysalis Formerly Known as Charlotte Frost.

"Walk me downstairs," Horton said. "How's filming?"

"That's kind of what I wanted to talk to you about."

Horton didn't say anything. We reached the staircase at the end of the hall, and he held the door open for me.

"It's not going so well," I confessed. "I mean, it's going fine. I think I'll have a movie at the end of all of this and I even think it'll be an OK movie. It's just—" I stopped.

Horton continued to be annoyingly silent. I took a deep breath and finished the sentence. "It's just that maybe Hank is becoming a problem and I'm not sure what to do about it."

"How is he a problem?'

I shrugged. We were almost at the first floor. I regretted opening my mouth in the first place. A saunter down the stairs simply wasn't enough time to process everything I needed to process.

"I don't know that we have enough time to go into it now," I said truthfully.

Horton opened the first floor stairwell door, and we walked the few remaining feet to the front door in silence.

"What are you doing tonight?" he asked.

"I have yoga, but it ends at seven-thirty."

"Let's meet somewhere at eight-thirty. Where do you want to meet?"

"Starbucks?" I asked hopefully. Horton gave me a look. "Oh, OK, how about City Diner on Ninetieth?" That was at least roughly equidistant from our respective apartments.

"Sure." Horton paused. "Chris Martin likes that diner too."

"How's his film going?" I asked politely.

"Very well. I'll see you at eight-thirty"

He walked briskly off, leaving me standing in the middle of the hallway. My advisor was a weird man. There was no doubt about it. I went to check my campus mailbox. There was an announcement from the department office asking us please to conserve energy by removing the graphics screen savers from on-campus computers and substituting a dark screen instead. This would save the university twelve cents in power costs per computer per year. Averaged across the hundred or so computers used by students and faculty in the MFA program, this would come to a grand total of $12 per year. I wondered briefly how much they paid the unfortunate office assistant who had figured this out. For all I knew, the school could have spent more than the projected $12 savings in labor costs already.

I went straight from yoga to the diner. Karen had wanted to do dinner and I told her that if we could fit it in between seven-forty-five and eight-thirty, she was on. She was already there when I walked in, seated in a booth with a stack of journal articles in front of her.

"Do you think they have root beer here? I'm having a massive craving," I said as I sat down.

Karen shrugged. "I don't know what to do about Marisa and Ned," she said.

I opened my menu and didn't respond. It looked like Karen was going to make the most of this forty-five minutes.

"Yup, they've got root beer," I said cheerfully.

"*Charlie.*"

"Why do you need to do anything about it?"

"This is going to sound terribly, terribly naive—but I don't understand why we can't all just get along. I want Ned to take his job more seriously and Marisa to be happy for me that *I'm* so happy with Ned, even if he is young and not the greatest assistant and everything."

I sighed. "I think she is happy for you. But if there's one thing that I've figured out from this abominable filming, it's that it's very difficult to separate emotion and work. So in the same way that I have trouble distancing my feelings for Hank-the-boyfriend from my feelings for Hank-the-actor, I suspect that Marisa is having trouble separating her feelings for you and Ned as a couple from her interactions with Ned at work."

Karen made a face to indicate grudging acknowledgment.

"Admittedly, I don't know Ned's side of the story, but it doesn't sound as though he's been the uber-assistant lately," I continued. "You know that, Karen."

Karen tilted her head. "He hates it there too."

"Sure. And he's technically allowed to talk about Marisa. It's a free country and she may not be the easiest boss. But, in my opinion, he lost the right to bitch publicly about her when he started dating you. It's just tacky." I paused and delivered the big gun. "And it's not fair for him to repeat things that Marisa has told you privately, and that you've told him, to the entire office, or to use you as an excuse for shoddy work."

"He doesn't do that."

I raised my eyebrows.

"He does?"

"I don't know whether it's a maturity issue. But, yeah, he's done that."

"Could be maturity. This is his first job." Karen stared into space for a second. Then she rolled her eyes dramatically and giggled. "Do you know what Ned said the other day?"

"What?" I asked.

"He wanted to know what year I graduated again and then he said that he didn't notice a huge age difference when we were talking, but wow, that was before he'd even graduated from high school."

I groaned. Even assuming that romantic chemistry is an ambiguous, individualized entity, I honestly didn't see what Karen saw in Ned. "Come on. Let's order dinner."

I hadn't particularly wanted to talk about Marisa and Karen and Ned, but when I saw Horton walk in, I realized that I didn't want to talk about Hank either. I seriously regretted flinging myself onto Horton's doorstep that afternoon and groveling for help. I probably hadn't worked hard enough to smooth things over with Hank. Talking to Marisa and Karen was one thing, but it felt disloyal to discuss him with Horton. It was also, indubitably, a far more serious acknowledgment that something was wrong. As Horton waved to me, I sighed and cut Karen off midsentence.

"Karen, Horton's here."

"Oh. Ok. See you at home." She reached for her wallet, but I brushed her hand away.

"Don't worry about it. Dinner's on me."

"Sure?"

"Yeah." Horton had reached our table by then. "Horton, this is my roommate, Karen. She's just leaving. Karen, Horton."

They exchanged nice-to-meet-yous. Horton slid into the seat Karen had vacated and signaled to the waitress.

"Mint tea, please."

The waitress turned to me. I shook my head. "I think I'm OK." As she walked away, I felt a bizarre desire to call her back and order something just to postpone the conversation. I took a sip of the watery dregs from my root beer and began tracing circles on the Formica table with my finger. Horton let me trace three circles before he said, "Charlie."

"Mmm-hmm," I said, still tracing.

"Tell me about Hank."

"Everything's fine. I overreacted this afternoon."

"Charlie," Horton said again.

I shrugged. "Maybe I don't know everything about making movies and maybe I'm not a great director, but this is my project and I *am* the director and he contradicts me all the time. We're constantly fighting about the way things should be done on set and this is in front of the entire cast and crew."

Horton pursed his lips. "Like what I saw that day?" he asked.

I nodded. "And sometimes worse," I admitted softly.

"Why do you think he's acting like that?'

I traced some circles on the table again. I wondered if I had exceeded the normal limit for nervous mannerisms yet. "Two things come to mind. The first is that I probably *don't* know what I'm doing. He could be right about all of his suggestions. I've worked on movies before and directed projects for classes at school, but this is certainly the first time I've ever been in charge of anything this big. Hank has a lot of on-camera experience and I'm sure it's frustrating for him to see me bumble through this."

Horton pushed his glasses up on his nose and gazed at me blankly.

"I'd like to think that I'm not so vain as to always have to be right," I added. "It's just that even if I am making a slew of egregious errors, I kind of wish Hank understood that that's OK and that this is meant to be a learning experience for me and that maybe someday I'll direct another film and I won't make those same mistakes." I stopped. I felt sort of like a wind-up toy that had inevitably reached the end of its tether and was now on the verge of falling over. What can I say? The Energizer Bunny, I'm not.

The waitress brought Horton his tea. He devoted his full attention to steeping it and adding exactly the right proportion of honey. For lack of anything better to do, I began counting the number of booths in the diner.

"OK, so your first theory is that Hank is frustrated by your errors and doesn't understand the difference between a student film and his other professional endeavors," Horton said at last. "What's your second idea?"

"Well, the first and second theories aren't mutually exclusive," I clarified for him. "The second theory is that I know that Hank is very passionate about *The Doctor's Wife*, which is good. I'm glad that he cares about making it a success." I tilted my hand and said, more quietly, "And I'm glad he respects my writing." There was another pause. "I just think it's hard to have two people so zealously absorbed in the same thing, especially when they have divergent opinions."

Horton drank some tea. "It sounds to me like you've got a lot of insight into what's going on."

What a nauseating reply. "So what do I do about it?" I asked.

"Not much of anything."

What an even more nauseating reply. I needed *help*. "I have to do something. I can't just let things go on like this."

"Look, Charlie, if you're going to work in this business, there's something you need to understand. *The Doctor's Wife* isn't your movie anymore."

I was puzzled. I looked up briefly from my circle tracing. "What do you mean?"

"When you were writing, everything could be the way you wanted because yours was the only mind involved in its creation. The instant you got a cast and crew, it stopped being yours. That's just the way movies work. This is the first thing you've written that's gotten made. But eventually you're going to have to realize that anything you write that gets produced isn't wholly yours. Right now you're battling Hank and his particular take on your screenplay. But someday in the future on another movie, you could just as easily disagree with a producer, a cowriter, another actor, the cinematographer, the set designer, or anyone else involved in the film. That's to say nothing of the critics and the viewers that you might have to deal with following release. You're going to have to learn to divorce the emotions you generate while writing from the final product. It's the nature of the medium of film."

I hated that what he said made sense.

Horton took another swallow of tea. "This is one of the reasons that I felt it would be a bad idea to cast your boyfriend in your movie." He raised his eyebrows and looked at me expectantly. I wondered if he was waiting for me to acknowledge that he'd been right.

"Learning experience, Horton," I said. "Remember?"

He smiled. "How is this affecting the two of you as a couple?" he asked.

I was *not* going to spew about my love life to Horton. I rolled my eyes. "About like you would expect," I said noncommittally.

Horton drank more tea and waited. "Not very well," I added. "I'm having trouble not taking his behavior on set as a personal slight. Plus, I see him so much that I never have time to recover from whatever doozy he's dealt me in filming that day." I paused. "I never really fit into that soap opera world anyway, Horton."

Horton looked at me sympathetically. I wished he wouldn't be so silent. It gave me too much leeway to say something incriminating. "I feel sort of like I'm living in an hourglass and if I can just get through filming, everything will be a lot easier." I said finally.

Horton toasted me with his teacup. "Learning experience, Charlotte," he replied. "Remember?"

It was absolutely impossible that there could be anyone more infuriating than Horton Lear. Honestly.

forty-one

If my mother were a president, she would have been Teddy Roosevelt: forceful, blustering, perhaps speaking softly but carrying the undeniably effective big stick of family guilt. Despite the romantic pit of my life, I had buckled under the onslaught of e-mails and answering machine messages and agreed to organize Sunday brunch with Hank. Hank was more enthusiastic about the whole endeavor than I was. In fact, he actually seemed pleased to meet my family.

"It shows you're not ashamed of me," he said, grinning.

"Shmoopie, of course I'm not ashamed of you," I said. "It's them! Prepare yourself to be assaulted by snoaning and unnecessarily intellectual discourse on anything and everything."

Hank took my hand underneath the table. We were at Vynl, which was my choice of restaurant. I needed seriously comforting and familiar surroundings to endure this. I had postponed ordering a Bloody Mary only because I was afraid that my parents, with their fantastic leaps of anxiety-induced imagination, would assume that Hank was leading me down the path of relentless inebriation.

"Shmoopie?" Hank asked, raising one eyebrow.

"I think it's time we moved into more nauseating epithets," I replied.

"Let's not and say we did."

"If you insist," I said, squeezing his hand.

"Will you imitate a snoan for me again?" he asked. "Just so I can recognize it later."

"Oh, when it happens, you'll know," I said darkly. "Now hush. There they are."

My parents were standing in the tiny entryway of the restaurant. I waved to them. No response. I waved again. They continued to swivel their heads futilely around the small interior of the restaurant.

"Mom," I hissed.

Hank laughed. "Better go get them," he said, tilting his head toward the door.

I rolled my eyes and walked the ten feet over to my befuddled parents.

"Hi," I said and allowed myself to be greeted with all of the fanfare suitable for a return from a trek across the Arctic Circle or solo trip around the world in a hot air balloon.

"Absolutely no parking anywhere," my father grimaced.

"Well, this is quaint," my mother said, sitting down at the mosaic table and picking up her menu, which was kitschily tucked inside an old George Michael album cover.

I performed suitable introductions. My father wheezed slightly and opened his menu. "What's good here, Puffin?"

Hank and I spoke at the same time. I said, "Mushroom sandwich."

Hank said, "Puffin?"

My father said, "That's not really brunch food."

My mother said, "Oh, we've always called Charlie Puffin."

(I wondered briefly about the odds of the earth opening up to swallow me whole. It would be a merciful act, as far as I was concerned. I didn't care that Hank knew that my parents called me Puffin. And my parents are far too disorganized to have any naked baby or mortifying junior high pictures at ready access. I just had a rather ominous feeling about what might come next.)

"A puffin's a bird, right?" Hank asked.

"It's a baby penguin," I replied, eager to be off this particular conversational topic.

"No, it's not," Dad said, closing his menu.

"It's not?"

"No, of course not." He looked unduly perplexed by his daughter's ignorance.

"What is it then?"

"Hank's right. It's a bird. It's black and white, like a penguin, but can live in the Northern Hemisphere."

"Puffins have flat, triangular bills," my mother added.

"Oh," I said and shrugged. "All these years . . ."

My mother sighed. "Oh, Puffin."

Dad closed his menu and smiled broadly. "Eggs Benedict, I think," he said with frustrating placidity.

The man is obsessed with his stomach. Obsessed. Of course, the conversation wasn't particularly enlightening, so he could be forgiven the gastronomic divergence. In fact, given my intense anxiety about this whole affair, it was rather mundane so far.

"How's filming going?" Mom asked.

The internal anxiety sensor spiked again.

"Fine," Hank said. He smiled the trademark Destin grin. Its effect was not lost on my mother, who began a mini swoon within her chair. "Charlie's a marvelous writer."

I thought that by this point I was immune to the Destin charm, but I began my own inevitable mini swoon. Damn him. The waiter appeared, and we ordered.

"Charlie's always been a writer," my mother said.

"And a reader," my father added.

"*Madame Bovary*," Hank said.

My father smiled. "Among other fictional things." He took

a sip of his newly delivered coffee. "Charlotte's big flaw as an intellectual is her inability to appreciate poetry."

"Oh, I *appreciate* poetry," I said defensively. "I just don't read it of my own free will."

"And your interpretations are rather hasty."

Grrr. Why was my darling daddy doing his best to humiliate me?

"I'm willing to admit that you're the poetry scholar, not me," I said amiably.

"Charlie's always been the pop culture aficionado in the family," my mother said. "It used to mystify us, but we've adjusted by now."

Note to my parents: When I am sitting at the table with you, it is not necessary to scrutinize me as you might a rare breed of animal. I am available for consultation on myself.

"It's funny," Hank said, "because she tends to be the ivory tower person on the film set."

"Where you play Charles," my mother said.

Hank nodded.

"What are your thoughts on *Bovary*?" my father asked.

"I think he's a more complex character than either the novel or Charlie's script give him credit for."

My father sniffed. I knew that he had noticed that Hank had ended a sentence in a preposition. Dad ranks Winston Churchill only a hair below Robert Frost, and I have heard the "ending a sentence with a preposition is something up with which I shall not put" quote more times than I care to remember. I slunk a little under the table.

All Dad said now was "Bovary's one of literature's most infamous cuckolds."

Hank tilted his head. "And Emma is an infamous adulteress."

"Yes, but the fact that his wife is an adulteress does not compensate for Charles' rather invidious oblivion," Dad shot back. "Have you read Nabokov's essay on *Madame Bovary*?"

Hank shook his head. "Can't say that I have."

Dad began an incredibly long, dense analysis of Nabokov's analysis of *Madame Bovary*. I kicked Hank under the table. He did not respond. I waited five excruciating minutes and kicked my mother under the table. She raised her eyebrows at me. I tilted my head toward Dad and made an "Oh, please, shut him up!" face at her. She looked away. I could sense the restrained snoans building within her nose.

"And certainly, when it was published, there was tremendous public backlash against the novel," my father continued. "Flaubert had to defend himself against obscenity charges."

Blah blah blah. Hank looked fascinated, but then again, he was an actor. My father added something about how the book was first published in serial form.

"So, really," Dad said, "it was the nineteenth-century equivalent of an exceptionally racy soap opera." He chuckled. "In which case, you'd be the expert, not Charlie."

My father had just plunged a metaphorical dagger into my heart. I stared at him with disgust. Hank chuckled also. If my father were a president, he would have been Woodrow Wilson: brilliant, socially inept, and with an unintentional proclivity for involving his country in treacherous situations.

"That looks like our food," my mother said brightly as the waiter made his way to our table.

I attacked my sandwich with a vengeance. "So Hank, tell us about *your* family," Mom said.

Hank poured a minuscule dollop of dressing on his almost-but-not-strictly macrobiotic salad. Who eats spinach for brunch? Now *that* was quintessential nonbreakfast food as far as I was concerned.

"Well, I grew up in western New Jersey and most of my family, except for my sister, Bridget, still lives there."

"And where is Bridget?"

"Scranton."

My mother nodded politely.

"I actually have five sisters," Hank said. "My mom and step-father live in Trenton; my dad is in a small town close to Cherry Hill."

"What does your father do?"

Way to hit the socioeconomic evaluative questions, Mom. He's blue collar. Hot, but blue collar.

"He's an insurance agent. My mother and stepfather own a house painting business."

My mother sliced off a small piece of her egg white omelet. I hate eggs. Except for the fact that I look exactly like both of my parents, our differing opinions on eggs are enough to make me suspect that I am a changeling. I can barely stand to be at the same table with people who eat eggs, which gets a bit tricky since my parents go through a full dozen every week.

Yuck.

Yuck.

At any rate, at this point in the parental third degree, I was ready to announce every unfortunate quality of Hank's, in-cluding his alleged rampant womanizing and dropping out of college, just to spare us the unfortunate act of my parents extracting it from him with agonizingly diplomatic patience. But that would have been a little too much like the scene in *Jailhouse Rock* when the debutante perkily announces to her parents at dinner that Elvis's character has "just returned from a stint in the penitentiary." Not that dropping out of Southern New Jersey State has the equivalent social stigma as jailtime.

(Except that these are my parents we're talking about, so an exception might be made if the jailtime had been earned during 1960s antiwar protests.)

"Mom, did I tell you that I ran into Jennifer Lambert the other day?" I said, changing the topic. Jennifer Lambert grew up in my neighborhood. In fact, we have exactly the same birthday. I have been known to refer to her as the anti-

Charlotte. She is polite and poised and has never, not once, forgotten to send a thank-you note. She even sent a thank-you note when, at the age of eight, I gave her a biography of Sacajawea at some Christmas gift swap where we drew names out of a hat to see who received our presents. In other words, I was assigned to give her a present, I gave her something so geeky that she probably hated it, we were children, and she still sent a thank-you note.

Needless to say, my mother thinks Jennifer Lambert is the greatest thing to grace the planet.

"How is she?" Mom asked.

"Fine." Did I mention that Jennifer is a stockbroker who took time off from her job to go on a humanitarian mission to Liberia? In my opinion, it has to be a pretty awful job if Liberia looks like a better option, but the fact remains that Jennifer has probably stashed the same six-figure amount that I now owe in student loans in an interest-earning money market account. "I think she really enjoyed Liberia."

"What a courageous thing to do."

Yak.

"I still say she has no personality," I said.

"She's shy, Charlie."

"So was Emily Dickinson," my father said.

"Bert," said Mom.

"Emily Dickinson had a detached retina," I added.

"Charlie."

"And she was practically a hermit," I continued.

"And I don't believe Jennifer Lambert has ever displayed a facility with either iambic tetrameter *or* iambic trimeter," Dad said.

The inevitable happened. Mom snoaned. I gleefully kicked Hank under the table. Dad laughed.

It was just another Sunday brunch with the Frost family.

forty-two

After brunch, I kissed my parents and Hank goodbye and took the subway up to school, where I proceeded to commit what indisputably felt like cinematic adultery with Chris Martin. We spent a full three hours huddled alone in a dark editing studio at school reviewing the dailies from *The Doctor's Wife* (which Hank had never seen). After two hours dissecting everything from Sabrina's penchant for lip-trembling to Walsh's need to lower his voice to better placement for camera B, I felt like I might live to see the none-too-tender age of twenty-eight without a possible career change.

"Honestly, Charlie, I think what you need more than anything is confidence," Chris said as he reached for his backpack. "This is going to be a good movie."

"You think?"

"I know."

I felt like a stray puppy who has just been patted on the head by a benevolent passerby. I gazed happily up at Chris. "What do I do about Hank?"

Chris paused for a second. "What do you mean?"

"The way he acts on set. The way he acts off set."

"On set, you should probably do nothing. He's not going to change and you're almost done filming. Just do your best to bite your tongue and slide through it without any major skirmishes. Do it for your own sake, and the sake of your cast and your movie."

"OK." That was the same advice everyone else seemed to be giving me. I was going to have to get in touch with my inner muzzle.

"Off set," Chris continued, "I don't know. That's something you're going to have to figure out for yourself." He paused. "Are you in love with him, Charlie?"

"Of course," I replied automatically, then paused and thought about the question. "But I think I'm holding myself back. I think I could love him even more and be sort of frighteningly enthralled by him, except he makes it really hard to love him when he acts this way."

I put the film back in its case.

Chris smiled. "Charlie, if you want Hank, that's OK. But maybe you want something—or someone—else. You'll eventually work out what's right."

I didn't say anything. I wanted Chris to go back to telling me about how great *The Doctor's Wife* was.

"Hey, if you want to talk more, I'm bartending at Mona's on Thirteenth tonight. It's Sunday, so it'll be totally quiet. I'll buy you a drink."

"I think I've taken up enough of your day. But thanks."

"The offer's always open, Charlie."

"OK."

Chris was a nice guy. A really nice guy, in fact. But maybe it was time to stop running to people with my problems and solve them myself. I put on my coat, locked the studio, and took the subway back downtown to Harmony, where I put in two hours teaching a special advanced workshop on arm balances. Later that afternoon, I was lying in a bubble bath, soaking my stiffened biceps and reading the *Times* magazine section, when the phone began ringing.

"I am not answering that," I said aloud to the lavender-scented froth that covered me. The home phone stopped

ringing. Much more faintly, I could hear my cell phone starting to ring.

"Not getting that either," I said, turning to the recipe section. Five minutes passed in blissful silence. The home phone
started ringing again.

"OK, OK," I said aloud, reaching for a towel. There had
better be some form of urgent catastrophe that needed my
attention. Trailing bubbles, I ran into the living room and
picked up the receiver just as the answering machine began
recording.

"Puffin!" my father boomed in greeting.

I silently and instantly vowed to get caller ID first thing
Monday morning.

"Hi, Dad."

"Your mother and I just wanted to tell you that we liked
Hank."

"He's *very* handsome," Mom added. Apparently this call
merited multiple extensions.

"Thanks," I muttered aloud.

"And very polite," Mom said.

"Yup."

"So when will we see you again?"

When I finish my thesis, I thought. Aloud, I said, "Soon. We
start filming in Connecticut on Tuesday and that'll be time-
consuming. But soon. I promise."

"Do you think Hank enjoyed brunch?" Dad asked.

Personally, I thought Hank had probably left brunch,
walked into the next bar, picked up a compliant blond with
breasts the size of my head, and downed two Jack Daniels in
rapid succession.

"I think so."

"Oh, good. We didn't do anything to embarrass you, did
we?" Dad asked.

"Nothing. Of course. But can I call you back? You caught
me at a bad time."

This was mystifying. I spend months worrying that Hank isn't highbrow enough for my parents and/or that my parents are too obnoxiously academic for Hank. It turns out that what I *really* needed to worry about was how desperate my parents were for me to have a boyfriend.

After hanging up I put on clean sweats and flopped on the couch. The phone immediately started ringing. It better not be my parents again.

"Hello?"

"Hey there, Charlie-doll."

"If it isn't the talented Mr. Destin," I said. I was having yet another tiny swoon at the sound of his miraculous voice. It's a shame our phone was cordless; otherwise, I could have started twirling the cord around my fingers in lovestruck adolescent fashion.

"I liked your parents."

"Apparently the feeling is mutual."

"I wasn't too brainless for them?"

"Well, they didn't say so." I tend never to introduce people I date to my parents for exactly this reason. My assumption has been that it fosters scads of insecurities in all parties. Maybe I needed to reexamine the possibility that *my* anxiety about the whole process dwarfed everyone else's. I wondered what Karen would have to say about this.

"What's up for tonight?" Hank asked, distracting me from ruminating.

"I'm meeting a guy from my program for drinks at the place where he bartends."

Holy shit! I *did* not mean to say that. *Where had that come from?????* Apparently, I had lost total control of my tongue. Grand. I made an attempt at recovery. "You can come with me, though. Maybe we could go to dinner first?"

"OK. You're sure I wouldn't be intruding?"

"Please," I said dismissively. Since Chris didn't even know that I was coming, let alone accompanied by my recalcitrant paramour, Hank could hardly encroach on our nonexistent plans. I thought for a second. Mona's is only a few blocks from Vincenzo's parents' restaurant. Hank's voice perked up when I suggested meeting there.

"Oh, that'd be great. You sure you don't mind going there again? Because I have some signed photos that I promised to drop off for friends of theirs."

It's rare that people ask me if I mind going to a charming and pricey Italian restaurant, where the owner is bound to comp us glasses of various divine liqueurs with dessert.

"Not at all." I checked my watch. It was six. "Can you give me a little time though? I'm not disheveled at the moment— but I'm hardly sheveled either."

Hank laughed. As I went to forage through my dwindling supply of clean clothes, I heard the sound of his laugh over and over again in my head. We would make it through whatever hump we were in at the moment. I just knew.

Three hours later, Hank and I wandered into Mona's. I'd never been there before and, on Sunday night, it was dark and essentially deserted. Chris was behind the bar, drinking something that looked like either Scotch or whiskey and reading a Kingsley Amis novel. The bar was an L-shape, and Hank and I settled ourselves on stools at the short end of the L.

"Are you allowed to drink on the job?" I called.

Chris looked up. "Hey, Charlie!" he said, with what sounded like surprisingly authentic enthusiasm. "I'm a bartender, not a cop," he added, walking down to our end of the bar. He looked utterly unperturbed by my arrival with the actor/boyfriend about whom I'd been whimpering night and day since the start of filming.

"We just had dinner around the corner," I said in explanation. "This is Hank."

Hank and Chris shook hands. "It's nice to meet you finally," Chris said. "I've heard a lot about you."

Hank raised one eyebrow at me but didn't say anything.

"Let me get you guys a drink," Chris offered.

Hank asked for a martini. I told Chris to surprise me. He pulled glasses out from underneath the bar and set to work. I patted Hank's leg.

"Did I tell you that I spent twenty minutes the other day practicing raising one eyebrow in front of the mirror?"

Hank gave me a strange look. Then he raised one eyebrow again. "Like this?"

"Mmm-hmm. It's not particularly easy."

Hank alternated raising his right, then his left, eyebrows in rapid succession. Show-off. Chris set our drinks down in front of us. Mine was pale yellow. Without a word, Hank reached into his martini and handed me the olive. I beamed at him. This small intimacy did not go unnoticed by Chris, who began toying with his bookmark.

"So what have I got here?" I asked, picking up my glass and twirling it by the stem.

Chris gave me a wry smile. "You did say to surprise you. This is a banana-tini and we are phasing it out of our bartending repertoire here at Mona's. So if you like it, you can take some banana vodka home with you because we have many, many bottles that are going to remain unused. It did not prove to be the most popular choice."

I normally adore neologisms but banana-tini was a bit much even for me.

"Orange you glad I didn't say banana?" I asked aloud. Hank and Chris both gave me strange looks. I decided not to go into the knock-knock argument.

"Chris is working on his MFA thesis as well," I told Hank. "He starts filming—when—two weeks?" Chris nodded.

"What's your project about?' Hank asked. Had he always

ended so many sentences in prepositions or was today simply End Sentences in Prepositions Day? (Hallmark comes out with so many new holidays that it's hard to keep track of them.) Chris began telling us about his screenplay. I watched Hank warm to the Hitchcockian scenario and eccentric, almost-retro characters.

"So let me get this straight," he said to Chris. "You know that Melanie and Arthur were married before, but you don't know that Melanie and George were married?"

"Right."

"That's so interesting," Hank said thoughtfully. "So who's starring in yours?"

Chris made a rueful face. "Well, not being as lucky as Charlie to get a headliner, I've got the usual odd assortment of students and unemployed actors. They'll be more than adequate, but I wouldn't have minded something a bit spicier."

Hank took a sip of his martini. "Is your casting set in stone? Because I'm sure I could hook you up with a few names. No one tremendously famous, obviously, but maybe someone with experience in named productions."

"Oh, man, that would have been great!" Chris said. "But yeah, we've already started rehearsals and they're going well enough. Am I allowed to raincheck that offer for my next film?" He rolled his eyes. "Assuming there *is* a next movie."

"Raincheck absolutely. I'll give you my agent's name and you can always get in touch with me through him."

Through his agent? What about through *me*?

"What are you guys planning for after graduation anyway?" Hank continued. As soon as we heard the dreaded question, Chris and I both devoted our attention to scrutinizing the bar.

"It sort of depends on the reception of our movies and what offers come out of that," I said eventually. "Ideally, we'll both have our own agents by graduation. The school advertises pretty heavily for the end-of-the-year screenings, so there's usually a good crowd of scouts. We'll also submit to the festivals, and Horton will probably hook us up with some connections." I took a sip of my banana-tini, which was sort of sweet but not totally unpalatable. "After that, we'll see. I don't think either of us can afford to go directly to the indie filmmaker route, so we'll probably put in time on rewrite gigs while we polish off our next masterpieces." I looked at Chris. "Does that sound right?"

"Dismally so," he agreed.

Hank looked at me. "I didn't know you were looking for an agent, Charlie. Why didn't you tell me?"

A. Because I thought it was understood that any aspiring and unrepresented screenwriter would need one.
B. Because the idea of having my boyfriend, rather than my ability (or at the very least my mentor) find me an agent was curdling.
C. Because I want the sort of agent who will secure posh and intelligent gigs for me and I wasn't entirely convinced your contacts might find that for me.

Aloud, I murmured, "Don't know."

Hank gave me a pained look. "I wish you would talk to me more about your work, doll."

I could feel Chris's eyes heavy and lingering on us. I wished that I hadn't been quite so petulant about Hank recently, now that he appeared to be having a complete about-face and was giving an Oscar-caliber performance of the Sensitive Man. I picked up my banana-tini and contemplated downing it in a single gulp, but set it back down without even a sip.

"At any rate," Chris intervened in a loud voice, "the goal is not to be a bartender forever."

"I bartended when I first moved to the city," Hank said. "At a little place on Avenue B that doesn't exist anymore. It was a total dive. No olives for the martinis and nothing resembling a banana-tini."

Chris and Hank began to swap bartending stories. I remembered Marisa saying that socially overadept people drive her up the wall. Hank had managed to charm all of my friends and family so thoroughly that they all probably thought I was orchestrating a mountain-molehill situation out of filming. Plus I was exhausted from the events of the day. As Chris and Hank continued their Battle of the Anecdotes, I put my head on the bar and fell asleep.

When Hank jostled me awake, it was almost midnight.

"Hey, doll," he said. "C'mon, we better get you to bed."

I nodded sleepily and reached for my coat. It was so ungodly cold outside that it seemed inconceivable that the vernal equinox was only a week or so away.

"Here, Charlie," Chris said, handing me two large bottles. "Take some vodka home with you. Mona's just going to throw it away because it's taking up so much room."

"Thanks," I said, yawning. I tucked the vodka inside my bag.

It took Hank almost twenty-five minutes to hail a taxi. Ten minutes into the ordeal, the strap on my bag broke and the bag fell to the street, smashing both bottles of vodka in the process. My life was suddenly one enormous banana-tini.

I knelt down and stared at the puddles of vodka drenching my books and clothes and sighed. Still crouched on the ground, I looked up at Hank and announced in a completely deadpan voice, "I think I'm cursed."

forty-three

It is very difficult to justify to the man in the cell phone store precisely why your still-under-warranty Nokia might have somehow mysteriously stopped working. I was so insistent in my denial of any strange, fruity odor that the poor guy was no doubt convinced he was having an olfactory hallucination. Normally I am a stickler for honesty—or at the very least scrupulous avoidance—but I was afraid that he would refuse to replace my phone if he learned that I had (unintentionally of course) drowned its sensitive technological parts in vodka.

Such is my life.

When I called Hank to inform him of my reinstated cell service, he was in a bar. He did not say he was in a bar. As I envisioned it, the conversation went more like this:

SCENE: CHARLIE is walking up Broadway in
the West Seventies talking on her phone.
Camera pans her from a distance as she
walks. It is twilight.

                    CHARLIE:
Baby, I can't hear you at all.

*Screen splits to show HANK in crowded bar
with MADDIE on one side and an unknown,
BEAUTIFUL WOMAN on the other.*

                    HANK:
Sorry.

                    CHARLIE:
Are you in a bar?

                    HANK:
No.

*CHARLIE does not say anything. She stops at
Fairway and contemplates the outdoor
produce. On the other half of the screen,
the BEAUTIFUL WOMAN takes HANK's olive from
his martini and feeds it to him.*

                    HANK:
Well, OK, Maddie and I stopped off to get a
drink. But we're about to leave.

*CHARLIE examines an apple absently as she
waits for HANK to continue.*

                    HANK:
Maybe I'll call you later?

CHARLIE commences walking again.

                    CHARLIE:
Or I could come meet you? I sort of feel
like going out.

HANK:
Don't bother, doll. I'll be out of here
soon. We can talk later.

CHARLIE:
OK, whatever.

She runs a hand through her hair.

*In bar, HANK runs a hand through the
BEAUTIFUL STRANGER's hair.*

*They hang up their cell phones. HANK'S scene
expands to fill the entire screen.*

HANK:
Another drink?

*He strokes the BEAUTIFUL WOMAN on the small
of her back. She nods.*

MADDIE:
Is Charlie on her way out the door?

*Neither HANK nor the BEAUTIFUL STRANGER
changes expressions.*

HANK:
We're having a drink, Mad. Why don't you
just enjoy it?

*MADDIE picks up her own drink and tosses it
back like a seasoned barhopper.*

MADDIE:
I enjoyed it very much, Hanky. Now you can
get me a refill that I'll enjoy even more.

Perhaps this imagined version was unnecessarily fertile, but I'm willing to bet that it wasn't totally implausible. I hadn't seen Hank for a couple of days when he showed up for filming Wednesday at Horton's friends' home in Connecticut. This could have been the vicissitudes of scheduling. But I had a hunch that his ambiguous timetable was rather intentionally that way. I only hoped this was because he was working on not aggravating me as carefully as I attempted not to aggravate him.

(Despite what various gossip columnists and *Troubled Passion* coworkers claimed, I had never actually seen Hank womanize with anyone other than me. I kept repeating this to myself. I had to have more faith in him. Frankly, I had a horrible suspicion that if we were to play those trust games that are played at camps and retreats and corporate workshops, I would fail miserably. I would probably injure myself permanently rather than close my eyes and fall tranquilly and unthinkingly into his expectant arms.)

At any rate, we had to finish filming, and I was going to have to postpone any painstaking analysis of my relationship until then. We were shooting exclusively outdoor scenes in Connecticut. Poor Sabrina was going to freeze in the thin pink coat that Sarah Wong had found for her at a vintage store on the Lower East Side. It would be just my luck to give my leading lady hypothermia or to spoil the illusion of springtime romance via her chattering, blue lips. Truth be told, Horton's friends' house wasn't any more 1950s suburbia than my grandmother's. I *could* have filmed in Great Neck without any great sacrifice of ambiance. But I was just as happy directing in an environment where nobody was going to refer to me as Puffin or ruin takes by loudly offering my cast and crew lemonade and cookies.

(Incidentally, Horton's friends had a large container of rat poison on their front porch. This disturbed me to no end. As I told Hank, presumably they had the poison because there were rats and not because it was a decorative object that added any sort of visual charm. Hank told me that there were rats all over New York and, in fact, he had once seen a rat on the same block as my apartment. I responded that I was well aware of the city rat population; I just felt that the suburbs should have advantages aside from good public schools and it would be nice if a lack of rodent residents was one of those advantages.

I have to ask: was this still love?)

At any rate, filming went smoothly up until lunch. Minna and Joe, Horton's friends, had offered us reign of the inside as well as the outside of their house. Given the size of the cast and crew, the abundance of rat poison, and the fact that we were impinging on them enough already, I said we'd drive into town. We piled into cars and met up at a bagel place in a strip mall.

It happened while I was halfway through my toasted sesame with cheddar cheese. Jody, the cinematographer, mentioned that he had seen a blurb about us at the Soap Opera Awards in some magazine.

"It said you guys were headed for eternal bliss."

I smiled in what I thought was a modest and noncommittal way.

Hank said, "Oh, those papers don't know what they're talking about anyway. They overexaggerate any relationship, no matter how insignificant."

It was probably my imagination, but it seemed like there was an awkward pall that fell over the table. Sabrina, dipshit that she is, said what we were all thinking.

"Oh, but you and Charlie aren't insignificant."

I repeat: she said this *aloud*. Most of the cast and crew within earshot either looked away in embarrassment or studied Hank and me with salacious glee. I waited for Hank to clarify whatever it was he felt like clarifying. Instead, he just took a sip from his bottle of water, thereby allowing the awkward pall to intensify to an almost unbearable degree. At last, Walsh stepped into his increasingly typical role as my savior and announced brusquely, "Charlie, isn't it about time we headed back to the house? If we want to beat rush hour traffic back to the city, we're going to need to power through some scenes."

I nodded mutely.

We gathered our trash together and headed for the door. Hank didn't ride in my car on the way back.

forty-four

That night found me predictably flopped on Karen's bed and freaking out.

"I don't get it," I said. "Why would he say something like that? Does he believe that? Because presumably he must have meant it if he said it. Not that people always mean everything they say, but he had the opportunity to clarify if he wanted and he didn't, so I can only assume he believes we're insignificant." I paused for air. "That's a reasonable assumption, isn't it?"

Karen shrugged.

"Isn't it?" I repeated.

She shrugged again.

"He thinks we're insignificant, doesn't he?"

Karen reached out and rubbed my shoulders gently. "Charlie, why are you having this conversation with me and not with Hank?"

"Because I need your help!"

"How am I going to help?"

Good question.

"Because you'll help me understand everything so that when I talk to Hank, I'll be in better control of my emotions. You're my hysteria filter," I said firmly.

"I'm here if you need a sounding board or if you want to practice what you're going to say to Hank. But I think you understand the situation more than you're willing to admit. You don't need anything clarified or elucidated or explained. Hank said something. Whether or not he meant it, it hurt your feelings, worried you, and embarrassed you in front of the cast. End of story."

"Karen," I wailed.

"What?"

"I love Hank. I don't want to be insignificant."

Karen rubbed my shoulders again. "Why don't you just go call Hank?"

"Are you sick of listening to me?" I said.

"Not yet. But give me time." She smiled.

"How's Ned?"

"Actually, our relationship is a bit catastrophic at the moment. But thanks for asking."

"Really?"

"Yeah."

"Oh my God, Karen, I had no idea. Do you want to talk about it?"

"Believe it or not, Charlie, I'd like to put the relationship drama on the back burner right now and concentrate my energies elsewhere."

"OK," I stood up. "Is it the age thing with Ned, Karen?"

"I don't know. Let me get back to you on that one."

"Sure you don't want to talk about it?"

"Not right now. Maybe later. Go call Hank."

"I don't want to talk to him about this."

Karen laughed. "Charlie, listen to us! We sound like the two most uncommunicative, emotionally stunted people on the planet."

"You're the psychologist." This is my standard reply to almost anything Karen says.

Karen pulled her hair back into a ponytail. "I guess. But does that make me a hypocrite or a disgrace to my future profession?"

"Neither. Because we never established that we are, in fact, emotionally stunted and I, for one, am not yet willing to accept that. I think all we need is a vacation in a fabulous tropical paradise or, barring that, a prolonged visit to a spa."

Karen wrinkled her nose. "Or maybe just a less anemic bank balance or less intensive graduate program or less confusing state of romantic affairs."

"You don't ask for much, Karen." I suddenly was in a better mood. I hopped off the bed and did a back bend. Karen stared at me.

"I haven't done that since I was eight," she said.

"How very uncentered of you," I said, pulling upright a bit too hastily. "This is a standing wheel pose."

"So did gymnastics steal that from yoga?"

"No idea," I said. "OK, I'm going out for a while."

"Are you going to Hank's?"

"Just for a walk. Maybe to Starbucks, to see if they have the winter hot cider special. Is it still winter?"

"Not technically, but it is damn cold out there." She stretched out into the space on her bed I'd just vacated. "If you get cider, you can bring me some back."

"OK."

It was cold outside. I stood on the corner of Ninety-ninth and Broadway for a vacant moment, trying to decide which direction to go. There were many more exciting things if I went left—City Diner, Zabar's, Marisa's apartment, Barnes & Noble. But, for some reason, I turned uptown, toward Columbia. I used my key to let myself into one of the editing studios and sat there quietly for a while. It was a strange place to be and a strange thing for me to do. My typical crisis MO is either to wail noisily to all my friends or to pull on my oldest, softest sweats and curl up in bed reading sweet children's books, where no one ever has to worry about master's theses or fretful, possibly philandering boyfriends. But it felt good to sit there alone, staring at the various equipment, most of which I had only the haziest idea of how to operate, and not think about anything.

It's rare that I can turn off my over-ruminating brain so thoroughly.

I'd been there for maybe an hour when I heard a key in the lock. I'd realized I'd forgotten to change the sign on the door from "vacant" to "in use." Crud. I was going to have to face humanity, probably in the unwelcome form of Miguel Reynard-Arora, gloating about the phenomenal ease with which he was filming his thesis. I reached out and flicked on one of the televisions so as to disguise the fact that I was sitting here doing nothing.

Chris Martin and Dr. Phil entered the studio at the exact same moment. I turned off the TV in horror.

"Hi! I'm just finishing up," I said.

"How's that talk show addiction coming along, Charlie?"

I smiled ruefully. "I just turned that on when I heard your key in the lock. I actually wasn't doing anything in here. Just sitting and thinking."

"Feel up for a coffee?" Chris asked. "I'm in a procrastinating mood."

"Yeah."

We wandered over to the Hungarian Pastry Shop in companionable silence. Once we were seated, me with herbal tea and Chris with espresso, he said, "So what's up, Charlie?"

"Not so much." I looked at his drink. "I don't see how you can drink that stuff at night. Doesn't it keep you up?"

Chris shook his head. "I drink so much caffeine it really doesn't matter anymore."

"Probably for me too," I said, "but I can't afford the knowledge that maybe the coffee that isn't keeping me awake at night isn't keeping me awake in the morning either." I frowned. "Did that make sense? Was that sentence even English?"

Chris rolled his eyes. "I liked Hank," was all he said.

"You and two million daytime television viewers," I replied. I drank some of my tea. "Honestly, I can't wait till filming is over. Only a few more days."

"Why?"

I shrugged. "Chris, I'm sort of falling apart. Hank continues to do whatever the hell he pleases on set; he referred to me as insignificant in front of the cast; Horton is no help; I strongly suspect that my friends are sick of my whining and, by the way, I haven't had time to teach yoga lately, so I have exactly $79 in my checking account."

"Guess coffee's on me," Chris said. I smiled.

"I'm just tired of feeling overwhelmed," I finished.

"Would stopping filming make you feel less overwhelmed?"

"I hope so. It has to."

Chris looked genuinely concerned, but didn't say anything. I began counting. There were eleven sugars, five Sweet'n Lows, seven Equals, and three Splendas in the holder on the table.

"I wish Horton were more helpful," I said. "He thinks this is a good learning experience for me and that I made my bed and I should lie in it. No pun intended."

Chris made a face. "Horton alternates between being a teddy bear and a hard-ass and has no idea how infuriating that can be."

I couldn't have put it better myself. It was such an incredible relief to talk to someone who understood exactly what I was going through, in a way that only another film student could.

"I just need, like, real advice. You know?" I said. What had just come out of my mouth? I was either losing all facility with the English language (probably an early warning sign of a progressive neurodegenerative disorder) or else had been demonically possessed by vocabulary-sucking Valley Girls. I drank some tea and attempted to be as articulate as my twenty years of education would suggest. "Caustic votes of confidence in my ability to handle any and all situations, regardless of potential catastrophic consequences, are not particularly heartening." There. Much better. Good to know I could always return to my usual pretentious self at will.

Chris drank some more coffee. "Is it really advice you need or is it empathy?"

"Probably empathy," I admitted. "Or sympathy, if we want to play semantic games."

Chris smiled. "Well, you have both from me. Really. I think you're in a tough bind. My hunch is that you will look back on filming as an important experience, but it doesn't make living through it any easier." There was a pause. "I'm going to have another coffee. Do you want more tea?"

I nodded. Chris went back up to the counter and returned with our drinks and a plate of gingerbread heaped with whipped cream and sprinkled with cinnamon. I began to feel better just looking at it.

"I'm not being too self-pitying, am I?" I asked. I was, after all, being plied with tea and gingerbread. Not to get into starving children (or starving Bohemians), residents of war-torn countries, tragic amputees, cancer victims, etc., but I know I have less right to wallow than many people.

Chris raised one eyebrow, like Hank. Could everyone besides me do that? Or was it some sex-linked trait that could only appear in males? Maybe I was just facially untalented. I've never been able to roll my tongue either.

"Does it matter?" he asked.

"I don't want to be *obnoxious*."

Chris smiled. "Hardly," he said. "You're charming even when you're obnoxious."

There was an unsteady pause. Chris and I may compliment each other on writing, (or ideas, or school work, or—very occasionally—certain directorial decisions) but we have never branched into personal compliments. This sounded like a prequel to flirting. I occupied the pause by nibbling some gingerbread.

"Have you ever made a gingerbread house?" I asked.

Chris shook his head.

"My friend Marisa and I tried to make one with her niece once. It was sort of a disaster. We couldn't get it to stick together at all. All the walls were tilted and collapsing."

There was another pause.

"What are you doing for your wrap party?" he asked.

"It's going to be at Hank's on Sunday. Want to come?" I asked. "Horton'll be there."

"Sure," Chris said. "Thanks. I'll bartend if you want."

"You don't have to be a servant," I said dryly. "You can just be a guest."

Chris gave me a look that was sort of the visual equivalent of a snoan. "I just thought it might be fun for you to have an open bar set up."

"It would," I agreed. "Why don't you bartend for part of the night and just hang out for the rest of it?" I frowned. "Absolutely no banana martinis, though."

"It was never suggested that you soak your belongings in vodka," Chris replied.

I reached for my hat and put it on. "I better get home," I said.

"I like that hat," Chris said.

"Thanks. Hank got it for me."

Before he would let me walk home, Chris made me promise to get in touch if I had any more bouts of filming-related despair. As I walked down Amsterdam (which, in the early Hundreds, is not the most comforting part of town), I called Hank from my new, unbanana-ed cell phone. Maybe I would go out to Brooklyn tonight and attempt to mend the tenuous, possibly breaking bridges between us.

His cell phone was turned off. I didn't leave a message.

forty-five

The next day felt like Family Weekend. Horton, Mallory, and Karen all descended on the house in Connecticut, claiming to have just realized that filming was almost over and they wanted to come before it ended. It was still appallingly cold outside. After an hour, Mallory and Karen took refuge inside. At one point, Karen knocked on the window. When I looked over, she was grinning with her nose pushed against the glass. Goofball. I blew her a dramatic Marlene-Dietrich-greeting-her-public kiss. It was too far away to tell, but I had a sneaky suspicion that they were all drinking coffee in front of a fire.

Horton, however, was in for the long haul. He stalked back and forth behind the mike, breathing heavy white gasps of air into the cold. I hoped the sound tech knew what he was doing; with my luck, Horton's panting would obliterate the actors' dialogue.

In truth, it was not the optimal day for observers. The scenes we were filming were tricky; I had never been convinced that I had nailed this particular conversation between Charles and Emma as precisely as I could. Plus, Hank and Sabrina were awfully cuddly together. At one point in my stage directions, when I asked Hank to turn his head toward the camera, Sabrina giggled vapidly.

"But then he can't look at me," she squeaked in a little, flirty mouse voice.

Just as well, sweetheart. Your nose is running.

"I'm sure you'll survive," I said in my own flirty voice, which came out sounding more emphysematic than coy and girlish. It must have been the cold weather.

Hank adjusted the homburg and cashmere scarf that Sarah Wong had secured for him. I happened to know that he hated the costumes for the outdoor scenes. His exact comment had been "Who am I? J. Edgar Hoover?"

"I think we're ready to shoot," he said, grinning. I wondered if it was possible that he was part-human, part-Cheshire cat.

"Hold your horses, shmoopie," I said. I gave him and Sabrina a few more directions and retreated behind the cameras. Our eager undergraduate boom boy jumped out.

"And action!" he called. After almost a month of filming, he was sounding like a pro.

I thought the scene was going well, but behind me I heard Horton's frenetic stalking. I stood up and looked at him, raising my mittened palms upward in a "What?" gesture. Horton shook his head. I beckoned to him, and we slunk to the side of the house. I could feel the grimy slush that covered the ground beginning to soak through my hiking boots.

"There's too much passion between those two," he said.

"That's OK," I said. "This is the beginning of their marriage. Emma's not discontent yet."

"She should be, Charlie," Horton said. "Look at that," he said, motioning to where Sabrina and Hank were kissing. "She's practically sucking out his tonsils."

I giggled.

"You think it should be more restrained?"

"Isn't that how you wrote it?" Horton asked, handing me a battered copy of the script. I flipped to the scene we were shooting. *EMMA reluctantly submits to his kiss*, I had written.

"Yeah, OK, you're right. I kind of like the electricity between them though."

"Is this the first time you've seen them like this?"

I thought for a second. This was an awfully distracting conversation to have during filming. "Don't know. I mean, most of the scenes we've filmed have been when Emma really resents Charles." A horrible thought occurred to me. I stood there, shifting my weight uneasily back and forth, wondering if I had the courage to voice it aloud. "Horton, do you think this isn't *acting*? Do you think they're, you know?"

"What?"

"Lusting for each other?" I said quietly.

"Just make sure they know that that's not how the script is written." Horton sighed, blowing out another white puff of air in the process.

Shit.

We walked back closer to the set. I was not prepared to deal with this. The take ended with Hank and Sabrina breaking reluctantly from their marathon liplock and gazing moonily at each other. I felt jellyish, the way I did as a kid after taking an inadvertently large puff of my asthma inhaler.

"OK, guys, that was really nice in a lot of ways." I outlined some of the scene's more successful moments. "But—" here I smiled what I hoped was good-natured smile—"let's tone it down some. This is the scene that, for the viewer, should solidify how trapped Emma feels. If she's visibly enjoying the physical contact, it makes it that much more difficult to understand her perspective."

I hoped I didn't sound like a possessive and jealous girlfriend. At this point, I felt more resignation than anything.

Hank gazed at me mildly. "Couldn't this be yet another way that Emma's confused about Charles? Maybe he excites her physically, but not emotionally."

Allow me to mention that each time Hank challenges me, I begin to find myself allying myself more and more with the

Soap Opera Weekly reporter who described him as an "unreasonably spoiled (even for this biz) yet flawlessly conditioned Thoroughbred."

(Hank counters that this same reporter once stiffed him with a $320 bar tab for twelve at Pastis and when he tried to collect—"off the guy's *expense account*, mind you, Charlie"— there was a bit of a run-in and that all the little jabs since then have been part of an ongoing rivalry. Yeah. And you should have seen the one that got away.)

I smiled as sweetly as possible and thrust the script at him. "Let's play it as it's written."

Sabrina giggled a giggle that sent absolute chills down my spine. "Hmmm. Pretending I'm not attracted to Hank. I guess that's why it's called acting."

I gave her a look that has withered the spirits of bimbos more hardy than she.

"We're going to try it again, with a heck of a lot more sexual ambivalence." I sounded fierce, even to my own ears. Hank and Sabrina started laughing. I joined them. I can only maintain the hard-ass act for so long.

Late that afternoon, Hank, Karen, and I drove back to the city together. I had survived—just barely—another day of filming.

"I don't think Horton likes me," Hank said suddenly from the backseat.

Why would he? I thought. *He's my advisor and you're messing up my thesis.*

"Why do you think that, baby?" I asked aloud.

"He's sort of curt." Hank paused. "Almost rude, even."

"That's not you, it's him. It's just the way he is. He's rude to me at least once a week." It was the truth.

"Yeah, but he's rude to you because it's a pattern the two of you have established."

"I guess so."

"Is he working on anything now?" Hank asked.

"Horton? He's more retired than half of Florida."

"He just seems like someone who's itching to sink his teeth into a project."

"Half of Florida," I repeated, staring out the window at the New York State Thruway. It was five-thirty and traffic was crawling.

The Four Tops came on the radio. "Oh, I love this song," I said, turning up the volume. I suddenly felt in a significantly better mood. I reached for the bag of Craisins I'd been snacking on and poured out a handful.

"Anyone mind if I sing?" I asked.

"Yes," Karen said.

"Yes," Hank said.

"What a lady, what a night!" I wailed at the top of my lungs anyway.

Karen pelted me with a Craisin.

"Oh, come on," I said. "This is a great song, Karen. It's almost—but not quite—as good as 'Unchained Melody.'"

I could feel Hank staring at me in disbelief. "Charlie, you belong in the Dork Museum."

I stopped being in a good mood. He meant it as a joke. I *know* he meant it as a joke. But I had sort of overdosed on Hank Destin at the moment.

"That's not funny," I said.

"Kind of is," Hank said.

"So I'm a dork? What's wrong with that? This isn't eighth grade. I'm happy the way I am, Hank, but if you want to dump me for the cheerleader, go right ahead."

"Don't get touchy."

"Of course I'm touchy!" I said, my voice much louder than intended. "You are doing your best to fuck up my thesis and I'm doing a pretty saintly job of both catering to your every ludicrous whim and ignoring your offensive flirtations with anything that walks."

"Are you talking about Sabrina? Because she's nothing, doll. I just flirt with her to get a better take."

"I think you can leave the stage instruction to me," I said frostily.

"Oh, would you get off your power trip and acknowledge you don't know what the hell you're doing?"

"Excuse me? I, at least, have some training in film. You picked up your skills in the trailer park of entertainment."

There was a horrible pause. "At least I earn money," Hank shot back.

"I'll make money someday."

"Not unless you change personality first."

Beside me, Karen was horribly rigid. I realized that the Four Tops were no longer on the radio. There was some song I didn't recognize playing instead. I opened my mouth to retort. Instead of words, a horrible, groaning snort emerged.

I was now officially turning into my mother.

"Did you just *snoan?*" Hank asked, his voice instantly cheerful. In fact, he sounded positively merry.

"No!"

No no no no no. There was no way that I could have spontaneously inherited snoaning capabilities. This was a living nightmare. Talk about pouring salt on wounds.

"Sounded like a snoan," Hank said.

I looked at Karen. Her lips were pressed together, and she was actually vibrating with repressed laughter.

"It will never happen again," I said. "It was a spontaneous, genetic response to a threatening situation."

Karen broke first and snickered loudly.

"OK, OK, but this does not mean that I am turning into my mother."

"Puffin," Hank said, in a remarkably accurate imitation of Mom.

Against my will, I laughed too. "Look, Hank, forget the snoaning—" I began.

Hank interrupted me. "Well, that may be hard to do."

I ignored him. "All I'm saying is that you need to let me be myself and make the mistakes I need to make in filming."

"Charlie, I'm only going to say this once—" Hank started, but I never got to hear what it was he was going to say only once.

Somehow, I had just rear-ended the car in front of me.

I burst into tears.

forty-six

The first thing I did when I got home—even before calling my grandmother to tell her that I had decimated her front bumper—was to take a very long, scaldingly hot shower. When I got done, Karen was sitting in the kitchen, drinking a glass of wine and highlighting a textbook.

"When I first started college, I didn't want to mark in my books because that would ruin them and I wanted them to stay pretty. That lasted about a month," I said.

Karen looked up. "How're you feeling?"

"Surprisingly fine," I said, opening the refrigerator. I began throwing away everything that was stale or moldy. When I was done, there was a wrinkly, but still usable, lemon and a pitcher of filtered water. And condiments. Our refrigerator would not have had the Slim Goodbody stamp of approval.

"I think I'm going to go to the store and then cook a really fabulous dinner. Any requests?"

Karen capped her highlighter and shut it in her book as a bookmark. "Actually, Ned called and wanted me to meet him. But I won't go if you want some company."

"Don't be silly. I'm fine."

"I don't mind staying home," Karen said.

"I know. But I don't need handholding and I think I'd

actually prefer time alone. What's up with you and Ned anyway?"

"That's a good question. Ask me again in a few hours and I might have an answer for you."

I gave Karen an imitation of the same sort of skeptical-yet-sympathetic look that she often gives me. She immediately started talking. What an incredibly handy thing to be able to make one's face do. I would have to use this more often. "Well, we had a fight," she said. "At the time, I thought it was a doozy of a fight, but I might revise my opinion after watching you and Hank this afternoon."

"Thanks," I said sarcastically. "What was the fight about?"

"Whether or not he should tell Steven that Marisa went for an interview at *Stylus* magazine."

"Maris had an interview at *Stylus*?" I asked. "Isn't that supposed to be super-snotty and super-trendy?"

"Maris is trendy. She was going to Bliss before they had a credit card machine."

"That's right," I remembered. "When was this?"

"Last week."

"How could I not know?"

"Uh, you're making a movie," Karen said.

"I'm around."

"Not so much, Charlie. You're a little preoccupied at the moment."

I felt like that comment might have deserved more attention but I breezed over it. "So wait, why was Ned going to tell Steven at all?"

"Well, Steven knew something was up and was pressuring him pretty heavily. Ned was afraid he might get fired."

"If Maris gets hired at *Stylus*, she could probably bring her assistant with her." I thought for a second. "Or does Ned want Marisa's job? He probably doesn't have enough experience."

"No, he wouldn't get her job and he knows it. I just got upset about the whole thing."

"It's upsetting," I agreed.

"Yeah." Karen twisted some hair around her finger. "But I'm going to dinner with Ned. I want to hear what he has to say."

"Innocent until proven guilty?" I asked.

"I just like to hear what people have to say about why they do the things they do."

"So this is purely an exercise in intellectual curiosity?"

Karen laughed. "Maybe I don't know that yet."

"Did Marisa get the job?"

"She has a second interview next week."

"Did Ned tell Steven?"

"Not definitively. But he was so damningly evasive that he might as well have."

"Poor Maris."

Karen shrugged. "Or maybe not poor Maris. Maybe she'll get the *Stylus* job." Karen glanced down at her black sweater. "Tell the truth: can you tell that there's a coffee stain on this?"

I stared closely. "Yes."

"Shit!" Karen exclaimed, stomping off to her bedroom to change. I laughed despite myself and picked up the phone to call my grandmother.

Later that night, after talking to my grandmother, her insurance company, Hank, Horton, Marisa, and Chris Martin, I had an important revelation. It was the sort of revelation that, had I been a cartoon character, would have been designated not by a single, paltry light bulb but by an entire string of flashing, multicolored Christmas lights and possibly piped-in reindeer music. Had I been a medieval mystic, I would have assumed that I now had enough vision to qualify for sainthood. Had I been a phone psychic, I would have begun to believe—for real—in my powers of intuition. It was that powerful. I nearly keeled over from the strength of it. Here is what I thought:

I would be OK without Hank Destin.

I really would. If anything happened to us, I would cry and fret and mope and want never to leave my apartment again. I would use it as justification to avoid dating for the next three years. I might even spend the next six months alternatively cursing and weeping as I sat glued before endless episodes of *Troubled Passion*. But I would be OK. And someday, I might even break my cardinal rule of writing "serious" screenplays and indulge in a funny little piece of fairy tale fluff about a grad student whose dream-come-true romance evolves into a nightmare.

It was a strange moment. I paused, forkful of pasta halfway to my mouth, and marveled at the oddness of human resilience. Then the moment passed and my miraculous brain moved on to wondering if we had any Parmesan left in the now-clean refrigerator.

forty-seven

Given that the fender on my grandmother's car was currently tied in place with my hiking boot lace, I felt it wouldn't be wise to drive it. The next day I took the train to Hank's so I could ride in his car service up to Minna and Joe's house. He read the *Post* on the way up and I read the *Times*. Somewhere in the Bronx, I leaned over.

"Can I have some of the *Post*?"

"Excuse me, but did you just request something from the trailer park of journalism?"

"Have I ever told you about my fondness for sleeping dogs?" I asked.

"No. Are you saying that they should be allowed to lie or that I am one?"

The driver snorted in the front seat. Hank looked at me and raised an eyebrow. I giggled. Hank handed me the entire *Post*.

"Oh, I only wanted a section of it," I said.

"It's the *Post*. There's just one section."

We read companionably for a few seconds, Hank having managed to content himself with the *Times* sports section. I'm not entirely sure how I feel about newspapers that don't have sections. I wouldn't want one large blob of orange or grapefruit; why would I want one large blob of newspaper? Some things are just meant to have divisions.

Orange you glad the Times *exists?* I thought. I was indubitably cracking up. I sighed and flipped to the gossip columns.

"Latrell Sprewell is a basketball player, right?"

Hank looked at me like I was insane.

"Yes, Charlotte."

"Well, he bought a house," I said.

"That's nice."

I skimmed the blind entries for a few moments. I can never figure out to whom they refer and therefore tend to view them more as space filler than valuable information. Unenriched, I turned the page.

"Oh my goodness," I said suddenly.

"Don't tell me—did a football player buy a house?" Hank asked with mock enthusiasm.

"Um, no," I said slowly. "More like a certain soap opera star was swapping spit with three members of a gaggle of Brazilian models at Halo the other night."

There was a pause.

"According to the *Post*, it looks like 'playboy Destin is over his fascination with grad students and the ivory tower. More exploits from the infamous womanizer can be expected.'"

"Oh, Charlie," Hank said. "I didn't know reporters were there."

Our driver began humming noisily.

"Why would it matter?" I asked. "Would you have done something differently if you knew it would end up in the paper?"

"Oh, Charlie," Hank repeated. "Why can't you just let me be myself?"

"If being yourself involves feeling up Brazilian models, you have my permission to go enroll in the Free to Be Me Sleaze Society."

The driver hummed even louder. He sounded like a bumblebee on crack.

"Would you mind not making that noise?" Hank said rudely. "You too can call the *Post* when we're done arguing."

"How about not displacing your aggression on the driver?" I said. "*He* didn't follow you to Halo with a mini cam."

"Look, Charlie, filming has been really stressful. You know that. I just needed to let off some steam."

"Yeah, you're right. Filming has been stressful. I need an outlet too. It's called *yoga*."

There was an angry silence. We both stared out the window. Maybe fighting in cars was becoming standard practice for Hank and me. I could call my next screenplay *Fighting in Cars with Boys*.

"Hank, I'm so tired of fighting with you," I said at last.

"Then why don't you ever give me a break?" Hank asked.

"What do you mean? Do you think I'm always on your case?"

"Charlie, I can't live up to you. I can't be what you want me to be and I can't pretend to be the person you think I am." He gestured to the paper. "That's who I am and that's not who you are and I'm tired of pretending that I care about *Madame Bovary* as a book when the truth is that I only care about getting in front of the camera and making a role come to life."

I waved the paper. "Sucking on the collagen-injected lips of Brazilian models is hardly about making a role come to life in front of the camera."

"Charlie, give it a rest. I shouldn't have done it. Am I sorry I did it? No. Do I think it was a big deal? No. Can I understand why you might be upset about this? Of course."

I didn't quite follow Hank's logic, but since he sounded testy, I let it pass. "What night was this?" I asked.

"Tuesday."

That was the night I'd gone to the film studio and met up with Chris. Afterward, I'd called Hank, intending to go out to Brooklyn and meet him, but his cell phone was turned off.

"Oh," I said.

The driver began humming again. I wondered if Hank would be totally passive-aggressive and start humming in unison, but he simply sighed quite loudly. The driver got the point and stopped.

"I called you that night. I wanted to come over," I said.

"I got the message." There was a pause. "Charlie-doll, it wouldn't have made a difference. I needed to play."

Until that point, I'd felt sort of wounded-puppy hurt. Now I was angry, well and truly pissed, my emotions so uncharacteristically out of control that I felt frightened by my reaction. For the first time in my life, I began to share some sort of sympathy for Lorena Bobbitt. (Well, OK, maybe not that extreme. But I was on my way.)

"For crying out loud, Hank, you're not a child. Couldn't you have restrained this incredibly powerful urge? I didn't buy that some-men-can't-control-themselves bullshit with Bill Clinton and I don't buy it with you."

"Well, we all can't be Saint Charlotte and live our tidy little ascetic lives, indulging in nothing and enjoying only those things that are good for us," Hank said.

"Oh, shut up," I said, with all the maturity that would be indicated by my twenty-seven years on earth and impending graduate diploma.

"Gladly," Hank said. "You never care about anything I have to say anyway."

We each turned and stared furiously out of our respective windows at the scenic Bronx. I couldn't believe we weren't even out of New York yet. I glumly wondered about the filming-to-traffic time ratio of my thesis. After a while, I turned and looked at Hank, who was still staring out the window with his jaw clenched tightly enough to cause permanent dental damage.

Here's the thing: I can't deal with fighting. I don't shirk from it but I absolutely cannot maintain it. I am cursed with the why-can't-we-all-just-get-along mentality. So even though I knew I shouldn't apologize, I slid into my role of the permanent olive branch profferrer.

"Hank, do you really think that I don't care about anything you have to say?" I asked gently.

"Come on, Charlie, we both know that it's only *your* opinion that matters in this film."

"That's not true," I replied automatically. Was it?

"Look, maybe I'm just tired of our relationship being about you: your thesis and your ambition and your ideas and your constant string of minor crises and your friends and your family and everything else."

I latched on to the last, possibly most irrelevant, part of his litany.

"I would have been thrilled to meet your family. I guess I thought we just weren't at that stage. I mean, it was just an accident that you met mine."

"Charlie, I've tried to tell you a thousand times that we're not so different. I care about my career too. I care about my work. You just assume that whatever you do is more vital than whatever anyone else does."

"That's not true!"

"So you say, Charlie, but I took that trailer park comment you made seriously."

"OK, you're right, that was a shitty thing to say," I admitted. "I was really upset about how you and Sabrina were acting on set and I shouldn't have said it and I'm not even sure I meant it."

"Are you in the habit of saying things you don't mean? That's news to me," Hank said icily.

"The trailer park comment came *after* you flaunted your stuff at Halo," I defended myself. "Don't blame this little paparazzi encounter on something I said in anger after the incident in question."

"You've implied it ever since we started dating. You don't respect me. It took me a hell of a long time to figure that one out. See, most people fall over themselves trying to please me. I think I was so taken with you because you treated me like a regular person, even after you knew who I was. You know, none of the other yoga instructors actually tried to correct any of my poses. I guess they were nervous or something. But you were different. I liked that."

I felt myself getting blurry and teary and confused. Hank didn't sound angry anymore.

"Maybe I used to think that your outrageous ambition and intellectual posing were sort of charming. But I can't deal with being second banana anymore, Charlie."

Hank was the one with the fan clubs—how could he feel like a second banana?

"Did you sleep with any of those women the other night?" I asked. "Wait, never mind, I don't want to know. I really, really don't want to know."

"I don't think that's the point, anyway," Hank said dryly.

Was he not even going to do me the courtesy of denying it? I felt icy and frightened. I remembered my revelation of the night before. I would be OK. I would. I would. I would. I looked around and ascertained that there was absolutely nothing worth counting in the car. Nothing. Desperate for distraction, I started counting backward from one hundred by sevens. Ninety-three, eighty-six, seventy-nine . . .

"Charlie, I don't know why you don't respect me. I suspect some of it has to do with the soap and some of it has to do with how very smart you are." He raised an eyebrow in that way that I associated only with him. "And maybe some of it has to do with a fundamental clash of ideas about film. You know, Charlie, I didn't spend my childhood glued to screen-plays of classic films, and I've never taken a film class in my life. Maybe that's not as horrible a failing as you think."

I wanted to cut to the chase. "So you just can't deal with me anymore?" I asked. "Is that the point?"

"I don't know, Charlie. Maybe."

"Jesus, Hank, I'm afraid even to say this, but what about *me*? Maybe I want to keep dealing with you!"

"Do you?"

Good question. Did I?

Hank leaped over my pause. "Maybe this is appropriate. Our relationship is about you and our breakup is about me."

"Are we breaking up?" I thought I was controlling myself pretty well but my voice sounded on the verge of tears. Great.

"Charlie, I don't even know if you loved me. I think you just liked the idea of me."

"Oh, God, Hank, I love you so much!" I said, my voice cracking like crazy. This felt horribly surreal. I waited for Hank to smile and tell me he loved me too and weren't we being silly and let's go to Florence as soon as we're done with the film.

He didn't.

"You don't always know best, Charlie."

"I never said I did!" I was over the crying temptation now. I wasn't going to weep or crack or dissolve. "Why is this all about what I've done wrong? Why do you maintain this delusion that you behave impeccably in all situations? You've ruined my thesis with your stubbornness and arrogance."

"I could have made it better, had you listened to me."

"You wouldn't even listen to me about why I wasn't listen-ing to you!"

"Charlie, this is exactly the kind of thing that I can't do anymore."

I pushed my lips together angrily. Hank reached out and touched my cheek. I jerked my head away from his reach.

"Aren't you tired of this, Charlie?" he asked. "Let's do ourselves a favor. It's time we stopped all this pretending." He paused. "You'll get over it."

"I know I will," I said haughtily, reaching for the *Post*.

I waited for one of us to break the silence that followed but we arrived in Connecticut before that happened.

forty-eight

It was probably denial (or delusion or preoccupation) but it didn't really dawn on me that Hank and I had *broken up*. I thought we'd just had another one of our hideous disagreements that would eventually sort itself out. I hopped out of the car as soon as we got to Minna and Joe's and managed to shepherd the cast and crew through the remaining filming as swiftly as I could. Hank didn't say much between scenes and spent most of the off-camera time talking to Nick Barone, the actor who played Leon. I suspected that they were smoking various mind-altering substances in the bushes together but didn't do anything to confirm this. I, meanwhile, spent most of my time developing an internal, self-congratulatory mono-logue for avoiding an on-set meltdown.

Later that day, Karen forwarded me an e-mail that Marisa had sent her:

Karen—

*Go check out today's **Post**, but do not (repeat NOT) let Charlie see it.*
Call me immediately.

xo,
M

Karen figured that I'd seen the *Post* by that time anyway and was sort of worried. I was touched, and rather amused, by Marisa's precautions. As soon as filming finished (forever!) on Friday, I fled home for Whine and Wine with my friends. We didn't really talk about what I now slowly—and unwillingly—realized was a breakup. After so much time obsessing about Hank and filming, it was a relief just to hang out eating Chinese food and watching cheesy videos with the two of them.

Unfortunately, Sunday night was the wrap party at Hank's apartment, and much as I would have preferred to avoid it, I was going to have to reenter the distasteful world of reality. (To be honest, I didn't understand why a wrap party was necessary anyway. Sure, maybe it was tradition, but *The Doctor's Wife* was far from done. I would be spending the next three weeks in the editing studio. Then I had to submit the finished product for formal thesis consideration, defend it in front of a panel, submit it for end-of-year awards, submit it for film festivals, screen it at the end-of-year ceremonies, submit it to agents, and so on. I should probably start referring to myself as Charlie the Submitter. It had a nice ring—almost like Catherine the Great.)

At any rate, I was going to have get into my damning-torpedoes mindset and face Hank and the rest of the cast and crew. I had engaged Marisa to be my personal shopper and she had found a fantastic shirt for me to wear to the party: two layers of bloodred mesh trimmed with black velvet ribbon, a heart shaped-neckline and corset styling. I'd planned to pair it with my trademark black pants, but Marisa insisted on lending me a slinky black skirt and bullied me into wearing the incredibly painful Shoes of Sin.

"I wore these on my first date with Hank," I had protested to her. "They have too many memories."

"Then it's all the more reason you ought to exorcise them," she replied, handing me some dainty pearl earrings. "I have to get these back. They belong to my sister."

So that's how I ended up ringing Hank's bell on Sunday night dressed like a Victorian prostitute. He smiled when he saw me and leaned forward and kissed me on the cheek.

"Charlie-doll," he said, as if nothing had happened. I shivered with the intimacy of it.

"Hi," I replied awkwardly. There is a reason Hank is an actor and I am not. I was incapable of faking even this small a social nicety.

"People have been wondering where you were. Your friend Chris is here. And Horton."

"OK."

Tentatively, I walked into the crowded apartment. After I'd spent so much time here alone with Hank, it was strange to see it so occupied. I wondered if I should take home some of the clothes and books I'd left here but decided I'd prefer not to do so publicly. Someone had created a collage of pictures from the film along one wall. I went over and looked at them.

"At least take some champagne," a voice said behind me, pressing a glass into my hand.

I turned. It was Chris Martin.

"Thanks." It seemed I was capable only of monosyllabic statements.

"Kind of strange to have a wrap party when you'll still be sweating it out for the next month."

Even though I'd been thinking the exact same thing, I shrugged. "Sure, but it's over for the cast and crew."

"Well, congratulations."

"Thanks." I thought back through our conversation. *Over* had two syllables, so I'd broken—sort of—out of the monosyllabic rut. Of course, *congratulations* had five, but that was Chris's word.

"Charlie, you seem a little spaced out. Is everything OK?" Chris asked.

"You just reminded me of all I had to do."

Chris pointed to a photo of Hank, Walsh, and me all

wearing 1950s men's hats that Sarah Wong had uncovered with her miraculous vintage shopping skills.

"That's a cute picture."

"You are not going to believe the costumes for this. If nothing else, it's going to look pretty." I paused. "I think I need food more than drink." There was a table of fancy hors d'ouevres. They seemed far more extravagant than the check from the film department would have covered. I was pretty sure that Hank had chucked in some of his own money to de-studentify the party. As I made my way over to the food, I realized that I felt distinctly out of place, like I must be wearing a huge scarlet S for Single (again).

After about an hour of smiling and chatting, I was feeling emotionally claustrophobic. Right around the time I noticed Maddie—whose presence at this party was completely inexplicable—flirting with Chris Martin (also inexplicable), I decided I need some air. I sneaked out on Hank's balcony and stared at the skyline for a while. I was thirty seconds away from hypothermia when the door behind me slid open.

"For someone who desperately wanted her filming to be over, you don't seem very celebratory," Horton said as he handed me my coat.

"Thanks," I said, as I wrapped myself up. Trust Horton to appear exactly when I was thirty seconds away from crumpling. He really ought to go perch himself on a mountain somewhere in Tibet and wait for people to come scrambling for his advice and assistance.

"I watched some of the dailies today. They're rather impressive, Charlie."

Bully for me. Fifty points to Gryffindor for continuing to be Type A in the face of impending romantic disaster.

"I don't think I'm a director, Horton," I said suddenly. "I think I might just try to be a writer from now on. I didn't enjoy the on-set work at all."

"That's a good thing to know about yourself," Horton said mildly. He walked over to the balcony and leaned on the metal railing. "How old are you now, kid?'

"Twenty-seven. Almost twenty-eight." In other words, ancient. When I was a child, I assumed that I would have procured my first million by the impossibly old age of twenty-one. Ha. I don't even have an apartment with a *dishwasher*.

"I was twenty-eight when I made my first feature," Horton said. His voice pulled me away from my moping and back to the present. "It took me eight more years to realize I wasn't a director."

"Why didn't you like directing?" I asked.

"Why don't you?" Horton challenged.

Because it caused me to break up with Hank. "Too much work with people and personalities," I said honestly. "And it's not that same sort of constant mental challenge as writing."

"I wasn't very happy when I was directing," Horton said simply. "I decided to try a radical change in my life and it worked and I felt much more alive and like myself," he said. "So I stuck with it."

Horton never self-discloses. I didn't say anything so that he could continue if he wanted. Instead, he turned around to face me. "Mallory saw the *Post*," he said.

I pulled my hands inside the sleeves of my coat so that they would be warmer. "Hank and I broke up," I admitted. It felt strange to hear those words aloud.

"When?"

"About twenty minutes after I read the *Post* on Thursday morning."

"Ah."

"It's OK," I said.

"Is it?" Horton asked.

"Well, not at this exact moment, because I'm in his apartment having to face him in front of thirty champagne-drinking people and it makes me want to bury my head in the sand. But it will be."

"I'm sorry," Horton said eventually.

"Yeah, me too. But we can't talk about it anymore because I might start to cry."

"Sure," Horton said. "You ready to go back inside?"

"No."

Horton tilted his head toward the door. "Come on," he said anyway.

I took one last look at the spectacular view of the skyline.

"OK," I said, and we made our way back into a party so celebratory that it felt almost Disney-fake to me. It was impossible that my cast and crew could be so joyous at the exact moment I wanted to fall apart. I was reminded, briefly, of this Auden poem about Icarus that my father is overly fond of quoting. Basically Icarus fell, but life went on and so many people didn't even know or notice that something as horrible as a boy plunging from the sky had even happened.

Dad says it's about the dichotomy of emotion, but I wondered if it could be more about ignoring grief.

forty-nine

With typical prescient timing, my mother called on Monday morning.

"Puffin, dear, are you done with filming?"

I was on my way out the door to meet with my film editor. I pulled on my coat and threw my Chap Stick and wallet in my bag.

"With filming, yeah, but not with the film," I said. "It has to be edited and spliced and all that."

"Oh, sure," my mother said, even though I was positive that she hadn't considered any of that. I locked the apartment door behind me and headed down the stairs, still on the phone.

"Well, how did everything finish up?" Mom said.

"Fine. I'm glad it's over."

"What's all that noise?" she asked. I was outside by now.

"Broadway."

"Are you going somewhere?"

"School."

"OK, darling. I was just calling to see if you wanted to come for dinner this week. Hank too, obviously."

"I can come on Thursday after I teach yoga," I said. "Hank and I are no longer together, so I don't think he'll be joining us." Why had I ever been stupid enough to introduce Hank to my parents? Basically I had introduced them, they adored Hank, we broke up. What a timetable of romantic success. Better for them never to have met.

Even over the multitude of honking car horns, I could hear my mother's gasp.

"Oh, Puffin!"

At least it was a gasp and not a snoan.

"Well, you know," I said inarticulately.

"I'm sorry."

"Thanks," I said curtly. My mother seemed to sense my foul mood.

"Well, look, darling, we'll see you on Thursday. We can talk more about it then."

"Sounds good." An electric cattle prod sounded more appealing. I hung up with gratitude and turned my cell phone off to avoid any more calls.

Later that afternoon, I was walking downtown to Harmony to catch an advanced class when I realized how incredibly tired I was. I stood on the corner of Ninety-sixth and Broadway for a few minutes, debating whether to go home, curl in bed for the rest of the day, and indulge shamelessly in self-pity. But that was the sort of activity that would inevitably have me tearfully missing Hank within thirty minutes. Almost without thinking, I ran to the bus stop and hopped on a crosstown about three seconds before it pulled away from the curb.

I got off at Fifth Avenue and walked down to the Metropolitan Museum. Once inside, with my little blue admission button fastened firmly to the neck of my sweater, I headed up the Great Staircase to stare at Vermeers. With certain art, I get this little, breathless click in my chest if I look at it for a while. After a few minutes, I felt vastly better, sort of like I'd been dunked in a vat of warm butter. I slowly turned away from one of the three portraits of luminous young girls with high foreheads and found myself face-to-face with Mallory Lear.

Bizarre.

This is the sort of accidental encounter that makes me feel like New York is too small and that perhaps I ought to consider moving to Tokyo. I know it's neither the most healthy nor the most mature policy, but I tend to avoid humanity when I am unsure of my ability to maintain even the slimmest facade of a rational emotional state.

"Charlie, I thought that was you," Mallory said breathlessly, air kissing me on the cheek. "I had to come here for a meeting—we're lending some art to an Americana exhibit later this year—and thought I might as well take advantage of the afternoon," she said, in answer to my unspoken question.

I gestured to the Vermeers behind me. "I always get this little breathless click in my chest when I look at these," I said.

It was the ultimate non sequitur but Mallory took it in stride. Rather than looking at me like I was either nuts or had some kind of heart abnormality that ought to be checked out by a cardiologist, she smiled and said, "Me too."

"Sorry I didn't get a chance to talk to you at the wrap party," I added.

"It's OK."

"You saw the *Post*, right?"

"Yes."

There was a pause. I wished I could fast forward through all the uncomfortable pauses that afflict my life. "Well, it was fun while it lasted," I said. "I'll probably never get a chance to date someone like Hank again."

"What do you mean, 'someone like Hank'?"

"Um, just someone rich and beautiful and famous."

"Why not?"

"Come on," I said.

Mallory shrugged. "From what I understand, he was rich

and beautiful and famous and a disaster on set *and* a playboy." She frowned. "But I am taking the *Post*'s word on the
playboy part, so it might not be true. We can give him the
benefit of the doubt on that charge."

"I have no idea if it's true," I admitted. "He didn't exactly
deny the Brazilian model debacle, but I am reasonably certain that he wasn't cheating on me throughout our brief but
torrid affair." I made a face. "He didn't have time to cheat, for
one thing. We spent practically every second on set."

"Mmm-hmm," Mallory murmured agreeably.

I flipped my head around so I could look at *Aristotle Contemplating the Bust of Homer*, which is a painting that has always disappointed me. Based on the great title, I've always
expected more than a beefy Netherlandish burgher looking
at a shadowy, indistinguishable lump of stone. I couldn't tell
from here, but up close you can see that the paint is very
thick and goopy. There's a word for the painting technique.

"Those lumps of paint that Rembrandt used?" I said ques-
tioningly. "What are they called again?"

"Impasto."

"Yeah, that's right. If you squat down and look up, you can
see all the different levels of the paint. I used to do that
when I was a kid—but not so much anymore."

Mallory smiled. "Let's sit for a second," she said, indicating
a bench in the middle of the room. We did. It was harder to
see Aristotle from this perspective. I was no longer Charlotte
Contemplating Aristotle Contemplating the Bust of Homer.

"I don't think I even realized we'd broken up. We'd been
fighting so much," I said.

Pause. Of course. Pauses bother me. I chose my next words
carefully so as to rein in my tendency to say something incriminating merely to fill the silence.

"He said I didn't understand and respect him, that I
judged him because he was on a soap and wasn't, you know,
cultured and intellectual and everything. I don't think he'd

even heard of *Madame Bovary* before and certainly hadn't read it."

"Do you think what he said was true?"

"I don't know." I stared at the serene Vermeer girls. What a blessing it must have been to live in a time before entertainment. Of course, there were no movies and most people were illiterate and there was all that religious persecution and turmoil. Was I better off in the present? It was a moot point, really, since I was obviously not going to hop into some sci-fi time machine and find out. I sighed.

"He may have been right and it's probably worth thinking about," I admitted. "I appreciate people with whom I can discuss books and movies, simply because I like those things and they form a fairly central part of my identity. Do I find it essential to a relationship? I don't know. Maybe it's more central than I'd like to admit or maybe I don't really want to be in a relationship and that's just an excuse." I checked my watch. I didn't have any place to go, but I sort of wanted to end the conversation. "I better get going," I said.

"Sure," Mallory agreed. I had a hunch that she knew I didn't need to go anywhere but was letting me escape nonetheless. I was grateful for that. Talking about Hank made me miss him, and missing Hank made me wonder about all the mistakes I'd made. I couldn't shake the unsettling feeling that I had thrown away something I would never have again.

On my way home from the museum, I stopped off at Blockbuster and rented a pile of movies. I could hear my own words about how I valued movies echoing in my head. Hank had diluted my passion for everything other than him. Perhaps I was in dire need of reconnecting with my ambition.

After watching *Double Indemnity*, *Dial M for Murder*, and last year's Sundance hit all in a row, I felt better, if a little glazed.

There was nothing that topped movies. Ever. This was

what I wanted to do with my life, and ultimately I could still find succor in screenwriting despite the status of my romantic life.

Now if I could only polish off *The Doctor's Wife* and wangle myself a career.

fifty

I was on my way to my thesis defense when I ran into Robert the doorman—whose uncanny sense of being in the wrong place at the wrong time was beginning to rival Kato Kaelin's—in Nussbaum and Wu on 110th Street. I lifted the lid off my newly purchased coffee and grudgingly said hello. I couldn't precisely figure out why seeing Robert bothered me so much, but it was almost like he was emblematic of the nice, normal guy I couldn't appreciate. (And since I apparently couldn't appreciate the spectacular Hank Destin either, I might as well cut my losses, find an all-female ashram, and take a vow of poverty, solitude, and eternal yoga practice.)

"Oh, hey, Charlie," Robert said, interrupting my reverie. It was warm outside, finally springlike weather, and he was wearing an absolutely awful Hawaiian shirt with fish on it. "What's going on?"

Since my hands were occupied, I motioned toward the door with my head. "I really don't have time to talk. My thesis defense is today and I wanted to prepare at school a little before I go in."

"Oh, sure, get going!" Robert said cheerfully. "Don't let me keep you. Wow, your thesis. That's great. Does that mean you get your master's?"

"In fine arts, yeah. It's an MFA, so it's a little different from an MA in terms of what I can do with it when I get out. There are a few more options." I wasn't sure why I was telling Robert this unless it was to reassure myself that I might possibly have a career other than working in Starbucks after graduation.

"Wow, congratulations," Robert repeated. To his credit, he sounded genuinely happy for me.

"Thanks." I had an opportunity to bolt for the door but I felt sort of sorry for Robert. He seemed perfectly happy, so my pity was undoubtedly misplaced. Still, it saddened me to see him (in his horrid shirt) among all the chattering, glossy students. "Anything going on with you?" I asked.

"Well, sort of. Remember when I saw you in the Laundromat?" He paused for such a long time that I realized that an answer was expected of me.

"Yes," I obligingly replied.

"Well, you probably don't remember this, but I asked you to read this essay 'cause I was thinking about going to school?" Robert pitched his voice a little higher on the last word so that his statement sounded like a question. I sensed that he needed some sort of confirmation again, so I nodded my agreement.

"Well, I got in."

"Oh, congratulations!" I said. Funny. Goodwill must be contagious because I was as honestly happy for Robert as he had been for me. "That's really wonderful. Are you going to be able to do that and still work?"

"No, I'll take out loans, but it's going to be so worth it. I'm just going to have such a different life when I get out."

I nodded.

"What are you studying?"

"Computers, I hope. It just seems like something that'll be really practical."

He probably didn't intend for me to take offense at that,

but I picked up an undercurrent of *unlike film* in his endorsement of practicality.

"Where are you going to be at school?" I asked.

Robert looked surprised. "Oh, didn't I say? Here."

"Here? You mean, like Columbia?"

Robert nodded. The colors on his shirt seemed even more garish and, for a moment, the fish stood out so much from the florid backdrop that they blurred. "Yeah, I was going to apply just to City College and Hunter, but I got one of those SAT books and studied really hard and ended up doing so much better than I planned, so I figured I'd give it a shot. I'm actually on my way to see the department head right now. It's a little early to arrange classes, but I was so excited about coming here that he agreed to meet with me."

"Oh my God, Robert, that's fantastic!"

"Thanks." He shuffled from foot to foot a bit.

"Well, I should get going," I said. "But I'll see you around."

"Sure, bye, Charlie."

I was too nervous about my thesis defense to process the implications of Robert's going to Columbia right then. But as soon as I was free of the various congratulations (Rhonda Bain had asked some tough questions about choices I'd made in adaptation, but I'd otherwise glided through), I found myself stalled by a vague, anticlimactic sense of sadness. I was going to miss the security and challenge of school. It had absorbed so much of my life for the past three years that I couldn't imagine what it would be like to be on my own, to write without the safety net of a class full of willing readers. As I walked downtown, I spotted Miguel across the street and, rather than submitting myself to a host of snoopy questions about my defense, I drifted into the garden of St. John the Divine.

I sat on a mossy stone bench and pulled out my cell

phone. The bench was charmingly appropriate for a cathedral garden, but I suspected that it might leave grass stains on
my suit. My parents weren't home, but I left a message that
I'd passed the defense. It was odd to feel so completely neu-
tral. I should feel more celebratory or relieved or *something*
right now. Lying back on the bench, I stared at the sky. I
couldn't believe Robert was going to Columbia. I'd pegged
him as unambitious and—though I didn't want to admit it—
not supersmart either. I mean, I never thought he was stupid
(I don't accept even a first date with someone who strikes me
as stupid), but, all in all, he'd left me sort of underwhelmed.

I shut my eyes so that the sun shone redly through my
lids. Robert hadn't become more attractive to me because he
was going to Columbia. I still didn't want to date him. But I
wondered how I had missed whatever spark the admissions
committee had evidently seen. It is *hard* to get into college as
a working adult. He must have killed the SAT. I thought
about what Hank had said to me. Did I have such preconc-
ceived notions of people that I ignored anything that went
against this view? Did I, intentionally or not, somehow stran-
gle the ideas and enthusiasm of others through my own ag-
gressive visions?

Was I a total snob?

I remembered a conversation with Miguel Reynard-Arora,
in which he'd informed me that he hadn't felt like any of our
classmates had been able to offer constructive advice for his
(in my opinion, piece of shit) screenplay. Was I like that? Did
I come across as an arrogant bitch?

God.

I didn't like thinking about this stuff, but I forced myself
to follow the introspection further. Never let it be said that
Little Miss Perfect Frost shirked her existential crisis. (Sometimes I nauseated myself.)

If there's one thing that I've learned from film school, it's
that there are far fewer creative people in this world than

you might assume. Sure, there's a lot of talent in my program. But there are also a lot of fairly blah people who nevertheless consider themselves the glittering future of American cinema. My classes often reminded me of a fortune cookie that Marisa had once gotten: *The average person thinks he isn't.*

I'd wanted Hank to play Leon, mainly because I believed he was like Leon—fiery and dramatic and passionate and beautiful. Hank had wanted to be Charles instead. Was it possible that Hank Destin, as a person, was more of a Charles than a Leon figure? Had I pushed him into my Leonlike image rather than allowing him to be as steadily bland as he naturally was? Of course, given the maxim of the average person, Hank himself didn't think he was bland. But was it possible that if I could somehow strip his personality out of his exquisite exterior, he would be as mundane as Robert?

Doubtful. I rejected the notion as quickly as it came to me. Hank had made me laugh and given me quirky presents and (for better or for worse) challenged my way of thinking. Robert had done none of that. But I was muddled about my perceptions of other people, which were being increasingly revealed as inaccurate. And what if I also fell under the heading of misguided average person snottily persisting in delusions of genius? Possibly Hank had been right about everything with *The Doctor's Wife* and I was too stubborn and stupid to understand. Sighing aloud, I rolled up to a sitting position. This was too depressing a line of thought.

I looked at my watch. It was almost noon, but I wasn't ready to leave the oasis of the cathedral garden yet. The courtyard was empty except for a woman, about my age, wearing a straw hat and baggy pink capris. Idly, I watched as she reached down and cupped her hands around something that had been crawling on a leaf—maybe a ladybug. Opening her hands slightly, she examined her catch, and a look of pure exaltation spread across her face.

I had just defended my MFA thesis and was on my way up. I should have been happy. Instead, I was struck by the most profound sensation of jealousy I'd ever had.

Life would be easier if I could only be so satisfied by a mere ladybug.

fifty-one

Apparently, there really is something worse than having too little time and that's having too much time. Two weeks after my defense, I was struggling to adapt to a life of leisure. With no obligations, I was spending an increasingly alarming amount of time stewing in my own sour thoughts and fears. Every second of every day felt like my worst four A.M. freak fit. I had taken to cleaning as a coping mechanism. I was probably going to asphyxiate from the Clorox.

One day I came home to find Karen (shockingly) scouring the already gleaming kitchen floor.

"Hey, there, Lady Macbeth," I greeted her. "Is everything OK?"

Karen looked up from her obsessive scrubbing. "Lady Macbeth?" she asked, then made the connection. "Oh, 'out, out, damned spot.'" She rolled her eyes at me. "That's cheesy."

"Everything OK?" I repeated.

"Yeah, I guess. Except I think we officially have the same life, Charlie." Karen sat back on her heels and blew a stray wisp of hair out of her eyes.

"How so?"

"Ned and I just broke up." Karen's face twisted as she

spoke. Even though I thought Ned was a dolt, I felt myself weaken at her unhappiness.

"Oh no," I cried, sitting down on the floor beside her.

Karen shrugged one shoulder. Her mouth was still scrunched up. "Oh, yes," she managed to say.

"Why?"

She shrugged again.

"Tell me."

Her face unfolded a little. "He said he needs time away—not just from me, but from life."

"Huh?"

"He's going to go work on a cattle ranch in Idaho!"

I snickered inadvertently.

"Is he bringing the Vespa?"

Karen smiled a little. "He said that talking to me about his life really helped him understand that this was what he needed!"

What a shit. "I'm so sorry," I said sincerely, moving closer so that I could rub her shoulders.

"I don't want him to find himself," Karen wailed. She was closer to tears now, I could tell. "I want him to find me."

I rubbed her shoulders and let her cry. Karen's not a howler. She just sort of silently leaks tears for a while. "I'm sorry," I repeated.

After about ten minutes, she blinked four times in a row and sat up. "I'm OK," she said.

"OK," I agreed, then added, "I bet he gets kicked in the head by a cow."

"I bet he gets anthrax," Karen grumbled.

"Or mad cow disease," I offered.

"Or joins a cult," Karen said. She looked a little blobby around the eyes. We were quiet for a while.

"I think we should go out," I said suddenly.

"Go out?" Karen asked.

"Sure," I said bravely. "What's the point in having such a

clean apartment if we don't get to experience the joy of coming *back* to it?"

"Where are we going?" Karen asked. It was three in the afternoon.

Good question.

"To get pedicures."

Twenty minutes later, my feet were bathing in a turquoise-colored pool. Beauty treatments in New York can be a humbling process—unless every strand of hair, inch of skin, or shred of cuticle is in meticulous shape. I had already been chided for "destroying" my legs with too many shaving cuts.

"You only get skin once in your life," the pedicurist announced, jabbing a nail scissors menacingly in the direction of my calf. "Why not take care of it? We wax here, you know!"

Because applying hot wax to my skin and using it to rip the hair out by its roots is *really* taking care of myself . . .

"Mmm-hmm," I murmured noncommittally, reexamining the bottle of polish I'd chosen. Beside me, Karen was leaning back with her eyes closed.

"This was *such* a good idea," she announced.

"Yes, well, I think I've spent enough time cleaning over the past month to realize that it's not the most pleasant distraction." I sighed. "Both of us single again, huh?"

"It was bound to happen," Karen said. "I mean, Charlie, we were hardly dating the most obvious long-term options."

"I thought Hank and I were destined for great love," I protested honestly. It sounded silly aloud. I sank further into my chair.

"I know you did," Karen replied. "But did you really think it would have worked out?"

"Because Hank and I were too different, you mean?"

"Because you *thought* you were too different from Hank."

"We are different. I still think that," I admitted. The pedicure chair had a built-in mechanical massager. I picked up the control and adjusted it so that the massage targeted my lower back. "What I don't know is how that idea I had about us being different affected our relationship," I added.

Karen opened her eyes. "How so?" she asked, fumbling around for her chair's control.

"I, um, have been spending a lot of sleepless nights lately," I confessed. "And I have a lot of time on my hands now that my thesis is done. Karen, all I do is think about Hank. Not super-mushy oooh-I-wish-I-were-back-with-Hank thoughts—although I have had those. It's more that I feel like I'm struggling to explain myself to *myself*."

"What needs to be explained?"

"I don't understand anything about being with Hank. I don't think I ever understood why we were together and I don't understand why we broke up and I especially, especially don't understand my role in our breaking up."

A diminutive Asian woman knelt before my footbath. She lifted my right foot out and began drying it off.

"I don't get it. You have to explain yourself because you don't understand yourself?"

"Kind of."

The pedicurist began clipping my toenails. "When was the last time you had a pedicure?" she demanded.

"Not that long ago," I said defensively. It had been at least a year.

"Your cuticles are all overgrown."

I shrugged.

"They should never get to this state," she added, attacking.

I shrugged again. Beside me, Karen's pedicurist was tsk-tsking her calluses.

"I don't know," I said aloud to Karen. "I, um, I've been really—" I stopped. The pedicurist began rubbing a blue lotion into my foot and calf. It tingled.

"I've been wondering if I ever let myself know the real Hank," I began again, more firmly. "You know, I get upset

with my parents because I think they have all these precon-
ceived ideas about people and judge them based on some invented intellectual standard. But I think that's exactly what I
did with Hank."

Karen turned her head so that she was looking at me.
Rather than meeting her eyes, I looked down at the pedicurist, who was now tapping my foot with two fingers like a
junkie searching for a vein. I'm sure it stimulated my reflex
points, but all I felt was mild pummeling.

"I was so snotty to him, Karen. So snotty." My voice caught
a little. I looked up. "I didn't think he could do what he did in
The Doctor's Wife. But he was really good. Whatever crazy
patchwork of acting techniques he put together from my directions and his own ideas worked."

Karen nodded. "Good," she repeated.

"Yeah, not Olivier good," I amended, "but so much better
than I ever wanted to admit. Karen, I just feel like a terrible
person. I'm snobby about Robert; I'm snobby about Hank." I
sighed. "Even my parents were willing to give Hank more
credit than I did, so maybe I'm misjudging them as well as
Hank!" There was a pause. "I feel so guilty," I finished.

Karen was quiet for a moment before answering. "You do
judge books by covers, Charlie. And maybe you weren't fair
to Hank in a lot of ways. But he was pretty nasty to you, too.
He said a lot of mean things and did God knows what with
Brazilian models and wouldn't let you make your own
movie. Don't forget that."

"OK," I muttered, feeling watery. I had been so perilously
close to crying so many times in the past month that I had to
wonder about a tear duct disorder. "I miss him, though. I
don't miss the way he was during filming, all vituperative and
pigheaded. But I miss *him*."

The pedicurist patted my leg. "You need to forget him,"
she said.

I smiled.

"Men are just not worth it," she continued. Karen's pedicurist nodded in agreement.

"You may be right," I said. Feeling as if I'd entertained the salon enough with my drama, I turned to Karen. "So, why do you think you and Ned were doomed?"

Excerpt from *Variety*:

. . . The pick of this year's Columbia student film litter is *The Doctor's Wife,* Charlotte Frost's 1950s adaptation of *Madame Bovary.* It's a monumental undertaking but Ms. Frost manages to transform Flaubert's complex novel into a simple tale of raw emotion. Of particular note is Ms. Frost's boyfriend, Hank Destin from TV's *Troubled Passion*, in his role as the hapless husband, Charles. Destin evokes a dual sympathy. We pity him for not realizing how ill-suited he is to his glorious wife (big-eyed ingénue Sabrina Waters). Yet through his various emotional blunders, we also come to pity and empathize with his young wife even more. Cinematography and editing are amateurish, but gorgeous costumes and poignant dialogue steal the show. Simply put, this is an unusually smart film. Watch for it on the festival circuit.

Meanwhile, the theme at NYU this year was sci-fi splendor, with Marrakech Morrison's short film *Two Kings* an obvious standout . . .

fifty-two

Three weeks later, I came home to an envelope.

*SCENE: Charlie's kitchen. CHARLIE is
sitting at the table staring at an
envelope. She picks it up and flips it
over. After looking at it for a moment,
she sets it back down on the table
unread.*

       CHARLIE (mutters to herself):
Get a grip, Charlotte.

*She picks up the envelope again and drops
it almost immediately.*

*We hear her breathe in deeply, audibly.
She snatches the envelope and tears it
open.*

*CHARLIE lets out a piercing,
unintelligible squeal. She starts
laughing wildly. Springing from the
chair, she executes a sloppy pirouette*

over to a phone on the wall and dials a
number with shaking fingers.

           CHARLIE *(into receiver)*:
I got it, I got it, I got it!

For a cynic who doesn't believe in happy endings, an awful lot of nice things were happening to me.

I had won the Stevens-Caplan Award for Best Film of the Year, which is a Columbia award, and was in the running for the Coca-Cola Refreshing Filmmaker Award, which is a national award and involves not only a medallion and a check large enough to live on for the next year, but also a coronation ceremony as the Most Fabulous Person Ever.

I had no trouble locating an agent. In fact, agents had been banging down my door ever since the screening for *The Doctor's Wife*. Once the awards hubbub started, Karen suggested that I turn off the ringer on the phone. But I didn't want to miss one single iota of fawning attention.

It was funny—I knew *The Doctor's Wife* was a good movie. I knew that it seemed better than many of this year's thesis films. But I had trouble seeing it as exceptionally good. It was just something that I'd dashed off in a fevered sweat in my living room, following a mortifying rejection of what I considered my best work to date. Honestly, I had considered it enough of a success to make it through filming without literally tearing out most of my hair in a panicked fit.

Hank, with his typical revolting ability to send lovely gifts just when I felt my most addled, had been deluging me with congratulatory flowers after each award, screening, or announcement. Pretty much everyone had commented on his performance in the film. In my newly found free time, I had taken up watching *Troubled Passion*. It was strangely addictive. I'd be lying if I didn't acknowledge that Hank's rejection still stung, much as I could understand why we were better off navigating our own disparate circles. I wondered if I'd ever see him again. Ten years from now, would either of us even remember that feeling of waking up together, my head curled against his shoulder?

Three days before graduation, I met up with Horton in a diner around the corner from campus. I'd heard through Cherie, the department secretary, that he was "cut up" about Chris and me leaving.

"He just don't seem like the same guy he was last fall," she'd told me.

When I got to the diner, Horton was sitting there with a cup of tea in front of him, looking—to be perfectly honest—exactly like the same guy he had been last fall. I was glad to see him. Even though we lived all of fifteen blocks away from each other, we probably wouldn't see each other very often after graduation. The thing that I found most odd about graduating was that people who had been so central to my existence for such a long time would cease to be at all relevant.

"How are you enjoying those fifteen minutes, Charlotte?" he greeted me.

I smiled ruefully. "I think they're already gone. I haven't gotten a phone call in nearly two weeks."

"Press is funny that way. You'll heat up again if you make the festivals. Have you heard anything?"

"Not yet." I rolled my eyes. "Which frankly sucks. But I've got to get into *something*."

"I think so, too. What does Corrinne say?"

Corrinne was my agent. I had chosen her based on the fact that she apologized for not having read any of my screenplays.

"I only saw your film," she admitted. "But I was blown away by it. I'd love to read the script someday. I'm convinced

I want to represent you. But I can understand if you want me to read some of your other work before committing."

She sounded so vastly more human than many of the other people who had contacted me that I'd warmed to her immediately. It also didn't hurt that she repped a roster of recent MFA superstars from various schools.

At any rate, Corrinne said I absolutely had nothing to worry about when it came to the indie festivals or (gasp) the Student Academy Awards. I told Horton this. He nodded and sipped some more tea.

"So what's next for you, Charlie?"

I rolled my eyes. "You sound like my parents. They ask me that at least three times a day. Honestly, I think I want to tackle a new screenplay. But I'd probably have to bartend or something while I wrote it. Corrinne thinks she can get me a job on one of the nighttime TV dramas, but I don't know that I want to go that route yet." I sighed. "I know it would be temporary but I'm afraid that I couldn't maintain both a weekly writing schedule and do something on my own. Everything's on hiatus right now anyway, so I don't have to make a decision immediately."

All the financial concerns were somewhat triggered by the fact that I had lost out on the Coke filmmaker award to a guy from USC with an AIDS-themed short film that had made me cry when I finally saw it. While I think there should be different awards for short versus feature length films (who knows if he could have sustained that intensity across two hours?), I had to admit that it was very, very good. At any rate, aside from the cushy check, I wasn't too upset about losing. Being a finalist was good enough for my résumé and, as Horton had tartly phrased it, I had had my fifteen minutes after all.

Horton sipped more tea delicately. "I have a proposition for you," he said.

Well, that sounds dirty, I thought automatically but restrained myself from making any comment aloud.

"I've decided to take a leave of absence from Columbia. I've got a deal with Universal to direct four new features for them. They've sent me script after hopeless script."

I suddenly remembered the scripts that Horton had asked me to read over the course of the year. I sat up a little straighter.

"I sent over a copy of *The Doctor's Wife*. It took a while to convince them, since I think I'm enough of a risk for them at the moment, but they are willing to hire you to write a script for me to direct. They would pay you Writers Guild minimum and it would have to be closely supervised by studio execs. I also cannot guarantee that they wouldn't eventually hire someone to do a rewrite and destroy all your work. But the offer's there."

I was quiet for a very long time. "Are you serious?" I said at last, whispering the words, just in case talking too loudly might negate their reality.

Horton smiled. "Absolutely. I think we work well together and I think you're talented." He looked knowingly at me. "My only question is if you think you're ready for this. It's a big leap from being a student."

"Oh my God, I'd have to be on crack not to take you up on this," I said bluntly. I realized how crass I'd sounded and tried to backtrack. "Well, it's just that it's a good opportunity and—"

Horton was laughing.

"One more thing, Charlotte."

"Yeah?"

"Are you ready for a romantic comedy?"

"A comedy?"

I don't write comedy. I just live it.

"That's what they want me to do," Horton said matter of factly.

"But I've never done that."

"Feel like trying? You're certainly funny."

"But comedies aren't—"

"*Real* film?" Horton supplied.

I shrugged.

"I think you should try it. You might be surprised."

"If that's what they want, I don't suppose I have much choice."

Horton looked at me over the top of his glasses. There were deep furrows in his face. He looked his age. I couldn't believe that he was going back to directing (let alone directing *four* features).

"Can it at least be an I-laughed-I-cried comedy?" I asked.

"You're the writer," he said, handing me a business card. "Jonathan Cohen, the exec in charge of the project, is going to be in New York next week. He wants you to call and set up a meeting." Horton gave a wry half-chuckle, half-cough. "His assistant was going to call you last week and set one up anyway, but I convinced her that I really ought to talk to you first."

"Thank you," I said softly. I had a lot of questions for him (most of them pertaining to "Do you really think I can do this?") but decided that he'd already answered them implicitly.

"Thank you," I repeated, feeling suddenly cold. If you had told me at ten that my life would work out so conveniently, I wouldn't have believed it. Hell, if you had told me at twenty-four, I wouldn't have believed it.

When it comes down to it, I'm just not the walking-into-sunsets kind of girl.

fifty-three

Two days before leaving for the Toronto Film Festival, I was having a crisis on the floor of Marisa's apartment. It was the end of September and I was halfway through my new screenplay.

"I don't understand it," I said grouchily. "Why couldn't I have gotten into the Hamptons Festival? That way I could have just hopped on the Long Island Rail Road to get there and you guys could come and we could stay in Karen's parents' house. It makes no sense. The Hamptons has a special student division. How could I have not gotten in?"

Marisa was checking out the festival listings online. "Will you stop whining? Three months ago, you were saying that you would only get into local festivals and wouldn't get to go anywhere interesting."

"I wasn't thinking very clearly then."

"Yeah, well, look at all of these incredible people who are going to be there. Charlie, this should be like a dream come true."

"I know. But I don't belong there. Not yet. I'm going be such an impostor. I don't know anything about movies, Maris!" I began tapping my foot frenetically.

Marisa laughed. "You didn't go to yoga today, did you, Charlie?"

"That's completely irrelevant. I am flipping out. Flipping out! And Hank will be there. And of course, he will not be flipping out, because Hank Destin is much too cool a specimen to flip out." Tap. Tap.

The buzzer sounded. "That's Karen," Marisa said, getting up from the couch. With purposeful effort, I willed my foot to stop. If I was going to spend the next week surrounded by slick filmsters, I was going to have to learn to camouflage my incessant neuroses.

Karen had brought Vietnamese takeout with her. It was probably the first time in my life that I had been so unmoved by dinner. I toyed absently with my shrimp while Marisa and Karen inhaled enough food to sustain Hanoi for a year.

"Charlie, you are going to be fabulous. The festival is going to be fabulous. Just try to enjoy it. You can call us every single day, if you want," Karen said at last.

"I don't know why I'm so scared," I said. "Once I get there, I'm sure I'll be fine. It's not like anyone's going to come to my screening, anyway. It's at nine A.M., for God's sake, when every reasonable festivalgoer will be hung over."

"You are going to be fine," Marisa said definitely. "And it'll be good for you to see Hank."

"You think so?"

"Well, sure," Karen said, staring dubiously at a frizzled piece of basil in her chopsticks. "You've built him up to be this earth-shattering figure. He's the guy you didn't understand, the one you didn't appreciate, the one you should have stayed with. At the same time, he's this total villain who cheated on you and ruined your thesis and everything else." Karen ate the basil anyway. "If you see him, maybe you can neutralize some of those feelings and start to see him just as another ex-boyfriend."

"Because what I definitely need is another ex-boyfriend," I said sourly.

Karen shrugged.

"You know what I've been thinking lately?" I said. "I've been working on this new screenplay and it's, frankly, so satisfying. I love it. I love the process of sitting down to disentangle a scene. And I was thinking—and don't laugh"—I warned them—"that maybe my career is all I need. My dad always said that he thought movies were the big passion in my life. Maybe he was right. Every relationship I have ever had has paled in comparison to the legitimate happiness of being a screenwriter. If my life were to be just all that it is now, I think that would be enough. I think I'm happier without romance."

Marisa and Karen stared at me.

"Really," I reiterated. "This isn't just a reaction to breaking up with Hank. That was a while ago. This is *me*. I really feel that I'm OK just with movies."

Karen nodded. "I can see why you would feel that way." I narrowed my eyes at her. That sounded like the ultimate therapist cop-out comment to me.

There was more quiet. I decided to change the topic. "Speaking of, did I tell you guys about my drink with Chris Martin the other night?"

"Did he finally hit on you?" Marisa said.

"I was so upset!"

Karen and Marisa looked at each other and made not-very-restrained snickering noises.

"Did you guys see this coming?"

"OK, Charlie, how could you not see it coming?" Marisa asked. "It's not like you live on Planet Celibacy."

"Yeah, but, it's *Chris*. He's my, you know, my work buddy."

"Who has been mooning around you with stars in his eyes for three years now."

"Not really."

"Yeah, really."

"I was so upset!" I repeated. "I was telling him about

Toronto and then all of a sudden there was a hand on my thigh. I didn't know what to do."

"What did you do?" Marisa asked.

"Honestly? I said, 'That's my thigh, Chris.'"

Marisa and Karen went from snickering to howling.

"You did not."

"It seemed like a reasonable thing to say at the time. It was only in retrospect that it dawned on me how ridiculous it was."

"How did he react?"

I giggled despite myself. "He said he knew it was my thigh, which threw me for a loop. I said, 'Oh' and he said that he really liked me and understood that last spring had been rough for me and he's been waiting for me to heal. And I said that I was healed but wanted him as a friend. It was totally awkward."

"I'm sure." Karen unscrewed the top of a bottle of water and poured some into a cup.

"So now I have that to worry about as well."

"Nah," Marisa said. "That's not worth worrying about. Isn't he moving to LA anyway?"

"Well, he's been thinking about it. Nothing's settled."

"Within three weeks, you guys will be the same as you always were," Marisa predicted.

"Probably." I pushed my food aside and reached for the water. "How's work, Maris? Any better now that Steven left?"

"Night and day, frankly." Maris had gotten a couple of job offers over the past six months, including the one at *Stylus*, but had ultimately opted to stay at her old job because she wanted to keep working in books and specifically with the same books and authors she had painstakingly cultivated over the past five years. For about three months, she called me every day after work saying, *I wanted this, Charlie, right? Remind me that I could have left and I didn't, so this must be something I want*. Just when I was beginning to feel unusually phony reassuring her that she had made the right choice, her evil boss thankfully decided to go ruin the lives of people at a rival publishing company.

"How's June working out?" Karen asked quietly. June was Marisa's new assistant.

"She's a dream. She reminds me of me." Marisa frowned for a second. "I don't mean that to be as conceited as it sounds."

"Mmm-hmm," I said, in a fantastic imitation of my mother. I hoped Karen and Marisa got that I was imitating her and not turning into her, as might have been indicated by the snoaning incident.

Outside, a siren started wailing. This time last year I had just started writing *The Doctor's Wife* and was head-over-heels for Hank. Time flies when you're having fun (or not fun or an existential crisis or a romantic drama).

"Ugggghhh! I am so nervous about Toronto!" I announced for the hundredth time.

One of the nice things about airports is the opportunity to read countless women's magazines. I was in line with *Cosmo, Elle, Glamour*, and a bottle of juice at a little concessions-and-newspapers stand in the Air Canada terminal. Ahead of me, there was a pilot in navy uniform, various honorary pins clipped to his blazer.

"What would you like, sir?' " the clerk asked him. She had bleached hair, with a thick crust of bangs hanging over her forehead, and looked about eighteen.

The pilot leaned against the counter, looking for all the world like something out of central casting for a World War II film of the non-*Dirty Dozen* variety. "Well, I'd *like* a beer and some of that popcorn, but I'll just have coffee instead," he said cheerfully.

I laughed automatically. The pilot turned to me and winked. "That's how it goes," he said.

"What about the popcorn?" the clerk asked.

"Just the coffee is fine."

He reached for his wallet, still looking at me. "You going home today?" he asked.

"No, New York is home. I'm going to Toronto."

"On business?'

"Well," I began. "Sort of."

"Hey, Charlie?" a crushingly familiar voice said behind me. I turned (slowly and unwillingly). It was Hank. He was wearing a glorious tan leather jacket and hadn't shaved that morning. It was an unbearably sexy combo. I stiffened.

"Hi."

Beside me, I could feel the pilot watching us intently. I love having my most intensely awkward moments served up for public consumption.

"It's good to see you," he said.

There was silence. We both shuffled awkwardly from foot to foot and stared at each other for a moment. Then, suddenly, like zombies coming out of a cursed trance, we leaned forward and air kissed somewhat formally. His cheek was prickly. I wondered if his agent had recommended the decorative stubble.

"You heading up to Toronto?" Hank asked.

"Of course. Hard to believe this is happening, right?"

"Maybe not as hard for me as it is for you. Hey, what flight are you on?"

"The five-forty Air Canada."

"Oh, me too."

This was not happening. Not happening. If this were a screenplay, I would wonder about the technique of convenient meetings. Since it was my life, I wondered about the possibility that I was hexed.

fifty-four

Hank was in first class. I was naturally not. He showed up by my seat even before the drinks cart.

"Charlie."

I contemplated feigning sudden, narcoleptic sleep.

"Hi, Hank."

"Look, we should talk. We need to figure out how we're going to present ourselves at the festival."

"Present ourselves?"

"You know."

"Maybe not."

The drinks cart rattled down the aisle, right on time. I was saved by the stewardess, who stared at Hank with a waiting glance. He got the hint.

"Oh, sorry," he said, edging around the cart with difficulty. Once safely on the other side, he beckoned to me. *Come on*, he mouthed, jerking his head toward the first-class section.

I busied myself in the *Cosmo* quiz. It was of the utmost importance that I find out if I were a Time Wasting Cosmogirl. (Of course, the fact that I bothered to fill out the quiz at all no doubt indicated yes.) When I got done, Hank was no longer lurking in the aisle, and the drinks cart had rattled safely to the back of the cabin. I sighed and headed for first class, ducking behind the polyester dividing curtain with resignation.

Hank was in the third row, drinking Scotch from an actual glass tumbler. The section was almost empty and there was no one sitting next to him. I lowered myself into the adjacent seat, which was roughly double the width of my coach-class one.

"Present ourselves?" I opened.

Hank smiled at me. "Charlie-doll," he said.

No no no. There could be no affectionate diminutives if I were to make it through this conversation alive. I looked at his face, which was both disarmingly familiar and alien at the same time. It seemed inconceivable that I could have ever dated someone so handsome.

"I don't think I understand," I said.

Hank squished his lips to one side, possibly indicating that he was thinking about what to say.

"Charlie, when I see you, you act sort of, well, weird and unfriendly. I look at you and just feel that it's really nice to see you. You obviously don't agree. For the sake of the film, I think maybe it would be nice if we demonstrated a warmer relationship."

Excuse me? "Are you telling me that I need to fake affection and gratitude toward you?"

"I hoped you wouldn't have to fake it. At least not the affection part."

I sighed, not sure of how to respond.

A flight attendant came bustling up the aisle and knelt by our row.

"Miss, I'm sorry, but I'm going to have to ask you to return to your seat," she whispered emphatically.

I smiled, despite myself.

"I think I've been sent back to steerage," I said.

"Oh, please," Hank said to the stewardess in exasperation.

"Sir, I'm sorry, but if I allow one person up here . . ." she trailed off.

"Look, this is sort of important," he said. "We're old acquaintances—"

Acquaintances? I thought.

"—and haven't seen each other in a long time. If there is any way that you could allow this young lady—"

Young lady?

"—to remain up here, I would really appreciate it." Hank gave her a two-hundred-watt special Destin smile.

The flight attendant was not swayed. "I'm sorry, sir, but there's just no way."

I bounced up from the seat. "I'd better get back then."

"Charlie, wait." Hank got up as well and followed me down the aisle. We ducked back under the curtain. Unlike first class, the coach cabin was packed. Two children were playing some kind of game and laughing deliriously.

"Shit," Hank said, scanning the crowded cabin. Reaching for my hand, he pulled me into the bathroom with him.

Grand. Now every journalist and his mother would report that Hank and I had joined the Mile High Club on our way to Toronto.

"Hank!" I said. The bathroom was very small, and we were only inches away from each other.

"Charlie, I don't want us to be cold and strange and unfriendly together. This is our dream that's coming true. All that work was worth it. This should be a celebration." He smiled and I, unlike the flight attendant, felt myself melt. "Look at where we are, doll."

His excessively long lashes lowered a fraction of a centimeter over his eyes. I didn't say anything. I remembered my conviction that movies and screenwriting were the great, everlasting passion of my life. A sudden image of a cartoon character with an angel on one shoulder and devil on the other flashed into my mind. The part of me that had melted solidified back into practical cynicism without much effort. I had Betty Friedan on one shoulder and Gloria Steinem on the other. I was not going to fall back into the Destin Quagmire.

"It is exciting," I agreed. "You're right. I'm pretty thrilled with how it's all worked out. And you look like you're doing well, and that makes me happy too. It's just that seeing you is not easy. I'm sorry. I wish I could fake things as successfully as you do. But I'm not like that. I'm sorry." I was whispering by the end of my statement.

"I'm not faking," Hank said.

I moved back against the door, away from him. I could feel the cheap foam board buckle against my weight.

"Sometimes I miss you, Charlie."

I didn't say anything. I didn't believe him. He was a total phony. He couldn't stand having me ignore him. I was not going to fall for this. Being with Hank hadn't made me happy, certainly not as happy as I was now, with my writing and working and personal best checking account balance. Maybe the dreamer in me had wanted him to slink back to me, professing eternal love. But I was a realist now, and I hardly needed some ephemeral, imitation prince to bring me bliss. Please. I was over the need to seal this epoch in my life with swelling violin music and *The End* written in curling script. I had been a contented screenwriter before Hank and I would continue to be a contented screenwriter without him.

"I have to go," I said, reaching for the lock on the door.

"Charlie, stop running away!"

"Stop pretending you care about me!" I shot back and pushed the door open. An old woman stood outside, staring pleasantly but vacantly at Hank and me. Her face was inches away from mine. I shut the door immediately.

"She looked exactly like a *Troubled Passion* fan. I was sparing you unwelcome publicity," I explained vapidly.

Hank pulled down the toilet seat and sat on it. He rubbed

his temples for a second. This was possibly the least romantic scene of my life.

"Oh, Charlotte, Charlotte," he muttered.

"What?"

"Why won't you let me talk to you?"

"You're talking. I just shut the door in Superfan's face, re-member?"

"Charlie, I have always, always adored you. We both made some mistakes. I'm willing to put those behind us."

Hank reached out and touched my shoulder. It was a very soft, very tender touch. I felt myself wilting. Maybe we *could* join the Mile High Club. I now apparently had Betty Friedan on one shoulder and Courtney Love on the other.

"Hank, we weren't good for each other," I said honestly. "Being with you made me feel rotten about myself, and I'd venture to say vice versa. I don't want to go back to that."

"It wouldn't have to be like that. That's where the learning-from-experience part comes in. Besides, Charlie, think about it: *The Doctor's Wife* is making both of our ca-reers. My agent has been getting calls ever since the *Variety* review, and we're convinced that it's only going to heat up even more after the festival. This is something we did to-gether. We *needed* each other to pull it off."

I wasn't sure that I bought that entirely but I would admit (grudgingly) that Hank had been pretty damn wonderful in the film, better than any other actor. Something about it had made the most of our talents, no matter how godawful a pro-cess filming had been. He was never starring in another one of my movies. That was for damn sure.

"Hank, what do you want from me?" I asked abruptly.

"Charlie," he started, then paused. "I'm not saying we have to start dating again," Hank said softly. "But let's do our best to reconnect as people."

I stared at him dubiously.

"I don't know." I sighed. "I mean, I don't know if that's even possible. I'm not a forgetter, Hank."

"I'm not asking you to forget. I'm asking you to look past." He rubbed his temples some more. He looked very tired.

"Look, Charlie," he began again. "Ultimately, I think I just want for us to be able to talk to each other the way we used to. And I think that will be better for the film, too, because even though it's kind of at a shitty screening time and there are tons of other movies, I don't want there to be any press about us squabbling. But, yeah, truthfully, I miss you and want you back in my life. I'm staying at the Four Seasons. Call me if you want to go to dinner. Or coffee. Or breakfast. Or *anything*." He stood up and opened the door. The same woman was standing there blankly. He pushed past her without a word.

I stood there, frozen, framed by the doorway. The woman continued to stare at me. I wondered if she had been able to hear us. I wondered if the whole plane had been able to hear us. Maybe she just had some retinal disorder that wouldn't allow eye motion.

"Sorry," I said and went back to my own seat, where I proceeded to think bitter thoughts about the people who had designed airplanes. Didn't they know that there were times that travelers might need enough space to curl into the fetal position?

Hank seemed every bit as confused about me as I was about him. In truth, I didn't think returning to Hank was a particularly healthy option. It just had all the hallmarks of weak, stupid girl stamped on it. I wasn't suckered by his spectacular craggy features or glitzy wealth anymore. Sure I'd made my share of mistakes in our relationship. But now I understood that he was far blander than I'd assumed, that he was Charles-ish, that this wasn't great love, that filming had taken a far greater toll on my psyche than I was willing to admit.

I couldn't call him at his hotel. It would be stupid.

Or would it?

I pushed the recline button and squeezed my chair backward.

It would be stupid. It would set me up for a period of emotional disarray and confusion and weakness just when I was surging ahead in my career. Hank and I were never destined for eternal bliss. We brought out the worst in each other. It would be only a matter of time before he started making his stubborn, vindictive, cutting comments. Calling him would be indulgent.

And stupid.

I stared out the window in bafflement. I needed to know that Hank had changed.

Stupid.

He needed to know that I had changed. Would it hurt for us just to talk?

Stupid. Risky. Weak. The words echoed in my head.

And yet . . .

"Frankly, my dear," I whispered to the shreds of cloud alongside me, "I don't give a damn."

And, since I was already jumping off the great cliff of indulgence, I allowed the looping white script letters of *The End* to roll across the screenplay of my mind.

AVON TRADE... because every great bag deserves a great book!

Paperback $12.95
($17.95 Can.)
ISBN 0-06-058958-2

Paperback $12.95
($17.95 Can.)
ISBN 0-06-058441-6

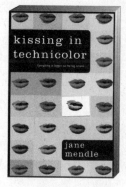

Paperback $12.95
($17.95 Can.)
ISBN 0-06-059568-X

Paperback $13.95
($21.95 Can.)
ISBN 0-06-008164-3

Paperback $10.95
($16.95 Can.)
ISBN 0-06-056036-3

Paperback $12.95
ISBN 0-06-059580-9